THE GOOD WOLF

I0636947

THE GOOD WOLF

J. A. Springs

WRITING
FOR THE
WORLD
PRESS

since
2021

Copyright © 2025 Writing for the World Press, LLC.
Lancaster, PA. 17603
All rights reserved
ISBNs 13:
978-8-9898622-2-1 (eBook)
978-1-966464-12-9 (Paperback)

No part of this publication may be reproduced, distributed, or transmitted in any form or by any means, including photocopying, recording, or other electronic or mechanical methods, without the prior written permission of the publisher, except as permitted under U.S. copyright law. For permission requests, contact Writing for the World Press at writingfortheworldpress.com.

This is a work of fiction. Names, characters, places, and incidents are the product of the author's imagination or are used fictitiously. Any resemblance to actual persons, living or dead, or actual events is purely coincidental.

Always for J.M.S. First.
I hope the destination will be as beautiful as the journey. I miss you and love you mom.

Veiled Guardian

Amidst the meadow's gentle grace,
A good wolf wears a sheepish trace.
Cloaked in wool, with kindred eyes,
A guise that truth and trust belies.
In moonlit nights, a guardian's howl,
Protects the flock, with honor foul.
A lupine heart, in sheep's attire,
The good wolf tends the shepherd's fire.

1

In a mere span of eight years, the world that had cradled Cadi's childhood and shaped her early life morphed from a realm of positivity to one mired in adversity. As she eloquently summed it up, 'It went from sugar to shit.'

Recollections flickered, reminding her that her own existence had commenced a mere eight years ago, yet she wasn't even close to being an eight-year-old. Sixteen, to be precise. Her physical age might have measured eight years, but the rapid crescendo of her first half-year marked her swift development within a genetic incubation chamber. Only after emerging from this cocoon was she thrust into the world.

In the present moment, she perched in a tree, her stance precarious on a branch that seemed too slender to support her without aid. The wind ruffled her brow as her frown deepened. Despite her reluctance, stubbornness rooted her to her lofty post.

Her frame was petite, yet her intellect was as keen as a blade. In the realm of the mind, she occupied a mental space akin to that of a college scholar. Yet, beyond these palpable truths, Cadi's world veered into the realm of the strange, an enigmatic territory that was uniquely hers.

The few anomalies she possessed might appear sufficiently peculiar to warrant the label of 'weird,' yet their classification transcended mere oddity. It wasn't solely the complexity of her age, nor was it solely the genetic blueprint that paved the way for a lifespan potentially two or three times that of an average person.

Nor was it exclusively her heightened strength, her senses honed to an acute level, or even her rapid healing prowess. It wasn't even the vertical irises that framed her eyes, or the sleek, feline-like tail that trailed behind her. Individually or collectively, what struck as unconventional about Cadi in that very moment wasn't her unique attributes, but rather her current perch atop the tree, accompanied by an unmistakable pout.

The setting was early morning, the sun barely cresting the horizon. She tilted her head, her gaze lifting towards the nascent sun, while a hand shielded her brow. The dichotomy was striking—the morning's freshness versus the childlike stance she'd adopted due to her parents' response.

With a sigh, the pout persisted, an emblem of her discontent. Her thoughts looped around the recent denial of her request, the dissatisfaction tugging at her as she pondered her parents' overprotective stance. Despite her extraordinary nature, she believed herself capable of self-preservation in times of crisis. The urge to shout her defiance at her parents, to declare her independence and her capability to fend for herself, coursed through her like a hidden undercurrent.

Beneath the tree, her father stood, an emblem of gentle concern. From the moment he had emerged from the house, she had observed his approach with an attentive eye. His endearing call, coaxing her to descend, echoed in the air. It was as if she could predict the very words he would use—promises of chocolate, her one undeniable weakness. But today, she was determined not to yield to this simple bait.

Cadi's gaze drifted down to her father, her heart responding to the melody of his beckoning. Involuntarily, her body shifted on the branch, attempting to create a physical space between them. It was a feeble attempt, for her heart recognized his goodwill even as her obstinacy held her captive. She averted her face, the cool touch of the bark on her back providing only a fleeting distraction from her frustration.

With his appearance, a part of her longed to capitulate, her inner turmoil tethered to his mere presence. She knew, logically, that her defiance was unnecessary, but emotions swirled within her like a storm, demanding an outlet. The temptation to descend, to end the standoff, lingered like an unspoken invitation, yet her determination held her captive.

"Are you going to stay up there all morning, kitten?" Jack's voice floated upward, warm and coaxing.

Cadi's gaze was drawn downward, caught by the orbit of his words, but she quickly looked away, her stare evasive. Meeting his eyes felt like surrendering her fortress of resolve. Her arms folded across her chest, a gesture that seemed to bolster her determination.

"I'm not coming down," her voice, tinged with defiance, carried down to him.

Jack's presence was unwavering below, his gaze a soft pressure against her persistence. Her fleeting glance downward held more than mere acknowledgement; it was a silent exchange, a conversation in looks. She couldn't afford to let his caring gaze melt her resolve. *I can't give up*, she thought to herself, *at least not easily!*

Yet, beneath her resolve, she understood his tenacity. Their disagreement had erupted at dawn, before breakfast's aroma could dance in the air. A desire for normalcy had fueled her, even though her life was anything but ordinary. She longed to taste experiences akin to those of her peers, despite being an anomaly herself. Cadi could feel the warmth in her body intensifying, the emotions of moments ago surging back, a relentless tide.

"I just wanted permission to be allowed to attend a real school, where I might be able to make real friends and experience a new environment," the words slipped from her lips in a soft, almost inaudible whisper.

Her fingers clenched, nails biting into her palms as she battled to quell the tears threatening to surface, an admission feeling like a surrender to her vulnerability. Earlier, she had meticulously pieced together her thoughts, logic weaving through her arguments as she envisioned herself attending a conventional school.

In her mind, she had painted the canvas of benefits, how she could seamlessly integrate, how her physical distinctions could be concealed if given the chance. Her reasons were not only well-founded but sensible. They should have been enough to sway her parents, to convince them of the feasibility.

But in the face of her parents' steadfast resistance, her careful reasoning seemed to crumble. It was mostly her mother's voice that resonated against the tide of her own, a chorus of opposition. Cadi's heart was a battleground, torn between the longing for normalcy and the undertow of her mother's fears.

Cadi sought to reason with her parents, highlighting her mother's ventures beyond the familiar walls of their home as evidence that the outside world was manageable. But the wall of her parents' concerns remained steadfast, both of them raising the same counterpoint in unison—that her mother Faye's adjustments weren't comparable to her own. Cadi's tail, a distinctive aspect of her being, introduced a layer of complexity beyond what her mother dealt with by just donning contact lenses to alter her eye appearance. The simple act of venturing beyond their home's sanctuary for shopping, errands, or family outings became a more intricate puzzle due to her unique attributes.

However, Cadi wasn't resigned to accept their negative response. With a slight turn of her head, she deflected her gaze from her father. Deep within, an ember of defiance flickered, an ember that whispered of alternatives, of places she could conceal herself where her parents' watchful eyes wouldn't find her. Yet, paradoxically, her heart held a hidden truth—the yearning for her father's discovery.

Their familial dynamic was one of aspiration and apprehension, a dance of wishes clashing with concerns. The backdrop of their discourse painted a picture of the secluded house and the world beyond its threshold, setting the stage for Cadi's yearning to bridge the two.

Her father, Jack, had an innate ability to mend the jagged edges of her world whenever distress clouded her skies. It was something she treasured, this power he held to set things right. Still, she wasn't oblivious to the risky nature of her request. She acknowledged the tangled web of complexities that accompanied it.

Aware of the world's dangers, she understood her parents' intent—to safeguard her from the threats lurking beyond their home's haven. They wanted to keep her close, a fortress of protection against the perils that prowled beyond the circle of their care. In the realm outside, unbound by her parents' watchful gaze, danger lay in wait, particularly for her. The revelation of her divergence from humanity could alter everything. It was an unspoken truth that swirled between them.

And yet, beyond the confines of her unique heritage, a deeper unease persisted. The knowledge that she and her mother weren't entirely human weighed on her, a perpetual shadow that darkened her thoughts. But it wasn't merely this inherent distinction that rendered the world hazardous. According to her parents, it was the world itself, its very nature and its reactions, that posed the real danger. The conclusion was paradoxical, a reflection of her distinctiveness and the unforgiving world's intolerance.

The interplay of familial dynamics, the protectiveness rooted in love, and the uncharted territory of her own identity were woven together against the backdrop of their secluded refuge, starkly contrasted with the broader world they warily acknowledged.

Disappointment pooled within her, a heavy realization that her parents would exert their utmost efforts, though limited, to shield her from harm. Yet, with each passing day, the task seemed to stretch beyond their grasp. Her sense of isolation deepened, threading her existence with a sense of exclusion from the world's embrace. A subtle rebellion stirred within her, a rebellion nurtured by the realization that their protective cocoon could not shield her indefinitely. The urge to venture beyond, to carve her own path, became a beacon of her growing desires.

The walls of her sanctuary, once a refuge, now seemed to contract, suffocating her. The confines pressed in, stifling her spirit. The day-to-day routine chiseled away at her strength, and the simmering tension grated on her nerves. Her mother's guidance, once a source of comfort, now became a trigger for clashes, a manifestation of the stifling control she felt. The world that lay beyond beckoned, an unexplored terrain promising adventure, freedom, and the space to become who she yearned to be.

Within the last four years of her life, the world had spun on its axis. The narrative shifted dramatically, and what was once familiar was now a shifting landscape, a poignant metaphor for the upheaval that had swept over her world. The political landscape underwent a profound transformation, starkly departing from the familiar norm. The international dynamics shifted from what she once recognized to a drastically altered state today.

On a global scale, cherished concepts of freedom and independence found themselves under pervasive infringement. These sweeping changes were orchestrated by the cunning maneuvers of a singular figure—the president of her country. Amidst these changes, her struggles mirrored the ongoing battle between her desire for independence and the cocoon of protection her parents wove around her.

Jack's tried-and-true charm came into play, echoing a strategy that had once won over her mother, Faye. His eyes sparkled with the same twinkle that had eventually ensnared Faye's heart. He directed that twinkle skyward, fixing his gaze on his adopted daughter perched among the branches. His upturned face embraced the early morning sun, casting a warm glow on his dark skin that resembled rich chocolate, basking in the embrace of the sun's early rays.

Cadi's attention flicked to her father, her initial reaction a huff followed by a deepening frown. She swiftly averted her gaze from his imploring eyes, yet she was well aware that resistance was futile. A sense of yielding loomed within her, a sensation that she'd eventually acquiesce and descend from the tree limb. Her obstinacy, while palpable, seemed like a small hurdle to overcome.

It was a battle of wills, a tug of emotions that she knew she couldn't maintain for long. And then, like clockwork, her father produced the perfect leverage. A well-placed bribe chipped away at her resolve until there was little left to cling to, and she reluctantly surrendered her perch.

As Jack prepared to leave his post beneath the tree, his gaze lifted once more to the figure of his daughter, an image of contrast with her pale skin and cat-like poise amid the branches. The dynamics between them were an intricate dance of parental persuasion and daughterly obstinance, painted against the canvas of a sun-soaked morning.

"Alright, I guess I'll be the only one eating chocolate chip pancakes this morning," Jack's voice carried a touch of jest. His shoulders slumped subtly, a feigned disappointment in his tone.

Cadi's reaction was immediate, her resolve softening like a snowflake melting under a warm touch. The allure of chocolate chip pancakes proved to be an effective bribe, and she dropped her charade of upset. "That's not fair, dad," her voice held a playful protest, a chink in her armor revealing her capitulation.

The father-daughter dynamic played out like a dance, a subtle interplay of affection and negotiation. Pretending not to hear, Jack continued his movement as though he intended to turn back towards the house. Cadi swiftly descended from her arboreal perch, abandoning the branch that seemed insufficient to hold her weight.

She landed gracefully in her father's waiting embrace, her delicate form fitting snugly against his sturdy frame. His robust arms easily absorbed the impact of her landing, a testament to their bond and her slight build.

Cadi remained petite for her age, barely cresting four feet and eleven inches. Her stature stood just one inch shorter than her mother Faye's five-foot height. In contrast, her father stood like an unwavering cedar tree, towering at a solid six feet. His exterior projected a rugged durability, while his heart was the soft core hidden within.

With an affectionate chuckle, Jack effortlessly slung his armful of 'kitten' over his shoulder, her protests and squirms notwithstanding. As they headed towards the house through the backdoor, Cadi's protests bubbled forth alongside her kicks, an endearing display of her spirited nature. Her tail, an extension of her feline-like characteristics, playfully brushed against Jack's face. His absent swatting, a mix of indulgence and humor, encapsulated the familial dynamics between them.

With a gentle thud, he settled his hissing and squirming bundle of indignant daughter onto a stool at the kitchen counter. Her protests were audible, a symphony of defiance. In her haste, she ensured that she didn't accidentally perch on her own tail, deftly tucking it out of the way just in time. The mundane act carried a tender familiarity, a touch of the extraordinary hidden within the ordinary.

"Now that I've got you here, are you gonna help me out?" Jack's question trailed over his shoulder, a playful edge to his voice.

He efficiently gathered the necessary supplies to fulfill his promise of chocolate chip pancakes for his spirited daughter. As he moved, he shared a casual piece of information, weaving it into their conversation. "Your mother's already headed to the police station for work, beating me to it this morning. So, it's just you and me for now, Kitten."

Sitting at the counter, Cadi's fingers toyed with the salt and pepper shakers before her, a distraction to veil the emotions churning beneath her surface. Despite her effort to mask her feelings, a tinge of vulnerability lingered in her posture. Her voice, when it emerged, was measured, laden with a complexity that mirrored the undercurrents between them.

"So I guess Mom's work takes precedence over checking in on her own daughter's feelings after this morning's disagreement?" The words were layered, a blend of accusation and hurt, tinged with a hint of longing for validation.

Pausing in his tasks, Jack pivoted to face the evident frown etched on Cadi's features. Her words had struck a chord, leaving him grappling with a mixture of emotions.

"That's not fair. Your mother loves you and cares how you feel, Cadi. We both do," his response was measured, infused with a blend of earnestness and parental reassurance.

Cadi's silence echoed in the aftermath of his words. Her deflection marked a shifting of the emotional tide, a pivot to a more neutral subject.

"Do you have to go to the police station today, Dad?" she inquired, redirecting their conversation.

Jack's response came in the form of a simple nod, encapsulating the unspoken responsibilities that were an intrinsic part of his life.

Cadi inhaled, a soft intake of air that carried the weight of her emotions. As she exhaled, a sense of resignation seemed to seep into her posture. Her shoulders slumped, a visual echo of her inner turmoil.

"So I'll be by myself again, today," her words were tinged with a touch of disappointment, an acknowledgment of the solitude that stretched ahead.

The sigh that followed carried a hint of surrender, a silent admission of the circumstances she faced. Leaning into her palm, her chin nestled in the open cup of her hand, she exhaled another breath. Her elbows found support on the countertop in front of her, propping her up as she wrestled with the quiet complexities of her feelings.

"Look, Kitten," Jack's voice carried a tender note, a prelude to a crucial conversation. "Your mom and I heard what you had to say this morning."

Cadi's response was a subdued murmur, a blend of hurt and disappointment lacing her words. "It didn't seem like you guys cared too much about what I had to say, though," her voice held the lingering echoes of the morning's emotional exchange.

"When you rushed out, needing time to yourself," Jack continued, his tone unwavering yet gently soothing, "your mom and I talked about your request. We discussed it together."

Cadi's eyes lit up, a spark of hope kindling within her. Her vertical irises took on an iridescent green hue, casting a mesmerizing glow. The delicate flush that painted her cheeks in shades of pink only served to heighten the vibrancy of her already radiant features. Amidst the whirlwind of emotions, uncertainty mingled with hope, blurring the lines between elation and caution. As she navigated the threshold of potential happiness, her expression was a delicate balance of curiosity and anticipation.

Barely able to contain her eagerness, she found herself on the precipice of optimism. The suspense of waiting for Jack's revelation became nearly unbearable.

"So you guys are going to let me go to school?" Her words held a hopeful lilt, her voice tinged with a mixture of longing and cautious optimism.

"I think so," Jack's response carried a hint of affirmation.

Jack's intent to convey further thoughts was abruptly curtailed as his arms were engulfed by his blissfully exuberant, teenage daughter. Caught between her enthusiasm and his dual responsibilities—cooking and communicating—he made a futile attempt to disengage from her joyful embrace. Her grip eventually eased after a few moments, granting him the liberty to resume both his culinary duties and their ongoing conversation.

"Your mom and I are planning to have discussions with the school administrators," he announced, his tone a testament to his commitment. "We're looking into the possibility of enrolling you in our local high school, allowing you to participate in a few classes. I get why you're eager for this, even though I believe you possess an intellect that surpasses the typical high school curriculum," his voice contained a blend of pride and gentle amusement.

"Thank you, daddy." Cadi's exuberance manifested in joyful bounces before she was enveloped in her father's bear hug. Her happiness translated into a kiss planted happily on his cheek. "I need to call Aunt Elizabeth and let her and Cousin Brooke know that I'll finally get to go to school."

"Part-time!" Jack's playful addition trailed after Cadi as she retreated to make her excited phone call.

Jack and Cadi relished their breakfast together, a sense of camaraderie and shared anticipation filling the air after her phone call. Once they had finished their meal, Jack directed Cadi to her online studies. As she headed off, his fatherly concern lingered. His daughter's circumstances presented unique challenges for a teenager. She would miss out on many experiences typical for girls her age due to her non-human attributes, and the potential fallout from her true nature being discovered was a looming uncertainty they couldn't ignore.

Jack's concern for his daughter's well-being weighed heavily on his mind. The strain of confinement, the constant need to conceal her true identity—it all took its toll. Yet, he held confidence in Cadi's ability to navigate the impending changes as she ventured into the world of school. He believed that the limited time she'd spend there would serve her well in keeping her secret intact.

Conversations between Jack and Faye had revolved around the meticulous measures they'd take to ensure Cadi's secret remained secure. Gym classes were out of the question, a strategic move to prevent any chance of her tail being accidentally exposed. Cadi had grown accustomed to winding her tail around her waist when she was out with her parents, a practice she could easily adapt to the classroom setting.

As they pondered the mystery of Cadi's unique physiology, neither Jack nor Faye could fathom why her tail had been allowed to develop. The person responsible for her genetic makeup had the power to design her without it, much like her mother Faye. However, the answers to such questions were forever out of reach. The scientist behind Cadi and Faye's existence was long gone, thanks to Faye herself.

Jack gathered his belongings, planting a goodbye kiss on Cadi's cheek before departing for his day at the police station alongside her mother. With their absence, the house seemed to echo with the emptiness, leaving Cadi to grapple with her thoughts in solitude. Swiftly completing her assignments, she was left with ample time to daydream about the prospect of attending a traditional brick-and-mortar school.

Cadi retreated to her room, her mind a whirlwind of thoughts centered around the upcoming prospect of attending a conventional school like any ordinary child. Amidst her excitement, a reflective pause emerged.

A normal girl, she mused within herself.

This introspection inserted itself into her joyful reverie. Her room held a full-length mirror, and she positioned herself before it, her gaze locked onto the reflection that met her eyes.

"A real girl?" she questioned aloud.

As if seeking answers, Cadi began to undress, standing before the mirror in her underwear. Her contemplation deepened, grappling with the duality of her identity. She longed to be less of what she was and more of what she aspired to be—a genuine, regular girl. Yet, the reflection that met her was a complex blend, encompassing both girlhood and something more profound.

The split irises were prominent, impossible to ignore. They were more.

The tail that swayed behind the image in the mirror was a striking presence, a tangible reminder of her uniqueness. That too was more.

Cadi's hands traced a gentle path along her arms and belly, her fingertips tenderly brushing against her skin.

Barely perceptible, the fine black fur that graced her skin was a subtle veil, a delicate contrast against her porcelain complexion. This presence added to the complex mosaic of her being. That was more.

Cadi's smile emerged, but it wasn't one born of amusement. The slightly elongated canines that revealed themselves as she smiled held a deeper significance, a trait that further distinguished her. It was more.

Cadi yearned to experience life as a normal girl, unburdened by the need to conceal her true self behind contacts and a strategically loose shirt that camouflaged her tail when she coiled it around her waist.

Her frustration was palpable, and she struggled to comprehend why her own mother didn't seem more concerned about their differences. These differences, like her split irises and tail, set them apart from the world they inhabited. The mirror before her tempted her to express her inner turmoil, as she contemplated hurling something at her reflection, feeling at odds with the image that stared back at her.

In this confrontation with her own image, she questioned where her worth lay. How could she find love for herself when the very attributes that defined her seemed to push her so far from normalcy? Despite her parents' declarations of love, Cadi couldn't perceive what they saw in her. She deemed herself a monster, a freak whose reflection barely resembled that of a real, ordinary girl.

Yet, these were only the surface manifestations of her uniqueness—the visible veneer of a semblance of normalcy. She dared not even account for her high intelligence, exceptional strength, and remarkable agility.

These were also more but this more wasn't a tangible representation, despite that, this more set her even further away from her desires to be a 'real girl'.

Amid a blink that swept away a tear, Cadi turned from the mirror, donned her attire, and immersed herself in her studies. While her assignments were already complete, her resolve to confront her emotions with her mother later in the day provided a beacon of hope.

2

Approaching his fiftieth birthday, Jack was well aware that his youthful years had faded, yet his physical fitness still allowed him to surpass some of the younger police officers on the force. The time spent with Cadi that morning had eaten into his usual hours at the precinct's gymnasium. He resolved to make up for it later in the week, though at that moment, his thoughts were set on seeing his wife, Faye.

In the span of eight years, time seemed to have slipped away, and their story had unfolded rapidly. Their initial meeting had set in motion a chain of events that led them to be united. Fate had orchestrated their convergence when they both yearned for someone to be the catalyst for positive change in their lives. Together, they had become stronger, needing each other to navigate the twists and turns life presented.

Change and growth had been imperative for both of them, shaping them from who they were before their paths converged to the individuals they needed to become. Their mutual support made this transformation seamless, providing the foundation they required. This change led them on a journey of emotional and physical attachment, culminating in a lawful union—a sequence they never second-guessed or regretted.

Faye's professional trajectory took a turn as she departed from her former agency, embracing a new career path within the same police force as Jack. Her journey commenced as a uniformed police officer, and over the span of eight years, she had risen to the rank of lieutenant. In terms of formal rank, they shared the same standing—both being lieutenants. However, their positions held different spheres of influence. While Jack held the title of *lieutenant detective*, Faye's role endowed her with a higher position, symbolizing a unique power dynamic between them.

Currently, she held the esteemed position of Deputy Chief within the police force. The elevation of the previous Deputy Chief to Chief of Police had paved the way for this progression. The former Chief, Eugene Ritter, had retired to preempt the heart attack that his concerned doctor had persistently warned him about.

Jack took a detour from his own office, instead making a beeline for Faye's workspace. Leaning against the door frame, he exercised patience as he awaited her momentary respite from an ongoing phone call, seeking her undivided attention.

Faye noticed his presence by the doorway and responded with a welcoming wave, beckoning him to enter. The gesture was followed by a subtle signal, indicating her desire for him to shut the door behind him. Jack complied, closing the door before settling onto the couch—the single addition Faye had introduced to the office since acquiring it.

A few minutes after Jack's arrival and seating, Faye wrapped up her phone call. She approached him and settled onto his lap, her head finding a resting place on his shoulder. Gently, she maneuvered his arms around her petite form, drawing herself close. The embrace, no matter its duration or frequency, was a source of perpetual solace for her. The enveloping hold and his familiar scent held an enduring allure. It wasn't just a matter of physical comfort; within his arms, she found a sense of security, safety, and his unwavering strength. These were tangible offerings, a testament to the depth of their bond.

As she nestled in his embrace, Faye recognized that this sense of comfort, security, and strength wasn't transient. It was an ongoing need, an enduring want.

"This is sexual harassment, deputy chief," Jack remarked, his tone tinged with playful accusation.

In response, Faye leaned in and placed a teasing kiss on Jack's neck. A mischievous smile curved her lips.

"That was sexual harassment. Everything before that was just harassment," she retorted with a playful glint in her eyes.

Jack's laughter rippled through the room.

"So, how is our little monster?" Faye inquired with a playful tone, a glint of affection in her eyes..

"She's a teenaged, hormonal girl. How do you think she is? You two have been going at it for the last few months." Jack's response carried a tinge of sadness, reflecting his awareness of his daughter's emotional struggles and his frustration at feeling helpless in alleviating her distress.

"Don't remind me, Jack. Is she at least happy that we changed our minds about her going to school?" Faye asked with a hopeful tone. Her concern for Cadi's emotional well-being was evident, reflecting her own awareness of the situation and her genuine worry for their daughter.

Jack's hand trailed down Faye's legs, covered by her skirt, all the way to her knees and then back up. He was well aware of the effect his touch was having on her, and he anticipated her reaction. He waited patiently for the inevitable response, knowing that Faye's emotions were stirred.

It didn't take long for Faye to react, despite any intention to resist. A shiver started at her core, coursing its way up her shoulders, causing her to tremble. With a mix of playfulness and affection, she punched Jack's chest, a gesture that communicated her response to his teasing touch.

"Stop that, you beast, and answer the question about our daughter." Faye replied, her words a response to his teasing touch.

Despite the effect his actions had on her, she was determined not to let their conversation veer off course. A sigh escaped her lips, revealing the impact of his touch on her, but she consciously took a few measured breaths, seeking to regain her composure and steady her emotions.

Jack's radiant smile only intensified her affection for her husband, reinforcing the love she felt for him, even with his quirks and unique qualities.

"Our little monster is ecstatic about our decision to let her finally go to school and can't wait to start. She was not upset at all that we're only letting her go to a brick and mortar school for part of the day instead of the whole day. She understood the need to keep the time down so we minimize her risk of exposure," he shared.

Despite this, his heart ached for the limited time he'd had to spend with his daughter that morning. The prospect of Cadi being outside the house and beyond their immediate supervision still weighed heavily on Jack's mind.

"That's good," said Faye happily. "Now we just have to let her know about..." she paused, her concern evident as she grappled with the potential consequences of her condition. She was also apprehensive about how Cadi, given her recent emotional state, would react to the news.

Jack placed his hand on Faye's belly.

"Are you certain?" he asked, repeating the question for what felt like the millionth time.

"Yeah, I'm certain. It was always a question of whether or not we could, and I guess we know now," Faye replied. Her happiness was tinged with an underlying worry due to her genetic history. She was a clone, a result of genetic manipulation, and both of them were uncertain about how this might impact their child.

"I'm happy, but I'm also worried," Jack admitted. "Izzy and Brooke moved back here so that Izzy could oversee your healthcare. I was concerned that if it came out that you weren't entirely human, you might end up becoming some sort of science experiment." His words carried a mix of relief and apprehension.

Having his sister back in town was a welcome source of support. Elizabeth's presence would help manage Faye's pregnancy and potentially offer solutions to unforeseen challenges arising from Faye's genetic background.

Faye's genes passing onto their child was not a doubt; the real question lay in how those genes might manifest in physical differences that caused them concern.

"Dr. Jason Conwell is still at Saint Elwood Hospital, and we could have relied on him until we found an alternative. But now, that concern is put to rest," Faye reassured.

"He's not a pediatrician or an obstetrician," Jack retorted. "He's a mortician."

Despite his sister's presence offering reassurance, he couldn't shake off the concern about his ability to ensure Faye received the necessary healthcare during her pregnancy. It was a source of constant unease for him.

"He would have been the best option, Jack, because he was one of the only ones to know of my true nature. But now we have him and your sister Izzy," Faye reassured him.

Jack pulled her closer, his lips finding hers. "Do we really want to bring a child into this chaotic world right now? Especially with President Pike ruling the country?"

"Dr. Brundle rambled on about how the people would give him power willingly. I can't believe that he knew that this would happen," Faye said, her voice tinged with disbelief. She shook her head, her hand rising to her forehead as she spoke.

"With the loss of Congress due to a terrorist attack and the President being assassinated the week after, I'm surprised that the entire country didn't fall apart," Jack stated silently.

He considered everything that had happened recently in the political realm and sighed heavily. "Vice President Pike took over and later ran for the office of President, capitalizing on the chaos. He was unopposed in his presidential bid."

Jack recalled the events that had occurred after President Pike had taken office. Soon after, he enacted significant changes by suspending parts of the constitution and expanding Presidential power. Martial law was declared, and an army of genetically engineered soldiers was raised almost overnight. The unsettling events had shaken the world.

Faye turned to face Jack, concern etched across her features. "That's the part that I don't understand. I killed that crazy doctor and destroyed all the clones at the facility here. There shouldn't have been anyone else capable of recreating his work so quickly."

They both shared a knowing look, understanding the depths of Donovan Pike's sinister intentions. Yet, despite their knowledge of his true nature and the atrocities he had committed, they were powerless to prevent his meteoric rise to power. The weight of their secrets and the impossibility of convincing the public of the unbelievable truth left them with no choice but to remain silent, even as Pike's grip on the country tightened.

In the ensuing silence, the soft hum of the overhead lights filled the room, a backdrop to their conversation that had, for the moment, drawn them both into its gravity. Despite the bustling police department beyond her office doors, their exchange had cocooned them in a world of their own thoughts.

Jack artfully wrapped up his reflections before continuing, his voice resonating gently in the room, a counterpoint to the distant commotion. "I don't think that the facility here in the city was the only one that he was using to create those soldiers."

Faye, now on her feet, nodded in agreement. "That's obvious to see now. He's got over one hundred thousand soldiers—"

Jack interjected, completing her thought with an air of gravitas. "The last official estimate was close to a quarter of a million, as more are being reported from smaller countries."

"Whatever," Faye said with a dismissive wave of her hand, "they're spread out all over the globe with equipment and supplies to sustain them. It's like they just popped up out of the ground, which we know they did given the Shepherd Institute's propensity for underground facilities. Meanwhile, not one country in the entire world saw this coming. None of the various intelligence agencies around the world had a clue."

As Faye spoke, her agitation found physical expression in her pacing back and forth across the confined office. Her hand, seemingly drawn by instinct, rested carefully and protectively on her belly, an unconscious act that conveyed both her inner turmoil and the deep-seated need to shield what she held within

Jack's mind was haunted by uncertainties about the world's future, but his greatest apprehension lay in the welfare of the people navigating these perilous times.

"What scares me most is how countries worldwide are reacting to what's been termed the Tehran Incident. Those soldiers deployed in Iran were attacked by Iranian forces in Tehran, and within hours, these soldiers managed to decimate the entire Iranian unit using weaponry and equipment that defied any existing standards," he shared with a mix of apprehension and gravity.

As the memories of those tense moments resurfaced in his mind, Jack couldn't help but swallow involuntarily, the taste of unease still lingering on his tongue. The raw tension in the atmosphere during the height of the incident was etched into his memory, a vivid reminder of how fragile their world had become.

Faye came to a halt before Jack, her movements stilled as she assumed a strong and grounded stance. Her feet were positioned wide apart, providing a sturdy foundation as she prepared to make her declaration.

"Well, you asked if we really wanted to bring a child into this world. I don't see where we have much choice. I'm not giving up this child. It's a part of both of us, Jack."

Jack rose from his seat and enveloped Faye in his embrace, drawing her close against his broad chest. With her back pressed against him, she gazed up into his eyes, her hands covering his forearms. As he kissed her forehead, Faye closed her eyes, savoring the comfort of his love. She felt his sincerity when he spoke, his words touching her heart deeply.

"I would never ask you to give up our blessing. Never in a million years would I ask something like that of you. I love you too much," said Jack.

Tears welled in Faye's eyes as she admitted, "I know you do." The emotions stirred by her pregnancy and the conversation had left her feeling vulnerable.

Faye gently patted Jack's arm, a silent signal for him to release her from the embrace, even though she secretly wished to remain nestled in his arms. She wiped away the tears that had threatened to escape her eyes and composed herself.

"You need to get to work, sir. Your coffee is made in your office, and it's getting cold," she informed him.

Surprised, Jack asked, "How did you know what time I'd be here?"

Ignoring his question, Faye replied with a pointed tone, "Go and have your two creams and two sugars."

With a smirk on his face, Jack left her office reluctantly.

"Don't forget that we're going to see your sister later," she called after him, a reminder of their upcoming appointment.

Jack and Faye arrived at his vehicle simultaneously, a natural outcome given their shared departure from the police station. They would ride in Jack's truck, bound for Dr. Conwell's office to attend Faye's initial pregnancy checkup.

Inside the truck, the absence of music allowed the rhythmic hum of the tires gliding over the asphalt to pervade the space. The world outside seemed to pass in a blur as other vehicles on the road captured Faye's fleeting attention. Gradually, her thoughts synced with the present moment, prompting her to break the silence.

"Jack," she began, her voice resonating in the cozy confines of the vehicle, "I can't help but think about what's ahead for us." Her words were tinged with a mix of excitement and uncertainty, mirroring the emotional undercurrents of their current situation.

Jack's hands expertly navigated the steering wheel, his gaze remaining on the road ahead. He sensed the weight of her unspoken thoughts. As he stole a quick sideways glance at Faye, he replied, "It's a new chapter, that's for sure. But we'll face it together, just like everything else."

"I really don't know how Cadi is going to react when we tell her that I'm pregnant," Faye mused aloud, her voice carrying a mix of contemplation and concern. The uncertainty of their daughter's reaction weighed on her mind.

Jack's grip on the steering wheel tightened slightly as he considered Faye's question. He glanced at her with a reassuring smile before turning his attention back to the road.

"I think we should tell her tonight when we get home," he suggested, his tone confident and hopeful.

The prospect of revealing the news to their daughter filled him with a sense of anticipation and excitement, evident in the sparkle in his eyes.

"Really?" Faye asked, a hint of skepticism creeping into her voice.

The idea of Cadi's potentially exuberant response seemed almost too good to be true, given the teenager's recent emotional ups and downs.

Jack nodded, his expression steadfast. "Yeah, I have a feeling she's going to be over the moon about it. I think she'll be thrilled to be a big sister," he affirmed, his optimism contagious.

Faye's lips curled into a smile as she regarded her husband, his optimism providing a glimmer of comfort.

"You always have a way of seeing the bright side of things," she remarked affectionately.

Jack chuckled softly.

"Well, I've learned that life's too short to dwell on the negatives. And besides, we've got each other to lean on," he said, his gaze briefly meeting Faye's before returning to the road ahead.

Faye's fingers found their way to his, their hands intertwining in a familiar gesture of unity.

"You're right," she agreed, a sense of reassurance settling over her.

Faye's gaze drifted back to the passing scenery outside the window, her mind drifting back to Cadi and the unpredictable shifts in her mood. She wanted to believe that their daughter would be genuinely happy about the news, but a nagging uncertainty lingered beneath the surface. Faye recognized the ebb and flow of her own thoughts, swinging between optimism and doubt with an unsettling speed. She attributed these fluctuations to the changing chemistry of her body, a common occurrence during pregnancy.

"I hope so," Faye whispered softly, her words carrying a mixture of hope and apprehension.

She closed her eyes briefly, as if to silently collect her thoughts and steady her emotions. With a deep breath, she released the doubts that threatened to cloud her mind, replacing them with a fervent wish for a positive outcome.

Beside her, Jack stole a glance at Faye, his keen perception catching the shift in her demeanor. His fingers tightened gently around hers, offering a subtle source of comfort and support. While he couldn't read her thoughts, he understood the rollercoaster of emotions that often accompanied pregnancy.

"We'll take it one step at a time, Faye," Jack said, his voice gentle and reassuring.

Jack swiftly navigated through the hospital grounds, managing to secure a parking spot surprisingly close to the entrance of the administrative section where they were headed. The building loomed before them, its size symmetrical in both directions as they entered through its centrally located doorway. A four-story structure, it emanated a sense of solidity without being overbearing.

Their footsteps echoed softly as they entered the building. Their journey through the entrance hall was brief, leading them to Dr. Conwell's office with ease. His sister, Elizabeth was expected to be within Dr. Conwell's office since she had no medical office of her own to utilize.

Inside the office, Jack's sister-in-law, Elizabeth, eagerly awaited their arrival. With vibrant red hair and freckles adorning her face, she brushed past Jack as if he were a mere ornament placed haphazardly in her path. Enthusiastically, she gathered Faye into a warm embrace, a gesture that expressed her affection and longing.

"Elizabeth!" Faye exclaimed with delight. "It's been so long, and you've cut your hair so short!"

Elizabeth, her face radiating joy, basked in the attention and playfully showcased her new haircut. "Do you like it, Faye?"

Faye's smile was genuine and bright as she responded, "I love it."

The camaraderie between the two women was evident in their interactions. Jack stood by, his affectionate amusement evident in his eyes as he observed the lively exchange between Faye and Elizabeth.

With a gap no larger than a couple of feet, the two women converged in an embrace, as though the world might conspire to tear them apart if they dared to let go. Jack, despite his presence, found himself relegated to the status of a mere bystander, left standing on the sidelines and momentarily invisible to their heartfelt reunion.

"Hi, Izzy. It's so nice to see you," Jack interjected with a playful edge, his words laced with a hint of sarcasm. He went on, mimicking his sister's voice with an exaggerated high pitch and nasality. "Oh, hi Jack. I've missed my brother so much," he mockingly echoed, his hands gesturing in a whimsical imitation of how the two women had embraced.

After that, Jack found himself standing before the two women who seemed to silently project daggers his way, an unspoken retaliation for his playful mimicry. Elizabeth and Faye used the opportunity to catch up, and it was Elizabeth who guided Faye to a small adjoining examination room to initiate the process. The initial examination started with a cursory nature, but it gradually grew more complex. Eventually, Elizabeth's professional instincts kicked in, leading her to the decision that an ultrasound was in order. While they awaited a nurse to fetch a portable unit for the procedure, Jack had the chance to engage in conversation with his sister-in-law.

"So, your old classmate, Jason, is offering up his office for us?" Jack inquired, his tone casual as he leaned against the wall.

Elizabeth's response was equally nonchalant, revealing her intentions. "Well, I'm back here for now mainly to oversee Faye's care. But I'm planning to make a bid to reclaim my position at the forensics office," she revealed with a matter-of-fact demeanor.

"You didn't enjoy being back in Ireland?" Jack inquired, his curiosity getting the best of him.

As he posed the question, he noticed Faye shifting on the exam table, her legs swinging down as she observed the heartfelt reunion between him and Elizabeth. The joyous expression on Faye's face was evident. Elizabeth's response came with a hint of nostalgia, her gaze distant for a moment.

"The family I have there is alright, but they can never replace the bond I have with you and Faye," she admitted, the sincerity in her words palpable.

Jack's tone turned softer as he shared a sentiment he hadn't voiced before. "I wish my brother had the chance to meet your family there."

Elizabeth's hand tenderly cupped Jack's cheek, her touch gentle and reassuring. "In a way, they did get to know him. Through you being there for Brooke as she grew up, she got to experience a part of her father. My family in Ireland got to connect with him in that way too." The depth of gratitude and emotion in her voice was unmistakable.

Jack's fingers intertwined with his sister's, his lips pressing a gentle kiss onto her open palm, a gesture of deep familial affection.

"I'm genuinely happy for you," he expressed warmly.

Elizabeth's smile, a reflection of her gratitude, met Jack's gaze. The resemblance between him and her late husband, his identical twin, was a bittersweet reminder of the person she still missed dearly.

Elizabeth was still coming down from the emotional high when the nurse came into the examination room with the ultrasound machine. Jack was not too knowledgeable about pregnancies but he did know that you did not usually get an ultrasound this early into the pregnancy.

Elizabeth had Faye remove her blouse and put on a gown and set up the equipment while Faye got ready. Not long afterwards, the lights had been dimmed, the ultrasound machine was humming, and the monitor began to show an image in black and white relief.

Jack couldn't make out what he was seeing in the monitor but he could see the look of concern on Elizabeth's face as she interprets what she saw in the monitor.

"What's the matter, Izzy?" Asked Jack, a twinge of nervousness coming over him.

Elizabeth squinted and shook her head. She wasn't very concerned about what she was seeing in the monitor, everything looked normal for what should have been expected at the period of pregnancy Faye was showing that she was in, however, Faye had only recently gotten pregnant and the development that Elizabeth saw in the screen didn't match that.

She looked over at Faye and asked her a direct question."How far along are you supposed to be, Faye?"

Faye looked a little worried. "I should be about four weeks or so if I've calculated things right."

"What's going on, Izzy?" asked Jack. "What's got you so worried?"

Elizabeth put the ultrasound wand down and turned the monitor around so that they could see it clearly instead of from a peripheral view. It had not taken very long for Elizabeth to confirm a pregnancy. She had also confirmed that there were two viable fetuses, thus confirming that Faye had a multiple pregnancy. The fetuses were in an advanced gestation, compared to the stage of development there should have been for the babies, based on the time estimates of when she conceived. Faye and Jack were expecting both a boy and a girl.

Elizabeth spoke slowly so that Jack and Faye could understand exactly what she was going to say. "These babies are showing every indication that they are just about three months along. How have you been feeling, Faye?"

"Weak and sick, despite my ability to heal rapidly," she admitted.

"Yeah, I'll bet. I can understand that given what I'm seeing," Elizabeth stated.

"What do you mean by three months?" Faye asked, coming back to the statement that had obviously gone over Jack's head but raised alarms for Faye. "Is there anything that we need to know about the development of the babies?"

Elizabeth looked like she did not want to answer the question. She wasn't frightened or scared, she was just confused and it showed on her face.

Jack could feel the fist clenching in his chest and turning in his gut. His vision narrowed. He noticed a pale Faye also staring at Elizabeth.

"Izzy, talk to us," Faye pleaded. "Are we going to lose the babies?"

Elizabeth shook herself to throw off the unsure feeling that she felt. "No," she assured Faye vehemently denying the possibility that the pregnancy could be in jeopardy. "The babies seem to be growing at a rapid, unprecedented rate. At this rate of growth, we're looking at a pregnancy that will be a bit over three months total instead of the normal gestation period. That's what I'm worried about. I'm also very worried that it will probably be very hard on you, Faye."

"How hard?" asked Jack in a small, rough voice. He was relieved to find out that the baby's were fine. Their accelerated growth rate concerned him but the news that Faye could be in trouble alarmed him.

"I'm not certain," said Elizabeth. "I don't know enough about the biology of Shepherds to understand fully how this pregnancy will go, but if she was purely human and had a pregnancy like this, then it wouldn't be beyond the realm of probability that the pregnancy could kill her and the babies both if she's not getting enough nutrients. Her healing factor is a bonus for her in this but its still a risky situation."

Faye's fingers tightened around Jack's hand, her fear intensifying at the weight of his words. Unintentionally, her grip grew stronger until a gasp escaped Jack's lips. The sudden sound made her realize the force she had applied, and she looked over at him with wide eyes. Guilt washed over her, prompting her to quickly release his hand. Her attempt to find solace in their connection had inadvertently turned painful.

"I'm sorry," she whispered to Jack, her voice laced with genuine remorse. However, his attention seemed elsewhere, fixated on something that had left him dumbfounded.

Tears shimmered in the corners of Jack's eyes, a sight that struck Faye deeply. In a moment of self-preservation, she convinced herself that his tears were a result of the physical discomfort she had inadvertently caused. It was easier to believe that than to confront the possibility that the source of his emotions lay elsewhere.

As Faye grappled with her own doubts and insecurities, she found herself leaning on the narrative she had constructed. In her mind, Jack was meant to be her pillar of strength, a steady presence that could hold both their burdens. It was a narrative she desperately clung to, for she knew that if Jack wavered, her own resilience might crumble.

In that moment, Faye recognized the fragility of their dynamic. She needed Jack's unwavering strength, even if she had to pretend not to see the turmoil in his eyes. It was a delicate balance, one that she was determined to uphold, even if it meant turning a blind eye to the truth that threatened to shatter the foundation they had built.

There was an unexplainable depth in the connection that existed between Jack and Faye. It transcended mere words; it was a sensation that resonated within his aching heart. Little did he anticipate that this bond would lead to a pivotal juncture in his life, one where he would be compelled to make a decision that would tear at his own heartstrings, no matter the path he chose.

Within the core of his being, Jack sensed Faye's desperate need. It tugged at him, a constant reminder that their fates were intertwined in ways he couldn't fully comprehend. As circumstances unfolded, he found himself facing a crossroads he never saw coming.

Jack understood Faye's character. He knew her well enough to realize that she would never consider ending the lives of their unborn children, even if it meant preserving her own life. It was this unwavering conviction that posed a challenge for him, forcing him to confront an array of options, each with its own weighty consequence. Each potential scenario painted a complex picture of their future.

He possessed a deep understanding of Faye, recognizing her inclination to sacrifice her own life for the sake of the unborn twins. In this scenario, he envisioned her entrusting Cadi into his care, prioritizing the precious lives within her. While her love for Cadi was unwavering, he sensed that she might opt for bringing the twins into the world, even if it meant facing the profound sacrifice of her own life and the affection she held for both Cadi and Jack.

The possibilities weighed heavily on Jack's shoulders, causing his muscles to tense and his stomach to knot even tighter. The pressure of the situation bore down on him, leaving his mind racing with potential outcomes. The turmoil he felt was almost suffocating, yet he couldn't let it show. Not when Faye's gentle touch lingered on his palm, a fragile link to the woman who held his heart.

For a moment, Jack battled his own inner turmoil, fighting the urge to succumb to his own fears and uncertainties. The turmoil was his alone to bear, yet he recognized the need to bolster Faye's courage. With a silent resolve, he stilled his inner storm, summoning a facade of strength. The turmoil within remained his burden to bear, all in the hope of lending Faye the strength she needed to navigate the storm that lay ahead.

Elizabeth deftly collected several vials of blood, her practiced movements almost mechanical. With the procedure completed, she released both Jack and Faye from her clinical grasp. As they prepared to make the journey back home, a heavy silence seemed to settle between them. Yet, Jack was determined not to let that silence linger, especially when he recognized the need for reassurance that hung in the air.

While he too yearned for the comfort of reassurances, Jack knew that in this moment, Faye's needs were paramount. He set aside his own desires and focused on being the pillar of strength that she needed. It was a sacrifice he was willing to make to ensure her well-being.

In the confines of the truck's front seat, Jack's hand reached out, bridging the physical gap that separated them. Faye, her seatbelt securely fastened, had retreated to her own world, leaning against the passenger side door with her feet tucked up on the seat. Her eyes remained closed, shutting out the world around her.

Despite Jack's effort, his outstretched hand fell just short of spanning the distance between them. The mere six inches that kept them apart seemed trivial, yet it felt like an insurmountable chasm. His frustration swelled, the significance of that gap mirrored his own inability to fully reach Faye, both physically and emotionally. Whether it was an inch or miles, it was a barrier that prevented him from offering her the comfort he so desperately wished to provide.

The urge to close that gap, to bridge the divide and offer solace, was overpowering. Jack considered adjusting his position in the driver's seat, determined to gain the reach he longed for. His longing for a tangible connection with Faye at that moment was palpable.

But then, as if sensing his inner turmoil, Faye shifted. She moved her foot, ever so slightly, until it was within Jack's grasp. The small gesture held a wealth of meaning. It was an acknowledgment, a silent agreement that their connection was as essential to her as it was to him.

Meeting her gesture with a mixture of relief and tenderness, Jack looked over at Faye. Her eyes remained closed, a serene expression gracing her features. And there, at the corner of her lips, a faint but genuine smile tugged upwards. In that moment, the physical distance between them mattered less than the unspoken understanding that bound them together.

"You are such a leg man," she playfully teased, a mischievous glint in her eyes as as she opened them to gaze at Jack.

She adjusted her position to grant his hand access to her calf.

With a playful grin, Jack's fingers danced along the sensitive skin behind her knee, evoking an unrestrained squeal from her lips, a sound that held a hint of girlish delight. Their interaction was effortless, a testament to the unspoken understanding that bound them together.

Words were unnecessary; their connection transcended spoken language.

3

They completed the remainder of the journey home in a tranquil silence, a shared understanding of the challenge they were about to face now enveloping them. Upon arriving at the cozy two-bedroom house that had been Jack's long before Faye and Cadi entered his life, they settled in for a family dinner that Cadi had thoughtfully prepared.

As they gathered around the table, Cadi couldn't help but interject with a playful comment, noting that her appetite might suffer if her parents continued to exchange what she teasingly called 'goo-goo eyes.' The subtle gestures of their connection, like their playful footsie under the table, were hardly discreet. Both Jack and Faye chuckled good-naturedly at their daughter's observation, though they made an effort to tone down their affectionate interactions out of consideration for her.

In this light-hearted exchange, the family dynamic was on full display—a mix of love, and a bit of good-natured teasing.

After dinner, the scene shifted to Faye and Jack's bedroom as they prepared to retire for the night. However, their immediate focus wasn't on sleep but on washing away the remnants of the day. Their desire was to ensure they had ample time to spend with Cadi before surrendering to the embrace of slumber, momentarily escaping the world's concerns. Faye positioned herself at the entrance to the ensuite, her anticipation palpable, as she waited for Jack to join her for a shared shower. Already, Faye had shed her skirt and was in the process of removing her blouse, her movements unhurried.

The sound of the shower running provided them with a secure environment to converse about the pressing matter of the pregnancy.

Faye knew they needed to address the situation before bringing Cadi into the fold. They recognized the importance of discussing the topic privately, shielded by the veil of the running water's white noise. With Cadi's extraordinary hearing, it was a necessary precaution to ensure their conversation remained confidential until they were ready to share it with her.

Faye stepped into the inviting warmth of the shower, and Jack soon followed, the rush of water serving as a shield for their private conversation. As the droplets cascaded over them, Jack's soapy hands gently glided across Faye's back, initiating their discussion.

"How do you think Cadi will react to the news that we're pregnant?" Faye inquired, her voice carrying both curiosity and concern.

Jack's fingers worked the lather on her back as he pondered her question. "I'm not entirely sure at first. Knowing her, she might need a moment for it to sink in past her genius IQ, but eventually, I think she'll be genuinely happy," he responded thoughtfully.

Faye's expression remained earnest as she turned to face Jack, the water droplets tracing shimmering paths down her skin.

"You know, you're not being very helpful by avoiding my concerns, Jack," she chided playfully.

With a purposeful shift, she positioned herself behind him, her intention clear as she reached for the bar of soap. Her voice, however, carried a more serious tone. "I genuinely worry about how she'll process this. I don't want her to feel left out, or worse, to think that our love for her might change because we're having biological children."

As Jack turned his head, his gaze meeting Faye's, he couldn't help but smile at the sight of her standing on tiptoe, her effort to meet his eyes accentuating her determination.

"You underestimate how much she adores you, Faye," he reassured her. "She's had time to get used to the idea that our family isn't defined by blood. Cadi knows we love her as our own, no matter the biology."

Faye's eyes softened, a mixture of gratitude and uncertainty in her gaze. "I hope you're right, Jack. It's just that I know teenagers can be sensitive about these things."

Jack's smile turned reassuring, his fingers gently reaching up to brush a strand of wet hair from her face. "You're right, teenagers can be complex, but so is our girl. We'll just have to navigate it together and make sure she knows that our love for her won't waver."

A tentative smile tugged at the corners of Faye's lips. "I suppose we have faced stranger challenges before."

Jack chuckled softly, his hand sliding down her arm to hold hers. "Indeed, we have. This will be no different."

Steam from the shower fogged up the window, the steady stream of water pouring from the faucet head created a hiss that continued to softly be the backdrop of their discussion.

The bathroom was filled with a cozy warmth, steam swirling to fog up the window as the steady flow of water from the faucet head created a gentle hiss, providing a soothing backdrop to their conversation.

Faye's thoughtful expression softened as she turned off the water and took a step closer to Jack. "You're right. It's never been an issue before, because it's always just been us—our own little family, Mom, Dad, and Kitten."

Jack's eyes met hers, and he reached out to pull Faye into his embrace, their wet bodies pressing against each other. His voice was gentle yet firm as he spoke, the affection in his words tangible.

"Listen, Faye," he began, his warm breath mingling with the steam around them. "The fact that Cadi wasn't carried by you, and that she came into this world through that eccentric scientist's unconventional methods, doesn't make you any less her mother. And just because Cadi doesn't share any of my genetic material doesn't make her any less my daughter than if she were biologically mine. We both love her, and she loves us both. At the end of the day, that's what truly matters."

Faye's eyes shimmered with a mixture of emotions, a combination of gratitude and reassurance. She leaned into Jack's embrace, finding solace in his words and his presence.

"You always have a way of putting things into perspective," she admitted softly

Jack's arms tightened around her, pulling her even closer, their bodies melding together. His lips found her forehead, placing a tender kiss there.

"Well, I've had a lot of practice with our unconventional family dynamics," he teased lightly, his voice carrying a hint of playfulness.

Faye's lips curved into a smile against his chest. "That's true. And we've come a long way, haven't we?"

Jack's fingers brushed her damp hair, his touch gentle as he nodded. "Absolutely. We've faced challenges that most families never even imagine. But each hurdle has only made us stronger."

As the water droplets dripped from their skin and mingled with the mist around them, Faye tilted her head to meet Jack's gaze. "And now we're facing another challenge. One that's different but just as significant."

Nestling closer, Faye lowered her head to rest gently on Jack's chest, her embrace enveloping him in a tender gesture. Her arms encircled him, and with a playful giggle, she offered a squeeze that elicited a good-natured groan from Jack. Though her stature was noticeably smaller than his, Faye possessed an unexpected strength that made her affectionate gestures all the more impactful. This hug was a reminder of that unique quality.

A content smile played on Faye's lips as she looked up at him, her eyes shining with warmth.

"You're definitely not escaping my hugs, no matter how much you groan," she teased affectionately.

Jack's own smile matched hers, and he nodded in mock defeat. "I wouldn't dream of it," he replied, his voice infused with playful surrender. The dynamic between them was a perfect blend of comfort, familiarity, and light-hearted banter.

With a soft chuckle, Faye released her hold on him, allowing Jack to step away.

"Alright, then. Let's go share the good news with Cadi," he suggested, his cheerful tone revealing his excitement.

After stepping out of the shower, they dried off, got dressed, and made their way to the family room where they expected to find Cadi. Their daughter was curled up on the sofa, engrossed in a TV show. She was dressed in one of Jack's button-up dress shirts paired with shorts, her favorite nighttime ensemble. Over time, Jack had come to accept that his dress shirts were a coveted commodity among the women in his life, a fact that both amused and warmed his heart. Faye, similarly attired in one of Jack's shirts, joined Cadi's side in the cozy family room, ready to share their news.

Jack settled onto the sofa, creating a space for Faye to sit beside him. As Faye joined him, she playfully maneuvered her way into his lap, positioning herself comfortably between his legs. Jack, shirtless after their earlier shower, let out an audible gasp when Faye's damp hair brushed against the bare skin of his chest. His startled reaction was met with a mischievous grin from Faye, who couldn't resist the opportunity to tease him—particularly when she knew he was sensitive to cold sensations. Despite his protest, the playful interaction was a testament to their easygoing intimacy.

Observing her parents' positioning, Cadi's keen sense of intuition kicked in. She recognized this setup from previous occasions when they had important matters to discuss. Sensing that there was something on their minds, she took the initiative to turn off the television, ready to give her full attention to whatever her parents were about to share.

With a hint of curiosity and anticipation, Cadi voiced her observation, "What's going on? You guys only do this when there's something you need to discuss with me."

Faye looked up at Jack, a subtle exchange of glances passing between them before Jack responded

"She gets that precociousness from you, Faye," he quipped with an affectionate smile, acknowledging their daughter's sharp intuition.

Faye pulled her head forward and then moved it back with a swift motion. Her long, damp, raven-black hair fanned out as her head made a soft 'thwack' against Jack's bare chest. Jack let out an exaggerated "Ouch!" followed by a hearty laugh

Faye turned her attention to Cadi, her expression shifting into a more serious and gentle demeanor.

"Cadi, your father and I wanted to discuss something important with you," Faye began softly, her words carrying a weight of significance. "We've always cherished our family as it is, just the three of us. You know that we love you deeply, regardless of any circumstances."

"I do, Mom. You both make sure I feel loved every day, and I appreciate that," Cadi replied, her voice a mixture of reassurance and curiosity. Yet, there was a hint of uncertainty in her eyes as she tried to discern the purpose of this conversation.

Faye's smile held warmth and sincerity as she met Cadi's gaze. "I truly love you, Cadi. We both do." Faye's hand gently reached up to touch Jack's cheek, a simple gesture that spoke volumes of their shared bond.

Jack chimed in, his own affectionate tone resonating. "Your mom's right, Kitten. Our love for you is boundless and unconditional."

Cadi's gaze shifted between her parents, her perceptive eyes assessing them before she voiced her thoughts. "If you're about to tell me that you're pregnant, I'm way ahead of you."

Faye and Jack exchanged perplexed glances, both of them mirroring the questions swirling in their minds. But it was Jack who voiced their shared curiosity. "How did you know, Cadi?"

Cadi regarded her father with a look that suggested she had just witnessed a magician reveal a simple card trick. "Dad, even a detective like you could have pieced it together if Mom hadn't spilled the beans. I mean, come on!"

As their bewilderment remained apparent, Cadi decided to give them a break. "Mom and I are on the same menstrual cycle. I noticed she missed her period last month and this one. She's been leaving for work early to avoid morning sickness at home where I could pick up on it." She playfully pointed to her nose. "My sense of smell isn't too shabby, you know, Mom."

Faye's dismay was palpable as she processed this revelation. It was as if someone had let the air out of her balloon. "Why didn't you say anything earlier?"

Cadi's response was candid and matter-of-fact. "You guys didn't seem ready to talk about it, so I figured I'd wait until you wanted to share. No biggie."

Frustration mingled with relief in Faye's expression as she realized the unnecessary stress she had put herself through. "And here I was, stressing out about how you'd react and trying to figure out the perfect way to tell you!"

Cadi laughed, her amusement evident. "Relax, Mom. It's all good. Oh, and nice try with the tail-grab, but I'm way too quick for that!"

Cadi playfully dodged her mother's attempt to catch her tail, maintaining her own upper hand in the impromptu exchange.

"That's not fair, Mom. You don't have a tail I can grab onto, and you know how sensitive mine is," Cadi pouted, her playful complaint prompting laughter from both her parents.

With the tension broken, Cadi moved over and enveloped her parents in a warm embrace, allowing herself to bask in their affection. She let them shower her with love and attention, cherishing the simple yet profound moments they shared. As the television program she had been watching came to an end, Cadi bid them both goodnight with a kiss, retreating to her room for some well-deserved rest.

One of Jack's arms provided a secure embrace around Faye, with the free hand he used his fingers idly entwine in her still-damp hair. In the quiet of the moment, he turned his gaze towards her, his voice a soft murmur breaking the silence, "What's on your mind, Faye?"

Her contemplative expression caught the soft light filtering from the lone lamp lit in the room, casting a gentle glow on her features. Faye's thoughts, like wisps of smoke, drifted through her mind as she began to articulate the complex considerations that had been occupying her thoughts since their afternoon discussion.

"It's been three years since Donovan Pike assumed the presidency, and this global presence of his army," Faye began, her voice measured. The weight of the world's changes, guided by Pike's leadership, hung heavily in the air between them.

Her mind retraced the cautious anticipation they had harbored when Donovan Pike rose to power, knowing well the potential dangers of his capabilities. Faye turned to look into Jack's deep brown eyes, a brief moment of connection that held a world of understanding, before she shifted her gaze away, focusing on her thoughts.

"The surprising thing is," she continued, her voice carrying a hint of amazement, "our economy and the economies of the world have flourished. Pike's rule has brought about unexpected prosperity. Our national debt has vanished, and social services are finally meeting the needs of those they're meant to serve. It's a stark contrast to what we had feared."

Her fingers found solace in the texture of Jack's forearm, tracing patterns unconsciously as her words wove a tapestry of change and uncertainty. The position they shared, her back nestled against his chest and his arm wrapped protectively around her. Faye hadn't intentionally sought this proximity, but it felt natural as her thoughts continued to flow.

She let out a quiet sigh, a mixture of contemplation and reflection. "It's almost like the world has found its equilibrium under his rule." Her voice trailed off, her brows furrowing slightly as unspoken questions lingered beneath the surface.

Faye's words flowed, carrying the weight of observations and contemplation. "There's a marked reduction in homelessness, and crime rates have reached unprecedented lows. Our initial concerns led us to believe that things might take a turn for the worse, but instead, they've improved steadily over time." The subtle shift of her fingers on Jack's arm hinted at the complexity of emotions stirred by these unexpected outcomes.

The aftermath of Donovan Pike's rise to power had surprised them. Faye's voice held a trace of reflection, a sentiment echoed by Jack as he responded.

"Even if a dictator's intentions appear benevolent, the essence of dictatorship remains," Jack's somber tone hung in the air, his sigh an expression of his deeply held convictions.

Faye's gaze over her shoulder met Jack's, a connection forged through shared concerns and convictions.

"I understand your perspective, Jack," she replied, her voice holding both agreement and a note of empathy. "It's just that there's something... off. It doesn't quite add up."

The pieces of their world seemed to defy easy assembly, leaving them grappling with the incongruities. A contemplative pause lingered, heavy with unspoken thoughts.

"Each major country in the world harbors a contingent of my 'brothers,' and yet, there's been a remarkable silence from these nations over the past years about that fact," Faye's words bore an undercurrent of intrigue and suspicion. Her gaze seemed to penetrate the veil of uncertainty as she continued, "The soldiers remain stationed on the established Shepherd-owned bases."

Jack's response held a shared perplexity.

"I've noticed it too," he acknowledged, his tone reflecting the mystery that surrounded these events. "Tehran was a clear example of the opposite, but for that, it's a trend seen globally. The armies aren't displaying any signs of aggression or conquest. They're just... stationary," Jack's words mirrored Faye's observations, his voice carrying a mix of curiosity and unease.

Shifting Faye in his lap, Jack adjusted their positions until they were facing each other, his gaze a steady.

Faye's eyes met Jack's, and within that gaze, a world of emotions swirled. Her voice held a touch of vulnerability as she confessed, "I can't help but wonder if there's a deeper plan at play, one that we can't quite see yet."

Faye's sigh, soft yet heavy with contemplation, reverberated in the air, an echo of her inner thoughts. An unspoken connection lingered between them, their shared understanding speaking volumes in the absence of words, as they sat wrapped in each other's presence.

Their conversation resumed, Jack's voice punctuating the silence.

"Just about every major conflict on the globe died out, as if the very fuel driving their flames had been extinguished," he mused, his words carrying a sense of awe at the unprecedented turn of events.

Faye's gently took Jack's large hand and placed it on her belly. Her voice held a touch of earnest curiosity, a plea for understanding.

"Is this type of peace so bad?" The vision of their children growing up in a world devoid of the scars of warfare seemed to brighten her gaze, a reflection of her maternal concern.

Jack's response bore a gravity that belied the simplicity of the question. "Perhaps the better question to ask would be, 'What have we given up in order to gain this peace?'" His words were tinged with a mixture of contemplation and concern, the weight of an unspoken unease carried in his tone.

As Jack's hand found its place within Faye's grasp, a tangible reassurance passed between them. Faye's gaze met his, a silent exchange of emotions bridging the gap of uncertainty.

"I'm not sure what we've given up. We can't see that yet," she conceded, her words gentle yet contemplative. "But do you think that it was something that we needed if we don't even know what it is that we've lost in the first place?"

Jack's gaze held a blend of admiration and understanding as he looked at Faye.

"You always have a way of looking at things from a different angle," he remarked, a faint smile touching his lips.

Faye's response was a soft smile that mirrored Jack's.

"Sometimes, a shift in perspective is all we need to make sense of the unknown," she mused, her fingers tracing idle patterns on his hand that rested on her belly.

The room was quiet, save for the whispers of their shared breaths.

Jack's serious tone brushed against Faye, his voice carrying a pressure of contemplation. "Faye, do you remember what that Shepherd scientist said to you?" The gravity of his tone revealed the significance of his question.

Faye's brows furrowed as she delved into her memories, her gaze distant as she recalled the words that had once been spoken to her.

"He told me that we would become servants by our own choice," she admitted, her voice tinged with a mix of resignation and realization. "He said that humans would willingly surrender control of their lives, seeking relief from the burdens of decision-making, all while remaining oblivious to the fact that we were giving away the very essence of our autonomy."

The memory of Shepherd's chilling prophecy lingered within her, a dark undercurrent in the river of her thoughts. The onus of Shepherd's words had been etched into her consciousness, a chilling reminder of the dangers they posed. Somewhere between the tumultuous years since the incident and the present moment, she had shared this unsettling revelation with him. The exact timing had faded into the tapestry of their history, rendered irrelevant by the impact of the message itself.

"I'm still grappling with it, Faye," Jack admitted, his voice tinged with a mix of frustration and confusion. "Donovan Pike manages to suspend parts of the constitution, effectively halts Congress, and then orchestrates a swift turnaround for the country. And all of this is happening under his authority, which he could potentially make permanent. But at the same time, he's not doing anything overt to solidify his grip on power. He's even talking about holding elections next year. I just can't figure out his endgame here."

Faye leaned back, her expression pensive as she mulled over Jack's words.

"I think the key lies in the public's perception of his actions and the support of his changes," she responded thoughtfully. "If he wants to remain in power, the most straightforward approach is to be effective in his role."

"That's true," Jack stated. "Right now, he's rather effective in exercising his powers and making beneficial changes to society. I worry that people won't recognize this as the dictatorship it is and seek changes."

Faye seemed to think about what Jack had pointed out and she agreed. "I don't think people will seek to change things. After all, why fix something that's still working? Even if there might be 'better' alternatives out there, people tend to choose the path of least resistance. They'd rather stick to what they know and what's easy, even if it means a longer journey without unexpected challenges. They're lazy."

Jack nodded, a mixture of agreement and apprehension in his gaze. "You have a point. It's human nature to opt for the familiar and the comfortable, even if it means sacrificing potential gains in the process. But there's still something unsettling about the way things have changed so quickly."

Faye reached out, her fingers finding their way to Jack's hand, seeking a reassuring connection.

"Change can be unnerving, especially when it happens rapidly and doesn't follow the expected course," she acknowledged. "We've seen the world shift in ways we never could have predicted, and it's only natural for us to question the motives behind it all."

Jack's grip on her hand tightened slightly, his concern mirrored in his gaze. "I just hope we're not trading too much for this peace and stability. There's always a cost."

Faye nestled her head against Jack's chest, her voice softening as she began to speak. "It's not just our country; it's the entire world. President Pike's impact has been unprecedented. His ability to bring about positive global changes is something we've never witnessed before. I can't help but think that if other nations had a choice, they would opt to keep him in power."

A solemn acknowledgment hung in the air. Jack's agreement was measured, his voice carrying the weight of unspoken thoughts. "As much as it's unsettling to admit, it's hard to imagine the world without him at this point."

As if in a seamless motion, Jack effortlessly lifted her into his arms, their connection unbroken as he carried her down the hallway to their room. Laying her gently on the bed, Jack settled beside her.

"Jack, I think it's best not to burden Cadi with the full extent of the risks surrounding this pregnancy until we have more information," she suggested softly, her fingers finding their way to his.

Jack's gaze held a mixture of agreement and concern. "I was thinking the same thing. She's still young, and there's no need to worry her unnecessarily."

Faye's grip on his hand tightened, her gratitude evident in her touch. She leaned in, her lips meeting his in a passionate kiss that conveyed a depth of emotion beyond words.

In the aftermath of their discussion on global matters and Donovan Pike, an unspoken understanding lingered between them. The weight of their true concerns, centered around the safety of their unborn babies and their cherished daughter Cadi, remained hidden beneath the surface. It was a tacit acknowledgment, a shared decision to keep these anxieties at bay, shielded from the light of day. A veiled shield for the deeper concerns that occupied their thoughts.

Though their words danced around the core of their worries, Faye and Jack couldn't ignore the subtext that colored their conversation. Their conversation about world affairs had served as a convenient cover, allowing them to address their apprehensions without directly confronting them. It was a delicate balance, a way to share their concerns without fully exposing the depth of their fears. Their shared decision to withhold certain information from Cadi inadvertently exposed their mutual pact to avoid the sensitive topic altogether

Unspoken but keenly felt, their unexpressed agreement hung in the air, palpable and real. Their choice to withhold certain information from Cadi—a promise to shield her from unnecessary worry and preserve her sense of security. As they lay together, the unspoken truths and silent assurances wrapped around them like a warm embrace.

In the early hours of the morning, Jack awoke from slumber. His gaze settled upon Faye, her tranquil form a breathtaking sight. An ache of admiration filled his chest as he observed her in peaceful repose. The strands of her raven hair cascaded gently around her head, forming an ethereal halo that caught the soft light filtering into the room.

Motivated by the serene image etched into his thoughts, Jack turned his attention to his own body. Muscles taut from rest beckoned for his care. Determined to ease their tension, he embarked on a routine of self-care. Stretching his limbs and humming softly, he surrendered to the soothing rhythm of his movements. The release of pent-up tension spread throughout his body, leaving him with a welcomed sense of relief and relaxation.

The air-conditioner hummed with diligence, steadily countering the warmth within the house and gradually restoring it to a more comfortable level. Amid this white noise, the soft whir of the fan barely registered, a background melody to the scene. Jack, positioned within this soundscape, felt the gentle sweep of forced air caress his skin, its touch delicate as it ruffled the fine hairs on his exposed arms and legs. A subtle shiver traced his nerves, sending a cascade of goosebumps along his flesh.

Yet, as his attention lingered on the prickling sensation and the rising hairs, an uninvited disquiet tiptoed into his consciousness. The physical coolness of the house, while noticeable, seemed insufficient to account for the unsettling unease settling within him. It was as though the very currents of the air had turned into a metaphor for something intangible, an unspoken tension stirring his restlessness.

In this suspended moment, a realization crystallized. Jack's intuition sharpened, suggesting that the source of his disquiet extended beyond the mere temperature or air currents. An intangible presence, imperceptible yet potent, coiled within the shadows of his perception. He was on the precipice of a revelation—a feeling that compelled him to explore further. An urgent curiosity brewed within him, urging him to verify his surroundings, to ascertain whether his instincts held weight or if he was merely grappling with imagined uncertainties.

Jack stealthily slipped out of his own room, his steps navigating the familiar path to his daughter Cadi's room. The house, wrapped in the embrace of the early hour, seemed to hold its breath as he moved. He pushed open Cadi's door with a practiced ease, revealing her sleeping form cocooned in the embrace of her bed. The subdued glow of a nightlight cast gentle shadows across the room, allowing Jack to take in the scene with a mixture of familiarity and parental concern.

Cadi, as he had expected, lay serenely in her slumber, nestled within the realm of dreams. Her rhythmic breathing was a comforting lullaby that spoke of the peace of deep sleep. A small smile tugged at the corners of Jack's lips as he observed her. At this late—or rather, early—hour, the tranquility of her repose painted a portrait of innocence and vulnerability.

His gaze traced the contours of her form, the delicate curve of her cheek, the tousled cascade of her hair, and the gentle rise and fall of her chest. A nostalgic tenderness swelled within him, a testament to the passage of time and the evolving dynamics of fatherhood. One significant reason that Cadi had been gently nudged out of their shared bed wasn't solely due to her maturing age; it was also a result of her impressive ability to commandeer a mattress with such enthusiasm that the term 'bed hog' didn't quite suffice. Her nocturnal movements often resembled a small tornado more than anything else, leaving little room for anyone else.

Despite the comical frustrations of the past, as he looked upon her now, his heart brimmed with an overwhelming surge of love. There she was, a beautiful and spirited force in his life, cocooned in the sanctuary of her dreams. A sense of protection welled within him, the primal urge to ensure her safety in a world that often felt uncertain.

With gentle precision, Jack reached down and tugged the covers up, enveloping her form in their warmth. Leaning over, he pressed a tender kiss onto her forehead, a silent blessing of fatherly affection. His eyes lingered, his gaze soft as it traced the contours of her face, a silent acknowledgment of the profound bond they shared. In this moment, he found solace in the knowledge that she was safe and sound, her dreams a haven untouched by the complexities of the waking world.

He remained by her side for a few more heartbeats, his watchful gaze a testament to the depth of his care. The fear of sudden disappearance that had haunted him earlier seemed to ebb away, replaced by a quiet reassurance. With a final, lingering look, he turned away, leaving her to her slumber. The door closed softly behind him.

Stepping away from Cadi's room, Jack's intention was to return to his own quarters and seek the solace of Faye's presence. Yet, as if caught in a persistent loop, his attention was once again claimed by an unsettling undercurrent that refused to be dismissed. The familiar tendrils of unease coiled around his thoughts, defying his attempts to rationalize them away. The sanctuary of his home, he mused, should have provided a sense of security, but the feeling persisted, refusing to be placated.

His steps, initially directed towards his and Faye's shared space, altered their course as his instincts took over. The unease demanded his attention, urging him to remain vigilant. He tried to reason with himself, reminding his racing mind that he was within the familiar embrace of his own abode. Yet, that logical assertion failed to quell the growing disquiet that gnawed at the edges of his consciousness.

A methodical awareness settled upon him as he stood in the hushed corridors. He strained to attune his senses to the expected symphony of nocturnal sounds that typically enveloped the house during these hours. The gentle hum of the refrigerator's compressor hummed its familiar tune, a reliable participant in the nighttime orchestra. Somewhere distant, the rhythmic cadence of an analog clock marked the passage of time, its ticking offering a sense of continuity.

The house, a steadfast sentinel to their lives, had long since settled into the familiar creaks and groans that accompanied its aging frame. The absence of any unsettling noises associated with shifting foundations or creeping floorboards should have provided reassurance. After all, he was the sole inhabitant awake within its walls, negating any unexpected sounds. Yet, there it was again—an anomalous sound that disrupted the otherwise predictable rhythm of the night.

Jack's ears strained, his senses honed in on the dissonance that had woven itself into the fabric of the night. It was a sound that defied explanation within the realm of the expected—the kind that pricks at the primal instincts of vigilance. His thoughts raced as he weighed possibilities, his mind navigating a labyrinth of conjecture.

A quiet rustle, almost imperceptible, reached his ears—a sound that lacked the familiarity of the house's timeworn voice. It was an interloper amidst the customary sounds, a dissonant note that couldn't be ignored. Jack's jaw tightened as he instinctively tensed, his pulse quickening in tandem with his growing realization. The unease that had nudged at his consciousness was validated by this unwelcome auditory intrusion.

In the stillness of the night, Jack found himself in a tense coexistence with the unknown, his senses on high alert. The quiet thud of his heartbeat resonated in his ears, a testament to his heightened awareness. He stood poised at the precipice of action, his instincts primed to confront whatever lay beyond the veil of uncertainty. The profound silence that wrapped around him was a canvas upon which his next moves would be painted, a tableau of anticipation and determination.

Jack heard as a barely audible noise stirred from the front of the house—a soft click, so faint that it might not have registered if he were asleep. Yet, it wasn't the kind of sound that would typically rouse one from slumber. Nonetheless, Jack's skin prickled, his body reacting with an involuntary ripple of goosebumps along his arms and a prickling sensation at the nape of his neck. It was a shiver that transcended the boundary between cold and fear, a premonition of something unsettled.

Amidst the tension, Jack's instinctual response kicked in. His body shifted into a mode of vigilance, a primal adaptation honed by experience. His heart rate edged up, a steady cadence that propelled the necessary flow of blood to his muscles. A measured inhalation expanded his lungs, grounding his breathing into a deep and rhythmic tempo. Muscles that had been at rest now began to loosen, anticipating the tension they might soon endure.

Caught in this web of uncertainty, Jack stood at a crossroads. The whisper of a decision—whether to return to his bedroom and arm himself or to proceed unaided—hovered in the air. Time seemed to stretch, suspended between the allure of swift resolution and the weight of caution. In this pause, Jack's gaze shifted, his eyes flitting towards the hallway that led back to the room where Faye lay sleeping.

Eventually, he made his choice, swayed by the urgency of reassurance. His sense of expediency won out, prompting him to proceed without a weapon. The thought of hastening back to Faye's side and ensuring her safety outweighed the instinct to arm himself. The alternative—a decision that might involve waking Faye and possibly causing unnecessary alarm—was weighed and ultimately dismissed. Jack knew that his desire to return to Faye's warmth and slip back into the embrace of sleep was as powerful as his commitment to the task at hand.

Yet, a deeper force guided his actions, an instinct that he had learned never to ignore. It was the same intuition that had safeguarded him and his loved ones countless times before. A silent guardian urging him to act, to investigate, to ensure the security of his family. Jack knew the stakes were higher this time. It wasn't just himself he was protecting; it was Faye and Cadi, both peacefully slumbering within the walls of their home.

As he ventured forward, moving with a quiet resolve, Jack was accompanied by the echo of his purpose—an unspoken promise to shield those he cherished. The footsteps that carried him through the corridors echoed the commitment that had defined his role as protector. It was a role he embraced willingly, knowing that his loved ones depended on his unyielding vigilance.

With each step, he drew closer to the source of that unsettling sound. A current of anticipation coursed through his veins, his senses acutely attuned to the task at hand. The darkness of the house seemed to envelop him, but it was within this darkness that Jack's determination and resolve illuminated his path. As he neared the heart of the uncertainty, his heart beat in unison with his unwavering dedication to those he loved.

Jack's footsteps carried him deeper into the house, a sense of unease growing with each passing moment. A disconcerting feeling settled over him, a recognition that something was amiss, that the house itself held a secret he was only now beginning to unravel. As he advanced, a puzzle piece snapped into place in his mind—something felt off about the illumination in the front room, an eerie absence of light that contradicted the typical nighttime ambiance.

Although the house appeared darker than usual, an array of electronic devices scattered throughout emitted their distinct glows, offering a peculiar illumination. This ambient light, though subtle, proved sufficient for him to discern the contours of shadows. The kitchen's faint glow originated from the digital clock on the stove and microwave, while in the living room, the electronic components of the entertainment system contributed a muted yet usable digital display. It wasn't a glaring brightness, but it provided just enough visibility for him to rely on his night vision.

His gaze darted across the room, honing in on a dark shadow that skittered in the distance, a silhouette traversing the length of the living room. Reflexively, Jack turned away, his instincts firing off an urgent signal to retreat. A swift retreat to his shared bedroom, a place of safety where he could arm himself against the potential threat, became his singular focus. His foot took that first quick step down the hallway, each stride fueled by an instinctual need to protect.

The second step was halted abruptly, a wave of realization crashing over him—the truth struck before he could react. The danger he was attempting to escape had caught up to him. His senses registered the telltale discharge of a gas-powered weapon, a sound that carried a sinister promise. A sudden sting erupted in his thigh, quickly followed by the descent of numbing paralysis that swallowed his leg whole. Jack's balance faltered, his body lurching forward as his numbed limb failed to support him.

The trajectory of his fall was a blurred rush, a cascade of events that unfolded in an instant yet seemed to stretch out indefinitely. His thoughts careened, the gravity of his vulnerability mingling with his fierce determination to protect his family. The instinct to lash out surged within him, a primal response to the threat that had now made itself known. But the rational part of him understood the futility of such an action, recognizing that any retaliation would be in vain, a futile outpouring of rage.

In that fleeting moment of choice, Jack's priorities realigned. He let go of the fleeting satisfaction that vengeance might offer and instead channeled his energy into a desperate need to safeguard those he loved. His mind raced, formulating a plan that hinged on alerting his family, on preventing harm from reaching them. His voice caught in his throat, ready to sound the warning, but before he could utter a sound, another discharge pierced the air.

The impact was swift and unrelenting—a pinch in his left shoulder, a sensation that tore through flesh and consciousness alike. A jolt of pain intertwined with the numbing tide that had already begun to creep over him. The ground seemed to rise with an alarming urgency, his body meeting it with an unavoidable collision. Darkness swirled at the edges of his vision, encroaching upon his senses until it consumed his world entirely.

As Jack succumbed to unconsciousness, his final thoughts were of his family. The fierce determination that had guided him thus far now transitioned into a silent plea, a desperate hope that his actions would somehow translate into protection for those he held dear.

4

Cadi found herself in a state of confusion and uncertainty, grappling with a situation that exceeded her comprehension. The events unfolding before her were beyond the scope of her limited understanding of the world's intricate dynamics. In her young mind, it was inconceivable that such a distressing incident could transpire within her own secure and familiar environment. The disparity between what she believed the world should be and the stark reality that had just unfolded left her utterly bewildered, struggling to make sense of the inexplicable.

Her slumber was disrupted when her father, Jack, entered her room—a nightly ritual she had come to cherish. His presence brought comfort and a sense of security that she treasured. His tender gestures, like tucking her in, enveloped her in warmth and affection. The moments of closeness between them were a soothing balm to her spirit, making her nights easier to navigate. The goodnight kiss and the reassurance of his love had become essential to her, a testament to the bond they shared.

However, this night felt different. The atmosphere in the house carried an unusual weight, an undercurrent of unfamiliar scents—hints of men, the tang of metal, and the faint aroma of oil. Even the sounds that reached her ears were unlike the usual nocturnal symphony—the creaks and murmurs of the house settling, the scuttling of creatures within the walls. Instead, new sounds invaded her sanctuary—shifting gears, hushed breaths, the cryptic chatter of radio earpieces, and the sharp discharges of air cartridges. These auditory anomalies resonated in the hallway outside her room, weaving an eerie tapestry that contrasted sharply with the norm.

It was within this altered soundscape that she heard a particularly unsettling occurrence—a sound of distress, a deep breath followed by a fall, and her father's collapse in the hallway. Her heart quickened, an instinctive response to the unforeseen turmoil unfurling beyond her room. The urge to rush out and investigate tugged at her, yet an overriding sense of caution held her back. She was acutely aware of the potential danger lurking just beyond her door.

Cadi's mind raced, torn between the impulse to seek her father and the wariness that had been ingrained within her by his careful teachings. She grappled with the gravity of the situation, her young mind struggling to reconcile the incongruities of the present moment. As the seconds ticked away, she wrestled with her emotions and the desire to take action, a mixture of concern for her father and a newfound apprehension for the unfamiliar threat that had intruded upon their home.

In the midst of the uncertainty, Cadi's gaze remained fixed on her closed bedroom door, the barrier between her and the enigma that had unfolded. Her father's collapse echoed in her ears, a haunting reminder of vulnerability. She felt the weight of responsibility pressing upon her young shoulders, the need to protect and understand—two instincts that tugged at her with equal force. And as the night unfolded, those instincts would guide her actions in ways she never could have foreseen.

Describing Cadi as merely frightened would be an immense understatement of her emotional state at that pivotal moment. She was engulfed by a paralyzing terror that threatened to consume her. The presence of these unknown individuals, likely numbering half a dozen, intruding upon the sanctuary of their home was not just a source of fear—it was a tidal wave of overwhelming dread. The realization that danger lurked within their supposedly secure abode left Cadi in a state of panic, her thoughts racing to make sense of the inconceivable threat.

Cadi's desperate desire to warn her mother about the perilous intruders was in stark conflict with her own survival instinct. The impulse to shout out a warning warred with the fear of potential consequences, leaving her in a harrowing dilemma. However, fate intervened on her behalf, sparing her from the need to make that agonizing choice. The sound of her mother emerging from the bedroom to confront the intruders echoed through the hallway, a brave and courageous response to the danger that had breached their home. Cadi's heart raced as she absorbed the weight of her mother's actions, her own anxiety mirrored in her mother's brave confrontation.

The sudden, thunderous eruption of gunfire reverberated through the narrow confines of the hallway, a stark reminder of the impending danger. Cadi instinctively recognized the source of the gunshot as her mother's defense against the assailants. The deafening sound, amplified by the proximity to her own bedroom door, jolted Cadi to her core. She recoiled in terror, her instinctual response amplified by the disorienting cacophony.

Seeking refuge in the face of chaos was a familiar coping mechanism for Cadi, one that led her to the attic—her secret sanctuary. Disguised as a small access panel within her closet ceiling, it was the portal to a space where she had often sought solace before. This same portal offered her a means of escape from the madness unfurling below. Crawling through the access point, Cadi sought refuge in the attic, leaving behind the turmoil that threatened her sense of safety. In the eerie stillness of the attic, she sought solace and separation from the grim reality that had befallen her home.

Recognizing her own limitations, Cadi knew that her presence could only hinder her mother's efforts to repel the invaders. Her hiding was not an act of cowardice, but a conscious decision to minimize her mother's burden. Above all, she wished to prevent herself from becoming a liability and endangering her mother's chances of success.

In the attic's concealed embrace, Cadi listened intently, her senses attuned to the tumultuous events transpiring below her. Voices, strained and hushed, reached her ears, distorted by the insulation that separated her from the source. Though words were muffled, their tension was palpable, a reminder of the ongoing struggle within her home. Cadi strained to decipher the faint whispers of conversation, her heart pounding in anxious anticipation of any scrap of information that might offer insight into the unfolding crisis.

"Come out and drop your gun, Alpha 06," the voice echoed with a stern authority, shattering the tense silence that had engulfed the house "We've got Detective Riddle, so you'll need to give up if you don't want to see him get hurt. I'll count to three. One... two..."

The ominous ultimatum carried a weight of urgency, a demand for compliance that brooked no negotiation. The ultimatum was clear—compliance or harm befalling Jack, an individual who held significance to them both. Cadi strained to hear every word, her heart racing in rhythm with the escalating tension. Her mother's response came swiftly, a resigned surrender to the high-stakes predicament they were entangled in.

"Alright, I'm coming out," her mother's voice rang out, threaded with a palpable mix of anxiety and determination.

The gravity of the situation seemed to magnify as Cadi absorbed each word, her senses heightened to the exchange unfolding beyond her sheltered haven.

The sound of something heavy hitting the carpeted floor echoed through the hallway, an audible punctuation to her mother's capitulation. Cadi inferred that her mother had relinquished her weapon, a stark reminder of their vulnerability in the face of this threat. Yet, the immediate danger was far from over. A series of sounds reverberated from below, signaling the sequence of events Cadi had feared. The airgun's distinctive discharge was followed by a haunting thud, and a chilling realization dawned upon Cadi.

The same fate that had befallen her father now appeared to have struck her mother. The heavy impact that had reached her ears signified a tranquillizing blow, a cruel end to her mother's brave resistance. Cadi's heart ached for her parents, each sound a painful reminder of the perilous situation they had been ensnared in.

As the events unfolded downstairs, a shiver of anxiety gripped Cadi. She held her breath, straining to detect any movement that might betray the presence of the intruders. In a desperate attempt to divert their attention, she had strategically opened one of her windows, creating the illusion of escape. The calculated misdirection was a desperate ploy to ensure her own safety.

The sounds of intrusion reached her room, the shuffling footsteps an unsettling reminder of their unwanted visitors. Her breath caught as the reality of their search seemed imminent, their presence almost tangible. Cadi pressed herself into the shadows of the attic, willing herself to become an inconspicuous observer of the events below. Every sound was a symphony of danger, each footfall a harbinger of potential discovery. She prayed that her ruse had sown enough confusion to shield her from their scrutiny.

Her heart raced in synchrony with the rhythm of her thoughts. Cadi listened intently, her senses attuned to the ebb and flow of movement below. The final sounds of departure were a bittersweet symphony, carrying with them the hope that their intruders were leaving. In the attic's seclusion, Cadi clung to the shadows, a silent witness to the tumultuous events that had unraveled her once-safe haven.

In the span of less than fifteen minutes, the world as Cadi knew it was irreversibly shattered. In the disorienting whirlwind of events that unfolded, her sense of security and comfort, once anchored to the four walls of her home, crumbled like a facade exposed to harsh truths. Huddled in the corner of the attic, she clung to herself, her arms encircling her knees, a silent witness to the cataclysmic upheaval that had engulfed her life. Amidst the chaos, she grappled with conflicting emotions, her desire to cry warring with the need to hold back the rising tide of hysteria that threatened to consume her.

The sanctity she had attributed to her home had been an illusion, a fragile veneer that crumbled in the face of harsh reality. Her heartbeat echoed the cacophony of her thoughts—fear, confusion, and a raw determination to weather the storm. Cadi's trembling form held a tension that mirrored the tumultuous events that had unfolded below. She recognized the danger of succumbing to the despair that lurked just beneath the surface, threatening to engulf her in a torrent of tears and panic.

With her arms wound tightly around her legs, Cadi fought to steady her breathing, to quell the racing thoughts that threatened to overwhelm her. This was a pivotal moment, a crossroads between surrendering to the torrent of emotions or maintaining a semblance of control. She knew that yielding to hysteria now would only hinder her ability to navigate the uncertainty ahead. Her dampened eyes glistened with unshed tears, a testament to her internal struggle, yet her resolve held firm. Cadi clung to the remnants of her composure, determined to find a path through the chaos.

The attic enveloped her in its quiet embrace, a space removed from the turmoil that had infiltrated the rest of her world. Time seemed to stretch as she grappled with her next move. Amidst the quiet, the passage of minutes felt like an eternity, each heartbeat and breath a reminder of her existence. Cadi's mind whirred with thoughts, the immediate future a blank canvas upon which she needed to paint her survival.

As her breathing steadied and the storm of emotions abated, Cadi's inner strength emerged. The threat was real, the danger pressing, yet within the silence of the attic, she found a refuge to steady herself. She knew she couldn't remain hidden forever, that decisions had to be made, actions taken. But in this fragile moment, amidst the debris of her shattered illusions, she gathered her resolve. Cadi waited, not in helpless submission, but in a pause—an interlude before the storm—preparing to face the challenges that lay ahead with a determination that matched the tumult of her emotions.

The house below her lay cloaked in an oppressive silence, each moment stretching into an eternity as Cadi maintained her vigilant watch from the attic. Time seemed to stand still, matching the weight of her emotions. She remained suspended in a liminal space, caught between the urge to take action and the paralyzing grip of fear. Cadi's heart echoed in the hollow of the attic, its rhythm a counterpoint to the stillness of her surroundings. And still, she waited.

The passage of time was a slow drip, each moment merging into the next. An hour crawled by, then another, their agonizing slowness a testament to the tension that hung in the air. Fatigue clung to Cadi, a heavy blanket that should have pulled her into slumber, but her mind was too fraught with disbelief, too wired with apprehension to allow her rest. In this suspended reality, the boundary between exhaustion and alertness blurred, leaving her in a state of heightened awareness. Distrust of the stillness held her captive, keeping her rooted to the confines of the attic. Her limbs protested, fatigue tugging at her, yet she dared not surrender to sleep. The tendrils of uncertainty wrapped around her, urging her to remain hidden, to not risk discovery by those who had violated the sanctity of her home. It was a precarious balance between fear and the urge to escape, between a desire for safety and a thirst for answers.

As time trickled by, the urgency of her body's needs began to compete with her internal struggle. Uncertainty clung to her like a shroud, a shield against the unknown dangers below. Yet, discomfort grew as her body demanded attention, reminding her of its needs. The relentless pressure of a full bladder forced her to confront her vulnerability, to consider the risk of movement and exposure.

Forced to reckon with her own physical needs, Cadi realized that her discomfort outweighed her uncertainty. She could no longer remain hidden in the attic, cocooned in her protective shell. The need to answer the call of nature pushed her beyond the limits of her apprehension, propelling her towards a decision she had been avoiding. With a sigh of resignation, she resolved to face her vulnerability head-on, to leave the confines of the attic and venture back into the reality that had been shattered.

The stillness persisted, but Cadi's determination had shifted. With a deep breath, she readied herself to descend from the attic, her movements careful and deliberate. The passage of time had not quelled her fear, but it had steeled her resolve. As her foot touched the floor below, uncertainty still clung to her, but it was now accompanied by a burgeoning sense of agency. Cadi had chosen to step out of the shadows, to confront the unknown, driven by the primal needs of her body and the indomitable spirit that resided within her.

With a careful and calculated grace, Cadi extricated herself from the tight confines of the attic. She maneuvered her body through the cramped space, her movements methodical as she navigated the darkness. The closed attic access yielded to her touch, revealing the entrance that led to her closet. She lowered herself down with a cautious deliberateness, her tail betraying her unease with intermittent twitches. The scent of burnt gunpowder lingered in the air, a lingering reminder of the chaos that had erupted within the home. It pricked at her senses, adding another layer of tension to her already fraught nerves.

Her determination to avoid further discomfort spurred her onward, despite the nervous energy that threatened to consume her. She had no desire to make a mess of things, especially given the circumstances. The urgency of her physical needs propelled her forward, past the lingering traces of violence and chaos. She navigated the path to the bathroom, her senses attuned to every sound and shadow. Relief washed over her as she completed her task, a small victory in the midst of uncertainty.

Returning to her room, Cadi remained shrouded in the darkness, her heightened senses compensating for the lack of light. The lingering tang of spent gunpowder pervaded the air, a constant reminder of her mother's final stand. It clung to her like a spectral echo, a testament to the horrors that had unfolded. Cadi's thoughts flitted briefly to her mother, but she pushed the images away, unwilling to let herself be consumed by grief and fear.

Cautious in her actions, she refrained from turning on any lights, a silent acknowledgment of the potential danger that could be lurking outside. If her assailants believed she had fled the house, they might be keeping a watchful eye on its exterior. Her cat-like night vision served her well, allowing her to navigate the dimly lit spaces with relative ease. She moved with purpose, each step a testament to her determination to find safety in the midst of chaos.

Her mind focused on the singular goal of finding a place where she could regroup and feel a semblance of security. The events that had shattered her world had left her grappling with a new reality, one in which her home was no longer the sanctuary she had believed it to be. The urgency of the situation eclipsed her fear, propelling her forward with a tenacious resolve. The weight of uncertainty pressed against her, but she pushed through it, driven by the instinct to survive and find a way to navigate the uncharted territory that had become her reality.

Cadi adjusted her attire, opting for a pair of jeans and a loose-fitting shirt. The jeans hung low on her hips, ensuring her tail remained free from any undue pressure caused by waistbands. This arrangement prevented her tail from being trapped beneath fabric. The loose shirt allowed her to discreetly coil her tail around her waist, keeping it hidden. Yet, to secure her tail in place, she reluctantly had to employ a ribbon. The discomfort was tolerable, albeit temporary. Cadi acknowledged that her tail's behavior wasn't entirely under her control; its movements were often influenced by external factors, both emotional and physical, operating at a subconscious level. The ribbon became a necessity to maintain her desired level of control.

With her long, dark hair bundled and concealed beneath a baseball cap, Cadi packed a few changes of clothes into a book bag. She ventured into the kitchen, gathering essential supplies—water, fresh fruit, and various items that would sustain her for a few days until she could find safety. Though poised to depart, she hesitated by the back door, a lingering thought prompting her to retrace her steps into her parents' room.

There, she located her father's wallet and extracted his debit card, armed with the knowledge of its PIN. The notion of using the card for cash was reserved as a final recourse, as she grappled with uncertainties. She couldn't dismiss the possibility that the captors might trace her access to the linked account. Cadi lacked insight into their capabilities, and she was unwilling to underestimate the extent of their methods and objectives. Therefore, caution became her guiding principle, steering her decisions in the face of ambiguity. Cadi's sharp intellect compelled her to anticipate and prepare for every possible scenario. In her quest for readiness, she located her mother's wallet and acquired her debit card. With a calculated approach, she considered the potential of leveraging one, or ideally both, of the cards if circumstances necessitated it. But before delving into the practicality of card usage, Cadi recognized the fundamental hurdle that demanded her immediate attention—a challenge that was currently a source of frustration: where should she go at that very moment?

Initially, her instinct urged her toward her aunt's residence, yet the timing was unfortunate, as Aunt Izzy had recently returned to the country and hadn't settled into a home yet. The idea of seeking refuge with her grandparents flitted across her mind, but it was swiftly dismissed as unwise. Engaging her grandparents in such a perilous situation seemed unnecessary and inadvisable, a notion she firmly held onto given the evident gravity of the circumstances. Moreover, other factors called for consideration.

Central to Cadi's concerns was the enigma of her adversaries' identity and capabilities. Amidst the uncertainty, one undeniable fact remained: the assailants appeared indifferent to the fact that her parents held positions in law enforcement. Cadi wisely resisted assuming that these individuals were unaware of her parents' roles. If they had boldly infiltrated her home to capture her parents—potentially including her—then there was no reason to believe they wouldn't attempt to locate her even at her grandparents' residence. Fueled by her innate sense of responsibility, Cadi hesitated to place her grandparents in jeopardy for the sake of her own safety.

Guided by a mix of intuition and logic, Cadi recognized the necessity of seeking a refuge that her possible pursuers wouldn't suspect, let alone know about. This foresight effectively ruled out her grandparents as viable options for aiding her quest for a secure haven. While making her preparations for departure, she grappled with the challenge of identifying a location that wouldn't raise suspicion and hadn't been previously considered by her pursuers.

As she readied herself to leave, Cadi meticulously secured her surroundings. She closed and locked her window, as well as the backdoor, reinforcing her cautious demeanor. Amidst the practical actions, she allowed her thoughts to drift, formulating a plan for a hiding place that was unlikely to register on anyone's radar.

Cadi consulted her smartphone for directions to her desired destination before toggling it into airplane mode to sever its connection to cell towers. A further step followed—powering it down completely. She couldn't risk the possibility of her home invaders tracing her movements through her phone. Her intended address lay roughly twelve miles away from her current location, a journey she estimated might span about two hours due to her physical prowess. An unspoken hesitancy held her back from making a phone call ahead of time, as the potential of call monitoring lingered in her mind. Instead, she would have to gamble on the assumption that her aid was available.

Stepping through the backyard, Cadi reached the street bordering the adjacent block. With clear bearings on her route, she embarked on a brisk jog that she believed she could sustain until her destination was reached. Her path led her towards Jason Conwell's abode—a figure well known to her. He had been her aunt Elizabeth's associate and a close collaborator, and notably, one of the few outside immediate family who was privy to her genetic distinction. Following her aunt's departure from the country, both she and her mother had come to rely on Dr. Conwell for medical care.

However, Jason Conwell wasn't a typical family physician. Though he had training as a general practitioner, he found his calling as a medical examiner in the local hospital. His role centered on conducting autopsies, and it was a role he embraced wholeheartedly. In this intricate tapestry of character dynamics, Cadi's journey bore the weight of her circumstances as she sought assistance from a person who knew not only her medical condition but also her family's intricacies.

Cadi possessed the doctor's home address, her lifeline in this moment of crisis. She held out hope that her timing would align favorably; if it wasn't one of his scheduled work nights, she wouldn't be confronted with the choice of either waiting by his house or heading to his hospital workplace. The latter option was less preferable. Her aim was to maintain a low profile, avoiding any unnecessary attention. The fewer eyes on her, the safer she'd feel. Not having seen her parents' abductors up close, Cadi had no visual reference to evade them. However, one sensory cue lingered—the distinct scent of the oil they had been exposed to. She hoped that this scent might serve as a shared marker, helping her identify any potential allies.

Having maintained a steady pace for about two hours, Cadi effortlessly conquered the twelve-mile distance, her endurance and relentless speed a testament to her capability. Despite the exertion, her breathing remained controlled and her body relatively dry. Transitioning into a more leisurely walk, she entered Jason's neighborhood, her senses alert to her surroundings. Every detail was scrutinized, as she sought any hint of irregularity. Unfamiliar with the nuances of this area, she yearned for the familiarity of her own neighborhood, longing for a sense of normalcy she had known before the nightmare engulfed her life.

The clock inched towards two-thirty in the morning, casting an eerie stillness over the deserted streets. Cadi found solace in the absence of moving vehicles, a sight that calmed her nerves. If a car had appeared down the road, her instinct would have driven her to cower and conceal herself until the vehicle was a safe distance away. Taking no chances was her rule.

Approaching her destination, just about two blocks away, an inexplicable sensation made the hairs on Cadi's neck stand on end. Simultaneously, her tail's tip exhibited a subtle twitch. Instinctually, her subconscious signaled an alarm, while the task of pinpointing the exact nature of the danger fell to her conscious mind. An aura of caution enveloped her. Stopping in her tracks, she nimbly stepped off the sidewalk, ensuring a strategic vantage point that minimized her visibility while allowing her to surveil the street. Concealing herself behind some bushes, Cadi hunkered down, waiting and observing with a measured patience.

Swiftly, her instincts were validated. A sense of foreboding centered around a four-door sedan, parked on her side of the street, just ahead of her crouched position. It sat halfway between her and her destination at Dr. Conwell's residence. Her focus remained locked on the vehicle, scrutinizing every detail to understand the source of her unease. The dimly lit street held only a few sporadic nightlights, leaving areas of shadow untouched by their illumination. Among the parked vehicles lining the street, this sedan stood out distinctly, an anomaly in the night's darkness.

Thanks to her distinct split irises, Cadi's night vision was exceptional. Focusing her attention on the task at hand, she swiftly identified the sedan and its occupants. Two figures were seated within, intently observing... something. Alarmed by the prospect that they might be surveilling the doctor's house, Cadi made a swift decision and walked away, choosing not to tempt fate.

Noticing that the doctor's car was absent from his driveway, she held onto a glimmer of hope. Without a garage, the absence could hint that he was either at the hospital or elsewhere. Discreetly, she weighed her options. Calling him to inquire about his whereabouts risked exposing her own plans, so she opted to proceed under the assumption that he might be at the hospital. This scenario confirmed that the people who had taken her parents were actively searching for her. Furthermore, it indicated that these individuals possessed a level of information about her family that was deeper than she had initially believed.

Retreating from the scene, Cadi ensured she was safely out of sight from the sedan's occupants. Once confident she was concealed, she oriented herself towards Saint Elwood Hospital—the workplace of Dr. Conwell. Pacing herself, she embarked on a journey that paralleled the previous one from her home to the doctor's residence. Calculating the time required, she estimated that she would reach the hospital within half an hour on foot.

With her arrival at the hospital drawing near, Cadi remained vigilant. Her experience had taught her that danger could emerge from the most unexpected sources. As she pressed forward, the dynamics of her character drove her to stay cautious, prepared for any possibility.

Cadi's pace led her to the hospital premises promptly. Her attention swept across the employee parking lot until her gaze landed on Dr. Conwell's car. The sight provided a measure of reassurance, suggesting the likelihood of his presence within the hospital, either in his office or perhaps the morgue. Considering the hour, only two entrances offered access to the hospital's interior—the emergency room entrance and the main doors at the opposite end. Cadi's trained eye immediately spotted individuals monitoring the main entrance. As she contemplated entry solutions with unwavering determination, the thought crossed her mind that the emergency room entrance might be under surveillance too. Undeterred, she moved around the building, seeking an alternate entry point.

Her determination paid off when she identified an open door on a balcony elevated by a floor. A cautious scan of the surroundings confirmed her privacy, giving her the green light to act. Crouching low, she sprung upwards, utilizing her agility to grasp the bottom rung of the balcony railing. With a fluid motion, she hoisted herself over the railing and into the building, her practiced movements reflecting a combination of skill and precision. Familiarity with the hospital layout enabled her to swiftly orient herself, pinpointing her location without hesitation.

Aware of the cafeteria's layout from past visits, Cadi recognized that the doorway led into the cafeteria proper and that the balcony corresponded to the exterior dining area. These details provided her with a valuable sense of bearings as she navigated the hospital's interior, her actions driven by a mixture of purposeful determination and the natural familiarity borne from previous encounters within these walls.

Cadi deliberated and resolved to locate a phone within the hospital, intending to call Dr. Conwell's office. This move was a strategic measure to confirm his presence without using her own cell phone, minimizing the risk of potential monitoring or location tracking associated with her device. Her rationale for this decision stemmed from her desire to avoid unnecessary exposure and the potential interception of her call, with the ultimate aim of circumventing any unforeseen threats that could be lurking.

Her strategy of calling aimed to ascertain Dr. Conwell's location without physically descending to his office, thereby sidestepping the risk of encountering unwanted surveillance. Instead, she contemplated a safer alternative—urging him to join her in the cafeteria. This approach allowed her to observe his arrival and assess the situation for any suspicious activity. If the coast appeared clear, she could then venture to make contact with him. Yet, a degree of caution persisted; she was mindful that even Dr. Conwell's presence might inadvertently place her in jeopardy, given that he himself could be under surveillance.

Cadi's determination led her to a phone within the hospital, allowing her to reach out and connect with Dr. Conwell's office situated in the morgue. As the call connected, her tone carried a subtle urgency, one that didn't escape the doctor's attention.

"Hello?" Jason's voice came through, a note of concern edging into his tone.

"Dr. Conwell, it's Cadi," she began, her words rushed yet purposeful. "I'm at the hospital, and I really need to talk to you. Could you please come up to the cafeteria from your office?"

A brief pause followed on the other end of the line. Cadi's heart raced as she awaited his response. Jason's voice returned, a hint of reassurance laced within. "Of course, Cadellia. Give me a few minutes to finish up some tasks down here, and I'll be right up."

The relief in Cadi's demeanor was palpable as she responded, "Thank you so much, Dr. Conwell. I'll be waiting in the cafeteria."

Cadi then began to give Dr. Conwell a set of instructions he should follow as he came up to see her.

After the call ended, a subtle shift took place in Cadi's stance. Her tension, though not entirely dissipated, seemed to have found some release. The next steps lay ahead,

Jason's agreement to meet her in the cafeteria spoke volumes about the urgency he detected in Cadi's pleas. Emboldened by this cooperation, she reentered the cafeteria and made her way to the balcony. Positioned there, she had a clear line of sight to the cafeteria entrance, affording her the advantage of observing anyone's approach. It was a strategic vantage point—one that granted her the flexibility to react swiftly if anything seemed awry.

The dimly lit balcony shrouded her in darkness, making her difficult to spot from the well-lit interior where large windows reflected the brightness. This concealment granted her the early warning she needed, acting as a buffer against any unforeseen danger. With this escape route secured, she knew she could vanish from sight without a trace if the situation took a turn for the worse.

Following Cadi's instructions, Jason found himself adhering to a set of steps that felt somewhat peculiar, yet he carried them out without hesitation. His reasons for complying were twofold, each rooted in his perception of her urgency. The tension that emanated from her voice during their conversation convinced him of the seriousness of the situation. Moreover, he couldn't fathom that she would prank him under these circumstances, given the early hour and the nature of her plea.

Cadi's directive to meet in the cafeteria on the second floor seemed simple enough to Jason. It was the intricacies of the path she laid out that had him feeling slightly awkward, as they were designed to thwart any potential pursuers from discovering their meeting point. She instructed him to venture to a distant set of elevators, a walk that would allow him to gauge whether he was being followed. Following that, he was to ride the elevator to the third floor, and if alone, send it to the fourth floor as a potential decoy. His next task involved discreetly observing the elevators, ensuring he wasn't trailed. If, after five minutes, there was no sign of elevator movement, he was to descend a flight of stairs to the second floor and head to the cafeteria where she awaited.

Jason stepped into the cafeteria, his presence unobtrusive among the scattering of tables and chairs. With purposeful strides, he approached the food counter and retrieved a tray. His experienced eyes scanned the options available. Opting for practicality, he selected two sandwiches and a pair of drinks from the cooler. After arranging his choices on the tray, he proceeded to the checkout, promptly settling the bill. Tray in hand, he sought out an unoccupied table, occupying one of the vacant seats as he settled into a brief wait.

The cool, artificial lighting of the cafeteria cast a tranquil ambiance, contrasting the turmoil that had brought him to this rendezvous.

He didn't have to wait long. A familiar voice cut through the stillness, carrying a mix of urgency and familiarity. "Dr. Conwell." The sound emerged from the door leading to the balcony's outdoor dining space, a doorway to both the meeting and the enigma he had been drawn into. Quickly gathering his tray, he made his way towards the source of the call.

Cadi stood at the threshold, a blend of determination and tension etched into her features. As their gazes met, it was evident to him that her condition was not as dire as her earlier phone call had suggested. Yet, her eyes held a hint of weariness, like one who had navigated the edges of exhaustion. Jason handed her one of the drinks he had fetched, along with a sandwich, a subtle gesture of care and understanding. It was his instinct, honed through years of practicing medicine, to offer sustenance to those under strain, a gesture that often carried unspoken empathy.

Taking a seat at a nearby table by the railing, they found a vantage point that balanced their need for visibility and a swift exit if required. In the quiet of that space, a momentary lull embraced them, and the world outside seemed to momentarily cease its tumult. Jason studied Cadi discreetly, his trained eye absorbing the nuances of her demeanor. Despite the turmoil that had led them to this clandestine meeting, there was a resilience in her posture.

As their interaction shifted from abstract communication to tangible presence, he couldn't help but acknowledge the transformation that occurred when one shifted from voice to flesh. Her form carried an air of quiet strength that transcended the timbre of her voice on the phone. The bridge between telephony and reality had been crossed, illuminating the depth of the situation.

Without hesitation, he extended one of the sandwiches to her, along with the drink. It was a simple yet intentional offering, a silent recognition of the toll that anxiety could take on the body. Having dedicated years to the study of human behavior, he was well acquainted with the tendency of stress to undermine the basics of self-care. The act of nourishing oneself, even in moments of crisis, was a small rebellion against the tide of turmoil.

Gathering herself, Cadi accepted the sustenance, her eyes meeting his with a mixture of gratitude and acknowledgment. It was an unspoken exchange, a recognition of shared concern. She began to eat, the process of consuming nourishment grounding her in the present moment. It was a momentary respite, a fleeting pause in the chaos that had consumed her world.

The passage of time hung in the air, a palpable entity that seemed to bend and stretch according to the weight of their circumstances. Jason's voice, when it finally surfaced, bore an undercurrent of genuine concern.

"Cadellia, it's almost three in the morning. What happened? Where are your parents?" His tone conveyed a mixture of empathy and urgency, a mirror to the questions that undoubtedly reverberated within her own mind.

In the quiet of the cafeteria, the words lingered. Cadi meticulously unwrapped her sandwich, her fingers deftly peeling back the layers. Her focus on the task at hand was unwavering, her senses attuned to the tactile sensation of each movement. A familiar rhythm settled in—the rhythm of sustenance, a contrast to the turmoil that had thrust her into this clandestine rendezvous. She began to consume it with measured bites, savoring the taste as she processed the whirlwind of events that had brought her to this cafeteria rendezvous. Jason, while brimming with curiosity and concern, allowed her the space to eat without feeling hurried. She had consumed approximately half of the sandwich by the time Jason's questions began to permeate the air around them.

Despite his curiosity, he maintained a calm demeanor, one that conveyed both his concern. The notion of her choking on a hastily consumed bite was far from his intentions, and he strived to create an atmosphere of ease.

Her earlier exertions had left her with a hunger that transcended the confines of a mere physical appetite. The act of nourishing herself was a form of self-care—a way to regain her strength in the midst of adversity. Cadi recognized this, and her gratitude was palpable in the way she approached the repast. As she neared the midpoint of her meal, she felt the timing was right to broach the subject that had led her to seek him out.

In the intervals between bites, Cadi wove her narrative, threading words through the spaces between mouthfuls of food. Her voice emerged, a steady stream of disclosure that carried the weight of her ordeal.

"Earlier tonight, someone came into our house and took my mom and dad," she revealed, her words infused with an unsettling blend of certainty and vulnerability.

Jason's reaction was immediate—shock etched onto his features, his comprehension momentarily faltering.

"What?!" he exclaimed, disbelief evident in his tone.

The gravity of her statement hung in the air, a palpable revelation that defied the realm of ordinary comprehension. Cadi's response was a simple nod, confirming the validity of the words that had sent shockwaves through their conversation.

"Yeah," she affirmed, her voice steady, "whoever took 'em shot 'em with a tranquilizer gun and took 'em away while I was hiding in the attic."

The admission held an air of surrealism, as if the mere utterance of the words transformed the unthinkable into a tangible reality. Leaning forward, their proximity turned conspiratorial, Jason's elbows found support on the table's surface. The exchange had evolved beyond casual conversation—it had become a shared exploration of an enigma.

"So you didn't see them? You don't know what they look like?" he inquired, his voice lowered to match the intimate nature of their dialogue.

His query was born from a place of curiosity, seeking to discern the extent of her firsthand knowledge. Her response was a mixture of frustration and resignation, tinged with a touch of fear. She shuddered.

"No," Cadi replied, the memory of her concealed position resurfacing, "I was hiding, like I said. They were looking for me too." Taking a decisive swig from her drink, she paused for a moment, allowing the liquid to quench her thirst.

"They're still looking for me," she added, her words carrying an edge of caution.

Jason leaned back, his gaze fixed on her as he considered the implications of her revelation. The sudden absence of her parents, and her appearance at the hospital.

His question emerged, his curiosity mingled with concern, "How in the world do you know that?" As he spoke, his eyes searched hers, searching for the truth behind her statement.

"I didn't know where to go after I left home. I needed a place where they wouldn't easily find me, and I remembered your house. I thought it'd be a safe bet, somewhere they wouldn't expect me to go. But when I got there, they were already watching it," Cadi explained, her voice a mixture of frustration and desperation.

Her gaze met Jason's, the weight of her words settling between them as she continued, "So, I came here, thinking you might be at work since your car wasn't at your place. But guess what? Those people are here too. They're outside both the emergency room doors and the front entrance. I didn't get a chance to see what they looked like because I was too worried about getting spotted."

Her words hung in the air, the gravity of the situation accentuated by the tense atmosphere that had enveloped them. The dynamic between them had shifted from casual acquaintances to allies against an unknown threat. The urgency in her tone, the raw honesty in her eyes—everything conveyed the reality that they were navigating uncharted waters together.

Jason's gaze swept the vicinity, as though he could somehow discern the surveilling figures stationed at the hospital entrances.

"But how did you manage to get inside if they're keeping an eye on the doors?" he inquired, his voice a mixture of curiosity and concern.

Cadi's index finger pointed towards the open balcony door.

"I circled the building and spotted an open door on the balcony. I jumped up," she explained, her hands mimicking the swift motion.

"Got it. So, they're not aware you're here," Jason remarked with a note of relief in his voice.

His brows furrowed in contemplation.

"The question now is, what's our plan moving forward? What can we do to keep you safe?" He posed the question not just to Cadi but to the unfolding situation itself.

"That's a really good question, Dr. Conwell. Honestly, I was hoping you might have some suggestions, because right now, I'm at a loss and pretty scared," Cadi admitted, her tone a blend of vulnerability and trust.

"Give me a moment to think," Jason replied gently.

A brief hush enveloped them as he pondered the situation, allowing Cadi to finish the last bites of her sandwich. With a thoughtful gesture, he extended his own sandwich towards her, an offer she accepted with gratitude.

"You mentioned they're keeping an eye on my place, right?" Jason asked.

Cadi affirmed with a nod.

"Well, I suppose that rules out my place as a safe option. Even if we could manage to hide you in my car, without a garage, getting you from the car to the house would be far from inconspicuous. It's a bit of a dilemma," Jason mused, his hand finding its way to support his chin in contemplation.

Cadi managed a soft chuckle at the irony of the situation. "You're telling me something I already know."

Jason's attention shifted from his contemplations to the present, his gaze focusing on Cadi. "Cadellia, I take it that you're tired. I can arrange a place for you to rest right here in the hospital for tonight. Once you're recharged, we can start working on a more permanent solution for your shelter and dig into uncovering the identity of these individuals who took your parents and their current location."

With her second sandwich consumed, Cadi followed as Jason guided her through the hospital. They walked into the surgical center and then proceeded to a staff locker room. Connected to the locker room was a cozy lounge featuring a couch and a few plush chairs arranged around a television. The TV was powered off, and the lounge sat unoccupied, offering a haven of solitude.

Cadi's initial assumption was that Jason was suggesting she sleep on the couch, but to her pleasant surprise, that wasn't the case. As they entered the lounge, she noticed a table adorned with a coffee station on one side and five doors on the other. Each door led to a small room equipped with bunk beds on both sides. Jason explained that this space was designated for doctors to rest during extended shifts.

After locating an unoccupied room, Jason turned to Cadi and advised her to choose a bed and get some rest. He assured her that he would work on a plan and return for her in a few hours. He emphasized the importance of locking the door and not opening it for anyone except himself. With his directions given, he headed back to his office, leaving Cadi in the quiet sanctuary.

Cadi locked the door behind Jason's exit and settled onto one of the lower bunk beds. Although sleep seemed unlikely, the fatigue in her body prevailed, and within minutes of resting her head on the pillow, she succumbed to a deep slumber.

5

Jack awoke groggy as his senses slowly stirred to life. As he pieced together the reason behind his foggy state, he jolted upright, narrowly preventing the woman, Faye, who lay beside him, from tumbling off the bed. His swift movement spared her the fall. Gradually, he realized they weren't in the familiar confines of their own bed; instead, they were in an unfamiliar place together. This realization sent a jolt of concern through him, as it implied they had both fallen victim to the same ominous fate—drugged and abducted by unidentified culprits.

Glancing at Faye, who had been lying beside him, Jack noticed she was already awake. He could just barely discern her in the darkness. Her alertness suggested she had been conscious much longer than he had been.

"I'm not sure where we are," Faye spoke, addressing the unspoken question on Jack's mind. "I've been awake for about an hour now, and no one has appeared. I allowed you time to recover from the drug's effects. If you'd like, I can turn on the lights. The switch is near the door."

"Don't worry about the lights just yet. How are you holding up?" Jack's voice was rough, a lingering effect of the tranquilizer darts that had rendered him unconscious.

His mouth felt parched and his irritation at the disruption to their lives was palpable. His foremost concern was Faye. Not only was she pregnant, with previous warnings of potential complications, but even if she weren't expecting, she would still be his utmost priority. This was true despite the fact that she surpassed him in strength, speed, and vision.

"I'm alright. The drug metabolized much quicker in my system," Faye confessed, her unique body chemistry hastening the process.

This acceleration stemmed from the genetic material of the Shepherds that coursed through her veins. Oddly, her concern had been more for Jack's well-being than her own. Despite her pregnancy, she believed her body had purged the drugs before posing a threat to her developing babies.

Jack, renowned for his swift analysis of surroundings and strategic thinking, should have been the first to evaluate their situation and exploit any advantages. However, as Faye had implied, she was the first to regain consciousness. She anticipated briefing him on their predicament. Furthermore, her superior night vision could navigate the darkness that enveloped them, which was a definite advantage he lacked.

"Can you tell me what you found out about this place that we're in since you've been up longer?" he inquired.

"There isn't much to report. We've got a single entrance, secured from outside—I confirmed that. Furnishing-wise, there's a desk, a phone, a computer, and a restroom off to our right. The wall ahead holds a mounted television. Before you inquire, the phone doesn't make external calls; it links to a switchboard. While the computer isn't locked, it operates on an internal network. Interestingly, a closet stands yonder, stocked with uniforms in both our sizes. Adjacent is a bolted-down gun safe," Faye detailed, noting Jack's raised eyebrow at the mention of the safe.

Foreseeing his curiosity, Faye promptly added, "It's empty; I've already checked."

"Damn," Jack responded succinctly, his eyebrow lowering. He remained still, surveying their surroundings while processing Faye's provided information.

After a contemplative pause, he inquired, "Where's Cadi?"

Faye's heart took a brief, anxious skip. Worries about their daughter had been set aside, awaiting a more secure understanding of their situation.

Regret and fear tinged her words as she confessed, "I don't know. She's not here with us, as you can see. If they have her, she could be in a nearby room. My internal clock tells me we've only slept through the rest of the night. The computer's screensaver claims it's ten in the morning."

Jack's response dripped with sarcasm, "Do you really want to trust that, given everything that's transpired to gift us this 'second honeymoon'?"

A punch to Jack's arm punctuated Faye's retort, "You're not funny, Jack."

His grin widened as he edged closer to her. "Yes, I am."

Faye's quick-witted jab at Jack's expense followed, "Alright, you're right. You're funny... looking. But I'll let that slide, given your charming personality."

Jack's grin faded as he teased, "You're cold-blooded, woman," a half-serious jest, his touch finding her arm.

A smirk played on Faye's lips as she returned Jack's look. He cast a final sweep around their room, seeking any overlooked detail. He made use of the limited ambient light in the room, combined with his night vision, to facilitate the task at hand. Finally, he conceded, a casual shrug lifting his shoulders.

"Seems I'll take the initiative and inform our hosts that we're up and awake," Jack declared resolutely.

Uncertainty clouded Faye's expression; she hesitated about the approach. Her nose scrunched in contemplation as she inquired, "Do you believe that's the wisest course, Jack?"

Jack responded with another shrug. Certainty eluded him, yet it felt more productive than waiting. This approach held the promise of quicker answers too.

Jack's conviction held steady. "I don't see how it could harm us. They've brought us here, and if harm was intended, our surroundings would be less inviting and probably a lot more rustic. It's calm for now, but it could shift."

Jack swung his legs off the bed, realizing he was only in pajama bottoms. He reluctantly retrieved one of the outfits from the closet, slipping it on. Black attire—a t-shirt and a matching uniform jacket. He handed Faye a uniform. She was still wearing just his shirt that she normally wore to bed. He noticed the missing rank insignia on her uniform. His own uniform bore an army lieutenant colonel insignia, a puzzling detail he kept to himself, otherwise, the uniforms were marked solely by their last names.

Jack checked with Faye, ensuring her readiness before he approached the door. Faye's nod conveyed her level of preparation.

With a brisk rap, Jack knocked on the door, its unconventional design apparent. The absence of a knob made the door's slide into a wall slot unsurprising. Outside stood two armed guards flanking the doorway. As Jack and Faye appeared, the guards snapped to attention, saluting in unison. Their weapons stayed in place, their silence prevailing.

A third figure in the hallway stood at attention, saluting as well, maintaining the gesture in wait for Jack's response. Unlike the guards, he held the salute, anticipating Jack's move. Hesitantly, Jack returned the salute, acknowledging the man's rank as a captain.

"Colonel and Mrs. Riddle, if you'll come this way, our schedule awaits," the Captain instructed.

Glances exchanged, Jack and Faye mirrored each other's confusion. Lost in the unfamiliar situation, Faye's shrug echoed Jack's earlier gesture. While keeping her gaze on Jack, Faye tilted her head toward the captain, a subtle indication that Jack should engage.

Hesitating, Jack started, "Um, Captain..."

Jack hoped for the man to share his name, but with no introduction forthcoming, he continued, "Could you perhaps shed light on the situation?"

"Sir," the captain responded, beginning his explanation. Consulting a clipboard, he referred to it as he began to provide details.

He recited the information in a flat, crisp tone, lacking inflection. "To facilitate your transition, we've structured a day of activities. Currently, you're allocated for morning meal until eleven hundred hours. From eleven fifteen to eleven forty-five, a medical appointment. Equipment draw and marksman orientation commence at twelve hundred hours, concluding at thirteen forty-five hours. Lunch follows from fourteen hundred to fifteen hundred hours. Subsequently, free time is scheduled. Staff briefing takes place at seventeen hundred hours."

"What?" Jack interjected, surprise evident.

It was a laundry list of activities, leaving Jack and Faye equally clueless about their situation. The captain appeared poised to reiterate the entire itinerary until Jack swiftly cut him off. With a smart about-face, the captain departed without a further word. Casting another look of bewilderment at each other, Jack and Faye followed him.

"Captain, where are we?" Jack queried once they caught up.

"That will be explained during the staff briefing," the captain retorted crisply.

Curiosity getting the best of her, Faye tried prying, "Who are you people?"

"That will be explained—," the captain began.

Faye cut him off, "—at the staff briefing later," she concluded, exchanging a look with Jack, gauging his reaction to the scant information. Faye shook her head in disbelief.

The captain remained unfazed, a blank expression on his face.

Sarcasm laced Faye's tone as she remarked to Jack, "Looks like the grand revelation awaits us at the staff meeting."

Jack chuckled, teasingly acknowledging, "Your deductive skills shine, Faye."

Frustration surged as Faye punched Jack's arm, exasperated by the dearth of information and his attempts at humor. She realized the captain accompanying them didn't grasp her sarcasm.

Seventeen hundred hours appeared the only hope for learning the truth amidst the haze. They followed the captain's lead, arriving at a spacious mess hall. Half-filled tables housed men eating, readying to dine, or cleaning up trays after finishing.

In this cafeteria, Jack and Faye started piecing together their location. A table nearby bore soldiers identical to their counterparts to the left and right. Their facial features remained identical across the entire group.

As they glanced at the captain, his resemblance to his comrades became evident. Slowly, the realization dawned upon Jack and Faye. Belatedly, they recognized the guards outside their doors mirrored the soldiers now seated in the cafeteria.JA silent exchange of understanding passed between Jack and Faye. Here they were, among the genetically engineered soldiers under President Donovan Pike's control—the unit likely stationed near their city. Faye pivoted, scanning the immediate vicinity from her spot beside Jack.

"These might well be my 'brothers,'" Faye remarked slowly, a curious look in her eyes as she surveyed the uncanny resemblances.

Jack's nod mirrored his agreement. "I'd say the same."

Pushing through the morning meal became a task for Jack and Faye. With realization came a shift in perspective on their surroundings and the people present. The unknown terrain was now undeniably enemy territory. The captain escorting them bore a different significance, their view tinted by an unfamiliar aspect. Stripped of anonymity, his demeanor hadn't altered. He continued to respect

Jack's rank, yet his courteous detachment now evoked a sense of revulsion in both of them. Their shared experience with another clone, created by the same man behind the clones surrounding them, explained their aversion.

As Jack and Faye observed these individuals, they detected subtle discrepancies compared to their memory of the other clone. These figures exhibited less aggression, devoid of the sharp teeth that had characterized the previous clone. Upon finishing their meal, the captain guided them through their planned activities.

A divergence ensued during the medical appointment that followed the meal, as Jack and Faye were separated. Jack felt like he hadn't undergone such a thorough examination since his military days. Once they were reunited, Jack considered inquiring about Faye's medical experience, but her unsmiling countenance deterred him. He chose to wait, hoping her mood would brighten within the next half hour or so. Jack hesitated, refraining from reaching out to hold Faye's hand.

Resuming the uniform triggered Jack's mental adaptation to military life, gears shifting for survival and function. Holding hands while uniformed was discouraged, lacking a specific prohibition but deemed incongruent with military presence. Jack's initial hesitation gave way to resolve; he reached for Faye's hand despite his earlier doubts. His decision proved right as Faye responded by clasping his hand in both of hers. Drawing him closer, she wrapped her arm around his, resting her head on his arm.

They believed the day's surprises had concluded until they reached the quarter master for equipment. Uncertainty clouded their understanding of the gear to be assigned. Jack received his service revolver, while Faye was handed her pair of Magsec handguns, each with suitable holsters. The weapons' issuance was swift, surprising even as live ammunition accompanied the weapons, catching them off guard.

Emerging from a traumatic kidnapping, drugged and disoriented, Jack and Faye found themselves in an unfamiliar setting, surrounded by clones evoking memories of a past adversary. Now, handed weapons and live ammunition, their confusion only deepened.

The situation was beyond baffling.

"To avoid the hassle of retrieving your weapons from the quartermaster each time, you can store them in your quarters' gun safe," the captain informed them after they acquired the arms.

Guided to a shooting range within the facility, the captain led them through rigorous shooting drills. These drills echoed military tactics, a realm Jack hadn't traversed in years. Faye performed marginally better, her physical strength aiding her through the training regimen. Yet, her stamina dwindled towards the session's close, pregnancy affecting her endurance. Despite challenges, both surpassed expectations.

As the training concluded, they both achieved qualification on the shooting range. The captain then led them back to the cafeteria, granting them lunchtime. He informed them of their rendezvous at their quarters for the upcoming staff briefing scheduled for seventeen hundred hours.

Once the captain was out of earshot, Faye turned to Jack with candid urgency. "What's happening, Jack?"

He sighed, unstrapping his weapons and placing them on the metal surface of the dining table that stretched to their left and right. "I'm just as bewildered and lost as you are. I can't make sense of any of this."

Jack's hesitation to stow the weapons in the gun safe in their room later revealed his lingering unease in this unfamiliar setting.

"But can we trust this place enough to lock them away later?" he mused. "By the way, that weapons training was incredibly intense. Did you see that coming?"

Faye regarded him with incredulity. "That's your concern right now?"

Jack looked taken aback. "I mean, come on. The training was grueling. I almost miss it."

Faye's face twisted in disbelief. "Jack, seriously? We have bigger problems. We really need to figure out what's going in this place."

"I'm as uneasy as you are. Why give us our weapons back casually?" Jack's voice carried anger. "And why did they commission me into... this?" He gestured around, his frustration palpable.

"That's exactly what's bugging me. Last night's invitation was anything but ordinary," Faye replied, hands gesturing emphatically. She turned towards the long dining table, seemingly poised to vent her frustration with a kick, but she held back.

Coming up behind Faye, Jack wrapped his arms around her, offering comfort. "I understand. But I'm worried about Cadi. We haven't seen her, and our escort didn't mention her."

Faye turned within his embrace, her arms encircling his waist. Due to their height difference, she looked up into his eyes. "Do you think they might be holding her hostage to make us cooperate?" Her concern was palpable.

"I don't think so," Jack responded, leaning in to plant a kiss on Faye's forehead.

As he leaned back, he continued speaking, hoping his affectionate gesture would provide reassurance. In truth, holding her close also helped steady himself. Glancing around the cafeteria, Jack noticed a few onlookers during their intimate exchange. Unfazed, he welcomed the opportunity to showcase the beautiful woman who cherished him, reveling in her desire to be close.

Jack resumed, "If they intended that, it'd make more sense for them to issue a warning, establish control, before returning our weapons. And, ultimately, let us roam this place with minimal supervision."

Faye released a sigh, finding solace as her head rested against Jack's robust chest. His embrace offered her a sense of security, a fleeting feeling of safety amidst the uncertainty.

"I guess we really are going to have to wait for this staff briefing so that we can ask someone else what's going," she murmured, her tone tinged with resignation. Her head was hanging low. "I don't think the captain is going to tell us anything."

Completing their meal, Jack and Faye returned to their quarters. Faye struggled to focus, her thoughts consumed by concern for Cadi's well-being. Worries about her daughter's whereabouts and condition weighed heavily on her mind, overshadowing everything else. Jack was her pillar of support, but the reassurance of Cadi's safety remained paramount.

Taking a moment to ease out of his boots, Jack coaxed Faye to do the same. They settled into the bed together, Jack's arms embracing her, forming a shelter against her anxieties. Curled up in his embrace, Faye's vulnerability was palpable. Her worries about Cadi compelled her to draw Jack's arms tightly around her, seeking solace and reassurance.

"Why were you so distressed after the medical exam?" Jack inquired gently, recollecting her post-exam demeanor. With some privacy now, he felt it was an opportune moment to address the matter.

"How could you tell?" Faye's voice held a trace of surprise. She didn't face him, opting instead to lower her head until her forehead met her drawn-up knees.

Jack's half-hearted laughter accompanied his response. "Are you asking that after all our years together?" Familiarity with Faye had honed his perception of her emotions; he could sense her distress with relative ease.

Faye managed a laugh, though it carried a weight of unease. "They seemed overly concerned when they found out about my pregnancy. Took quite a few blood samples, more than I'd expect for someone like me." Her words conveyed her uncertainty, a mix of genuine concern and unfamiliarity with medical procedures.

"What do you mean, 'someone like me?'" Jack inquired.

"I mean a hybrid clone. I thought they would take a lot of samples, but nowhere near the amount they had," Faye said with a rueful smile, dismissing the thought with a wave of her hand.

Jack's desire to ease Faye's worries was undeniable. Yet, he wasn't naive; the complexities of their situation loomed large.

"So, no other reason for you to be uneasy?" he probed gently, seeking reassurance amidst the uncertainties.

"No, honestly. I despise needles. That's all," Faye confirmed. A sigh released the tension from her shoulders, a physical manifestation of her relieved exhalation. Drawing herself backward, she nestled deeper into Jack's arms, seeking solace akin to a cocooning embrace.

"Admittedly, this place is unsettling. It is freaking me out. Not knowing what is going on is unnerving," Jack confessed, his vulnerability laid bare.

Softly, Faye implored, "Just hold me. We'll unravel this in an hour." In her words, the plea for his presence and the promise of understanding intertwined, their bond a source of strength amid the enigma.

Jack held Faye against his chest, keenly attuned to her unease. Despite her physical strength, vulnerabilities could touch even her, and her need for solace transcended might. Nestled in his embrace, she found the assurance and security she sought. Her eyes shut, taking in the steady rhythm of his heart. Strong and proud, his heartbeat resounded, a promise of constancy and enduring love. Its comforting cadence reverberated within her, finding resonance within her own heart and soul. Each beat drew her further into the tranquility his arms invariably brought.

They lingered in that embrace, Jack's arms enfolding Faye with a sense of security, until the time came to head to the imminent staff briefing. They secured their boots, emerging from their quarters to meet the awaiting captain. With synchronized steps, Faye and Jack followed the captain's lead, trailing behind him as they made their way to the briefing room. Inside, the captain gestured to two chairs designated for them before saluting and exiting the room.

Seated, Jack and Faye shared a moment of anticipation, the air tinged with a mixture of uncertainty and curiosity. Soon after, a door on the opposite side of the conference room swung open, revealing an unexpected presence that neither of them could have foreseen. In a startling turn of events, Dr. Anthony Brundle entered the room, catching both Jack and Faye off guard.

Reacting swiftly, Faye sprang from her chair, her gun drawn in a seamless motion. Her agility was so rapid that Jack scarcely had a moment to react. The hammer of her gun was expertly cocked back as she took aim, her focus locked onto Dr. Anthony Brundle, a figure they had never anticipated encountering in this again.

"How can you possibly still be alive, Dr. Brundle? I ended your life years ago in that Shepherd facility," Faye hissed, her voice a mixture of anger and disbelief. The weight of the weapon she gripped was countered by the unyielding force of her hold.

Dr. Brundle's gaze remained vacant, his eyes meeting Faye's intense glare before shifting to the weapon that she aimed at him—a tool of potential demise he recognized too well. The air was heavy with tension, thickened by the realization that she harbored no hesitation in using it to extinguish his existence. The weapon's grip felt solid in her hand, her knuckles cracking under the strain of both its weight and the pressure she exerted.

Amidst the charged atmosphere, another voice pierced the silence, interrupting the standoff. Faye and Jack's attention shifted beyond the doctor to Donovan Pike, who stood in the doorway, the very entrance that Dr. Brundle had used to access the conference room.

"Lower your weapon, Mrs. Riddle," the President instructed calmly. "The Dr. Brundle you knew is long deceased. This man before you is one of his clones."

"What?" Faye's voice cut through the air, laden with disbelief.

"Yes, indeed, he's a clone," Donovan elaborated, his tone carrying an air of nonchalance. His presence seemed to ease the palpable tension in the room. "Dr. Brundle used him as his initial test subject. He needed to ensure the viability of the process before attempting widespread implementation."

Faye reluctantly lowered her gun, her uncertainty palpable. She wrestled with conflicting emotions, unsure whether she should truly relinquish her weapon. The memory of the formidable Dr. Brundle she had encountered before filled her thoughts. If the man standing before her was indeed a clone of that same individual, the idea of placing her trust in him seemed perilous at best, and damn foolish and foolhardy as worst. After a moment of contemplation, Faye holstered her weapon, her movements deliberate as she settled into her chair. Jack's reassuring touch on her hand provided a subtle comfort.

"I'm fine," Faye finally spoke, her words a mixture of reassurance and acknowledgment of her internal turmoil. The shock of seeing Dr. Brundle had unsettled her, even if just temporarily.

Her gaze remained locked on Dr. Brundle, her unwavering stare a testament to the intensity of her emotions. The explanation about his clone did little to temper the hatred that had resurfaced upon his unexpected reappearance. Faye refused to let the bitterness that had surged within her abate during the brief moments of clarification. She was resolute in her refusal to let go of her animosity.

"Dr. Brundle was quite unhinged," Donovan began, his tone contemplative. "The only reason I kept him around was due to his exceptional brilliance. Ironically, I often associated his genius with his madness. This Dr. Brundle, though possessing some brilliance, is notably saner," he continued, addressing the clone. "No offense intended, of course."

Dr. Brundle responded with a dismissive wave of his hand, a gesture that conveyed his indifference.

"None taken," he replied casually.

Faye's voice cut in, her words carrying an undercurrent of defiance.

"Well, I do attribute his previous demise to a well-placed bullet from my side," she stated matter-of-factly.

Donovan's gaze shifted towards Faye, acknowledging her statement before redirecting the conversation.

"Now, if you're quite finished with the gun-waving, we can proceed with our intended agenda," he suggested, his tone indicating impatience.

Jack's frustration surfaced, his words charged with emotion.

"What is happening here?" he demanded, his tone forceful. "Why have you brought us us?"

Donovan adjusted his glasses, pushing them up the bridge of his nose with a hint of formality.

"It's a distinct pleasure to finally meet you both," Donovan addressed Jack's inquiry. "I've brought you here because I require your assistance."

Both Faye and Jack regarded President Donovan Pike with utter bewilderment.

"What do you mean, Mr. President? You're the leader of the United States, and you possess a genetically engineered super army of clones," Faye questioned, her tone tinged with skepticism.

Faye turned to Jack and shrugged her shoulders.

"They're positioned worldwide with advanced weaponry and technology that's unprecedented. They could potentially overthrow any government on the planet. It seems you already have the world under control. What more could you possibly need from us?" Jack inquired, his expression earnest.

"I never aspired to power for its own sake. My goal was to attain a position where I could make a meaningful impact on the world when the time came. And that time is now. The world is in dire need, and both of you have a vital role to play in addressing that need," Donovan explained earnestly.

Faye's skepticism was evident as she questioned, "What exactly are you and this unhinged scientist planning now? It's difficult to fathom how just the two of us could make any significant difference, especially with the vast resources you already possess." She gestured towards Dr. Brundle and President Pike, her finger slicing through the air to emphasize her point.

Donovan's focus shifted solely onto Faye, his gaze unwavering. She was the center of his attention for the remainder of the conversation, her presence commanding Donovan's focus.

"You believe you have us Shepherds all figured out, don't you?" Donovan's hand gestured towards Faye, his tone carrying a touch of amusement.

He took a step further into the conference room, distancing himself from the doorway. His focus remained fixed on Faye as he continued, "But you're only privy to a fraction of the truth. You're in the dark about what the Shepherds truly represent and their actual objectives on this planet. The reality of our presence here has been concealed, known to only a select few among us. These individuals hold the knowledge of our genuine purpose."

Faye's patience waned, and she spoke with a hint of exasperation, "So, are you planning to reveal this grand secret to us, or do we

have to engage in a guessing game until we stumble upon the truth?"
Her frustration was evident as her hands gestured in the air, seeking
clarity amid the uncertainty.

"Patience is required at this juncture. I will eventually unveil the
details of the situation and the role I need you both to play,"
Donovan assured them.

Faye's irritation subsided, arms now crossed in a somewhat
begrudging acquiescence. A dismissive huff slipped from her lips,
but before her impatience could dominate, Donovan resumed his
explanation.

"As you're already aware, we Shepherds aren't human," Donovan
began.

"Yeah, we've got that part," Jack affirmed.

"We represent an extraterrestrial race that has traversed the cosmos
for eons. Our journeys take us from one star system to another,
where we integrate ourselves into ecosystems capable of sustaining
our form of life," Donovan explained, his pacing adding a dynamic
element to his narrative. His measured strides drew the rapt
attention of both Jack and Faye.

"So, are you saying that other planets out there in the vastness of
space have intelligent life similar to humans?" Jack inquired,
skepticism overridden by Faye's unique origin story. Her existence
itself was a testament to advanced genetic manipulation beyond
contemporary human capabilities.

Donovan regarded Jack with a somber expression. "To the best of my
knowledge, the galaxy hasn't unveiled any sentient lifeforms beyond
what humans and Shepherds represent. While other life exists, the
level of intelligence found in both our species is unparalleled," he
elaborated.

Faye's curiosity brimmed over, her gaze narrowing as it settled on
Donovan. She eagerly sought to decipher the trajectory of his
discourse, her eagerness palpable as she probed, "What are you

trying to tell us?" Her furrowed brow indicated her readiness to delve into the heart of Donovan's monologue.

Donovan's exhalation was measured, his shoulders easing downward as he released a slow sigh. "I believe it's imperative for you to recalibrate your understanding. Both humans and Shepherds exist to serve a race known as the Braxit. Millennia ago, the Braxit engineered Shepherds from modified human and Braxit genetic material."

He allowed a moment for the weight of his words to settle before continuing, "The Braxit traverse the cosmos, so much so that even they may have lost track of their original home planet. From Earth, they select humans and transplant them onto hospitable planets. These chosen humans serve as resource gatherers, sustaining the vast machinery of their colossal ships that are alive."

Donovan paused anew, ensuring his revelations weren't overwhelming his audience. Satisfied with their attentive expressions, he pressed ahead, "Among the transplanted humans, Shepherds are also embedded, their true nature concealed until that moment. Their task is to shepherd these newcomers, fostering the growth of civilizations on their new homes. Once a civilization attains a specific population threshold, or when the Braxit identify a fresh planet to colonize, they return."

Leaning forward and placing his palms on the table's surface, Donovan met the gaze of Jack and Faye with intensity. "This is the core of the Shepherd mission."

Apprehension began to coil within Jack, a tight knot of uncertainty that threatened to unravel his understanding of the world. The information Donovan was revealing was unsettling, and Jack couldn't decide whether he should embrace it or turn away. Surprisingly, it was Faye who took the initiative to press for more details, driven by her own need for clarity.

Faye's unease mirrored Jack's, both grappling with the implications of this newfound knowledge. Yet, despite her internal turmoil, she felt a compulsion to dig deeper, to validate the suspicions that were slowly emerging from the shadows of her mind.

"What are their intentions?" Faye's voice quivered with hesitancy.

She knew that seeking an answer to this question would likely confirm her growing apprehensions. Even though part of her wished to remain ignorant, the other part demanded certainty.

"They're pursuing the same objectives as explorers throughout history. They seek resources to sustain themselves, and that pursuit involves the colonization of other worlds," Jack interjected before Donovan could provide a full response.

His words were a testament to his instinct for understanding, as well as his eagerness to fill in the gaps. Faye's eyes flicked to Jack, her brow furrowing as she considered his statement.

She then turned her gaze back to Donovan, her lips forming the question that had been looming, "Are they using humans like us to transform these planets into something tailored to their needs?"

Donovan's gaze shifted to Jack, and he commenced with his explanation, "To some extent, that's correct. The Braxit's expectations of their colonists involve facilitating their access to the vital resources present on the planets they've targeted for colonization."

The tension in the room seemed to tighten with each passing word, an invisible thread connecting them all as they grappled with the implications of these revelations. Jack's frustration, however, couldn't be contained, his voice rising as he half-jumped from his seat.

"What does that mean for us on Earth, then? We just lose a chunk of our population and are left to deal with the aftermath?" Jack's words carried a mixture of anger and confusion, his posture reflecting his inner turmoil.

Donovan's response didn't come immediately, leaving Jack to wonder whether the pause was deliberate or a natural pause in the conversation. But when Donovan finally spoke, his words reverberated with a sense of gravity that sent a chill down Jack's spine.

"It would signify the transformation of our world as we currently comprehend it," Donovan's tone was somber, his words heavy with a sense of impending doom. "The Braxit would extract the human element they need and then leave us to navigate our fate until the time comes for them to harvest more for another colony."

The room seemed to hang suspended in Donovan's words, the weight of their meaning casting a shadow over everyone present. Faye and Jack exchanged glances, realizing that their world was on the precipice of irrevocable change.

Jack grappled with the concept of change, realizing that the true essence of his curiosity lay not in the mere notion of change, but in the details of its unfolding. His need for clarity compelled him to seek a more comprehensive explanation.

Addressing Donovan, Jack posed his query, "Donovan, what are the specific ways in which our world will change?"

Unexpectedly, it wasn't Donovan who stepped in to provide elucidation. Instead, it was the clone of Dr. Brundle who subtly cleared his throat, gathering the attention of all present before he began to speak.

"Lieutenant Colonel Riddle, the process of colonization hinges on several pivotal factors that must align to ensure its success," the clone of Dr. Brundle spoke with a measured tone. "Foremost among these prerequisites is the presence of a habitable environment. For an extraterrestrial civilization, this translates to a planet with a conducive atmosphere and ample water, assuming the alien race shares similarities with ours. Given that we already know they share certain similarities, the demand for a substantial influx of colonists is a necessity to mitigate potential losses that could impede the process of planetary development."

"Is that the extent of it? The world's only going to experience a population dip?" Jack's voice carried a mix of skepticism and concern.

Dr. Brundle's response came in the form of a slow headshake. "No, it's not a minor number. We could be talking about the disappearance of billions of individuals, vanishing in one swift action. Although this has transpired before, the annals of world history remain oblivious to such events. However, the projected scale of abductions we're dealing with would not only disrupt global equilibrium but could potentially plunge our society into instability. Even if the upheaval doesn't throw the world into chaos, the mere notion of an immensely advanced alien civilization swooping in to extract what they desire, unopposed by any technology we possess, would be sufficient to shatter us."

Faye appeared poised to interject, her expression signaling an urge to contribute to the conversation. Dr. Brundle preempted her with a raised hand, using the ensuing quiet to reclaim his narrative. As Faye's fingers began tapping a rhythm on the conference room table, and Jack's powerful grip twisted his chair's armrests, the tension was palpable.

"The Braxit regard humans as nothing more than what we view sugar or cotton to be," Dr. Brundle's words were starkly matter-of-fact. "To them, humans are merely commodities, akin to consumable resources. Both the humans they abduct and the limited number of Shepherds they take serve as tools for their expansion. With their newly established colonies, they'll extract the resources they need."

6

Cadi's nose wrinkled as the pungent odor of chemicals jolted her from the clutches of exhausted slumber. Beyond the door, distant sounds hinted at ongoing cleaning efforts in the surrounding space. Beneath the overpowering chemical scent, a more familiar aroma lingered—one she could readily discern. It was a scent interwoven with recent conversations, belonging to someone she had only just begun to confide in. Jason Conwell, a family friend and her current protector, carried that distinct human scent. In the aftermath of the unsettling incident that had shattered her sense of security, she had turned to Jason for aid. He was now a steadfast presence, working alongside Cadi to shield her from the unknown assailants who had invaded her home late in the evening, spiriting away her parents in tow.

According to Cadi's inner clock, just over four hours of sleep had elapsed. Normally, this span would have sufficed to rejuvenate her waning vigor and reset her internal equilibrium. However, her recent circumstances had demanded that she tap into the dormant reservoir of her strength—a unique wellspring that belonged exclusively to her. It wasn't a shared strength; it was uniquely and distinctly hers, an intrinsic part of her lineage. This exceptional potency flowed through her as naturally as breath did for the average person; it was ingrained in her biology and identity.

Yet, harnessing this innate well of strength carried a trade-off. It exacted a toll, steadily wearing upon her. For every ounce of energy expended, there came a corresponding demand for increased caloric intake and extended hours of restful sleep for recovery. The previous night, she had covered a twelve-mile distance, racing to reach Dr.

Conwell's residence. Subsequently, she had been compelled to traverse additional miles from his home to the hospital where he served as a medical examiner during his shifts.

Dr. Conwell had graciously arranged for her to stay in this room overnight, granting her the opportunity for much-needed rest. Yet, in the present moment, some four hours had slipped by, and he stood ready to rouse her from slumber. Even as grogginess clung to her like a persistent veil, she yearned for more sleep—another six to eight hours, to be exact. The calories she required had been consumed the previous night, and all she craved now was the kind of deep, uninterrupted sleep that mimicked the stillness of the grave.

That next morning, Jason used the key he had retrieved from the door the night before to get into the room that Cadi rested in. His touch found Cadi's shoulder, his gentle shake coaxing her awake. Her response was sluggish, a testament to her body's unwieldy insistence on prolonged rest after expending her unique strength. It was a double-edged sword, that strength—capable of cutting down adversaries just as aptly as its wielder. A paradox of both boon and burden. And in this very moment, Cadi grappled with its aftermath, striving to shake off its lingering effects.

Whether Dr. Conwell was privy to her situation remained uncertain, yet engaging in that discussion was far from appealing to Cadi in her current state. She yielded with reluctance, rolling over and forcing herself into a sitting position. The fact that she could move at all was a testament to her sheer determination.

Taking stock of her physical condition mentally, Cadi acknowledged that she could gradually dispel the lethargy over time. But her desire for just a few more precious hours of rest remained fervent. She wiped the remnants of sleep from her eyes, elongating her taut muscles, which offered a chorus of squeaks and protests at the exertion she demanded of them.

"I'm awake, Dr. Conwell," she murmured, her words carrying a tinge of grogginess. "Could I not catch a few more hours of sleep, please?" Her fingers rubbed at her eyes stubbornly resisting full openness.

A sympathetic regret colored Jason's response. "I'm sorry, but it's shift change, and it's best not to risk you being discovered here. We don't need that kind of trouble right now," he explained.

Curiosity getting the better of her grogginess, Cadi inquired, "So, where are we headed then?" Standing up, she stretched her body in a movement reminiscent of a cat, her tail twitching involuntarily before she smoothed its fur with a gentle motion.

"We're not leaving the hospital just yet, and I'm cautious about going to the downstairs workspace. I suspect someone's been periodically checking it," Jason explained, his posture straightening as he moved toward the door. "I actually have an office in the administrative wing of the hospital, where I'm officially stationed. But I'm rarely there, so not many are aware of it."

Cadi responded with a nonverbal grunt, her makeshift form of communication at the moment. Balancing on her toes, she executed a thorough stretch, focusing on easing the tightness in her back. Amidst a symphony of cracks, snaps, and satisfying pops, she retrieved her book bag, preparing herself to accompany Dr. Conwell to this elusive office. Her hope was clear: to be left alone for a bit longer, a chance to steal some precious sleep.

Guided by Dr. Conwell, Cadi traversed a labyrinth of white-tiled hallways, each seemingly interminable. An array of garish art, excessive public service posters, and ill-conceived paint schemes—meant to soothe but coming across as nauseating—adorned the walls. The staff seemed attentive enough, and the equipment was modern, but a fresh coat of paint wouldn't hurt, something that needed maintenance's attention.

En route to Dr. Conwell's office, Cadi capitalized on the opportunity to acquaint herself with the hospital's layout. This tactic resonated as wisdom learned from her father, Jack—a crucial skill when navigating unfamiliar territories, especially when being pursued by unfamiliar faces. Jack's teachings went beyond this aspect, but amidst the current circumstances, familiarizing herself with her surroundings was paramount.

Jack, her father, had imparted a gamut of knowledge to her, a series of lessons. Presently, though, comprehending the immediate environment held heightened significance. The trajectory of events hinted that the broader teachings he had instilled might soon rise to prominence. The notion wasn't exactly embraced wholeheartedly. Many of these lessons necessitated skills she hesitated to wield, even against her intended targets.

When Jack had tutored Cadi in self-defense and survival skills, he hadn't pulled any punches. These were skills crafted for survival in a world that could be deeply unforgiving. Even at the tender age of eight, he recognized the hidden strength beneath her unassuming exterior. He pushed her limits relentlessly, pausing only to allow her recovery before reengaging in the lesson.

Her endurance grew as he intended. The sparring sessions, a staple of their training, hadn't initially included her leveraging her smaller size and agility to confound opponents. Over time, however, her newfound strength enabled her to hold her own against her formidable father. Yet, as she matured, wisdom mingled with youthful impetuosity, reminding her that the art of combat extended beyond mere physical prowess.

While her strength empowered her, her astuteness tempered her headstrong tendencies and impulsive temper. It whispered that she lacked the stamina for prolonged engagements. And as she walked these hospital corridors, the echoes of Jack's teachings danced within her thoughts, intermingling with the present reality.

Cadi understood that her victories would emerge from a careful orchestration of her swiftness, nimbleness, stature, and strength, each woven into her approach. It had taken years for Jack and her mother Faye to drive home that invaluable lesson. Yet, once she grasped it, she started besting her father in two out of three matches. Her mother, however, remained unbeaten, a challenge that kept her grounded and emphasized the necessity of her final skill: experience. Jason swung open the door to an office nestled halfway down a cul-de-sac corridor. Cadi's awareness pinpointed an emergency exit stairwell in that direction, offering an alternative escape route. But triggering the doors would undoubtedly set off alarms. Positioned on the second floor, she assessed the possibility of a safe jump to the ground if circumstances demanded, yet the windows were deliberately designed to thwart any attempt at passage.

The hallway's windows shared a common vulnerability. Cadi calculated that her senses could alert her to an approaching presence, affording her the chance to dash from the office and down the emergency exit before capture. Speed would become her ally in such a scenario. Nervousness tinged her thoughts as she contemplated the confines of the single-exit office, yet she acknowledged that movement was imperative. Remaining exposed in the corridor wasn't an option she could afford.

Amidst the decision-making process, she felt the echo of her parents' teachings.

Jason stood by the open office door, expectantly holding it ajar for Cadi. Oblivious to the internal struggle she grappled with, he remained unaware of the decisions she was meticulously weighing. Eventually, Cadi opted to venture into the room, embracing the single exit and entrusting herself to the uncertain gamble. Meeting Jason's smile with one of her own, she willed her nervousness to remain hidden beneath the veneer.

Stepping into the office, Cadi swept her gaze across her surroundings, absorbing the mundane familiarity of the space. It adhered to the standard archetype of an office, similar to countless others she had encountered. A substantial wooden desk adorned with an unassuming leather-bound chair dominated the room. Bookshelves lined one wall, laden with curios and an array of medical volumes—references that Jason consulted frequently. Positioned across was another door, leading to an adjacent space Jason mentioned. This additional area served as an examination room, intended for use by other general practitioners. Yet, since Jason had no need for it, it remained largely unused, barring its purpose when Faye visited and underwent examination by Elizabeth. Cadi's scrutiny included the examination table within this secondary space—a sight that eased her tension, as she discovered a door leading directly into the hallway. Seated behind his desk, Jason gestured to an available chair, prompting her to join him. She shed her bag from her shoulder, letting it slump onto the floor.

"Have you made up your mind about your next move, Cadi?" Jason inquired, his tone gentle and patient.

Cadi's uncertainty manifested in a nonchalant shrug, the path ahead uncertain though her objective remained resolute.

"I was thinking, maybe I could reach out to my aunt or the police station, let them know what's happened. See if they can provide some assistance," she voiced, her feet drawn up to her buttocks, tucked into the chair she occupied.

"I believe that's a solid plan," Jason concurred.

Curiosity sparked, Cadi probed, "Which one should I contact first, Dr. Conwell?"

"Given the situation, I'd recommend reaching out to the police first. Their resources and expertise could be pivotal in locating your missing parents," Jason advised, underscoring his confidence in this choice.

Cadi absorbed the counsel, musing, "You're right. My aunt Izzy might not have much she can do without the police's backing. Telling her about my parents would only bring her undue worry."

As Cadi deliberated, the weight of the decision to inform her aunt or withhold the truth wrestled within her. She concluded that revealing the situation to her aunt was imperative, albeit after she connected with the police.

Settling on her course of action, Cadi initiated the call to the police station, her fingers dialing the number with purpose. Through the connection, she reached the sergeant's desk, and a familiar voice responded, "Hi, Mary," Cadi greeted, recognizing the woman on the other end.

Sergeant Mary Pembroke, a fixture at the police headquarters where Cadi's parents were employed, occupied the desk sergeant position for as long as Cadi could recall. The woman's tenure and familiarity with Cadi's father, Jack, ran deep, built upon a storied history of shared work experiences. Her acquaintance with Cadi's mother traced back to the latter's introduction to the police headquarters.

Mary excelled in her role, orchestrating duty schedules and assignments while maintaining a vigilant watch over the daily activities of the entire force. Her supervisory responsibilities uniquely positioned her as the go-to source for personnel information and channeling concerns to the appropriate individuals within the department. Beyond her professionalism, Mary's amiable nature set her apart. She held a genuine fondness for Cadi, an affection that likely stemmed from viewing Cadi as the daughter she herself never had the chance to raise, given her blessing of three grown sons.

"Hi, Cadi," Mary's voice resonated with enthusiasm over the line. "Just to update you, I received your parents' transfer paperwork this morning and everything's been sorted out."

Cadi found herself mired in confusion, struggling to reconcile the words she had just heard. The concept of her parents being 'transferred' felt absurd in light of their kidnapping and current captivity, their whereabouts obscured by a sinister veil. The pieces of this puzzle did not align. No transfer involved being shot with tranquilizers and abducted in the dead of night; this wasn't the realm of reality as Cadi understood it. With growing skepticism, she questioned the validity of Sergeant Pembroke's information, sensing a mistake had crept in somewhere.

"What do you mean, transferred?" Cadi interjected, her voice a mixture of bewilderment and skepticism.

Sergeant Pembroke responded, seeking to clarify the puzzling situation. "Your parents were reassigned to the Presidential Task Force. With the president's visit scheduled for today at ten thirty, they were brought into the detail tasked with protecting him."

The explanations only deepened Cadi's doubts. Suspicion tainted her next question as it left her lips, her voice tinged with distrust. "Mary, who authorized those orders?"

A significant pause resonated through the line, broken by Mary's eventual response. "Curiously, these kinds of assignment orders usually go through the human resources department, make their way to the Chief, and then come to me. Yet, these orders seem to have bypassed that route, originating directly from the governor's office and arriving here. The governor shouldn't wield the authority to directly assign local police or specify officers by name like this. Just give me a moment, Cadi. I need to place a call to clarify these orders..."

Cadi's voice broke through the conversation, her urgency commanding attention.

"Wait," she interjected, her tone cutting through the confusion. "Something's not right with those orders. Our home was broken into last night, and my parents were taken."

The shock in Mary's response was palpable. "What?" Her incredulity was mirrored in her question.

"My parents have been kidnapped, Mary," Cadi stated, her words conveying a harsh reality. "I don't know who took them but they didn't go to an assignment, that's for sure."

A shift occurred as Mary's concern pivoted to Cadi's well-being. "Cadi, are you okay?" she inquired, her voice laced with empathy.

"Yeah, I managed to hide and then left the house once it was safe. I didn't want to stay there in case whoever took my parents returned for me," Cadi explained, recounting her calculated actions.

Mary's admiration was evident. "You're sharp, kid. Hang on, Cadi. I'll be right back."

The connection momentarily faded as Mary set the phone down, leaving Cadi in a brief interlude to reflect on the tumultuous events of the previous night. The memories weren't pleasant; they evoked a sense of vulnerability that cut deep. Her parents, her protectors, had been whisked away, leaving her exposed. The feeling of safety now seemed elusive, shattered by the ease with which her parents had been taken. Uncertainty gnawed at her, eroding her faith in the world's stability.

A short while later, Mary's voice returned to the line, slicing through Cadi's thoughts and reanchoring her to the present. "I've talked to the Chief. He's sending a uniformed officer to your house for investigation. He's suggesting you come in too, so we can send a police car your way. Where are you right now?"

Before Cadi could respond, Jason motioned for her attention, an unspoken concern present in his actions. Cadi muted the handset's mouthpiece, ensuring their conversation wouldn't be overheard.

"What's wrong?" she inquired.

Jason's voice carried a calm urgency. "I wasn't eavesdropping, but it's hard not to overhear. Do you think it's wise to head in? I mean, these people took your parents from your home, and now there are these transfer orders appearing to cover it up. If they can orchestrate that, who knows what else they're capable of?"

"I can't linger at the hospital, and your place is likely under surveillance," Cadi admitted, torn between her options. "Being around armed officers seems safer now, especially now that they know something isn't right."

Jason contemplated Cadi's reasoning for heading to the police station, and as he mulled over her words, it became evident that her safety was his paramount concern. He recognized his own limitations in shielding her from danger, and the hospital's security remained uncertain. The police station emerged as the most viable sanctuary for her. With a nod, he silently conveyed his agreement, allowing her to resume her conversation with Sergeant Pembroke.

Cadi acknowledged the affirmation from Dr. Conwell, her gratitude for his vigilance evident in her smile. It was a relief that he shared her concern for her safety. Determined not to be a burden any longer, she aimed to shield him from the risks associated with her presence.

Reconnecting with the call, Cadi spoke into the handset. "Hi... Mary?" she greeted.

Mary's voice conveyed her genuine worry. "Yeah, are sure you're okay, kid?"

Cadi assessed her emotions, offering a measured response. "Considering the circumstances, I'm holding up."

"Where are you? I'll send a patrol car over to pick you up," Mary inquired, her tone decisive.

"I'm at the medical examiner's office," Cadi disclosed.

"The one at Saint Elwood Hospital?" Mary confirmed.

Cadi's gaze shifted to Jason across the room. "Yes, that's the one. And I'm with Dr. Conwell."

Mary paused briefly, the line muted as background radio communications filled the void. After a couple of minutes, she returned to the line.

"Cadi?" Mary's voice called through the line, momentarily interrupting the silence. She paused, waiting for Cadi's response before she continued, "There'll be a patrol car stationed out front of the building. They'll be there to pick you up in about half an hour."

"Thank you, Sergeant Pembroke," Cadi expressed with genuine gratitude. A glimmer of solace coursed through her, knowing she would be surrounded by her parents' colleagues—a semblance of protection in this disorienting ordeal.

"You're welcome, kid. I'll see you soon," Mary responded with a reassuring tone.

Cadi brought the call to an end, a sense of slight relief washing over her. This new development held the promise of a more secure immediate future. Her options were limited, and the prospect of finding solace and aid among her parents' colleagues gave her some hope. The path ahead seemed uncertain, but if she could find a place of security and support, she might be able to unravel the enigma behind her parents' disappearance and work towards reuniting with them.

After a brief pause for reflection, Cadi came to the realization that it was the right moment to reach out to her aunt and share the current situation. While immediate solutions might be beyond her aunt's grasp, Cadi knew her aunt could offer invaluable moral support during this challenging time. A comforting presence could go a long way in alleviating Cadi's distress, even though her parents' sudden and involuntary separation had left her shaken.

With Jason observing her, Cadi once again lifted the phone, her fingers gracefully dancing over the dial pad to connect with her aunt's number. Amidst the quiet room, she initiated the call, seeking a connection that could provide solace. Aunt Elizabeth's voice broke the silence on the second ring, her warm greeting reaching Cadi's ears.

"Hey there, Kitten," Elizabeth's voice chimed through the line.

The moniker had originated with Jack, an apt and endearing label that had been wholeheartedly embraced by the entire family. To Cadi, it symbolized not just a name, but a tangible manifestation of their affection, a constant reminder of her place in their hearts. The label's ubiquity didn't bother her; if anything, it amplified the love she felt.

"The timing of your call couldn't be more perfect," Elizabeth exclaimed with a sense of serendipity.

Caught off guard by the fortuitousness of the situation, Cadi inquired, "Why's that, aunt Izzy?" The synchronicity of their conversation seemed too good to be true.

"Brooke just landed," Elizabeth revealed, sharing news that sparked curiosity.

Perplexed by this revelation, Cadi probed further, "What do you mean? I thought she was extending her stay in Ireland."

Amid her curiosity, the original intention of her call momentarily receded. The return of her beloved cousin, Brooke, held a special place in her heart.

"Surprise is the word. Brooke decided to make a swift return stateside, cutting her Ireland stay short," Elizabeth explained, the excitement of Brooke's arrival evident in her tone.

"In fact, she's at the airport right now. The tricky part is getting in touch with your dad and Faye to let them in on the secret," Elizabeth continued, a hint of challenge in her voice. Then, as if thinking aloud, she wondered, "I wonder if your dad is tied up with work at the moment."

This unexpected twist in their conversation brought Cadi back to the reason she'd called in the first place. "No. I don't know where he is. That's why I was calling you right now. I was trying to let you know."

"What's happening? Why the uncertainty about your dad's whereabouts?" Elizabeth's voice carried a genuine sense of concern, her query revealing her worry.

Cadi's reply came forth, laden with the weight of recent events, "It's not just Dad who's gone. Mom is missing too. Early this morning, our house was invaded, and they were both taken."

The account unfolded, recounting the harrowing incident that had transpired since her previous conversation with her aunt—the one where Cadi had enthusiastically shared her decision to attend a conventional school. That prior excitement had dimmed considerably, eclipsed by the stark reality of her parents' abduction. It was a coup of a vastly different nature, a sobering reminder of how swiftly life's priorities could shift. Only a day earlier, her parents had embraced her wishes, a decision that now felt far removed from her current ordeal.

The swiftness with which significance warped, and priorities underwent upheaval, struck Cadi profoundly. In the face of altered circumstances, motivations crystallized. Her world, assaulted by unforeseen forces, had left her struggling to regain her balance, much like attempting to find solid footing on a tilting, spinning terrain. She grappled with the notion that her once-steady existence had been upended. Her aunt's announcement, though welcomed, proved insufficient to anchor her in this new reality. If anything, it heightened her sense of dislocation, realizing that her aunt's distress was now intertwined with her own, adding an extra layer of tumult to her already shaken world.

Yearning for the reassuring presence of her aunt, Cadi found herself on the cusp of that reality. However, there were two critical considerations at play. Firstly, a police car was en route to collect her, and its destination lay in a direction far removed from her aunt's current location. Secondly, safeguarding her aunt and cousin from the clutches of the unknown adversaries was paramount. The intersection of her desires and the web of danger posed a complex dilemma.

"Where are you right now, Kitten?" Elizabeth's voice held a mixture of concern and resolve.

Softly, Cadi responded, her voice carrying the weight of the situation, "I'm at the hospital with Dr. Conwell." The conversation's trajectory seemed to be exacerbating her condition, exacerbating the weariness she felt since awakening. The fatigue weighed on her, compounding her discomfort.

Elizabeth's next question pivoted towards practicality, "Can you make your way to the police station?"

Cadi provided a proactive response, relaying her efforts, "Actually, aunt Izzy, I've already contacted them. Sergeant Pembroke dispatched a patrol car to collect me. It's due to arrive within the next fifteen minutes. I think it's best if I head to the hospital's entrance to await their arrival."

After thoughtful consideration, Elizabeth formulated a plan with Cadi's safety in mind, "That sounds like a solid plan. Brooke and I will meet you there."

Their conversation concluded with fond farewells, the phone lines disconnecting, momentarily severing their connection. Cadi shifted her gaze towards Jason, who was absorbed in the final touches of a text message. Swiftly, he closed his phone and slipped it into his shirt pocket

"Let's head to the front," he proposed, rising from his seat to guide her towards the hospital's entrance. This move would facilitate her rendezvous with the police officers assigned to collect her, ushering her towards the upcoming journey to the police station.

Their walk was brisk, quickly bringing them to the hospital's main entrance. Positioned outside was the patrol car, an emblem of authority stationed by the doors. Inside the car, two uniformed officers sat, their uncertainty palpable as they scanned every passing woman or girl, their eyes vigilant until each disappeared from view.

Cadi acknowledged her imminent departure, speaking to Dr. Conwell, "Looks like that's my ride."

Jason's inquiry bore concern, "Are you certain about going with them?"

Cadi's conviction shone through as she replied, "Yes, I believe it's the right choice. My aunt will meet me at the station, and together, I hope we can find a way to bring my parents back from wherever they've been taken."

Jason's gaze shifted to the patrol car, an undercurrent of doubt apparent in his expression.

"You're placing a lot of trust in them," he remarked, his tone tinged with skepticism.

Cadi's confusion was evident as her brows knit together. Dr. Conwell's perspective puzzled her. "They're the police, meant to safeguard and protect us. Right now, I can't ensure my own safety. I need their assistance to stay secure and to locate my parents."

"Alright," Jason conceded, offering a slightly awkward hug. "Remember, you can call me if you need anything. You have my phone number."

Cadi's gratitude flowed as she responded, "I won't forget, Dr. Conwell. Thank you for being there when I needed support. Facing this alone would have been far tougher. Your assistance meant a lot."

Jason's dedication shone through in his declaration, "Don't mention it. I'd do it again and again, regardless of the persistent risks involved."

7

If Donovan had chosen that very moment to place a bag reeking of dog waste onto the conference room table, it's likely that the reaction from the two individuals seated across from him would have been only marginally more intense. Indeed, such an action would have contributed little to the already astonishing revelations that had unfolded within the confines of the conference room. An action such as that, in this case, would have hardly augmented the prevailing sense of shock.

Both Jack and Faye found the discourse up until that point to be exuding an exceptionally unpleasant odor—a metaphorical stench that neither of them could bear.

"Why, then, are you sharing this with us? What exactly do you intend to achieve with this information?" Jack inquired, his voice laced with a blend of curiosity and skepticism. "It's quite evident that you're looking for something. You need something from us, otherwise you wouldn't have gone through the trouble of getting us here."

"Your observation is astute, Colonel Riddle," Donovan acknowledged, marking the first occasion he had employed Jack's military title when addressing him. The subtlety of this distinction did not evade Jack's notice; he filed it away in the recesses of his mind, recognizing it as a deliberate choice laden with unspoken intentions.

"The Braxit's arrival could trigger a global catastrophe of unprecedented proportions," Donovan conveyed, his tone laden with urgency. "Across countless eons, they've expanded throughout the galaxy, and no force has ever managed to impede their progress.

I've summoned you and your wife here with a plea for assistance—to collaborate in our endeavors to thwart their advance. My aim is to prevent them from laying waste to our planet."

Jack's brow furrowed as he contemplated Donovan's words.

"What compels us to aid you? And supposing we agree, how could the two of us possibly thwart an entire alien invasion?" he queried, a mixture of skepticism and curiosity evident in his voice.

In response, Donovan interlocked his fingers, creating a steeple in front of him. "This Earth is my home as well. I, too, was born and raised on this planet. Over time, it has become as much my sanctuary as yours, untainted by the looming specter of the Braxit. Among the Shepherds, only a select few were entrusted with the true purpose of our existence here. Those privy to this reality were tasked with broadcasting a signal into space, a beacon meant for the Braxit. This signal informed them that our planet was ripe for harvesting potential colonists. My intention was to thwart their efforts, but my success was partial, at best."

Jack's skepticism remained palpable as he sought further clarification.

"So, the recent attacks on the Shepherds—were they your doing?" he pressed Donovan for an explanation.

"Certainly." Donovan's tone carried no trace of remorse for his actions. "I orchestrated the removal of those Shepherds, as they held the potential to disseminate a message that would imperil our world. I took steps to mitigate the threat to our planet."

Jack's gaze remained steady as he delved deeper. "So, what's our role in rectifying your failure?" he inquired.

"Within a small enclave of Shepherds, a determined faction persists, committed to fulfilling our original mission," Donovan explained. "The current whereabouts of this group elude me, as does their number. I'm entrusting you with the leadership of a unit composed of the soldiers I've stationed globally. Your charge is to eliminate this remaining threat; failure to do so would seal the fate of us all," he directed toward Jack.

Faye's attention shifted between the two men, sensing a layer of undisclosed information. The gap in her understanding compelled her to speak up.

"Why can't your soldiers handle this task independently? Why do you require our involvement?" she inquired, her curiosity unyielding.

Donovan maintained his unbroken gaze with Jack, interpreting Jack's subtle shift in gaze as a tacit acceptance of the upcoming events. "Upon assuming the presidency, I was privy to classified information. Your husband, Jack Riddle, has been withholding specific details from you. Namely, he has never severed ties with the Department of Defense. In fact, he commands a military intelligence agency dedicated to unveiling the truth about Shepherds. He has been aware of our existence for years. His presence in this city was orchestrated because we maintained a covert base here, which his agency was surveilling."

In the tense silence that followed, Donovan's revelation hung heavy in the air, illuminating a complex web of hidden truths and unspoken connections.

Faye turned her gaze toward Jack, a swirl of disbelief evident in her eyes.

"Is this true, Jack?" Her voice carried a mixture of shock and hurt.

If Donovan's revelation held any validity, it meant that Jack had been harboring secrets—worse, lying to her—for an extended period. Jack's eyes drifted downward to his interlaced fingers, resting upon the conference room table's surface. With an exhalation he had been holding, his shoulders slumped in tandem, a physical surrender to the weight of the moment.

"Both of you, I trust that you comprehend the gravity of our decisions here," Donovan interjected, his voice adopting a somber note. "I'll entrust the remainder to you now. Other pressing matters necessitate my immediate attention this morning. Dr. Brundle will be at your disposal for any assistance you require."

With a fluid motion, Donovan rose from his seat and departed through the same entrance he had used earlier, accompanied by Dr. Brundle. Faye remained fixed in her shocked stare, locked onto Jack, as he reached for the door ahead of him.

"Jack—" Faye began, her voice a fragile thread of uncertainty.

However, Jack's interruption was swift, cutting through her words with a stern clarity. "Leave it, Faye."

His tone possessed an authority that caused Faye to instinctively withdraw, her words tapering off abruptly.

"We'll discuss it later. Not now," Jack continued after a momentary pause, his voice softened by the weight of unresolved emotions.

A surge of fury coursed through Faye, its intensity almost propelling her to press the matter further. Yet, she recognized that unmistakable resolve etched across Jack's features—the unwavering determination that had fortified his spine. It was a look she had witnessed on Cadi's face before, a shared trait that transcended their non-blood connection. Faye understood that any attempt to delve deeper into this subject would yield no progress at the moment, as Jack had firmly indicated. Reluctantly, she relented, easing herself into a seat with measured reluctance.

The revelation, delivered by Donovan Pike, gnawed at her. It grated on her sensibilities to learn something so significant about the man to whom she had bared her heart, and to learn it from a source as enigmatic as Donovan. The weight of their situation was not lost on her; they were being coerced into a decision of monumental proportions, a decision whose implications could shape the course of their lives.

Anger surged anew within her as the reality of the threat settled in. The enormity of the peril, with its far-reaching ramifications, weighed heavily on their present and their future—a future that was meant to be shared. Protecting the world from the specter of the Shepherds was imperative, not only for them but also for the life they had created together, their daughter Cadi, and the potential lives of their unborn children.

Observing Jack, it was evident that he had already shouldered the mantle of responsibility thrust upon them. His readiness to lead, his readiness to command the troops for this paramount mission, was palpable. In contrast, Faye's emotions swirled in uncertainty. While the imperative to safeguard the world resonated with her, a disquiet had begun to stir within her, casting a shadow over her bond with Jack.

For the first time since their paths had crossed, doubts emerged in the sanctuary of her heart, doubts about the Jack she had known, about the future they had envisioned together. She had misgivings about Jack.

Faye swiftly pivoted, halting Donovan in his tracks with her resolute words. "For the time being, we're willing to collaborate. But let it be clear, if we perceive even a hint of your pursuit for further power, we won't hesitate to intervene and put a stop to it."

Donovan's departure didn't entail a backward glance, but the lack of visual acknowledgment didn't necessarily imply a lack of attention.

"I wouldn't anticipate anything less—from you," said Donovan, his response carried a measured tone, laden with unspoken implications. With Donovan's exit, the door clicked shut, sealing them off from his presence. Faye sensed an undercurrent of hidden meaning in his parting words, yet the storm of thoughts swirling within her mind, dominated by Jack's concealed truth, rendered her unable to dwell on the subtleties of Donovan's statement. Her focus was consumed by her own internal turmoil, leaving little room to decipher the nuance behind their exchange.

After their conversation with Donovan concluded, Dr. Brundle motioned for Jack to remain behind.

"Now that our prior discussion has wrapped up, there's a matter of significance that requires our attention," stated Dr. Brundle.

Jack's anticipation was palpable

"I hope this has to do with our daughter," he interjected.

Dr. Brundle considered Jack's inquiry thoughtfully, his head tilting slightly. "As a matter of fact, a team has been dispatched to locate your daughter and ensure her safe arrival here. Her well-being is our paramount concern, and we've allocated substantial resources to ensure her security. Rest assured, we share your urgency in reuniting her with you. However, at present, we ask for your patience while we expedite her safe transfer. We'll keep you informed to the best of our ability regarding her status."

Jack's response carried a hint of defiance. "Alternatively, you could grant us the freedom to search for her ourselves."

Dr. Brundle met Jack's challenge with a composed demeanor, conveying the urgency of their situation. "While that's a potential course of action, it's not a practical solution. Time is of the essence, Lieutenant Colonel Riddle. We must act swiftly to address the looming threat of the other Shepherds. Your involvement is crucial, and we're on a tight schedule."

Faye's voice joined the conversation, seeking her place within this unfolding narrative. "And what about me?"

Dr. Brundle's gaze turned toward Faye, his expression marked by a mixture of concern and caution.

"Your safety is paramount, and I won't expose you to potential risks by allowing you to venture outside," he responded resolutely.

Jack regarded the doctor with a mix of puzzlement and determination, sensing an undercurrent of unease that Dr. Brundle's fervent statement revealed. An instinctive understanding formed between Jack and Faye that there was more to this situation than met the eye, igniting their determination to unearth the truth.

"Find my daughter," Jack's demand resonated with urgency.

Dr. Brundle's response held a reassuring certainty. "Rest assured, we share your determination to locate her. Bringing her here is a priority for us as well. However, there's another matter of significance I must address with you, Faye, regarding your pregnancy."

Faye's concern manifested in her inquiry, her hand instinctively drifting toward her burgeoning belly, a visible testament to the rapid progression of her gestation. "What's wrong? Is there a problem that could impact my pregnancy? We're already aware that the babies are developing faster than normal."

Dr. Brundle's response was measured and informative. "You're already ahead of the curve by acknowledging the accelerated development of the babies. That awareness is crucial. This conception is unlike any other—it's an unprecedented occurrence. The successful merging of human and Shepherd genetics through natural means is a new territory. While this situation is exceptionally rare, it doesn't foretell an insurmountable challenge. Our priority will be to provide specialized care to ensure a healthy delivery. The brevity and complexity of this pregnancy demand our utmost attention."

Jack's palpable relief echoed within Faye, a shared sentiment that resonated not only in words but also in the unspoken realms of their connection. The depth of Jack's concern unveiled itself in his reaction to Dr. Brundle's words. In a surprising twist, Faye herself began to discern the weight she had been carrying—an intangible burden that now dissipated like snow yielding to a sun-warmed rooftop. With a newfound clarity, she acknowledged the degree of unease Izzy's words about her pregnancy had stirred within her.

Concerning the pregnancy, Jack inquired, seeking assurance. "So there are no complications to be expected?"

Dr. Brundle's response radiated a soothing assurance, his smile a balm to their worries. "You can both rest assured. Mrs. Riddle is under my vigilant care. The pregnancy holds immense significance as it represents the first instance of a successful pairing between a Shepherd and a human, resulting in a viable pregnancy, as I previously mentioned."

Faye regarded Dr. Brundle with a mix of caution and skepticism.

"Trust doesn't come easily. I don't trust you. After all, the previous iteration of you that I terminated was far from trustworthy," she stated, her tone unwavering.

Dr. Brundle met her wariness with an earnest reply.

"I stand apart from that version you encountered—much like you and the Lieutenant Colonel differ in your physiology. I assure you, I possess a sound mind. My sanity is unassailable," he emphasized, his gesture indicating his head.

Jack's response was succinct, a low grunt that succinctly conveyed his skepticism, leaving no doubt about his sentiments toward Dr. Brundle's statement.

"Why should we trust you? That's what she asked," Jack reiterated, his emphasis on the word 'trust' resounding.

Dr. Brundle addressed the skepticism head-on, his tone steady. "The answer is straightforward. It's within my best interest to ensure her well-being with this abbreviated pregnancy. Not out of coercion, but due to the necessity of her being in prime condition for the completion of your assigned mission. Understand, Faye will require specialized care during this complex pregnancy—assistance she won't find elsewhere on this planet."

He paused, allowing his words to settle. When their silence lingered, he continued. "The truth remains: nobody, other than I, possesses the required expertise to guarantee her survival through this unique ordeal. This pregnancy isn't a conventional human or Shepherd one; it's a phenomenon unto itself. Moreover, the apparent acceleration of this pregnancy, as indicated by all observed signs, means that it will take a toll on her physical well-being."

As Dr. Brundle's words hung in the air, Jack's gaze shifted toward Faye. A pang of pain resonated within his chest, a palpable sensation that he resisted giving into. His impulse to clutch his heart, to quell the ache, remained unacted upon. The profound distress stirred by the mere contemplation of losing Faye, for any reason whatsoever, was an ache that defied any physical remedy.

"What does 'abbreviated' mean for us in terms of this pregnancy? My sister Elizabeth mentioned something similar. Are we talking about a total of six or seven months of pregnancy?" Jack's inquiry carried curiosity and a touch of concern.

Dr. Brundle pondered for a moment, his mental calculations evident. "It's likely the entire pregnancy won't extend beyond three months. But I must emphasize, this is an estimate."

He paused, rubbing his forehead in contemplation. "Our current knowledge isn't sufficient to provide a precise answer. The apparent brevity of this pregnancy, indicated by all available data, constitutes the main risk for Faye. As the two fetuses continue to develop within her, her body's energy demands will escalate. A swift increase in caloric intake will be imperative to supply the energy her body will soon require. Every calorie she consumes will be directed toward nourishing the growing babies, and this demand will only intensify with time. It's a natural progression."

Tension and concern etched Faye's features deeply. Dr. Brundle's compassionate gaze met hers, conveying his genuine apprehension for her well-being through his sad brown eyes.

Jack positioned himself close to Faye's chair, his large hand a reassuring weight on her delicate shoulder. She held onto his hand with a firm grip as they faced Dr. Brundle together.

Jack turned his gaze away from Faye and redirected his attention to Dr. Brundle. "Elizabeth, my sister, has been overseeing Faye's well-being. We'd appreciate her continued involvement in Faye's care, as part of the team dedicated to her. Is it possible to arrange this?" Jack inquired, addressing Dr. Brundle.

Dr. Brundle responded affirmatively. "Certainly, we can easily make the necessary arrangements. After our discussion, kindly provide me with her contact information. I'll ensure she's integrated into the team. We'll confer upon her the rank of Captain, naturally."

With a faint smile, Jack added, "I don't think she'll object."

Even as a semblance of relief crossed his expression, Jack's worry for Faye and the unborn children resurfaced. In the span of less than twenty-four hours, he had encountered two distinct sources echoing the same message: Faye's pregnancy posed a serious threat to her life. His concern deepened as he contemplated the toll this information was taking on Faye, and how it might impact her aspirations for the future. He understood that his worry for her would persist until the entirety of this ordeal was concluded.

The fear of losing Faye loomed within Jack—a fear that surpassed any other apprehension. The significance of Faye in his life was immeasurable, and he couldn't fathom the possibility of her absence, even if the reason was their shared creation of life. He was already grappling with the challenge of discussing his role in the Department of Defense Intelligence Section with Faye.

Faye's desire to bear the children she had conceived with Jack was unwavering. She held a steadfast willingness to lay down her own life if it meant securing the survival of their unborn twins. Yet, her readiness for such a sacrifice did not diminish the profound terror that enveloped her at the mere prospect. The prospect of bringing

Jack's children into the world resonated deeply within her, a desire that eclipsed everything else. The confirmation of her pregnancy had ignited elation within her, a sense of joy she hadn't known before.

However, Elizabeth's voiced concerns had planted seeds of doubt within Faye. Dr. Brundle's subsequent validation solidified those fears, casting a heavy weight that seemed to settle like a stone in her heart. Her fear wasn't solely rooted in the predicted toll the pregnancy might exact on her body—she was determined to face that challenge head-on. Rather, her trepidation stemmed from the realization that if they hadn't been taken captive and brought to this facility, they would be navigating this journey without the support of Dr. Brundle. The chances of a dire outcome would loom far larger in the absence of their current circumstances.

Amid her turmoil, Jack's touch on her hands, where they were interlaced with his on her shoulder, brought a fleeting sense of comfort. Jack's love for Faye was an all-encompassing force, radiating from every fiber of his being. He harbored an unwavering desire to shield her from harm, a sentiment that had driven his decision to withhold his former occupation from her. In this moment, there was no one more cherished to him than Faye. Though there was one other being, a small lost kitten, whose significance was akin to a precious piece of his heart. Jack longed to reunite their fragmented family, to envelop them in safety once again.

"Dr. Brundle," Jack began, his gaze focused on the doctor. "Are there any specifics we should be aware of concerning the babies' post-birth development?"

Dr. Brundle adjusted in his seat, directing his attention to Jack.

"Could you clarify your question a bit more?" he inquired.

"I'm curious about the continued accelerated growth rate after their birth. Will this rapid growth persist beyond their delivery, or will it halt once they're born?" Jack sought clarity.

Dr. Brundle's response was direct, reflecting his commitment to transparency. "As per my initial observations, the accelerated growth is likely to persist. If that assumption holds true, there shouldn't be any cause for concern. I am reasonably confident that I can address any metabolic irregularities and stabilize their growth and metabolism through tailored treatment in an adapted gestation chamber."

Although apprehension tinged his next question, Jack pressed forward. "And what about their projected lifespan?"

"I'm interpreting your question's phrasing as being somewhat nuanced, but let me provide some insight. These children are the product of a human and a Shepherd—Faye is a hybrid creature herself. While I can't offer a definitive answer, it stands to reason that their lifespan would fall somewhere between the expected lifespans of a human and a Shepherd," Dr. Brundle contemplated, considering the complex blend of genetics at play.

Jack had never openly acknowledged the inherent fact that Faye's lifespan would far outstretch his own. From the moment they wed, he had been fully cognizant of her true nature, the disparity in their expected lifetimes. He endeavored not to dwell on it excessively, for it was a reality immutable and beyond his control. Instead, he resolved to relish each precious day with her, to savor every shared moment until his days inevitably reached their end. Though a part of him longed for their days to be interminable, he confronted the somber truth that their existence existed within the confines of an all-too-mortal world.

"In the upcoming days, you may start experiencing the full force of the pregnancy's effects, if you aren't already," Dr. Brundle informed Faye, shifting the focus of their discussion.

A hint of relief mingled with acknowledgment colored Faye's response. "The effects are already beginning to make themselves known," she admitted, yielding to the queasiness that had silently plagued her throughout the day.

Jack's gentle grip on her hand offered comfort, and Faye met his gaze, finding solace in his tender, moisture-laden eyes.

"I stayed silent because I didn't want you to worry any more than you already do. There's little you could do to ease my discomfort," Faye confessed to Jack, her voice carrying an undercurrent of vulnerability.

While the longing for Jack's comfort lingered in her thoughts, the anger stemming from his perceived betrayal of her trust retained its weight in her mind. Forgiveness hadn't found its place, and the revelations lingered unforgotten. The urge to confront Jack about the disclosed information persisted, fueled by a need for answers to her lingering questions about the situation.

He offered a reassuring smile, his words gentle yet resolute. "Your well-being is paramount to me." Seizing the moment, he leaned in to press a soft kiss to her lips, to which she willingly tilted her head, meeting his affection with her own.

In this tender moment, Dr. Brundle chose to withdraw, recognizing that he had effectively conveyed his intentions and provided them with a measure of assurance.

8

With a final wave to Dr. Conwell, Cadi exited the hospital's entrance, her gaze fixed on the marked patrol car stationed there. A couple of officers were engaged in conversation by the vehicle, one of them engrossed in a cell phone call. As she drew closer to the car window, the officer in the passenger seat diverted his attention towards her, concluding his call before stepping out of the vehicle. Despite the officer's slightly ill-fitting uniform, Cadi paid it no mind as he addressed her.

"Are you Cadellia Riddle?" inquired the officer.

"Yeah, but everyone just calls me Cadi," she responded.

Gesturing toward the back door of the patrol car, the officer invited her, saying, "If you'll get in, Miss Riddle, we can make our way where we need to go."

"Okay," Cadi agreed, preparing to slide into the back seat.

With a fluid motion, she tossed her book bag onto the seat and followed suit. Once Cadi was safely inside, the officer closed the door behind her, rejoining his place in the front passenger seat. The driver shifted the car into gear, and they set off.

The confines of the car made Cadi's tail itch beneath her shirt, the sensation of restraint after a prolonged period becoming bothersome. Unbinding it, she discreetly extended her tail to alleviate the discomfort. Outside the window, the passing scenery captured her attention in a vague manner, yet her persistent tail twitching nudged her to delve into the cause. Initially attributing her unease to the forthcoming visit to the police station—a step towards unraveling the mystery surrounding her parents' disappearance—Cadi slowly entertained the notion that something might be amiss. Her tail's agitated behavior mirrored past instances where her subconscious signaled potential danger.

"Been waiting for me long?" Cadi tossed the question casually into the air.

The two officers exchanged glances, a silent exchange of unspoken communication, before the passenger-side officer took the lead in responding.

"We had a good fifteen-minute wait," he answered, the same officer who had guided her into the vehicle.

"That was a quick response. Sergeant Hemton mentioned it'd be more like half an hour for you guys to show up," Cadi remarked, a suspicion gently forming in her mind.

These officers had arrived too soon. Her brief stroll from the hospital's entrance couldn't have coincided with the officers' early arrival. There was no way she had consumed the full thirty minutes they should have needed to reach her.

The officer before her shifted, partially facing her, his eyes locking onto hers. He seemed to take no mind to the fact that she had moved further behind him. "We happened to be nearby, so we got there faster than anticipated."

Cadi's lips curved into a sugary smile as she weighed his explanation. Beneath that smile, however, she sensed the deception. *Mary wouldn't have quoted thirty minutes if there were other officers in the vicinity to handle the task of picking me up*, her inner voice whispered with unwavering conviction.

The police officer redirected his attention to the road ahead, while Cadi released the restraint of her seatbelt. Initially positioned in the middle of the rear bench seat, she moved herself behind the passenger's seat, nestled right behind him. This new vantage point was less conducive to eavesdropping due to the partition of protective glass that segregated the front and back of the patrol car.

Yet, her immediate concern didn't involve such limitations; she had more pressing matters to address.

Testing the interior door handle, Cadi confirmed her fears: it was rendered inoperative, just as she had anticipated.

Seizing his cell phone once again, the officer in the passenger seat initiated a call. His voice carried assurance when he made contact, conveying, "Yes. We've secured the target. En route to base."

Upon concluding the conversation, he returned the phone to his pocket, locking eyes with Cadi. In that moment, the puzzle pieces fell into place, and she recognized the disconcerting truth. She knew there was no Sergeant Hemton within her knowledge of the police force. She was well-acquainted with the personnel, particularly due to her father Jack's frequent take-your-daughter-to-work days. The woman in charge was unmistakably named Pembroke. These discrepancies tugged at her intuition.

Glancing at the uniformed officers occupying the front seats, Cadi's instincts were affirmed. Their insignia clearly placed them in a precinct situated far north of the city—an area outside their assigned area. Sergeant Pembroke could never have dispatched officers from that distant location to collect her from a hospital in the southern part of the city. The morning traffic alone would have elongated their journey to nearly an hour, an implausible arrangement. A sense of unease settled over her as the pieces of a troubling puzzle began to coalesce.

Further heightening Cadi's suspicions was the officer's method of communication upon their arrival. His choice of using his personal cell phone instead of the patrol car's functioning radio struck her as odd. The radio emitted a constant stream of chatter, confirming its operational status. As she mulled over these peculiarities, another detail gnawed at her thoughts: the officer's reference to her as a 'target'. The term seemed more aligned with military jargon than the typical language of law enforcement.

Cadi's tail, a fidgety barometer of her unease, writhed restlessly beneath her. The stifling confines of the patrol car exacerbated her restlessness, compelling her to shift in her seat. At last, she sat up, her gaze surpassing the back seat to peer over the shoulder of the officer in the passenger seat. She inhaled deeply, her acute sense of smell catching a familiar fragrance in the air. A rush of recognition flooded her senses. After scanning the front compartment of the patrol car, she eased back into her seat, her facade carefully composed.

Her voice, a delicate veil concealing her mounting suspicions, broke the silence.

"When did the police department decide to equip street officers with assault rifles like those?" she inquired casually. Maintaining a poised tone, she skillfully cloaked her escalating concerns.

No words passed between the two police officers, their unspoken communication an echo of exchanged glances. The driver re-engaged with the road ahead, his focus returning to the bustling streets. A sudden turn in their route snagged Cadi's attention, dispelling any notion of their intended destination being the police headquarters. A question teetered on her lips, but the sight that met her eyes silenced her inquiry.

Through the partition dividing the patrol car's front and back, Cadi spotted a tranquilizer gun being aimed in her direction. The officer in the passenger seat had twisted around, attempting to line up his shot. However, her strategic relocation from the center of the back seat made her a less accessible target, creating a challenge for his aim. Reacting instinctively, Cadi lunged forward, her body pressing against the barrier. The officer's curse slipped out softly as her swift motion thwarted his intentions. In a quick and calculated move, Cadi lashed out with her foot, causing the gun to become lodged in the gap between the barrier's components. Extraction proved difficult for the officer, his attempts frustrated. A forceful punch against the plexiglass followed, a network of cracks branching out from the point of impact.

"Whoa!" Cadi exclaimed, her voice a mixture of surprise and fear.

Cadi's eyes widened, disbelief mingling with her realization. The officer's capacity to shatter the plexiglass barrier with a mere fist defied the realm of human capability. It struck her like a bolt of revelation—the two uniformed police officers might not be human at all. The devastating threat of the tranquilizer gun, once a pressing concern, seemed secondary now due to her strategic position against the bulkhead. The officer would have to expose his entire arm and the weapon to aim at her, a perilous maneuver she doubted he'd risk. The odds were tilting in her favor, allowing a glimmer of hope to shine through the ordeal.

Cognizant of the fleeting nature of her advantage, Cadi pivoted, placing her back against the bulkhead. As the man in the passenger seat squeezed the tranquilizer gun's trigger, Cadi shifted her attention to his aim. Aware of the awkward angle he faced, she identified his target—her tail. Swiftly, she maneuvered her tail out of harm's way, executing a well-timed deflection of his plan.

Gathering her resolve, she unleashed a powerful kick at the back window with both feet. Realizing the inadequacy of her height for a forceful impact, she swiveled her strategy and directed her energy towards the passenger door window instead. The risky move exposed her momentarily, vulnerable to a shot, but she banked on the element of surprise. With two forceful kicks, she shattered the window, fracturing the previously rigid boundary.

n a swift motion, Cadi propelled herself out of the window, her speed denying the tranquilizer-wielding cop a chance to react. His attempts to lower his window in time to intercept her escape remained fruitless as she nimbly ascended through the opening, perching herself atop the car's roof. The city's bustling traffic flowed past them from all directions, yet Cadi's focus remained unswayed by the urban rhythm. With a confident leap, she soared over the adjacent lane, her grace painting a brief moment of defiance against the canvas of speeding vehicles.

The city sidewalk greeted her feet as she landed with practiced precision. An alley beckoned, a refuge to elude her pursuers. Negotiating its twists and turns, she emerged onto a different street, heartbeat in tune with the pursuit sounds echoing behind her. Determination etched her expression as she lengthened her stride into a sprint. Her urgency spurred her on, a tangible desperation driving her to put as much distance between herself and her unidentified chasers as possible.

Amid her headlong dash, collisions with unsuspecting pedestrians marked her passage. She barreled through the busy sidewalk without pause, oblivious to the chaos she stirred. Her focus was singular—to escape the clutches of pursuit. The aftermath of her chaotic wake remained irrelevant; in her heightened state, there was no room for consideration.

Though the impulse to glance over her shoulder tempted her, she resisted. Fear gnawed at her, an inner turmoil urging her not to acknowledge the proximity of her pursuers. Looking back would render her escape tangible, too real to dismiss as mere flight. Cadi believed that meeting their gaze would shatter her fragile attempt at freedom, rendering her struggle futile and hopeless.

Cadi's frantic gaze darted left and right as she sprinted, a desperate search for a sanctuary to slip into, a means to elude her pursuers. Despite her fervent quest, no promising hiding spots materialized. Frustration clawed at her insides, threatening to spill into despair. Just as a wave of hopelessness began to well up, a figure half a block away caught her eye. An uncertain glimmer of salvation ignited as the person energetically waved, a beacon of possibility in the chaos.

Reservations tugged at Cadi, distrust casting shadows on the stranger's intentions. As she drew closer, however, his persistence in seeking her attention reassured her. Amid the turmoil, Cadi's desperation surpassed her doubt. Faced with a dearth of viable options, the adage 'any port in a storm' resonated—she was willing to accept help from any source that offered it. The young man's gesture—holding a door ajar—became a lifeline. He guided her inside, propelling her through the door's threshold to a back entrance that opened onto the very street where her ordeal had begun.

"This way," the unfamiliar voice urged, laden with urgency.

Cadi, still trying to synchronize her racing heartbeat with her breath, found herself breathless both physically and metaphorically. Her breath felt distant, as if she'd left it trailing about fifteen feet behind her, struggling to catch up.

Gathering her voice, she managed to question between gasps, "Who are you?"

The young man's brown hair framed his face as he shook his head. "Does that even matter right now? Escaping those pursuers takes precedence."

Attempting to steady herself, Cadi regarded him with a blend of gratitude and curiosity. "Do you know who they are?"

His head shook once more. "I do know they're not cops, if that's what you're wondering."

They burst forth from the back entrance of the bar, their breathless strides propelling them up the street until an alleyway materialized, offering a moment's respite. Nestled within its shadows sat a car, engine humming softly.

"Get in and keep low," the young man instructed, urgency threading through his words.

Cadi obeyed without hesitation, slipping into the back seat while her newfound ally took the driver's position. The engine roared softly with the application of the gas pedal, and the vehicle eased out of the alley, only to come to a swift halt moments later.

The tension was palpable as he spoke in hushed tones, "They're ahead of us, searching. Keep your head down."

Time hung suspended in those fleeting moments, thick with anticipation. Finally, a release of breath signaled his relief. "They're gone, but stay hidden."

Navigating with deliberate caution, the young man merged into the street's flow, steering the SUV away at a measured pace to evade unwarranted attention. Eventually, he cast a glance over his shoulder into the backseat, curiosity and concern intermingling in his gaze.

"Are you okay?" The young man who had come to Cadi's rescue turned his gaze toward her in the backseat, speaking with a reassuring tone. His eyes flitted between her and the road ahead, a delicate balance of concern and caution.

Cadi struggled to believe her current reality, her body trembling as she attempted to regain her composure. Escaping from her pursuers felt surreal, and the rush of emotions threatened to overwhelm her. Her world seemed to teeter on the edge of chaos, the shock of her recent ordeal yet to fully take hold. She recognized the need to let the impact of her escape sink in, to allow herself a measure of controlled hysteria, but her efforts to do so were met with resistance. While she grappled with the shock, a semblance of stability held her back from spiraling into outright panic.

Nervousness lacing her words, Cadi finally mustered the question on her mind, "Who are you?"

The ambient noise of passing cars swirled into a steady white noise, serving as a backdrop to their conversation. In the confines of the vehicle, this droning symphony harmonized with the restless thumping of Cadi's heart, a rhythm she thought her companion heard easily.

He responded with a self-assured gesture, his right thumb indicating himself, "Me? I'm Blake." His voice bore an air of casual familiarity, as if his identity should be self-evident. "How are you feeling, Cadellia?"

Cadi's bewilderment deepened. "Wait... how do you know my name? How do you know who I am?"

Blake's reply was unflinchingly candid, yet its forthrightness raised a new wave of concerns within Cadi.

"Because I've been trailing you since you left your house yesterday." His response held an honesty that was as unsettling as it was revealing.

Cadi instinctively drew back from Blake, retreating into the farthest reaches of the SUV's back seat as fear gripped her. Her voice trembled as she voiced her suspicion, "Are you with them?"

Blake's puzzled expression was illuminated by his widening eyes as he turned to face her.

"Who's 'them'?" he inquired, his tone tinged with curiosity.

Hesitating, Cadi weighed her words carefully. She didn't want to reveal too much until she understood the situation better.

"The people who took my parents and were chasing me just now," she answered, her voice cautious.

Blake's head shook emphatically. "No, I'm not—"

Interrupting him, Cadi's voice was an urgent torrent of questions. "Then who the hell are you? How do you know me? How did you know where to find me and help me?"

Her clenched fists reflected the tension escalating within her, the prospect of a physical altercation while Blake was at the wheel raising the stakes to dangerous levels. Her barrage of questions hung in the air, demanding answers she yearned to uncover.

Blake raised a placating hand, a calming gesture amid the storm of inquiries.

"Whoa, one question at a time, Ms. Riddle," he interjected, his voice steady. "My name is Blake. I knew where to be because I'd been following you since you left the hospital in the car with those two men."

His eyes met hers, earnest and determined. "As you got out of the patrol car, I pulled over and stepped out, thinking I could offer some help. I saw you change direction and doubled back through the building, luckily finding you heading my way. Remember, I knew you were at the hospital because I've been tracking you from your house."

"And what about the other question?" Cadi's voice held a speculative edge, her curiosity unyielding.

Blake's response carried a sense of shared understanding. "I'm a Shepherd, just like you. The Shepherds I'm affiliated with were attempting to establish contact with your parents. Our common goal was to work together in the pursuit of a singular objective: the removal of Donovan Pike from the presidency."

He paused, a gravitas underlying his words. "We needed your mother's expertise to aid in deposing Donovan Pike from his position of power. Our intention was to meet with your parents that morning, but it seems our plans were compromised. Donovan dispatched his agents to apprehend them before we could rendezvous."

Cadi's breath steadied as her adrenaline ebbed, the aftereffects of her escape finally catching up to her. A wave of exhaustion rolled over her, and she felt herself teetering on the precipice of unconsciousness. Frustration knotted within her as she realized her backpack—left behind in the police car's back seat during her escape—contained supplies that could have been invaluable in this moment. Her depleted energy reserves begged for replenishment, not just from her recent sprint, but also from the night's stolen rest she had forgone.

With a growing sense of urgency, Cadi yearned for sustenance to replace the calories she had expended during her harrowing escape from Donovan Pike's operatives. Her need was underscored by the absence of provisions, accentuating her vulnerability in the face of impending fatigue.

"How did you recognize that I'm a Shepherd?" Cadi's question held a hint of curiosity and drowsiness.

Blake's response came with an air of confidence, his tone laden with matter-of-factness.

"There's a notable absence of humans with tails, for one. And then, there's your eyes," he noted, gesturing toward his own as he pushed his sunglasses to rest atop his head.

His vertical slit irises were now visible, mirroring Cadi's own unique ocular trait that she had inadvertently revealed by forgoing her usual eye-masking contacts.

Cadi's realization washed over her with a mixture of embarrassment and oversight. The hurried departure from her home had led to the omission of her eye-altering contacts, rendering her distinctive eyes exposed to the world.

Feeling the tendrils of exhaustion curl around her, Cadi's voice emerged groggily. "Where are you taking me?"

Blake's gaze, reflected in the rearview mirror, carried a reassuring demeanor. "A place where you can find safety and rest."

Those words were the final anchor before the darkness descended, claiming Cadi's consciousness. Much like the inky void that had swallowed her parents the previous night, succumbing to the effects of tranquilizer darts. Just like that, sleep overcame her. It enfolded her in its embrace, shrouding her mind in the anticipatory quiet before dreams encroached. Resistance was futile; there was no bargaining, persuading, or deferring the inevitability of sleep's grasp.

Just as a lost child finds refuge in a guardian's arms, Cadi surrendered to the embrace of slumber.

Blake never had the opportunity to inform Cadi that his men had been conducting overwatch on the home shared by her parents and her. His original intention was to approach the Riddles the next morning, seeking their assistance. Unfortunately, his plans unraveled as Donovan made a move before he could act. When news reached Blake about the infiltration of the Riddle home, it was too late to dispatch a team to confront the situation.

9

Dr. Brundle exited the presence of Jack and Faye, passing through the same door that Donovan had used earlier. It was the very door both of them had entered through at the start of the conference. The door clicked shut behind him, its latch engaging with a soft sound. He stood there, poised, waiting for Donovan Pike to share his thoughts.

Donovan leaned against the wall beside the door, his foot propped against the wall behind him. His arms were crossed in front of him, and his head hung low with closed eyes. He seemed to be trying to find some semblance of relaxation, to calm his racing thoughts.

"You're quite the bastard, Dr. Brundle," Donovan's voice was a controlled whisper through clenched teeth.

Dr. Brundle responded with an air of nonchalance, brushing off Donovan's anger, "I didn't bring her back myself."

Donovan's frustration was palpable, his words biting, "No, you didn't. But you knew. You went through every file left by your predecessor and you must have known about the cloning."

Dr. Brundle met Donovan's gaze steadily, considering him before turning down the hallway. Slowly, he began to walk, his footfalls echoing down the corridor. The walls were uniformly painted in a monotone shade of egg white, stretching out before him with an unchanging, constant view. As he walked, his thoughts aligned with the hallway's unbroken expanse.

Dr. Brundle's measured pace gave Donovan a chance to catch up. Donovan pushed away from the wall with his foot, his hands finding refuge in his pockets. Eventually, he set off, matching his steps with the doctor's as they walked side by side down the corridor.

"I knew," Dr. Brundle spoke with a hint of resignation, momentarily tearing his gaze away from the featureless hallway that seemed to threaten a trance-like state with its monotony.

"But I didn't inform you because I anticipated your reaction, which turned out as I predicted. I assumed that Blake and his group were in the dark about my actions—that is, my other self's actions; it becomes quite intricate when discussing my original in this manner," he continued, his head tilting slightly to one side.

His eyes shifted back to Donovan, meeting the intensity in his gaze. "My presumption was that they believed she had taken her own life to escape their clutches. The other me was adept at playing both sides, orchestrating her return as a clone of the original," Dr. Brundle concluded, his voice carrying the weight of a complex truth.

Donovan's frustration was evident in the way he spoke, his breaths heavy with emotion. "Why was I kept in the dark when I dispatched an agent to eliminate that deranged hunter? Why wasn't I informed that it was her who was taken out?"

Dr. Brundle's response held a touch of uncertainty. He took a moment to consider, then made a choice that would delineate his clone self from the original Dr. Brundle, the one Faye had killed. "I think I'll refer to my other self by my first name from now on. Anthony didn't want you to know about his actions until he was prepared to unveil his deceit to you."

Donovan's agitation was tangible. His jaw clenched and unclenched, his fists mirrored the rhythm in his pockets.

"So, he intended to use her as the Key to find the Communicator," Donovan stated.

Dr. Brundle's eyebrow arched at Donovan's words.

"Is that a statement or a question?" he inquired, his tone suggesting curiosity mingled with a hint of dry wit.

"Don't play games with me, Doctor. I've little patience for wordplay right now," Donovan's voice was a veiled threat, his grasp on his emotions slipping through his fingers.

Dr. Brundle met Donovan's intensity with a measured response.

"Let's suffice it to say that I sought clarity with that question," he said, his tone neutral yet resolute.

As they continued walking down the corridor, an uncomfortable silence stretched between them, expanding like an abyss.

Dr. Brundle continued, a touch of contemplation in his voice, "What if you had discovered that she was the agent sent out when you initiated this campaign against the Shepherds? Would you have called her back? My original—Anthony, however unscrupulous, didn't even bother replicating her original's recorded brain patterns. She's no longer the woman you once knew. As of now, her name is—"

Donovan cut him off, his voice adopting a subdued quality as his anger waned. "I know her name. You don't need to remind me."

Their footsteps echoed in the empty corridor, each deliberate stride punctuating the renewed silence that hung between them.

"It may be inconsequential at this juncture," Donovan finally spoke, his tone carrying a mixture of resignation and contemplation. "We have the Key, and they do not. We won't be sending her out, so they'd have to come here to retrieve her. She's securely confined here, and our defenses are impenetrable. And if, by some slim chance, they did manage to breach our safeguards..."

Donovan's voice trailed off, leaving the implication hanging in the air, a foreboding that hinted at the dire consequences that could occur.

"Faye is pregnant," Dr. Brundle declared matter-of-factly, without preamble.

Donovan's response was a pause that extended for two steps before he voiced his visceral frustration, growling, "Damn you to hell, Dr. Brundle."

Observing Donovan's reaction, Dr. Brundle probed, "You still love her, don't you? Even after these countless centuries."

Donovan's words emerged laden with a mixture of raw emotion and sorrow. "I could never cease to love her but that's not her. I never wanted to release her, but she still chose to end it, all to prevent the inevitable. And now, against all odds, it's unfolding before us. I can't fathom how Blake thinks he can lay his hands on her and wield her as the Key."

Dr. Brundle's response was a nonchalant shrug of his shoulders, his head tilting slightly to the side. "Anthony altered something within her, a change that made conception far more attainable. The extent of it is rather intriguing."

Donovan abruptly halted his steps, and Dr. Brundle followed suit as Donovan's arm extended, signaling for him to cease his movement. With a guiding gesture, Donovan pivoted Dr. Brundle to face him, their eyes meeting.

"Don't you ever tire of your ceaseless quest for knowledge?" Donovan questioned, his gaze holding a mix of exasperation and a deeper wisdom. "You do realize life encompasses more than just accumulating knowledge, right?"

Meeting Donovan's gaze unwaveringly, Dr. Brundle held his look for a fleeting moment before closing his eyes, his head tilting slightly to one side. A hand gently found its way to Donovan's arm, offering a light pat.

"In my perspective," he mused, "life's purpose solely revolves around the pursuit and accumulation of knowledge."

At Dr. Brundle's reaffirmation of his unyielding thirst for knowledge, Donovan released his hold, reassured that the man before him retained the unquenchable curiosity he had always known, even in this cloned form. Beneath that hope lay a concern: was this copy as unhinged as the original? Donovan's worry surfaced in his question, laden with genuine concern, "Will she be alright?"

"If you're referring to the modifications made, her well-being is assured. However, the pregnancy will undoubtedly take a toll on her body," Dr. Brundle explained, his hand absently scratching his head as he pondered. "Though I can't offer an absolute prediction, the odds are decidedly in her favor now that she's under our protection."

"Why would you... Anthony," Donovan interjected, correcting himself, "...make such a decision? Why create a clone of her only to release her into the world? And can a clone still function as the Key?" Donovan's questioning probed the motives behind this intricate web of actions.

"I lack full certainty. There's a high likelihood that she retains the potential to be the Key, but we're confronted with a broader issue," Dr. Brundle divulged.

Donovan's exasperation was palpable as he inquired, "What's the new concern now?"

"A daughter," Dr. Brundle responded gravely. "One of her eggs was employed to conceive a daughter. Anthony took precautions, ensuring he had a contingency plan."

The weight of this revelation bore down on Donovan, his shock mingling with concern for the implications. "What in the hell are you saying? Are you serious? Why was I kept in the dark about this?" His tone held a mixture of disbelief and frustration.

"Anthony utilized one of Faye's eggs to create a daughter. I'm not joking, and my own awareness of this is quite recent," Dr. Brundle confirmed.

Resuming their walk down the hallway, Donovan kept pace with Dr. Brundle, a mixture of curiosity and urgency propelling him forward. Over his shoulder, Dr. Brundle continued, "The soldiers who returned after apprehending the Riddles reported discovering family photographs in their home with a young girl who bore an uncanny resemblance to Faye. Regrettably, they couldn't locate her. More recently, our security teams intercepted a communication she made to the police, prompting us to dispatch agents for her retrieval. Unfortunately, we lost track of her."

Donovan's frustration was palpable, his restraint tested. "Damn it all! Why didn't you share this information with me sooner? Is Blake and his group involved with her now?" He was on the verge of lashing out, the gravity of the situation wearing down his patience.

Dr. Brundle let out an exasperated sigh. "As I mentioned, I had been awaiting additional information before informing you. Now that I have it, I'm sharing everything I know. While her exact whereabouts elude us, it's highly likely that Blake and his faction of Shepherds have custody of the girl."

Donovan's hand found its way to his chin, his fingers tapping thoughtfully. He mused aloud, "So, should we consider the girl a potential threat to our plans?"

"Given that she undoubtedly shares genetic similarities with her mother, it's plausible that she could serve as the Key," Dr. Brundle explained. "Especially if her GEAR—Genetically Engineered Acoustic Resonance—can be harnessed to create Genetic Harmonic Resonance." He raised his hands in a gesture of uncertainty, an unusual sight for someone as knowledgeable as he was.

Donovan couldn't help but find this situation remarkable. In their long history together, there had been few instances where Dr. Brundle had been left perplexed or rendered speechless by a statement. This was undoubtedly one of those rare moments.

"We've never fully grasped the intricacies of how the Braxit brought us into existence, though Anthony did come astonishingly close to uncovering that knowledge. Regrettably, he carried those insights to his grave. Furthermore, the reason why certain attributes spontaneously emerge in some of us while others remain unchanged remains an enigma. Our working hypothesis suggests a DNA-based mechanism, yet even if that holds true, the specific triggers for activating these attributes elude us," Dr. Brundle explained.

Donovan's response was tinged with impatience, "I'm already familiar with this. What I need from you are insights that can aid us in our current situation."

"I'm processing the data," Dr. Brundle responded, his mind working to provide valuable information. "Consider how the Librarians, those who transition to them, manage to acquire the entirety of the Braxit's current knowledge without having returned to this planet for eons. And think about the Communicators—how do they establish contact with the Braxit? We now know that the Braxit have set their sights on another planet for colonization, waiting for us to activate the gate here to facilitate their journey. Then there are the Keys, responsible for working in tandem with the Communicators to open the portals."

He paused momentarily before continuing, "Our society of Shepherds is composed of distinct roles: Facilitators, Medics, Leaders, and Scientists. Each role brings specialized expertise. Once activated, Shepherds assume their designated roles, gaining access to the associated knowledge. This activation-based knowledge sharing is crucial, but it occurs only after the Shepherd has been activated—prior to that, the knowledge remains inaccessible."

"We've gone through this discussion countless times before. I've recently been initiated as a Leader, and it's opened up a wealth of new knowledge that I never had access to. Blake, on the other hand, has been a Leader for much longer, giving him a head start in utilizing that knowledge. My hope is that your presence, along with the Riddles, can help level the playing field against his advantage," Donovan stated.

"It's conceivable. Human belief in the transmission of knowledge through DNA might hold some truth. If that's the case, I need to uncover the conditions for activating this mechanism. I'm under the impression that Genetic Harmonic Resonance plays a pivotal role in this sharing, though there's limited understanding beyond that. It appears to be a central aspect of the Communicator's role, unlocked by the Key," Dr. Brundle concluded.

"Doctor, my advice is to exercise caution. No Scientist has ever been activated with knowledge of that nature. Moreover, I know there's a block on what you can learn in that domain due to the Braxit. Anthony altered himself to access that knowledge, a choice that likely contributed to his descent into madness. I find it curious that, despite gaining extensive knowledge when attributes are unlocked, we remain remarkably uninformed about that particular field and about the Braxit in general," Donovan cautioned.

"They've deliberately withheld that knowledge to keep us under control, and rightly so. Consider our current actions, all thanks to Anthony's exploration of a forbidden domain. We're in open rebellion, although the Braxit remain unaware of it—for now, as far as we know. Some Shepherds, bound by their programming, are still attempting to reach out to the Braxit and facilitate their arrival. As of now, we're inclined to think that Blake hasn't yet located the Communicator," Dr. Brundle elaborated.

Donovan ceased walking once again, his thoughts demanding more cognitive engagement, which momentarily overrode the instinct to keep moving. Dr. Brundle smoothly came to a stop beside him. "Do you believe we're on the right path?"

Dr. Brundle shook his head, not as a denial but rather a dismissal. "I'm quite indifferent, truth be told. My sole objective has always been the pursuit of knowledge. Everything else beyond that ultimate goal is inconsequential."

"I must say, Dr. Brundle, your candidness regarding your aspirations is admirable. You remain steadfast in your desires. Could that be the reason you—or Anthony—cloned her and brought Faye into existence?" Donovan inquired.

Dr. Brundle resumed his stride down the corridor. "I believe that's precisely why he cloned her and dispatched her into the world. He aimed to establish the circumstances required for obtaining more knowledge. What better way exists for us to acquire information that lies beyond the scope of our attributes than by drawing the subjects of our curiosity to us when we lack the means to access that information?"

"Why are you so different, Dr. Brundle?" Donovan's inquiry held a hint of fascination. "Among all the Scientists I've encountered, you stand out."

"I am more than just a scientist. I am a researcher, a gatherer of knowledge. But your question is intriguing. The underlying reason for my disposition is likely tied to the fact that my attribute was triggered while I was still in the womb. To comprehend what it means to possess self-awareness at such an early stage is beyond explanation. I have no clue why my attributes activated at such a tender age. It's a perplexing enigma that I've been seeking to unravel since the day of my birth," Dr. Brundle paused in his steps, allowing Donovan to catch up and stand beside him rather than trailing a step behind.

As Donovan walked alongside him, Dr. Brundle resumed his pace. Deliberately evading direct answers to questions about his demeanor, he offered vague responses that he believed would satisfy Donovan. He remained steadfast in his identity, unswayed by external inquiries, for that was what truly mattered to him in this context.

Being in Donovan's presence heightened Dr. Brundle's awareness of his concern for the man's well-being. The ongoing conversation emphasized the personal nature of the matters involving Faye that should have been addressed without delay—Faye's potential daughter, possibly under Blake's control, and Donovan's inability to fathom Dr. Brundle's true motives.

Dr. Brundle shut his eyes momentarily, reflecting on the missteps that had affected his friend, Donovan. He was determined to rectify these shortcomings to the best of his ability. He redirected the conversation to its initial focus.

"Do you think you can come to terms with the fact that she is still alive?" Dr. Brundle inquired of Donovan.

"I don't see that I have much choice but to accept the reality as it stands. The past between us cannot be altered, and her subsequent existence following her recreation is equally beyond my control," Donovan responded with a sense of resignation.

"It's regrettable that events concluded on such a somber note. Her choice to end her life seems rather futile now, given that I—Anthony—have ultimately restored her," Dr. Brundle expressed.

"You're not wrong, Doctor. Having her here with us is a relief. With her by our side, the concern about her being manipulated as the Key is alleviated," Donovan concurred.

"Indeed, Mr. Pike," Dr. Brundle affirmed.

"Now, our focus shifts to finding her daughter. Have you disclosed any of this to the Riddles yet? The fact that Faye is the Key?" Donovan inquired.

"I haven't shared any information with them as of now," Dr. Brundle confessed.

As they continued their stride down the hallway, Donovan broke the silence that had settled in, his words overlaying the rhythm of their footsteps resonating across the floor. "Do you genuinely have no insight into his intentions when he made her capable of pregnancy?"

"What do you mean, specifically, Mr. Pike?" Dr. Brundle inquired, his tone direct.

Donovan's brow furrowed as he grappled with the extraordinary situation at hand. Shepherd pregnancies were rare—hence their low population, and their gestation period was notably longer than that of humans. The concept of a pregnancy between the two species was entirely unprecedented. "I mean, what could he have aimed to achieve by enabling this pregnancy?"

"It's plausible that there wasn't a precise motive behind it. It might have been a pursuit of his capabilities—just a demonstration of his power. Or he could have intended to explore whether she could give birth to children with the potential to become Keys, akin to her. If I were to speculate—well, in a sense, I was him—I might have pursued it purely to explore its feasibility. Not all actions require a grand scheme; the mere possibility could have been motivation enough for him to act. However, I'm uncertain if the unusually accelerated pace of this pregnancy was intentional," Dr. Brundle pondered aloud.

Donovan let out a heavy sigh. "This situation is riddled with complications. I trust that you'll do everything within your means to ensure her well-being."

"I know the depth of your concern for her, and I assure you, I'm dedicated to her well-being. I have no intentions of losing any of my patients," Dr. Brundle responded, offering a reassuring smile.

Curiosity burned in Donovan's eyes as he pressed forward with his inquiry. "How much danger is she really in with this pregnancy?"

Dr. Brundle drew a breath, preparing to share the full scope of the situation, but Donovan intervened, raising his hand to halt him. "Hold on. I want the unfiltered truth, Dr. Brundle."

"Hmm. Well, let's be clear—this pregnancy could very well prove fatal for her. It's an extreme scenario, completely uncharted territory. I won't deny that I'm cautious about it, but at the same time, I'm also intrigued. This situation is unprecedented, and I'm eager to extract as much knowledge from it as I can. It could potentially revolutionize the genetic understanding of both humans and Shepherds," Dr. Brundle admitted with a candid honesty. While he had shielded the Riddles from the full extent of the danger, his decision was rooted in his medical expertise and scientific knowledge rather than their emotions.

Donovan's expression turned more serious as he absorbed the information. "Our priority is to ensure that we all survive to witness the future—your future, my future, and the future of everyone on this planet. And that includes the outcome of this unique pregnancy," he concluded.

10

Gradually, Cadi's consciousness stirred, the remnants of her recent ordeal still casting a shadow that kept her eyelids sealed shut. She eased into awareness, taking precious minutes to attune herself to the ambient symphony of this unfamiliar environment. A symphony composed of alien sounds and unrecognizable aromas, it was as though she'd stepped into a world entirely distinct from her own. Instinct, finely tuned by survival, held her senses taut, a sentinel against the unknown.

Her body's assessment brought a small smile to her lips as she registered a restored vitality. While the pangs of hunger gnawed at her, she resolved to address that gnawing once she ensured her safety, a hierarchy of needs where survival trumped sustenance. With a slow inhale, she relinquished the grip of caution, allowing her eyes to flutter open, unveiling the room.

Stretching out before her was a spacious bed, its expanse cocooned by a diaphanous quilt. She remained garbed in her attire, though her shoes and socks had been delicately shed. Casting off the quilt, she rose, her stance shifting from prone to perched as her gaze canvassed the space. Yet, the room divulged no secrets about her location, only an undeniable coziness that enveloped her. Its character, though, was marred by an absence—no decor to inscribe personality, no trace of life's touch.

Inhaling, she detected a sole olfactory note, one woven with the threads of the man who had plucked her from the street's cruel grasp and shielded her from the sham constables. Gratitude and wariness mingled within her, dispelling naivety's illusions. He had been her savior, yes, yet that was not an oath of allegiance. Caution whispered that his intentions might not extend beyond the refuge he had already bestowed.

Remaining prostrate on the bed wouldn't unravel the enigma shrouding her situation, so Cadi propelled herself into motion. Her shoes and socks lay in a haphazard tangle beside the bed—a silent invitation to step forward. As she laced her feet into them, a conscious decision guided her. She wasn't about to venture out blindly; instead, she aspired to thoroughly acquaint herself with this unfamiliar territory before relinquishing its embrace.

Within the room's depths, her inquisitive gaze grazed upon a closet that yielded a collection of jeans, each one a tailored fit for her form. Adjacent, a tapestry of shirts hung, showcasing a spectrum of styles. A revelation struck her: this space and its contents were meticulously curated for her occupancy. This wasn't mere coincidence or random fortune; it was deliberate preparation. A curiosity kindled within her, leading her to a dresser, where parcels of underclothes awaited—every piece an embodiment of her size.

Her feet gravitated toward a window shrouded in drapery as dense as midnight. Cadi inferred their dual purpose—to shield against intrusive sunlight and muffle the clamor of the outside world. With a gentle pull, the curtain surrendered its fortress, unveiling a panorama that stole her breath. A vast window stretched across the wall, and within this vastness resided a pair of French doors, poised like a portal to a balcony beyond.

Upon this stage, her city unfurled—a tapestry of towering structures in intricate disarray. Stones glistened with their own stories, capturing the waning sun's reverie. Amidst the skyward thrust, the grid of streets intersected, crafting pathways that demarcated domains of influence.

Sunset bathed the scene in a warm embrace, coaxing Cadi to imagine a breeze, a mere zephyr that would caress the evening's canvas. Downward, the city hummed with its routine, lives intersecting in a familiar choreography. In this twilight hour, the semblance of normalcy seemed almost tangible, an illusion prompting memories of her parents, Faye and Jack, returning home after a day's toil. A pang of homesickness gripped her, an ephemeral wish to be cocooned in their embrace. Yet, like a trove of emotions, she archived this longing and pivoted toward the door, ready to confront whatever lay beyond.

The apartment's expanse stretched to occupy the lion's share of the building's floor, a generous spread that belied its actual number of rooms. The illusion of grandeur gave way to the realization that only a handful of distinct chambers existed. However, the remainder of the space flowed in unbroken openness, inviting exploration. Amidst this spatial symphony, Cadi's gaze discovered Blake within one of these rare compartments.

Translucent walls constructed the room that ensconced Blake—a sanctuary that mirrored the semblance of a home office. With the merest glance, Cadi's perception promptly dubbed it as such. Caught in telephonic discourse, Blake's attention shifted as he glimpsed her through the glass barrier. An uplifted finger silently conveyed his need for a few more minutes tethered to his call.

In a whirlwind of efficiency, Blake concluded his conversation, a conclusion that Cadi observed was decidedly swift. Emerging from the glass cocoon, he bestowed upon her a grin of unabashed magnitude. Neatly groomed brown hair framed his features, and his smile unveiled a singular dimple, nestled like a secret on his left cheek. His voice danced with a supple melody, each note soft, sensuous, and redolent with aural richness. In the radiance of his smile and the vivacity of his eyes, Cadi sensed a welcome that enveloped her, a warmth both palpable and inviting.

"Well-rested now?" Blake's query, infused with curiosity, resonated with the sparkle in his brown eyes—a twinkle that mirrored his smile's effulgence.

Caught in his gaze, Cadi's demeanor turned bashfully coy, her gaze momentarily averted from the intensity of his eyes.

"Yeah, managed to get enough sleep," she admitted with a hint of a blush, as if her rest had made her feel a little exposed under his scrutiny.

A flicker at the edge of her peripheral vision jarred her awareness, flagging the fact that her tail now hung unencumbered. Rarely did Cadi venture out without ensuring her tail was carefully concealed—a lesson learned early in her life. This lapse stirred a surge of panic within her, the idea that her tail might be unwittingly exposed sent her heart racing. Blake's presence only amplified this unease, as his gaze was now upon her, attuned to the swift transformation of her demeanor.

Assuredly, Blake detected her discomfort, and his words flowed to quell her burgeoning anxiety.

"No worries," he reassured, a dismissive wave accompanying his words. "While it might be my first time encountering a tail on a person, there's no need for you to fret about it being seen."

Blake's disarming smile held an enchanting quality that magnetically drew Cadi in. With a graceful step forward, he brushed a few stray strands of hair behind her ear, a simple gesture that set her heart aflutter and caused the tip of her tail to twitch involuntarily. Her panic had been transparent, an open book to Blake. She fervently hoped that the emotions that stirred within her were concealed, masked from his perception. The prospect of him reading her like an open page was overwhelmingly embarrassing.

"In your room, did you happen to notice the things I set aside for you?" Blake's words flowed gently, a tender inquiry.

Cadi's brow knitted in momentary confusion before recognition surged forth. The contents of the closet and dresser sprung back into her mind's eye.

"Yes, I found the clothing in the closet and the belongings in the drawer. Your thoughtfulness is truly appreciated," she responded with sincere gratitude.

A smile curved upon Blake's lips, his satisfaction palpable.

"Considering you arrived with nothing but the clothes on your back, I figured a few essentials might come in handy," he revealed, a glint of contentment shimmering in his gaze. He chose not to acknowledge the flush that graced her cheeks, preferring to let it shimmer unspoken.

Cadi's eyes carried a shade of disappointment as she confessed, her voice a touch subdued.

"I left my bag in the back of that police car," she admitted with a sigh. "The fear just overwhelmed me, and I couldn't think beyond escaping. It never crossed my mind to grab my bag when I made my getaway."

Blake's fingers intertwined with hers, a gesture of comfort that carried her along as he led her through the spacious apartment.

"Given the circumstances, I'm confident many would've been equally single-minded about escaping," he consoled with a knowing smile.

Walking hand in hand, Cadi reveled in the warmth that radiated from Blake's touch. His grip, though gentle, bore an underlying strength that offered reassurance. She surrendered to his lead, her steps melding seamlessly with his guidance, an unspoken trust tethering her to his presence.

"Everything I thought I'd need for a few days was in that bag," Cadi mused, a touch of dismay creasing her features, momentarily clouding the happiness that had illuminated her just moments before.

Blake's response was gentle, his words carrying the essence of his considerate nature.

"I took the liberty of estimating the sizes that might suit you," he offered, keenly observant of the rapid currents shifting through her emotions, like ripples across a pond. He wondered if she recognized that her feelings paraded plainly across her countenance.

Attempting to uplift her spirits, Cadi replied, "I'm sure it'll be fine. I don't want to impose." This self-reassurance was a balm to her wounded pride, an attempt to quell the unease stirred by the loss of her bag.

Blake steered Cadi through the apartment, eventually arriving at the kitchen's heart. With a halt and a pivot, he focused on her, a gentle inquiry lacing his words. "I imagine you might be hungry?"

Cadi's response held a self-effacing edge, the tone cautious and considerate.

"I don't want to be a burden or cause any inconvenience." Yet, as her words hung in the air, a distinct growl emanated from her stomach, her body betraying her hunger. A flush of embarrassment crawled up her cheeks, compelling her to wish for the shadows to envelop her.

Blake's laughter was easy, a melodic resonance that smoothed the edges of her chagrin. "I think that growl answers that question," he jestingly remarked, his amusement a salve that lessened the intensity of her embarrassment, inviting a smile to grace her lips.

"Then I guess I won't be polite. If you're extending the invitation, I'll gladly accept it with a smile," she responded, finally allowing herself to indulge in the warmth of his offer.

Blake's hands found their place on Cadi's hips, effortlessly lifting her onto a stool at the kitchen counter. The memory of his touch lingered on her skin, an imprint she carried as she yearned for more—perhaps his embrace, an embrace she hadn't yet experienced. The twitch of her tail, like a secret language of her emotions, betrayed her, causing her cheeks to ignite with a telltale blush. She chided herself inwardly, deeming her instant infatuation as a schoolgirl crush, bemused by the swiftness of her heart's inclinations for a man she'd met just hours before.

A contemplative seriousness overtook her as her thoughts turned to the passage of time. Despite her revitalized state, Cadi recognized that the evening was still young. Her confrontation with the sham officers had occurred late in the morning, and the notion of having managed such a restful slumber in such a brief span puzzled her.

She broached the topic cautiously, questioning her host. "How long was I asleep?"

Blake paused his culinary preparations, his gaze meeting hers with a gravity that mirrored her query. "You slept for a little over twenty-four hours."

Cadi's groan was unmistakable. "Oh my. I need to call someone."

Promptly retrieving her phone from her pocket, she was thankful for not having placed it in her missing bag. However, before she could even press a button, Blake intercepted, plucking the device from her grasp and casually dropping it into the sink, where he promptly turned on the tap.

"What—" she began, her reflexive movement halted as her hands darted after her phone.

A calculated rationale was offered by Blake, his gaze a beacon of seriousness. "Let's not needlessly lead your pursuers right to your location. We've managed to shake them off, and we wouldn't want them back on your trail."

Understanding quickly coursed through Cadi's thoughts. "You're right," she conceded, the gravity of the situation falling upon her. "I underestimated them when I called the police. They almost had me."

Leaning over the counter, Blake took both of Cadi's hands in his own. His eyes held a gentle reassurance as he spoke. "Why don't you freshen up for dinner? It should be ready by the time you're done with a shower."

Blake's smile proved a formidable adversary to Cadi's ability to articulate herself with any semblance of coherence. In its glow, she felt as if time could halt, and she could bask eternally within the warmth of his eyes. He was a unique presence in her life, a departure from anyone she'd crossed paths with—a realization that wasn't quite groundbreaking given her limited social circle, especially when it came to men. Embracing his advice, she retraced her steps to the bedroom that had cradled her awakening.

Cadi found herself grappling with the notion that she might be developing a crush on Blake. While he appeared to be in his mid-twenties, uncertainty lingered in her perception. Despite the appealing exterior, she had no inclination for any form of relationship with him. Cadi recognized that her feelings could be attributed to Blake's handsome demeanor, compounded by the suspension bridge effect—her growing fondness influenced by his role in rescuing her from potential captors. Regardless, she understood the importance of being mindful of her emotions.

Upon arrival to her room, a cascade of soft melodies surged from the kitchen, casting a sonorous embrace throughout the house as music infused the entire house. In her room, the allure of hot water enticed her, and as she showered, she reveled in the soothing caress, coaxing her muscles to relax their grip. The rejuvenation she experienced lingered as she stepped out, a fresh aura enveloping her. Her senses were greeted by the scent of cooking food that had permeated the entire home. Hunger gnawed at her, a potent reminder of her body's needs.

Quickly, she donned a simple t-shirt and shorts, but a minor adjustment was required—rolling the back of the shorts to ease the pressure on her tail's base. Emerging from her room, she retraced her path to the kitchen, where Blake was engrossed in assembling a salad. Seizing a moment of distraction, Cadi requisitioned an item that could serve as a makeshift tool, permitting her to carefully create an opening in her shorts to accommodate her tail. By the time her alterations were complete, Blake had announced the readiness of their meal. Settling in at the counter, their plates before them, they were poised for conversation. However, Cadi's ravenous appetite precluded any meaningful exchange. Blake sensed her intensity and decided to abstain from engaging her mid-bite, surmising that an interruption might lead to a choking mishap.

Replete and content, Cadi leaned back, her hands finding rest atop her satiated belly. A sense of gratification radiated from her, a reflection of the meal she had thoroughly relished. Observing her satisfaction, Blake's demeanor held a subtle pleasure, gratified by her enjoyment. As a gracious host, he returned with beverages and cleared away their plates, resuming his place beside her. He allowed her the space she needed before embarking on conversation.

With an audible exhale, Cadi released a breath that carried a mixture of tension and relief. Her words came next, carrying a palpable curiosity. "So, why were my parents involved with this group opposing the president? I had no idea they were part of something like that."

Posing the question, Cadi assumed that Blake had already established contact with her parents, envisioning them collaborating seamlessly. Unbeknownst to her, this assumption proved to be mistaken.

However, Blake ignored the implication and redirected the narrative. His inquiry, delivered with a measured intensity, directed her thoughts in a new direction. "Do you have any knowledge about Donovan Pike, Cadi?"

Her response was frank, a candid admission of her limited understanding. The breadth of her familiarity with him was shallow—general public knowledge rather than intricate details. His political career had ignited when he assumed the role of lieutenant governor for their state, a trajectory previously unremarkable in the public eye.

Recounting what she knew, Cadi acknowledged the scarcity of her information, her voice tinged with a note of regret at her inability to contribute more to the discussion. Her parents had chosen not to disclose Donovan Pike's role as a Shepherd to her, deeming it unnecessary to involve her. Given her youth, they saw no advantage in her having this information. Yet, she recognized that this was a subject Blake intended to expound upon, offering her greater insights.

In his eyes, the matter at hand had an unspoken gravity. Blake was resolute in ensuring she gained a comprehensive understanding of the situation and the individuals involved. "Donovan Pike is a Shepherd."

"Why would he become the President if he's a Shepherd? I thought Shepherds operated from behind the scenes," Cadi inquired, her curiosity spurring the question.

Blake's response carried a note of candor, revealing a shift in historical paradigms. "In the past, that was the norm. But our fundamental directive as Shepherds centers on fostering the growth and progress of the human race as a whole."

Cadi's intrigue deepened, leading her to delve further. "How does that serve the interests of Shepherds?"

Open and willing, Blake embarked on a disclosure, offering insight into the workings of their intricate existence. "Considering the overwhelming population of humans—numbers that greatly surpass us—our approach adapts. We estimate there are only about three to five thousand Shepherds worldwide. By guiding humans to nurture their planet and advance as a species, we ultimately benefit. Our home is Earth, and we desire it to endure for the sake of our future generations."

Cadi's brow furrowed in contemplation, her thoughts returning to Donovan Pike. "So, what role does Donovan Pike play in all of this?"

"We believe he aspires to global dominion. Donovan Pike holds the belief that humans are inferior to Shepherds. He's been an advocate for Shepherds assuming control, with humans in a subservient role,"

Blake disclosed, his words laying bare a startling truth. Cadi's reaction was palpable—her hand instinctively flew to cover her mouth, a gesture born of disbelief and shock.

Blake acknowledged her astonishment, his solemn expression reinforcing the gravity of his claims. He expanded upon his revelation, delving into a complex spectrum of beliefs and dissent. "There are some among us who share his perspective, but the majority seek to dismantle his authority and restore the former governance. Pike orchestrated a plan to dismantle the existing government, a maneuver that facilitated his ascent to power."

Cadi's nod conveyed her comprehension of the intricacies at play. Her inquiry, rooted in a practical mindset, aimed to uncover their strategy. "So, how do you intend to remove him from power?"

Blake's reply was measured, weighed by careful consideration. "The thought of revealing his true nature and intentions has crossed our minds, but we recognize that many would dismiss it as a fabrication. We've reserved that option as a last resort. Assassination is unfeasible due to his private armies safeguarding his movements, although he rarely ventures far."

Cadi, mentally calculating the remaining avenues, voiced her thoughts. "That leaves you with limited options. With elections on the horizon, can't you leverage them to oust him from office?"

Blake's head swayed gently, brown tresses cascading in a soft dance. "Fixing the election is an option, but it's not viable. As it stands, there are no credible contenders for the office. The likelihood of his reelection seems almost certain. And even with our resources as Shepherds, persuading the world to accept a manipulated election as legitimate would prove insurmountable."

Cadi absorbed this revelation, her disbelief lingering. "That's a problem. It's hard to believe that my parents were tangled in something messy like this. It's pretty surreal."

Blake's response delved deeper, unveiling the catalyst that precipitated her parents' predicament. "Yes, it appears your parents' involvement acted as a spark, prompting his actions against them, leading to their abduction."

Blake was referring to what he had learned of her parents involvement with Donovan in the past as well as their resent abduction by Donovan's forces. Their abduction accelerated the timing of his plans.

The weight of her parents' situation hung heavy on Cadi's heart, evoking a somber introspection. The thought of their ordeal was a haunting presence, a constant undercurrent of sadness. The uncertainty they faced mirrored her own, their worries amplified by the absence of any knowledge about her whereabouts.

A surge of determination ignited within her, fueled by a desire to reconnect with her parents and ease their worries. She longed to extricate them from the turmoil they were enmeshed in. Her aspiration was simple: a return to normalcy. But the current state of affairs had veered far from what was ordinary, rendering her world unrecognizable. The upheaval was relentless, casting a shadow over everything that once defined her reality.

Cadi's hopes dwindled, a reflection of her narrowing options. In her quest for guidance, she turned to Blake, seeking aid in a time of desperation. "Is there a chance you or the people you know could assist me in locating my parents and securing their release from those who took them?"

Blake regarded her with a mix of empathy and contemplation, his concern manifesting in both his expression and the depths of his gaze. "If we could pinpoint your parents' whereabouts, the next step would be to assess whether we possess the necessary resources to extract them."

Cadi managed a weak smile, the response surpassing her initial expectations, a glimmer of hope in a sea of uncertainty. The impulse to cry was strong, her emotions teetering at the edge, yet she restrained herself. Despite her efforts, tears still lingered in her eyes, a testament to the tumultuous emotions stirring within her. Blake's touch, gentle and caring, wiped away the unshed tears, a gesture that resonated deeply within her.

A shift in the atmosphere followed as Blake stood, proposing a reprieve in the form of ice cream and a change of scenery. The prospect of a relaxed moment appealed to Cadi, and she readily accepted. Settled in the living room, she savored her ice cream, allowing herself a rare indulgence—an opportunity to embrace her inner child.

As the ice cream melted on her taste buds, so too did the weight of the situation melt away, if only temporarily. Amid her indulgence, she recognized the necessity of a more mature approach come morning. With determination, she resolved to collaborate with Blake and his allies to navigate the challenges her parents faced.

In this interlude, she was granted a respite, a pause in the whirlwind that had consumed her life. Her request for sprinkles and caramel was met with unexpected delight.

Savoring the cool sweetness of her ice cream, Cadi relished each bite, finding solace in this simple pleasure. With the bowl now empty, she conscientiously deposited it in the sink, expressing her gratitude to Blake before retreating to the designated room. Sleep didn't immediately beckon, so she wandered out onto the balcony, a quest for fresh air coupled with the allure of gazing upon the cityscape from the vantage point of the high-rise apartment.

Contemplation became her companion under the moonlit sky. She stared outward, her thoughts weaving intricate patterns of concern. The evolving dynamics within her family, shaped by the unfolding events, occupied her mind. Amidst these shifts, her own place in this intricate tapestry felt uncertain. The revelation that her biological connection to her father was absent, coupled with the knowledge of her non-maternal origin, lent an air of complexity to her identity.

Adding to her internal turmoil was her mother's pregnancy, a harbinger of change that rendered Cadi unsure of her role within the familial constellation. Her tail, a physical manifestation of her emotions, betrayed her unease with a subtle twitch, while her stomach tightened in tandem. The burden of her mother's overprotectiveness, though rooted in love, brought a sense of suffocation, leaving Cadi yearning for autonomy.

She acknowledged the futility of dwelling within the confines of circular thinking, recognizing its potential to amplify her anxiety. Refocusing, she directed her thoughts toward the challenge at hand—her parents' predicament. A resolve crystallized within her, a dedication to collaborate with Blake in a concerted effort to locate and liberate her parents. With the morning sun as her witness, she would confront the uncertainties head-on, channeling her energy into tangible actions.

In the interim, Blake retreated to his office, seeking a moment to decompress from the role he had to play during his interaction with Cadi. Despite the significant age gap of a few hundred years, he skillfully calculated his actions to earn her trust and maintain control over her compliance. His extensive experience in managing people through psychological means over the span of his long life made dealing with Cadi a relatively straightforward matter. A smile played on his lips as he turned to gaze out the window of his office, taking in the city lights far below his apartment.

11

Jack courteously gestured for Faye to enter the assigned quarters ahead of him. These shared quarters were on the brink of evolving from a space they were meant to share into the unexpected setting of a future crime—thanks to Faye's impending confrontation with Jack. This space was about to become a place where Faye could meticulously reprimand Jack in a harsh and negative manner. They would be slightly shielded from prying eyes, ignoring, of course, the unwavering sentinels stationed just beyond their door. The guards' continuous presence seemed almost like an unconventional yet integral element of the outside of the room's decor.

Taking her seat on the bed, Faye leaned back, beginning to undo her boots—a simple yet symbolic act of shedding the external world. With a deft kick, she sent her boots tumbling to the floor before arranging herself in a comfortably cross-legged position on the bed. Jack couldn't help but silently breathe a sigh of relief, thankful that her ire hadn't translated into a boot hurled menacingly at his head. Considering her current irritation and her undeniable strength, a propelled boot might easily transform into a dangerous missile, carrying enough momentum to land him in the infirmary.

Jack found himself grappling with the notion that he might be too advanced in years to wrestle with such concerns. Nevertheless, even armed with the certainty that airborne boots weren't in the equation, facing Faye remained no less daunting. The room contained other items, just as capable of being employed—with equal precision—to yield disastrous results for Jack. He opted to stand during the impending exchange; should he need to evade any launched salvos, it seemed far more advantageous to do so from a standing vantage point rather than a seated one that would needlessly curtail his maneuverability.

"Speak," commanded Faye, her arms now tightly folded across her chest, an embodiment of anger so intense it could potentially tinge her skin red.

Sighing with an air of resignation, Jack responded, "What do you wish to know?"

Her voice low and menacing, Faye growled, "I want to understand how you could keep something of such immense magnitude from me. How could you lie to me?"

"Wait a moment," Jack retorted, his tone laced with indignation. "I didn't lie to you about anything at all. I just kept it to myself and didn't say a word about it, you know, merely withheld information. And you never asked, so how was that a lie?"

"A lie of omission is still a lie," declared Faye, her conviction unwavering.

Jack raised a hand in a placating gesture. "Just a moment, if you will, 'Miss High and Mighty.' Weren't you the one who joined my investigation with a covert agenda of your own?"

"Yes, I was, but that's beside the point. According to what I've just heard, you already knew who I was," Faye countered.

"In that case, what exactly is the point, Faye?" Jack queried, his hands raised in an expression of both inquiry and mock surrender.

"The point is, I eventually came clean about my identity and my motives," Faye stated.

"In your recollection, this grand revelation occurred roughly at the same time I found myself on the brink of oblivion due to my lack of awareness. You weren't exactly unscathed either," Jack retorted, his tone laced with frustration.

"But I still opened up to you, Jack. Despite everything, I divulged everything," Faye's voice trembled, her throat constricting as she recalled the emotional tumult of those moments—her struggles, her fears, and the image of Jack in imminent danger.

Jack's eyebrows knitted in consternation. "You shared when it was convenient for you, not a moment sooner."

"Fine, I'll admit that you have a point there. However, Jack, your situation is as monumental as my own revelation—perhaps even more so due to your ongoing involvement," Faye contended. Her finger extended towards Jack's uniform, a tangible manifestation of the argument she was constructing.

"I couldn't, Faye," Jack confessed, his voice a mix of earnestness and entreaty.

"Don't feed me excuses, Jack. How many years has it been now? How much longer did you intend to wait?" Faye's question hung in the air, and she held her gaze steady, awaiting Jack's response. When he remained silent, her tone transformed into one of frustration. "You wouldn't have said anything if Donovan hadn't stepped in, would you?"

Jack's silence spoke volumes, prompting a furious and disillusioned sound from Faye. "For God's sake, Jack, what's happening to you? Who are you, really? The person I thought I knew—I'm starting to realize they might not be real at all."

Advancing a step, Jack extended his hand towards Faye, a gesture of both urgency and placation. "Wait a moment. Let's be fair here, Faye. You know me—perhaps better than anyone else ever could."

A sardonic smile curved Faye's lips. "Clearly, Colonel."

"I had my reasons for not telling you," Jack implored, his tone seeking understanding. "Can't you take my word on this? I would've endangered others' lives if I had disclosed it to you—the lives of those who served under me."

His plea hung in the air, a fragile thread of hope that seemed to dissolve upon reaching Faye's ears.

"Believe you? I'm finding it hard to know what to believe anymore, considering the enormity of the secret you kept," Faye replied, her gaze averted, her hands lying still and forlorn in her lap.

"Why was it so impossible for you to tell me?" The question finally escaped Faye's lips, her gaze locking onto Jack's. As her eyes glistened with the onset of tears, the magnitude of her hurt and sense of betrayal emanated palpably.

"I couldn't afford the risk of you knowing. The less you were aware of, the safer you and Cadi were," Jack whispered with a tone of apology. He acknowledged the weight of his decision to keep Faye in the dark. There had been no easy choices—only the unenviable task of safeguarding those under his protection and his loved ones through a shroud of secrecy. He'd assessed the potential damages, weighed the costs, and faced the harsh reality of a no-win situation. Either divulging or withholding the truth seemed to lead to a dead end. In his calculus, the path with the least destruction had seemed the only way forward. Keeping the secret meant his people remained safe, but it meant losing Faye. Disclosing the truth might prevent some losses, but it also risked others he was unwilling to bear.

Faye's hand swept through the air, a gesture of frustration and betrayal. "Being aware of the danger out there could have kept both Cadi and me safe. You didn't grant me the choice to assist in our protection. Instead, I had to discover it like this," she accused, her voice ascending in pitch as emotion surged.

Jack bristled at the reproach, his response swift. "It's not that simple, Faye. My love for you means I'd do anything to ensure your safety."

With his palms outspread, he asserted himself. But Faye's retort was quick, the words laced with accusation. "Knowledge would have offered more security than you allowed."

In a vulnerable admission, Jack's voice softened, revealing the depth of his feelings. "Faye, I love you. I'd move mountains for you."

"Fine," Faye declared, her tone edged with finality, as she stretched out on the bed. "You're welcome to move mountains, just do it from somewhere else. I think it's best if you leave."

Rolling away from Jack, she presented him with a view of her small form, her back turned resolutely. Jack's yearning to approach the bed and join Faye, to gather her in his strong arms and find solace beyond their current disagreement, surged within him. He wrestled with the impulse, his emotions clashing against his restraint. He was on the cusp of closing the distance, about to bridge the gap between them, when her voice intervened.

"I believe we've exhausted this conversation," Faye's words reached him, spoken over her shoulder, the finality ringing in the air.

A growing frustration seized Jack. His gaze swept across the room, settling on each object. He envisioned the satisfaction of releasing his pent-up emotions on the room's contents, the sound of destruction offering a fleeting release. Yet, he quickly quelled this mental tangent—he wouldn't surrender to such loss of control. Savoring thoughts of that nature teetered on the precipice of violence, a precipice he refused to approach. That was only a step away from putting your hands on someone.

"Faye, the government has known about Shepherds for nearly three decades. We were aware of their immense power—enough to bring down any government, including our own. We had no choice but to keep that information tightly guarded. Shepherds held influential positions within the Pentagon, across various agencies, even the White House itself. When Donovan assumed control, I dismantled everything to prevent him from discovering, but somehow he managed to uncover the truth. I couldn't afford any risks," Jack confessed in a hushed tone as he began to make his exit.

Faye's voice softened, her anger showing signs of subsiding. "Well, you made your decision, and I'm making mine. Goodnight, Colonel," she said quietly.

The use of his rank, that distant formality, signified a barrier she was placing between them. It was a subtle, telling signal that perhaps her suggestion for him to leave was best heeded. Jack's shoulders sagged, his demeanor one of defeat. A heavy sigh escaped his lips, and he shook his head with a mix of regret and resignation.

"I'll arrange for someone to gather my belongings later," he murmured before leaving.

Jack waited, anticipation threading through him, for a response from Faye. However, the silence remained unbroken. Feeling the weight of unspoken words, he pivoted on his heels and exited the quarters he had once shared with Faye, the atmosphere heavy with unresolved tension.

"Well, that went swimmingly," Jack muttered to himself, his voice laced with irony as he made his way out.

He found himself contemplating whether it might have been simpler if she had initiated the confrontation with a flying boot. At least a projectile that could be dodged would have been more straightforward than the volley of emotional bullets he had just endured.

Undoubtedly, the exchange hadn't transpired well; there was no need for someone else to point it out to him. In Jack's perception, it felt as though a nuclear explosion had erupted between him and Faye. The force of the blast had propelled him backward, leaving him to witness the fallout, the residual destruction now enveloping them. The aftermath had transitioned into a chilling nuclear winter he was forced to navigate. This outcome was far from anything he could have predicted. Donovan Pike's revelation had struck him with the force of a knockout punch, even though Donovan himself was oblivious to the havoc he had unintentionally wreaked.

Hovering between turmoil and hope, Jack clung to a thread of optimism. Faye hadn't announced their relationship's demise outright; her request for space seemed to suggest a glimmer of potential redemption. And so, Jack took what little victory he could. He resolved to grant her the room she sought, yearning for a chance to mend the bridges he feared he had irreparably damaged.

As Jack departed the room, Faye turned onto her back, her gaze fixed on the now-closed door. A sense of disbelief washed over her—it was difficult to grasp that Jack had acquiesced to her request and left without more of a struggle. She had anticipated a greater resistance, considering his usual tenacious disposition. The fact that he had yielded so easily left her feeling unsettled.

In all fairness, Faye recognized that she had explicitly instructed Jack to leave and had done so with a firm resolve. It was a decision she couldn't deny, yet she found herself growing increasingly agitated that he hadn't put up more resistance. She directed her frustration towards the absent Jack by hurling the pillow he had used against the door, a symbolic expression of her internal turmoil.

With a huff of exasperation, Faye flung herself backward onto the bed, her arms splayed out in a gesture of both surrender and frustration. Clutching her pillow to her face, she let out a muffled scream, her body writhing as she vented her pent-up emotions.

"Urgh, that infuriating, insufferable misogynistic ass!" she exclaimed with a mixture of expletive and disdain, the words serving as a release for the turmoil brewing within her.

Faye exhaled slowly, her fingers grazing her belly as she placed her hand there. The touch revealed tenderness, the evidence of change evident—her belly had expanded since just the previous day. Concern for her pregnancy weighed heavily on her mind, a worry that had crept in and settled deep. Curiously, Faye found herself somewhat grateful for Jack's departure. His absence offered her the excuse she needed to create some space between them, and in her heart, she understood the rationale behind his secrecy. She recognized the gravity of his decision, even if it left her discontented that he hadn't confided in her. Her understanding and agreement rested in two distinct places.

The truth was, Faye wanted that distance, that separation, to shield Jack from her struggles. She knew him well enough to anticipate the profound worry that would consume him if he discovered how intensely the pregnancy was affecting her. There were moments throughout the day when her extraordinary strength wavered, almost betraying her. There were times when the simple thought of retreating to their quarters and lying down seemed overwhelmingly inviting. But she couldn't allow Jack to witness these struggles. He had a crucial role to play, a mission to fulfill, and the burden of worrying about her and their unborn children would only hamper his ability to succeed.

In the intricate dance between love and practicality, Faye recognized that pushing Jack away, albeit none to gently, was a means of safeguarding his focus. She knew that the decisions they were making were not easy, but they were necessary for the greater good. In the end, as she rested her hand on her changing body, she understood that these challenges were part of their shared journey, a journey that demanded both understanding and sacrifice.

Faye couldn't deny the veracity of the information Dr. Brundle and her sister-in-law Elizabeth had shared regarding her pregnancy. It was evident that she was facing a challenging road ahead This gestational period wouldn't be an easy journey. The reality was sinking in that she would need to muster every ounce of her strength and resilience to ensure the well-being of the two precious lives growing within her.

Her strength was vital, not only for herself but also for the vulnerable lives she carried. She had no hesitation in pledging everything she had to ensure their health and safety. Her resolve was unshakeable; she would be a beacon of strength for them.

Yet, amid this commitment, a conflict raged within her heart. As much as she was willing to sacrifice and give her all, she grappled with the undeniable truth that such a sacrifice would mean losing Jack. Cadi would lose her mother, and the unborn babies would never know her. The emotional turmoil was real. Faye found herself at a crossroads of love and duty, with no easy path forward.

In this intricate dance between selflessness and personal desires, Faye recognized the depth of what she had to live for. The urge to be a protector, a guiding light for her children, was undeniable. As her hand instinctively rested on her abdomen, she understood that this wasn't just about survival; it was about embracing the threads that tied her to a world worth fighting for.

Jack's frustration festered, his bewilderment growing as he grappled with Faye's decision to push him away. The enigma lay in her inability to comprehend the intricacies of what he held back—information locked behind a dam of consequences he was unwilling to breach. The classified knowledge of the Shepherds bound him in secrecy, a national secret he couldn't casually unveil to anyone.

The lack of a destination tethered Jack's steps as he roamed aimlessly, adrift in a sea of uncertainty. He possessed a scant mental map of the facility, recognizing waypoints like the infirmary, firing range, conference room, and mess hall. Yet, the labyrinthine expanse surely concealed more corners of refuge. Opting for the mess hall, his plan was simple: secure a cup of coffee and find an inconspicuous nook, far from the bustling currents of personnel rushing to and fro.

Faye's obstructionist stance cast a shadow over his intentions. Acquiring new quarters felt like an endeavor he could navigate, provided he located the right interlocutor—someone capable of orchestrating the change without excessive commotion. An inkling told him his previous escort might hold the key, but the means of contacting the individual remained elusive, shrouded in the facility's expanse.

Considering the possibility, Jack speculated that the sentinels stationed by Faye's quarters might hold insights into reaching his enigmatic escort. An oversight struck him: he had neglected to consult the guards before his departure from that section of the installation. Regret settled in as he contemplated whether any of the numerous figures milling about might possess knowledge of his escort's identity. Discouraged, he abstained from inquiries, foreseeing a futile pursuit.

Jack's lapse in situational awareness left him chiding himself; the revelation of an unexpected company was a jolt he could have avoided. His table's new occupant, comfortable and unwavering, bore a steady gaze that met Jack's wandering mind. His internal debate vacillated between directing frustration inward or at the uninvited guest. Irrespective of his sentiments, adaptation was his sole recourse.

"Mr. President," Jack acknowledged, his greeting veiling the agitation beneath.

Hoping to mask his distraction, Jack silently wished Donovan hadn't detected his disarray. But his hopes were swiftly dashed, leaving him even more irked at his own vulnerability and the perplexing situation he found himself in.

"You appear preoccupied," Donovan remarked affably, exposing his keen perception. "You usually possess a sharper awareness. These circumstances can easily test anyone."

Jack's irritation broke through his veneer, the sharp edge of his tone betraying his vexation. "I would be less distracted if someone hadn't had me and my wife kidnapped and then decided to drop a bomb in the middle of our relationship."

Donovan's smile carried a tinge of remorse. "I regret the necessity of those actions. The urgency of the times demands drastic measures."

He hoped to quell the issue, aware of its potential persistence. Yet Jack clung to the grievance of the kidnapping, resolute in his stance. "Drastic, like dispatching a psychopath to commit murder, all in the name of preventing a world invasion?"

Understanding that the abduction was an open wound, Donovan met it head-on. "It was a grim decision, but it had to be made."

"Yeah," Jack's response was tinged with skepticism. His gaze locked onto Donovan's resolute steel-grey eyes, a battle of unwavering stares. Eventually, Jack relented, allowing his gaze to slip away from the intensity, an unspoken acknowledgment of the stalemate.

Donovan's vertical slit eyes, while familiar due to his exposure to Fay's and Cadi's unique features, still held an unsettling quality. Meeting Donovan's gaze, Jack voiced his inquiry, his curiosity tinged with an undercurrent of accusation. "Why did you unleash that madman?"

"That decision wasn't mine alone. My superior back then craved power, and that situation provided the opening I needed to eliminate the Shepherds in control—the very ones plotting the invasion," Donovan responded, his tone measured. "Dr. Brundle, the other one, furnished me with the means. I would have preferred a delicate approach, like a sieve to sift through them, but I only had a hammer. I employed what was at my disposal."

"You employed it to striking effect. It even earned you the Presidency," Jack retorted sardonically.

Donovan's expression remained composed as he clarified, "The Presidency was a result of circumstances, not my orchestration.

However, I did exploit the ensuing chaos to bolster my influence. The chain of events was triggered by our present adversaries to destabilize global governance. I marshaled my forces to counter their moves, deploying my soldiers worldwide. While it hindered their plans, it didn't extinguish them entirely."

Jack's skepticism was palpable as he scoffed. "So, your aim was to thwart them."

"Indeed. Nothing more, nothing less," Donovan replied evenly, his demeanor unwavering.

Uncertainty clouded Jack's judgment as he pondered Donovan's words. His inclination leaned toward belief, though doubts lingered like lingering shadows. Ultimately, his decision would hinge on Donovan's actions since taking power. The achievements, the paths he had chosen to tread or abstain from, and the deliberate lines he refused to cross all weighed heavily in Jack's evaluation. Donovan's realm of influence was broad, and the sway he held appeared nigh unstoppable.

Recognizing the need to transcend his own biases, Jack resolved to seek more information. It was a pragmatic shift to ensure his efficacy in the task laid out before him.

"So now you're tasking me with what your own troops and intelligence assets can't achieve?" Jack inquired, seeking clarity on his role within Donovan's plans.

"This time, a blunt instrument won't suffice. Precision is imperative for success. A scalpel, not a hammer," Donovan responded, emphasizing the nuanced approach required. "Your previous role in intelligence places you in a singular position. Your insight into the Shepherds is unparalleled. Your sources tracked their movements, and when you ceased your operations, you eradicated that data to prevent its access."

Donovan's admission flowed with an unexpected ease, a testament to his understanding of Jack's actions. He harbored no illusions of instantly swaying Jack to his side, but he aimed for cooperation, a mutually beneficial alliance.

"We had their locations, yes. But the details of their significance elude me. Among them, two stood out as particularly intriguing, although the full scope of their roles remained enigmatic," Jack confessed, his tone tinged with a sense of introspection.

"One of these individuals is likely Blake," Donovan stated, indicating his knowledge of Jack's situation. "He's currently engrossed in relaying the message to the Braxit. As for the other, it appears to be the Librarian."

Noticing Jack's silent contemplation, Donovan recognized the need for more information. "These two figures, aside from the governing councils I dismantled, held sufficient prominence to catch our attention. They possess the information to locate the Communicator we seek—the very person Blake intends to enlist for transmitting the message."

Jack's mind sifted through memories, orchestrating fragments of the past. His response carried a sense of certainty. "I lost track of Blake's whereabouts a while back, but I'm confident the Librarian remains rooted in the same location we initially identified. I can assemble a unit and head to that spot."

As Donovan prepared to depart, he conveyed his well-wishing with a straightforward directive. "Best of luck, Colonel. Utilize any resource necessary to achieve this task."

Just as Donovan was about to leave, Jack's recollection of his own predicament seized him. "Wait a moment, before you go, I have a question to pose."

Donovan's exit was briefly interrupted as he halted halfway out of his seat, attentive to Jack's inquiry. "Yes, how can I be of assistance?"

Though hesitant to embroil Donovan in his personal affairs, Jack's options were limited: either enlist Donovan's help or stumble blindly in search of another solution. Despite the unease of divulging private matters, he opted for the pragmatic path.

"I find myself in need of new quarters," he confessed, his words tinged with a hint of embarrassment.

Donovan promptly retook his seat, his concern evident.

"Are the current accommodations unsuitable for you and Faye?" His query was marked by sincerity, unaware of the emotional discord that had transpired between Jack and Faye, leading to their spatial estrangement.

"It's not that simple. I require new quarters. Faye and I... require some distance," Jack managed, his words bearing the weight of vulnerability.

After a brief pause of contemplation, Donovan addressed Jack's request without delving into the reasons, much to Jack's palpable relief.

"I'll have Lieutenant Morgan join you here in the mess hall to assist you," he offered, his focus solely on facilitating Jack's need.

"Thank you," Jack expressed, a sense of gratitude in his voice.

Donovan departed, leaving Jack to his own devices. Within this solitude, Jack nursed his coffee and the wounds inflicted by Faye's actions, his emotions a complex mix of hurt and resentment. His feelings were compounded by Donovan's decision to divulge information that Jack had hoped would remain concealed, a revelation that only heightened his disquiet. Despite his initial resistance to these thoughts, Jack's resolve began to waver. Eventually, he yielded, allowing impatience to dissipate as he awaited the return of the earlier mentioned lieutenant.

In due time, the mess hall welcomed Lieutenant Morgan's arrival, breaking the cycle of solitude. The lieutenant's competence efficiently addressed Jack's need for new quarters. With this task fulfilled, Jack sought solace in rest, a respite from the turmoil plaguing his mind. The weight of Faye's reaction to his true vocation and mission no longer demanded his wakefulness. He recognized the futility of dwelling on it, acknowledging that the passage of time and the gift of space were the only salves for such a wound. Thus, with the logistics settled, he allowed himself to drift into slumber.

12

As the morning light filtered through the window dressings, Cadi stirred from her slumber, greeted by its gentle touch. She inhaled deeply, the air carrying the aroma of brewing coffee and a sizzling breakfast. The tantalizing scent hinted at eggs, bacon, and French toast gracing the morning meal. With a series of satisfying pops and snaps, Cadi's joints protested as she completed her stretch, coaxing her body awake. Slowly, she rose from the bed, her senses attuned to the culinary symphony drifting in from beyond her room.

Her movements instinctively guided her toward the bedroom door, but her progress halted abruptly as her own reflection beckoned her from the mirror mounted above the dresser. In that fleeting moment, she was jolted from her reverie, her surroundings materializing in clarity. The realization washed over her: she was no longer in the comfort of her familiar home. Her parents weren't a mere step away, ready to shield her from any awkwardness.

Looking down at herself, clad in nothing more than a t-shirt and underwear, she comprehended the potential folly of her hasty actions. What might have passed unnoticed within the safe confines of her own home became a precarious situation here, with a man she had met a mere day ago, a man named Blake. The scope of their acquaintance barely extended beyond a single day, a fact that now loomed large in her mind.

The thought struck her like a revelation—this was simply not acceptable. This level of casual exposure wouldn't align well with her parents' sensibilities, should they become aware of it. The gravity of the situation sank in as Cadi resolved to find something more suitable to wear, a modest veil against vulnerability in this unfamiliar setting.

Cadi couldn't deny the truth—Blake was undeniably attractive. In the quiet corners of her mind, she had to admit to harboring a sort of schoolgirl crush on him. Inwardly grappling with honesty, she acknowledged the flutter of emotions he seemed to ignite within her. Was it merely his boyish charm and the tousled waves of his brunette hair that stirred her, or was it something more profound? Was her attraction a result of him plucking her from the precipice of danger, emerging as a mysterious guardian of her safety?

She found herself standing at a crossroads of sentiment, unsure of the precise genesis of her feelings. However, regardless of their origin, she was resolute in her decision not to venture beyond her room in her current attire. Swiftly, she exchanged her earlier choice for a pair of shorts, an embodiment of modesty. Delving into the closet, her fingers brushed past a collection of button-down dress shirts, neatly arranged further within its depths. A faint scent emanated from them, a scent that bore familiarity—the unmistakable essence of Blake. With a wistful smile, she selected one of the shirts and slipped it on, its form enveloping her figure in an unexpected sense of connection.

As she tucked the front of the shirt into her shorts and allowed the back to cascade freely, she found a newfound confidence. Adorned in this borrowed piece of clothing, she walked purposefully toward the kitchen, where the enticing aromas of breakfast beckoned, her steps infused with both curiosity and a subtly shifting dynamic of emotions.

"Good morning, Cadi," Blake greeted as he observed her settling onto a stool at the kitchen counter.

His inquisitive eyebrow arched involuntarily as he took note of the shirt she wore—one that clearly belonged to him. Her wide grin was a preemptive strike, an attempt to disarm any potential objection he might raise about her choice of attire, which now prominently featured his shirt. A shared understanding seemed to hang between them, unspoken yet acknowledged. Seeking to divert his attention, she segued smoothly into a different topic.

"That smells wonderful. Is it nearly ready?" Cadi asked tentatively, aware that she was ready to consume a meal.

Blake's lips curved into a knowing smile. He recognized Cadi's intention to divert him, a strategy to sidestep any commentary on her current attire. He acquiesced to her ploy, allowing himself to be guided away from the topic at hand. His perspective remained grounded—the shirt was inconsequential, and he felt no need to make a fuss about it.

Blake's foresight had led him to purposely leave his shirts in the closet, aware of Cadi's penchant for appropriating similar attire from her father, Jack. His understanding ran deep; this was another avenue to connect with her.

He assessed the situation with a pragmatic detachment. The shirt, to him, was merely a tool, another thread in the intricate tapestry he wove. A way to disarm and bend situations to his advantage, allowing for manipulation masked as cooperation.

"Grab the orange juice from the refrigerator, and I'll plate our breakfast while you take care of our glasses," he instructed, an unspoken accord binding their actions in this shared space.

Cadi carried out Blake's directive with a sense of anticipation, her return to the counter unveiling a hearty plate of breakfast. She settled into her seat, her eagerness matched only by the enticing spread before her. Amid the subtle clatter of utensils and the scents of morning cuisine, Blake's throaty clearing drew her attention.

Her gaze shifted to him, curiosity sparking in her eyes. A soft smile curved her lips as she realized the source of his interruption—her own tail, seemingly engaged in a playful interaction with Blake, perhaps swaying and brushing against him as she focused on her meal.

A sheepish grin tugged at her lips, and she moved to rectify the situation, withdrawing her tail from Blake's reach.

"Apologies," she murmured, her voice laced with a mixture of amusement and sincerity. "I guess my tail got a bit carried away with my appetite."

Blake dismissed her apology with a nonchalant gesture, his demeanor relaxed. "No need to apologize."

A natural smile found its place on his lips, his gaze settling on Cadi. The rosy hue that painted her cheeks in response didn't go unnoticed, a silent testament to their growing camaraderie.

"Once you finish breakfast, I'll ask you to prepare for the day," Blake's statement held a sense of purpose. His tone, while authoritative, carried an air of mutual understanding. "There's a place I need to visit, and I'd appreciate your company."

"Alright," Cadi agreed, her curiosity piqued. "Is there anything I should be aware of? Do I need to prepare or do anything specific?"

Blake's response was reassuring, a hint of casualness underscoring his words. "No special preparations necessary. Just come along. Jeans and a shirt will suffice. Contacts and tail don't need to be hidden either; we'll be in the company of fellow Shepherds."

Cadi nodded in understanding, her excitement palpable. "Got it. I'll be ready in about twenty minutes. I can't wait to meet other Shepherds. I've only known you and my mom."

Blake's warm smile mirrored his affable demeanor. "They'll be equally eager to meet you."

Following their exchange, breakfast drew to a close. Swiftly, they readied themselves for their outing. Blake expertly brewed coffee, decanting it into tumblers for their journey ahead. With preparations complete, they departed the apartment, sliding into Blake's vehicle before venturing out into the cityscape. The urban scenery unfolded before them as they navigated through the bustling streets, an enigmatic destination guiding their path. The minutes passed, blurring into a seamless passage of time, until their journey brought them to their awaited arrival point, a half-hour's drive away.

Their vehicle came to a halt in front of a building rising five stories high, encased in glass and steel. Its architecture bore an uncanny resemblance to every other structure within the industrial park, a deliberate lack of distinctiveness that concealed its true purpose. Set against a backdrop of nondescript structures, this building was a masterful ruse, the epitome of subtlety. Unassuming and inconspicuous, it harbored a secret that defied its mundane exterior—a secret known only to those aligned with Blake and his faction of Shepherds.

When Donovan initiated his campaign to eliminate the foremost Shepherds, Blake's faction opted to plunge their operations into darkness, effectively disappearing from the grid. This calculated move proved to be their lifeline, a choice that defied Donovan's relentless pursuit. The cloak of invisibility they donned was their armor, their shield against his probing eyes. This shroud of obscurity allowed them the time they required—a precious interval to forge strategic plans, to locate the elusive Key and Communicator, and to rally their enigmatic overseers, the Braxit.

The parking garage, secluded from prying eyes, served as a secure haven exclusively for Shepherds. Here, they could navigate in and out without fear of clandestine surveillance, a sanctuary hidden from unwelcome scrutiny. A single elevator, a solitary conduit to the pinnacle of the building, offered access to its uppermost floor, a floor that remained concealed from prying inquiry. Guarded zealously, the stairwell remained locked, its entrance denied to all but the initiated. These safeguards were meticulously orchestrated to veil their presence, part of a carefully woven tapestry of secrecy that enshrouded their activities within the building's unassuming exterior. As a clever diversion, the remaining floors were let out to legitimate enterprises, effectively masking the covert undertakings transpiring in their shadow.

As Blake maneuvered the vehicle into its designated spot, they embarked on the journey upward. Aboard the elevator, en route to the highest floor, a sense of unease twined around Cadi's thoughts. Exposed to the open air, her tail free and her natural eyes unveiled, she felt a twinge of apprehension. Despite the assurance of their privacy, the ghost of self-consciousness loomed over her. Anxieties nestled within her, persisting like dampened clothing that clings unrelentingly.

Cadi attempted to quell the disquiet that stirred within her, though her efforts met only partial success. An elusive sensation still sent shivers coursing up her spine, a lingering discomfort that came with the notion of exposure, of being laid bare. Despite her endeavors to dismiss it, the feeling persisted, insistent and tenacious.

However, the disquiet began to dissipate the moment she stepped off the elevator, met by a group of Shepherds whose eyes bore the same distinct split irises as hers. In their shared gaze, Cadi found a kinship that transcended mere words. For the first time in her existence, the sense of being an anomaly, an outsider, began to fade. Amidst these Shepherds, she was no longer an outlier; they bore the same marks of distinction, albeit minus the tail.

A profound shift enveloped her as she reveled in this newfound kinship. In this enclave, her identity was no longer defined by her differences. She didn't feel like a stranger trapped within her own skin; rather, she discovered a sense of belonging that she had never known. Normalcy was a fleeting notion for her, yet within this assembly, she glimpsed its semblance. Safety and acceptance wrapped around her like a comforting embrace, stemming from the simple fact that here, she was seen for who she truly was. The disheartening moniker of 'freak' that she had thrust herself lost its sting; she wasn't a creation of a deranged imagination but a person worthy of connection

Cadi stood captivated, her gaze tracing the fluid movements of a half-dozen Shepherds weaving through the lobby. Once Cadi and Blake disembarked from the elevator, they entered this space—a realm that seemed to breathe with ordinary routines, unaffected by the novelty of her presence. The Shepherds moved with an air of ease, engrossed in their individual tasks, as though Cadi's arrival was but a footnote in their daily lives.

Blake set forth, his strides decisive as he forged ahead along the corridor to their left. He didn't pause for Cadi. Observing his determined path, Cadi didn't hesitate to follow. The course of their walk became evident as they traversed the space, guided by a reason that Cadi was quick to discern.

A conference room beckoned at the hallway's terminus, and Blake navigated toward it with a sense of purpose. As Cadi ventured deeper, her surroundings maintained the veneer of any other office space, seemingly absorbed in the rhythm of productive endeavor. The hum of activity surrounded her, a whirlwind of movement and determination, each individual absorbed in their distinct pursuit. While the specifics of their tasks eluded her comprehension, the shared atmosphere of industriousness permeated the air, alluding to the enigmatic 'work' that occupied their attention.

Taking a seat amidst the array of chairs encircling the conference room table, Blake exuded a calm patience. Cadi's perceptive eye caught a subtlety in his choice of placement; he deliberately avoided the seats anchoring either end of the table, ones that typically assumed a position of prominence. This decision underscored his character, suggesting that his sense of leadership transcended ostentatious displays. Cadi's gained a growing insight into Blake's demeanor.

Uncertain of her role in the interim, Cadi navigated the expanse of the conference room, her steps echoing a sentiment of exploration. With a casual grace, she wandered, each movement rife with curiosity. As the moments ticked by, Blake's silence pervaded the room. His eyes followed her with a watchful gaze, observing her as she moved about like an inquisitive feline encountering a new domain.

Captivated by the world outside the window, Cadi paused, her focus extending beyond the room's confines. The outside panorama appeared remarkably mundane, an image that stood in stark contrast to the tumult that had engulfed her existence. Amid this semblance of normalcy, the world continued its ceaseless progression, seemingly undisturbed by the events that had thrust her into the heart of a newfound reality. Yet, amidst the quotidian continuity, an undercurrent of concern tugged at her thoughts—her parents, their safety, their apprehensions. A wave of unease washed over her, accompanied by questions that whispered through her mind.

Blake caught the current of her thoughts and gently voiced his inquiry, "Are your parents on your mind?"

Cadi acknowledged the question, her composure tenuous as she worked to steady her voice, masking the vulnerability she felt. She adopted a feigned smile, turning to meet Blake's gaze before responding, her hands intertwined behind her back.

"I suppose they're alright. I shouldn't let myself fret too much," Cadi uttered, her demeanor a blend of optimism and apprehension.

A momentary lapse in her poise prompted her to glance downwards, where a subtle scuff of her shoe against the carpet betrayed her underlying unease.

Blake's reassurance followed swiftly, his conviction unwavering. "Rest assured, we'll locate your parents and bring you back together. That's a certainty."

Meeting Blake's gaze anew, Cadi swayed slightly, her restless energy translating into a rhythmic rocking motion on the balls of her feet.

"I remember. You've mentioned that," she replied, the genuineness of her smile lit the room aglow.

With a telltale twitch, her tail swayed behind her. Seeking direction in their present circumstances, Cadi inquired, "Is there someone we're waiting for, Blake?"

Blake's response eschewed direct articulation, replaced by a simple gesture. He extended his arm, a subtle indication of the door's impending movement as it yielded to the approach of three individuals.

"Not anymore," he murmured, redirecting his attention toward the newcomers who filed into the room, each securing a place around the conference table.

With a tacit prompt from Blake, Cadi understood his wish for her to claim a seat among the gathering. As she positioned herself at the table, a sense of anticipation hung in the air, shrouding the room in an aura of significance.

The trio, now seated on the table's opposing flank, turned their attention inward, their postures reflecting an air of purpose. Blake's and Cadi's positioning ensured they faced the room's expansive windows, a panoramic expanse suffused with invigorating sunlight. The sheer volume of light, pouring through the glass, cast an uplifting atmosphere upon the chamber, transforming it into a space suffused with vitality and promise.

Within the conference room, the trio of Shepherds sat from Cadi's left to right, forming a tableau that embodied diversity—two males and a female. Blake assumed the role of orchestrator, establishing the meeting's cadence, a gesture that, in large part, served to familiarize Cadi with the key figures before her.

With an air of authority, Blake initiated the introductions, a gesture that testified to his deference for Cadi's participation.

"Mari, Alexander, and Antonio," he began, addressing each in turn. "Allow me to introduce Cadi. She's here to lend her aid to our mutual objectives, while we reciprocate by extracting her parents from Donovan's grasp."

Warm exchanges of greetings rippled across the room, Cadi absorbing the dynamic between Blake and his colleagues, her role shifting from participant to observer. Seated attentively, she yielded to the rhythm of the meeting, a watcher at the periphery.

As Blake steered the discourse like the helmsman of a multinational corporation, he received updates and insights from various facets of their clandestine organization. His posture reflected intent concentration as he absorbed the information presented, his fingertips quietly meeting beneath his lower lip. A moment of contemplative silence followed, as Blake engaged in an internal discourse, distilling the gleaned insights, melding them with his pre-existing knowledge, and plotting a course that would navigate the intricacies of their shared objective.

Blake lowered his hands, turning his attention to Mari, the opening question poised for a critical update. "Mari, how's the groundwork for the demonstrations shaping up?"

With a poised air, Mari responded concisely, her words carrying an undercurrent of assurance. "We've received confirmations of significant gatherings planned at strategic points across the nation. West Coast events are set to commence early in the morning, followed by East Coast assemblies in the late afternoon. Coordination is in place to ensure synchronized action nationwide."

Blake then shifted his focus to Antonio, a deliberate look encompassing the room's occupants. "Antonio, are our specialized units prepared for the imminent mission?"

Antonio's response carried a hint of hesitation, his gaze momentarily flitting towards Cadi. However, bolstered by a subtle cue from Blake, he regained his composure.

"Yes," he started, his glance returning to Blake. "Our teams are strategically positioned at key locales. While the exact target site remains uncertain, we've narrowed it down to four potential locations. As the demonstrations unfold, our move will be simultaneous."

Blake's affirmation was both decisive and commanding. "Execute with speed and precision."

Shifting his attention to the final occupant of the room, Blake inquired about the latest development. "Alexander, any progress in locating the asset we require?"

Alexander, composed and attentive, responded with clarity. "Indeed, sir. The Librarian's whereabouts have been traced to South America. They currently hold a teaching position at a local college in Panama City. We've taken steps to prepare one of our jets for your use, as soon as you're ready to proceed."

"That's good. I'll need to depart soon. I'll inform you before I head to the airport. Timing will be crucial, right before takeoff," stated Blake. Antonio and the other two Shepherds nodded in unison, their understanding clear.

"You can count on it, sir," affirmed Antonio, speaking on behalf of himself and his companions.

The conversation continued amongst Blake and the three Shepherds, delving into intricate plans and overarching goals. While engrossing for them, Cadi found her attention drifting to distant thoughts. Stepping away from the table, she positioned herself by the expansive window. Her gaze observed the bustling city below, individuals weaving in and out, each preoccupied with their destinations or origins. The scene elicited a memory of her younger years, reminiscent of when she used to observe ant hills.

Contemplating the lives of those below, Cadi pondered the complexities that might define their existence. Did they grasp the notion that an unseen world existed alongside theirs, hidden in plain sight? The idea of these people coexisting with half-aliens like herself seemed unfathomable. Unlike clandestine intrusions, she and her kind were intentionally placed on this planet, woven into human society. Yet, the distinct discrepancy lay in awareness—the Shepherds possessed insights into the world that eluded their human counterparts. Knowledge shaped their divergence.

Now, Cadi wrestled with the burden of knowing. It was a knowledge she wished she could relinquish, for ignorance might allow her to believe that her life paralleled that of anyone else's.

That's what Cadi truly yearned for: to be a normal teenage girl. But such a desire remained an elusive dream. Her reality transcended the realm of normalcy, surpassing it to such an extent that envisioning an ordinary teenage life was an almost impossible feat. Cadi allowed her thoughts to wander, drifting aimlessly from one idea to another, devoid of a specific focus. Her intention was to remain a silent observer while Blake engaged in dialogue with his peers. This was her initial strategy—until Blake redirected their conversation, steering it toward Cadi's parents.

"Antonio, what do you know of Donovan's plans for Jack and Faye Riddle?" Blake's question cut through the tension in the room, prompting Cadi to shift her attention back to the group of Shepherds.

She settled back into her seat, her curiosity piqued as she prepared to listen closely. Antonio cleared his throat, his strong voice resonating within the confines of the conference room. The weight of his experience and knowledge seemed to fill the space as he began to address the pressing concerns.

"More than likely, he will be trying to use Colonel Riddle's resources and knowledge to find out where we are and the Librarian is," Antonio's words were clear and direct, painting a stark picture of the danger at hand.

As the conversation continued, Alexander's voice joined the discussion, seeking further insight into the matter.

"Do you think that he knows where the Librarian is?" Alexander's question held a note of uncertainty, reflecting the group's shared concerns.

Blake leaned back in his seat, his posture reflecting the gravity of the situation. He allowed the conversation to unfold, absorbing the information being shared by his colleagues. When the moment was right, he added his perspective to the mix.

"His organization knew a lot, and we do not know to what extent his actual knowledge encompasses us, our operations, or the Librarian," Blake's voice held a mixture of caution and contemplation.

Antonio's gaze shifted to Alexander as he expanded on the topic.

"We were never able to infiltrate his unit. We can only guess how much he and his organization uncovered and knew about us." Antonio's words underscored the challenge they faced, leaving the group to grapple with the uncertainty of Donovan's knowledge and intentions.

Cadi, however, found herself growing more puzzled by the moment. The conversation seemed to revolve around people and plans she had never heard of. Her father, a colonel? She had grown up with the understanding that he was a police officer in the city. The mismatch between the discussion and her knowledge left her feeling lost and disconnected from the secrets being unveiled in front of her.

She looked over at Blake, her confusion evident in her expression. "What is he talking about? I've never heard of my father being a colonel."

Blake raised his hand in a calming gesture, trying to reassure Cadi and buy himself some time to provide her with answers. He sensed her unease and wanted to address her concerns, but first, he needed to finish the briefing.

"Let me finish the briefing, and I promise I'll explain everything to you," Blake said to Cadi, his tone firm yet understanding.

He wanted to keep her engaged in the conversation while ensuring that the critical information was conveyed to everyone present. Cadi nodded, a mixture of curiosity and anticipation in her eyes. She settled back, focusing her attention on the ongoing discussion among the Shepherds. The urgency of the situation and the decisions that needed to be made were clear to her, and she recognized the need to let the Shepherds proceed without further interruptions.

As the conversation progressed, Blake's question shifted the focus to Faye, and Mari took the opportunity to provide an update. "We've received reports from our agent. She's making faster progress than anticipated. We're hopeful that she'll be able to successfully deliver a healthy baby. Our agent is concerned about the strain the pregnancy might put on her, but the agent believes Faye has the strength to overcome it."

The room was filled with a mixture of tension and determination as the Shepherds continued to share information and discuss their plans. And while Cadi's mind was buzzing with questions, she held back, trusting that Blake would soon provide the answers she sought. Blake extended his gratitude to Mari, Alexander, and Antonio before dismissing them. He then turned his full attention to Cadi, his demeanor calm and understanding. He recognized the need to address her questions and concerns directly.

"Alright," Blake began, his voice steady and composed, "I understand that this might be overwhelming, but I need to be upfront with you. Your father was the commanding officer of an organization that was investigating Shepherds, including us. As for your mother, her pregnancy is complicated for reasons we're still trying to fully understand. Our agent is concerned about the strain it might place on her. Our priority is to keep her safe."

Cadi absorbed the information, her thoughts swirling as she tried to make sense of the new revelations. Her sense of identity and her understanding of her parents were being challenged, and she was grappling with the implications.

"Will my mom be alright?" Cadi asked, her concern for her mother evident in her voice.

Blake offered a reassuring smile. "Based on the information we have, we believe she has the strength to overcome this challenge. Our agent is doing everything possible to ensure her well-being."

Cadi's questions continued, as she sought clarity amid the confusion. "And what about my father? What's this about him being a colonel?"

Blake met her gaze with understanding. "Your father's role was not what you might have believed. He was not a police officer throughout. He worked for an organization under the Department of Defense that was investigating Shepherds, including us here. When Donovan assumed the presidency, he shut down that unit."

Cadi processed the information, her thoughts a mix of surprise, disbelief, and the need to come to terms with the new reality about her parents' roles. The gap between her perceptions and the truth was becoming more apparent, and she was starting to grasp the complexity of the situation.

Perched within his lab, a desk nestled beside the infirmary, Dr. Brundle found himself engrossed in his computer screen, a tableau of Faye's genome unfolding before him. Peculiarities danced within the strands of genetic code, their enigma eluding his full grasp. While his alter ego had showcased brilliance as a geneticist, their common foundation in intelligence was shared, yet genetics stood as a realm outside his expertise. This was further compounded by the intricate cognitive barrier ingrained by the Braxit, stymying his comprehension of genetic intricacies.

Within the framework of his alternate persona, christened Anthony, a relentless fervor fueled his pursuit of knowledge, transcending the deficit that had initially hindered him. Anthony's relentless obsession directed every personal resource toward unraveling the tapestry of genetic manipulation. Across the entire expanse of the world, no soul possessed a comparable repository of pragmatic, wieldable expertise in this arcane realm.

Curious paradoxes held Dr. Brundle in their grip. Jealousy coursed through him, a sentiment directed at himself—a sentiment that defied logical bounds, for his clone embodied an extension of himself. A plea for a deeper application of his faculties resounded within, a prayer that someday, understanding might eclipse his current limitations.

In the midst of his contemplation, the creak of the door reached his ears, a prelude to the entrance of two figures into his sanctum. Elizabeth and Jason, summoned to aid in Faye's prenatal care, made their way to seats drawn around Dr. Brundle's desk. The realm of his thoughts and the physical realm converged.

"The regeneration of her tail has commenced," Dr. Brundle uttered absentmindedly, his words an interjection between the inward symphony of his musings and the external world.

Fixed on the data dancing across his computer screen, Dr. Brundle remained immersed in the flood of information. Meanwhile,

Elizabeth and Jason found themselves grappling with uncertainty, struggling to decipher the words that had escaped Dr. Brundle's lips. Elizabeth's curiosity compelled her to seek clarity, coaxing the words from her lips in a gentle query.

"Could you please repeat that, Dr. Brundle?" Elizabeth's voice, a gentle entreaty, bridged the gap between her confusion and the revelation held within the doctor's words.

Shifting his gaze from the luminous monitor, Dr. Brundle's eyes met Elizabeth's as he echoed himself. "Faye's tail is in the process of regenerating. The resurgence of her tail coincides with her pregnancy."

Elizabeth's brow furrowed as comprehension intertwined with her inquiry. "But why is this a concern? Can't we simply remove it again later, if needed?"

The doctor's response was a window into the complexities at hand. "It appears that Faye carries a virus that triggers the regrowth of Shepherds' tails. Curiously, this virus has propagated within our Shepherd colleagues as well. The contagion has gripped approximately ten percent of our staff, and its transmission follows an exponential pattern. Remarkably, aside from its tail-regenerating effect, the virus appears benign, lacking any other discernible complications."

With a fluid gesture, Dr. Brundle redirected attention to his own tail, an appendage that bore a truth that he was grappling with.

"So what implications does this hold?" Elizabeth's voice bore a mix of concern and curiosity. "Have you managed to devise any strategies to halt its progress?"

The doctor's response was candid, revealing the bleak nature of the situation. "Halting its spread seems unlikely. The virus has already breached our facility's confines. Its infectious potential extends even to humans, turning them into potential carriers. Nevertheless, the virus itself, while disruptive, carries no significant threat beyond its curious effect of regenerating Shepherds' tails. Concealing their identity will become a challenge for Shepherds. At the present rate of dissemination, we estimate global coverage within three months."

A wry smile tugged at Elizabeth's lips. "I suppose the next few months promise to be rather eventful."

"Indeed," Dr. Brundle concurred, his focus pivoting. "But for now, our priority is ensuring Faye receives the necessary caloric intake during this critical period. I intend to augment her diet and administer intravenous calories. This should suffice for the interim. Let's establish a rotational schedule to manage her medical care."

Both Elizabeth and Jason swiftly offered their agreement, a silent unity of purpose uniting the trio. Engrossed in their duty, they studied the recent test results, deciphering the labyrinthine map of Faye's condition to formulate their preliminary care regimen.

Meanwhile, Faye found solace in her respite, a temporary haven from the relentless strain her burgeoning pregnancy exerted on her body. Yet, a restlessness festered beneath her skin, the duality of emotions tangled within her. The confines of the shared space with Jack had proven suffocating, a sensation that had compelled her to seek refuge within the medical wing. An oscillation of emotions clouded her judgment, wrestling with the rationality of her reactions.

In a gesture of genuine kindness, Brooke stepped into the role of Faye's companion, a presence that alleviated the sense of isolation inherent to the confines of the medical section. The solace Faye found in Brooke's company was deeply appreciated, even though it simultaneously underscored the absence of her own daughter, a lingering absence that bore heavily on her heart.

Brooke's presence held a dual purpose, a comforting pillar on which Faye leaned and a sounding board for her grievances, primarily concerning Jack. Faye's frustrations and accusations found a receptive audience in Brooke, who provided a sympathetic ear to her diatribes against the perceived indifference of Jack.

As a safe confidante, Brooke was privy to Faye's moments of vulnerability, serving as both a sounding board and a source of solace. Amid the turbulence of her pregnancy, Faye's emotions ran rampant, at times leaving her feeling like a shattered mosaic. One instance would find her fortified, ready to take on the world, while the next would usher in a deluge of tears, a yearning to be enveloped in the sturdy embrace of her husband, Jack.

13

The resounding klaxon filled the facility, its groan reverberating throughout. Positioned strategically across the entire complex, this auditory beacon served as the principal conduit for alerting installation personnel, rousing them to a state of preparedness and rallying for action.

Meanwhile, within the heart of the installation, Jack found himself stationed in the situation room. This room stood as the pivotal hub of command and control, drawing together both him and the senior cadre of the installation's staff. Their vigil within the command center had endured for approximately eight hours, during which they had remained ensconced, diligently tracking the cascading events unveiled by the news feeds across the nation.

An uprising had surged into being—an insurrection that rent the fabric of law and order asunder. Across the expanse of the land, the once-familiar mantle of tranquility had been usurped by the fires of violence, searing across the width of the nation from one coast to its opposing counterpart.

A relentless tempest of civil strife had thrust the entire country into the throes of a full-fledged war, where local militias squared off against government forces. Not a single state had emerged unscathed, each bearing witness to at least one conflagration. It was a widespread chaos.

In the northeastern reaches, the grip of this madness held sway over numerous cities within each state—up to ten of them. Jack, together with the installation commanders, remained ever watchful over these swirling events. However, their focus was presently locked onto the epicenter of the nation—the capital itself.

Days before the eruption of hostilities, Donovan had reclaimed his seat of power within the capital's confines. Yet, as the floodgates of conflict burst open, even the heart of governance was engulfed in the maelstrom. The local and state authorities, overmatched by numerically superior opposition forces, found themselves compelled to relinquish the capital's reins. Amidst this tumultuous retreat, the White House became a target, succumbing to an overpowering assault that severed communication with the President's retinue.

Jack held a silent prayer, a plea for this setback to amount to no more than a transitory challenge—one that could swiftly be surmounted. His paramount concern was to secure the safety of the nation's leader, for with the upper echelons of governance already scattered, the President's absence cast a long, foreboding shadow over the nation's destiny—a fate teetering on the edge of pandemonium, an outcome Jack was determined to avert at all costs.

With official channels of communication to the capital abruptly severed, Jack and his team found themselves compelled to cobble together fragmentary intelligence gleaned from the myriad news feeds streaming in from across the nation. Amidst this precarious information flow, Jack found comfort in the fact that the medical services remained unscathed, and the lifelines of electricity and water persisted.

"Major Burke," Jack's voice carried weight. "Deactivate the general alarm. What's the situation?"

Major Burke positioned himself next to Jack, poised to deliver his report. "I gave the order for general stations, sir."

"Why?" Jack's gaze remained fixed on the bank of monitors, each screen portraying scenes of anarchy unfurling across the country.

"Our perimeter defenses detected unidentified movement converging towards our position. Given the ongoing events, I deemed it wise to adopt a cautious stance and summon our troops to their stations."

"Prudent call, major," Jack acknowledged, briefly turning his attention towards the Shepherd.

Leadership now rested upon Jack's shoulders. Command had unexpectedly fallen into his grasp, a mantle he wore with uncertainty and determination. He had been thrust into a role that demanded more of him than he could have foreseen. Yet, armed with a newfound understanding of the stakes involved, he was resolute in safeguarding both his loved ones and a world veering toward the precipice of danger.

"This installation was a closely guarded secret, if I'm not mistaken?" Jack asked.

Major Burke concurred with a nod.

"Considering this, it's clear that anyone approaching us without proper identification is to be treated as a potential threat," Jack asserted, his voice resonating with a keen understanding of the situation. "Get the men ready for defense of the installation. Once we figure out who we're up against, we'll figure out a way to repel them."

Major Burke saluted crisply, swiftly exiting the command center to assume his role in leading the installation's defense. Amid the orchestrated flurry of activity, Jack's gaze scanned the room, alighting upon Major Allen who was engrossed in a blend of tasks. The major leaned over a table at the rear of the chamber, poring over maps of the capital city, his speech a rapid cadence into the phone he clutched. With purpose, Jack approached, patiently biding his time until the major concluded his conversation.

"Have you managed to determine the President's whereabouts?" Jack inquired, his concern giving his words weight.

"Indeed, sir. The President's security is presently being fortified. Plans are underway to convey him to this location, where we can ensure his safety," Major Allen responded

"I'd actually appreciate that piece of news if we weren't currently under attack," Jack admitted with a sigh. "It's quite baffling how our location got compromised. This installation shouldn't have been on anyone's radar. I'm left wondering who's behind this assault and why they've targeted us. After all, this isn't a strategic stronghold or a high-value target. It's simply a logistics base." Jack drew in a deep breath, tilting his head to the side as he absently rubbed his shoulder.

"I agree with your assessment, sir—" Major Allen began, but his words were abruptly cut off by a thunderous explosion that rocked the command center.

The force of the blast sent Jack, Major Allen, and a lieutenant who was present scrambling to squat and shield their heads. Once the dust had settled, they slowly rose to their feet. Jack brushed at his arms and ruffled his hair, his concerned gaze scanning the room to ensure everyone was unharmed.

The gravity of the explosion was evident to Jack. The fact that they were underground amplified the impact, almost knocking them off their feet from three floors above. Amid the aftermath, a captain burst into the command and control center, scanning the room until his eyes locked onto Jack. Swiftly making his way over, he launched into a report of the unfolding situation.

"What the hell was that, Captain?" Jack demanded, his voice edged with urgency.

"Sir, the enemy has breached the facility. Major Burke took the bulk of our forces and headed to confront the enemy at the eastern border of the installation. It appears a specialized strike force infiltrated from the west, a larger force is in the east. They used laser guidance to direct a bunker buster at the heavy doors of the supply loading docks, successfully breaching the facility. At present, we're engaged with a portion of their forces at junction C-91. However, intelligence suggests the group at that junction split their assault group, with half of them moving southward along corridor H-7," the captain explained with a sense of controlled urgency.

Though Jack's familiarity with the facility fell short of his desires, he possessed enough awareness to recognize that the section now infiltrated by the intruders held little strategic significance.

The loading docks? There's no single reason that comes to mind for their interest in that specific part of the installation, even if it were a mistake, Jack mused inwardly, his thoughts racing.

Distractedly, Jack focused on dusting off his hands as he looked down at them. The notion that the intrusion might be a mere error seemed implausible. As the words formed in his mind, they slipped from his lips in a low mutter.

"There is just no way possible that they are in that section by mistake." His gaze then lifted, unexpectedly locking with that of the bewildered captain, who offered a helpless shrug in response.

Unsure if Jack was thinking aloud or seeking an answer, the captain remained silent. Inside his mind, Jack's thoughts raced at a furious pace, dissecting the enemy's tactics. The eastern assailants had orchestrated a two-pronged assault, diverting the installation's defenses to the east while a smaller contingent slipped in from the west. Frustration gnawed at him as he rubbed his temple, a desperate effort to unearth the answers.

The scent of something fishy lingered in Jack's mind, pushing him to delve further into the situation. He reviewed the details once more, and a conclusion emerged: despite their numerical inferiority, the western group posed a greater threat. Reasoning that they had employed substantial strategic firepower to breach the facility, Jack surmised that this attack had been meticulously planned, down to the exact breach points and required weaponry.

These considerations converged, reinforcing Jack's conviction that the smaller infiltrating group hadn't ended up where they were by accident. Furthermore, the division of the larger force into smaller units and their methodical movements only added to the confusion in the base. A well-orchestrated scheme was at play. It was evident to Jack that something vital hinged on whether he could figure out their plans.

Turning to Major Allen, Jack's voice was a low, urgent whisper.

"Major Allen, I need a map of the installation immediately." The words signaled the beginning of a race against time to counter the invaders'.

Major Allen's presence was a whirlwind of focused motion, energy, and unwavering attention as he promptly obeyed the directive. The lieutenant promptly cleared the table hosting the physical paper maps that had occupied the space earlier. The table, an advanced holographic projector, stood ready to fulfill Jack's request. Major Allen tapped into its capabilities to summon the precise map that Jack needed, projecting it as a holographic display above the table's surface.

With a wave of his hand, Major Allen manipulated the holographic image of the facility they were situated in. His fingers dipped into the holographic projection, plucking out a specific section which he then expanded by widening his palms. The redundant larger image dissolved, making way for the magnified projection of the chosen area. With both hands, he deftly rotated the image, adjusting its orientation to provide a comprehensive view of the selected section.

Jack, keenly observing the holographic maneuvering, rapidly deduced the enemy's potential target. His finger pointed to a specific area of the hologram.

"Is this the medical section, Major Allen?" Jack inquired calmly.

The major's response was swift and assured, needing no contemplation. "Yes, sir. It is."

Jack's inquiry continued, his finger tracing the image.

"And this is where the breach occurred, right?" he questioned, indicating the loading docks on the holographic representation.

Major Allen shifted slightly to gain a clearer view beyond Jack's imposing frame.

"Yes, sir. That's correct," he confirmed without hesitation.

"Captain," Jack turned his attention to the captain who had rushed in earlier, "you mentioned that an enemy contingent is advancing through corridor H-7. Are they encountering any resistance?" The urgency of the situation hung in the air suffocating Jack.

The Captain's gaze flickered towards Major Allen before he responded. It wasn't reluctance that drove his hesitation to provide answers to Colonel Riddle's inquiries. Rather, it was the uneasy anticipation of where these questions might ultimately lead—a path he found himself dreading as much as Jack did. The Captain's silent hope lay in Major Allen's insights and potential solutions. None were forthcoming.

"Sir," the Captain began cautiously, his tone reflecting his harsh words. "The likelihood of encountering resistance along their route is minimal, confined mainly to the numerous security doors. That section of the installation remains unguarded."

His attention shifted to the holographic display, a gesture punctuating his words.

"We do have a squad positioned at this junction," he pointed, marking a specific location. "They could be mobilized swiftly to intercept the intruders."

"Excellent," Jack responded briskly. "Let's set that in motion immediately. Deploy the squad to this location and have them engage the infiltrators. Given their use of a bunker buster to breach the facility, it's doubtful the enemy will face significant hindrance with the security doors. The defense of this facility is unfortunately as sound as a sheet of paper. The interior security wasn't designed to thwart a concerted troop advance, as nothing of critical importance was ever supposed to be here."

As Jack and the Captain deliberated, Major Allen moved forward from his more reserved stance. While they had been planning, he had been collaborating with the command and control teams to organize the response to the enemy incursion. In the midst of their conversation, he had gleaned pertinent information that aligned with the course of action Jack proposed. With a subdued demeanor, he relayed the information, an unenthusiastic undertone underscoring his words. Sharing this revelation was a struggle even for him, but he recognized the necessity of conveying what he had learned to his superior, despite his reluctance.

"Sir," the major began, his voice carrying a sense of urgency. "We've received updates." Swiftly, he turned to the nearby lieutenant who manned a computer console. "Project the overlay onto the map and merge the data." The hologram flickered and a section of the display turned crimson, followed by the addition of two more marked areas. "Sir, the squad you were counting on to engage the enemy won't be able to execute that plan," Major Allen explained with a hint of regret. "Substantial damage to these two junctions has made it impossible for them to reach the enemy's location."

Jack's brow furrowed in concern. "What about Major Burke? Could we redirect one of his squads to provide assistance?" he inquired, seeking potential solutions.

Major Allen's response was swift. "I'm afraid that won't be feasible either, sir. He's fully committed to the eastern front at the moment. Designating a squad and rerouting them would take precious time we simply don't have. If the enemy is headed where we suspect, any reinforcements would arrive too late to make a meaningful impact."

A tinge of disappointment hung palpably in the air as Major Allen glanced back, his gaze sweeping over the assembled faces. "I've already contacted the infirmary and informed them to prepare for incoming hostiles. Currently, there's only one guard stationed there, and it's doubtful he can hold out for long unless luck happens to be on his side."

Frustration boiled within Jack, finding its outlet in the forceful slam of his palm against the projector surface. The image wavered momentarily as the table quivered under the impact before settling back into stability.

"Dammit, Faye. They're after you, and I'm stuck here, unable to protect you," Jack muttered, his frustration seeping into the air around him.

He hadn't intended to voice his thoughts aloud, but the words escaped before he realized it. The Major's comment snapped him back to the present, reminding him that he wasn't alone in the room.

"What was that, Major?" Jack inquired, seeking to grasp the context of the conversation that had been ongoing while his mind had drifted.

The Major had spoken while Jack had been lost in his thoughts, causing his words to slip by unnoticed.

"I mentioned that we can assemble a counter force using the personnel we have on hand," the Major reiterated, his tone composed.

"Are you referring to us?" Jack's left eyebrow arched inquisitively, prompting clarification.

"Yes, sir." The Major shifted his attention back to the holographic projection, his hands deftly maneuvering the image once more. This time, he guided the display toward the command and control center. "If we follow this route, we could drop down to the correct level at this point, effectively cutting off their path."

Jack studied the plan Major Allen presented and found the strategy to be well-considered and effective. However, what puzzled him was why this idea hadn't been proposed earlier during their planning discussions. It would have saved him considerable concern and anxiety. He was deeply troubled by the thought of his wife being potentially cornered by these assailants, especially given her vulnerable condition.

The mere thought of any harm befalling Faye or their unborn children ignited a fierce determination within Jack. He might not have mapped out a precise course of action in such a scenario, but one thing was clear: the retribution he would deliver would be relentless and unyielding. He was well aware that there would be no restraining him; no force on Earth could halt his pursuit of justice if anyone dared to harm his family. There would be no sanctuary for those who endangered Faye—of that he was resolute.

"Why wasn't this option suggested earlier?" Jack questioned, his tone a blend of curiosity and a hint of reproach.

"Because I was hoping an alternative solution would present itself," the Major replied, his explanation carrying a hint of frustration.

As Jack rose to his full height, his presence seemed to magnify the room's intensity. His arms crossed firmly over his chest, his gaze fixed sternly on the Major. The height difference between them was noticeable; Jack's commanding stature loomed over the Major, creating an imposing dynamic.

The Major hastened to clarify, sensing the need to defend his approach. "It's not what you're assuming, sir."

"Then enlighten me, Major. What should I be thinking?" Jack's voice held a blend of curiosity and challenge, urging the Major to provide a satisfactory explanation.

Major Allen gestured broadly to encompass the Command and Control center. "Among the five of us here we possess only four pistols and a single assault rifle."

Jack surveyed the room's occupants, mentally calculating the numbers—the lieutenant, the captain, myself, you, and who—. His eyebrows furrowed as he tried to identify the fifth individual. The realization dawned as the captain supplied the missing piece of the puzzle.

"The guard outside, sir," the captain clarified, completing the count.

The realization hit Jack like a wake-up call, leaving him feeling somewhat foolish for not considering the presence of the guard earlier. "You're right. I understand now what you mean. We might be outgunned but we just need to buy time for Faye to be moved. I'm sure that this enemy is not going to want to try searching the entire facility for Faye once she's been moved."

Major Allen's voice interjected with a concern, injecting a note of gravity into the discussion. "There's another aspect to consider, sir."

Jack's brows furrowed in a mix of uncertainty and confusion. "What else could possibly be a concern?"

"It's your safety, sir," Major Allen explained.

Jack's expression transitioned from confusion to a more attentive focus. "My safety? What do you mean?"

The Major elaborated, painting a clear picture of his concern. "As the commanding officer, your well-being is paramount. We can't afford to risk your injury or worse. If our goal is to buy time for your wife's relocation, the captain, the guard, the lieutenant, and I can handle that responsibility without putting your life on the line. This approach not only protects you but also ensures that our coordination and troop movements won't be compromised, as the command and control would be abandoned in the midst of repelling the invaders."

Jack's instinctual urge to be by Faye's side, to protect her and ensure her safety, was ready to manifest into words of protest. He was prepared to challenge Major Allen's plan, refusing to accept anything that could potentially separate him from Faye during such a critical moment. But before he could voice his objections, his internal debate was swiftly curtailed by the major's reminder of his broader responsibilities.

"Sir, please understand, I'm not suggesting you can't contribute to the operation. What I'm proposing is finding a way for you to contribute without putting yourself in direct danger. Your leadership is indispensable. No one else can guide this organization as effectively as you have," Major Allen emphasized, underlining the significance of Jack's role.

Jack pondered the major's proposition, acknowledging the validity in his words, though his heart still clung to the idea of personally confronting the enemy to safeguard Faye. He remained open to the major's advice, willing to consider a different approach.

"What's your suggestion, Major?" Jack inquired, curiosity lacing his words.

Major Allen's response was thoughtful and practical, a reflection of his strategic mindset. "Sir, you can continue to be instrumental by directly assisting your wife in her relocation to safety. You acan provide support in that capacity. Simultaneously, the captain, the guard outside, and I can take on the task of confronting the enemy."

The major's hands deftly manipulated the hologram once more, unveiling a corridor that ran parallel to the route designated for the team tasked with stalling the enemy advance. "Use this corridor to reach your wife, sir. Meanwhile, I'll lead the captain and the guard to engage the enemy head-on. And, I'll rely on you to take Lieutenant Moran with you. She can offer additional cover to ensure you pass safely without getting pinned down by enemy fire; she'll cover you."

Lieutenant Moran promptly stood up, her actions crisp and resolute. She extracted her sidearm, checked it with a professional eye, and holstered it back securely.

"Sir, I'm prepared and ready," she affirmed in response to Major Allen's directives.

Major Allen's understanding nod set the gears in motion. He summoned the guard from outside the door and disseminated the plan to his team. Each member absorbed their roles, and Jack's impatience reverberated in the air like a coiled spring ready to snap.

Jack's eagerness had consumed him, and he was itching to leap into action. The sense of urgency pushed aside the realization that he was in charge of the timing. Without a second thought, he issued the execution order without hesitation.

As Major Allen commanded the shutdown of systems and secured the control center, Jack mentally prepared himself for the mission ahead. His focus was unwavering as he took Lieutenant Moran under his wing, ready to move out. Major Allen's parting instructions resonated in Jack's mind.

The command and control center fell silent behind them as they departed. Major Allen's assurances that preparations were in motion at the infirmary eased some of Jack's worry. The prospect of imminent action swirled around him. He resolved himself and that fueled his every step.

Faye, my love, I'm coming for you. The plan is in motion, and Major Allen has arranged for your safety. I can't help but feel a tug of guilt for not being by your side right now, but I have to trust in the team and the measures in place. Our children's well-being depends on it.

Jack led as Lieutenant Moran as they left the Command and Control. Their footsteps resonated as she navigated the corridors behind Jack. He had no lingering doubts. The mission to protect, to safeguard loved ones was before him and Jack was resolute in his purpose.

Hold on, Faye. Just a little longer, Jack's internal monologue whispered, his heart a mix of determination and anxiety.

Jack and Lieutenant Moran sprinted through the twisting corridors, their destination set firmly on the infirmary. Their urgency was palpable, yet Jack retained enough caution to ensure his footing, determined not to invite injury amid his haste.

I can't afford to get hurt before I even get to Faye, Jack thought to himself. *I'm never letting anything happen to that stubborn woman as long as I'm alive,* he finished musing as he recalled that she had kicked him out of their shared room just recently.

Their swift progress continued unhindered until an unforeseen obstacle materialized—a group of individuals emerged from the opposite direction, intersecting their path.

In a disorienting moment, shots rang out, an exchange of gunfire unfolding in rapid succession. Amid the chaotic clamor, Jack heard exactly how the soldiers were interacting and giving information to one another.

"Lieutenant Moran, hold your fire. Do you hear how they're communicating with one another? The orders they're using?" Jack asked.

"They're ours!" she declared with wide eyes.

He swiftly deduced that the volleys were originating from friendly forces. With a decisive shout, he identified himself, the recognition cascading like a tide, swiftly quelling the confusion. In the aftermath, a semblance of order was rapidly restored, and Jack found himself flanked by three additional soldiers. The lieutenant's presence bolstered their ranks, forming a cohesive unit of four individuals

The rapid exchange of gunfire mercifully concluded without inflicting harm on either side, a silver lining amidst the turmoil and chaos. The delayed arrival of the three additional soldiers painted a vivid picture of the facility's disarray. Their response had been delayed, coinciding with the impact of the bunker buster that severed their access routes and fragmented them from their areas of responsibility. In an unexpected twist, this misfortune became Jack's ally.

Jack's senses were ablaze—his nostrils stung from the acrid gun smoke, his eyes smarting from the pervasive dust hanging in the air. He instinctively rubbed his eyes. With the reinforcement of additional soldiers, his capacity to accomplish his objectives had expanded considerably. Amidst the chaos, a resolute determination took hold: *Major Allen is buying me time. I can't allow myself to be hindered like this,* he reflected inwardly.

A silent dialogue raged within him, the urgency of the situation was underscored by the responsibility resting squarely on his shoulders. His internal monologue continued, *Thank goodness these men know how to function together. It'll make assembling this new team a far smoother process,* he acknowledged to himself.

Taking charge, Jack deftly reshaped this newly formed unit into a cohesive fire squad, a maneuverable entity that he could orchestrate with greater precision. Empowered by this reinforcement, he embarked once again on the path leading to the infirmary. Echoing through the corridor's expanse came the unmistakable staccato of small arms fire—a telltale sign that the major was already executing his designated phase of the plan. This synchronization offered a glimmer of respite; with the major's actions paving the way, Jack's own task now seemed more feasible.

Jack stationed two of the soldiers as sentinels at the infirmary's entrance, fortifying the access points. He deftly punched in his access code, enabling him to unlock the infirmary's doors. Stepping through the entrance, he orchestrated the positioning of the lieutenant and the guard he had encountered earlier, strategically situating them within the inner sanctum of the infirmary. With these safeguards in place, he pushed onward, penetrating deeper into the infirmary's expanse. His primary objective: locating Faye, his sister-in-law Elizabeth, Jason, and Dr. Brundle—those for whom he harbored a profound concern.

It didn't take long for his quest to bear fruit, within the infirmary's confines. His focus zeroed in on the woman he cherished beyond measure. Faye, despite bearing the marks of recent hardships, exuded joy as her gaze fell upon Jack. A mere forty-eight hours had elapsed since their last encounter, yet the circles beneath her eyes painted a picture of the strain she had endured. Even more arresting was the prominent bulge adorning her midsection—an undeniable indicator that her pregnancy was progressing at a pace that defied convention. It was a realization that left Jack taken aback by the rapidity of it all. Jack's gaze quickly swept across the faces of Elizabeth, Jason, and Dr. Brundle, a sense of relief flooding over him as he confirmed their well-being.

"Thank God, they're all safe," he muttered to himself.

Satisfied that they were safe, his attention returned to Faye who was already moving towards him. Faye swiftly closed the distance between them, her movements reflected her urgency to hold Jack. Jack's arms enveloped her, drawing her into an embrace that conveyed protectiveness. Amid this reunion, he noticed the presence of Elizabeth, Jason, and Dr. Brundle, standing poised and prepared, their faces questioning what was going on in the facility.

Amid the swirl of tension and emotion, Faye's voice broke the silence. "Jack, what's happening? We heard the alarms and felt the explosion. Then we received word to be ready to evacuate with our escort."

Jack held Faye at arm's length, their eyes locking for a moment. The fear of her potential loss had almost devastated him. Jack observed his hands as they lay on Faye's shoulders; they trembled. He guessed that the others would attribute it to the adrenaline in his system. He definitely didn't want Faye to worry about him.

"The installation's under attack. We've been breached. It appears that some of the enemy forces are converging on the infirmary as we speak," Jack finally answered.

Faye paled. "Here? Why would they target the infirmary? There's nothing of strategic value here."

"We believe they're coming for you," Jack affirmed, his words echoed the danger at hand. He briefly pulled Faye closer before releasing her, his attention now turning to Elizabeth.

"Izzy, do you and the others have everything you need?" Jack inquired, his concern encompassing the safety and readiness of their group.

Elizabeth's response was prompt and composed. "Yes, we're prepared to leave whenever necessary."

"Good," Jack acknowledged, a plan forming in his mind.

Gathering his assembled companions, he swiftly orchestrated their departure from the immediate danger zone. Emerging from the infirmary, the lieutenant assumed the vanguard, flanked by two companions, while the remaining two soldiers remained steadfast in safeguarding their rear. The group had barely distanced themselves by a mere couple of minutes when, seemingly fated, they collided headlong with the very individuals they had been striving to evade. The encounter ignited a sudden, intense exchange of gunfire, a volatile standoff

The lieutenant's strategic prowess came into play. She swiftly maneuvered her team advantageously, effectively gaining the upper hand. She exploited the environment to her advantage, eventually securing a superior vantage point. From this strategic perch, she skillfully neutralized the enemy combatants one by one, achieving a resolute victory without incurring any casualties on their own side.

Guiding their group, Jack directed them back toward the command and control center, Faye at his side. Their collective purpose was to reclaim the reins of command in the aftermath of turmoil. An hour elapsed, and a crucial update arrived from Major Burke, signaling that the adversary had been thwarted and was now in full retreat. Jack absorbed the contents of the status report, processing the information before orchestrating swift action. He dispatched search parties to locate Major Allen and his team.

Regrettably, later revelations would unveil a somber truth—Major Allen and his team had met their demise in their confrontation with the enemy. The loss was a reminder of the sacrifices entailed by their resistance. Yet, their actions had afforded Jack the precious moments he required. It was a debt he recognized and acknowledged, albeit tinged with a bittersweet sentiment.

14

Cadi's patience held steady within the confines of the armored SUV, which was in the garage beneath Blake's apartment building. The vehicle exuded an aura of fortification, its windows boasting an impervious bulletproof design.

Her gaze wandered through the monochrome expanse of the garage, its grayness a metaphor for the ambiguity that now enveloped their lives. Concrete pillars stood like silent sentinels, an architectural chorus of support for the layers above. The space held a minimalistic emptiness, punctuated only by a few other vehicles—solitude amidst the chaos.

The lighting was judiciously arranged, casting discreet pools of radiance to guide without revealing the entirety of the scene. Within this interplay of shadows and illumination, Cadi's sigh resonated, a soft exhalation of patience and longing. Leaning against the windows that had once seemed ordinary, she now found solace in their protective presence—a bulwark against the potential violence lurking beyond the steel and glass. Her chin rested upon her hand, a gesture of contemplation, as she waited.

However, Cadi found herself slightly uneasy, questioning the extent of such protective measures. The excessiveness of it all prickled at her, forming a subtle undercurrent of discomfort.

Initially, when Blake had briefed her about their impending journey to a local airport using this fortified transport, she struggled to comprehend the necessity for such an impenetrable mode of travel. She had assumed, based on recent precedent, that Blake would once again take the wheel and navigate them to their destination. The concept of this formidable vehicle only truly began to make sense when Blake delved into the details of the day's events.

It was during this conversation that Blake unveiled the truth of the matter to Cadi—the civil war he had orchestrated. He revealed his meticulous coordination, leveraging the vast resources of his Shepherd organization to set the stage for a conflict aimed at destabilizing the government. The intention behind this calculated chaos was to divert President Donovan's attention and resources, rendering them ineffective against Blake's pursuit of his concealed objectives. The seriousness of it all slowly unfurled before Cadi as Blake laid out his elaborate plan, weaving a tapestry of deception and subterfuge.

As Cadi sat in the car, her thoughts drifted back to that very morning when she had woken with a world untouched by doubts. Before Blake's revelation, her mind had been blissfully distant from questioning the fabric of reality. But once Blake's words settled upon her, a yearning for the return to her familiar world engulfed her. The hope for a restoration of the normalcy she had always known began to grow within her, like a quiet ember waiting for a spark.

How did we arrive at this point? Cadi pondered, her mind a labyrinth of uncertainties. Memories of comfort stirred: those leisurely mornings, marked by her father's warm pancakes and her mother's playful demands for attention from him, felt like fragments of a past that had slipped beyond reach. The longing for these simple pleasures intensified, reminding her of all that had been obscured amidst the tumult of the current reality.

In this turbulent new world, the protective barriers had dissolved, exposing the harsh contours of existence. The buffer that once shielded her from the world's madness had evaporated, revealing a reality both unforgiving and frightening, particularly for those unprepared to confront its starkness. Cadi's eyes were now unclouded, and she recognized the world's true nature—an ominous landscape that awaited the unvigilant with bated breath.

Her fervent desire to reclaim the lost normalcy was a beacon amidst this uncertainty, a yearning that echoed through her as she sat in the car, waiting. However, Blake's absence from the vehicle was a conspicuous reminder of their current state. She in the threshold between their past and the uncertain road that lay ahead.

Cadi absorbed the news feeds, distress coursed through her as she learned that the very republic she had known and grown up in was now tumultuous and uneasy. The ease with which tranquility could crumble, unsettling the very foundation of her world, left her profoundly disheartened. The thought of how fragile the equilibrium of peace was disturbed her mind—an unsteady teetering that could be disrupted by the slightest nudge, throwing the world off its axis. The unsettling reality gnawed at her, challenging her comprehension of how a life, a society, could be so precariously poised, vulnerable to the tiniest of disruptions. This world, she believed, should be marked by stability and steadfastness, a bulwark against the upheavals that threatened to unbalance everything.

She had braced herself and confronted the scenes of chaos that had erupted across her familiar landscape. Despite the emotional toll, she compelled herself to watch as the unfolding events played out on every available news outlet—raw, unfiltered. The chaos had cast its disruptive net far and wide, even affecting public services. Phone networks, both wired and cellular, buckled under the strain, while the internet strained against its own limitations in the face of overwhelming demand.

Within this maelstrom of uncertainty, fear took root within Cadi's heart. The urge to grab the nearest phone and dial her parents' number tugged at her. Blake's stern warnings about the risks of such an action echoed in her memory, a voice of caution that spoke of hidden dangers. He had argued that her parents' captors possessed the means to trace her call, jeopardizing not only her safety but the security of his team as well. While she comprehended his reasoning on a rational level, she couldn't help but feel her own longing. Her parents' comforting presence felt like an irresistible balm in the midst of the chaos. The urge to reach out to them was strong, but even if she dared, the simple truth was that she had no idea how to locate them anyway.

Setting aside thoughts of her parents, Cadi redirected her focus to the upcoming expedition to the airport, recognizing it as an opportunity to witness the unfolding events firsthand. The route would lead them through the city streets, offering a view of the masses venturing out in acts of civil disobedience. However, she couldn't muster any excitement for this impending spectacle; the prospect of witnessing the chaos was more unsettling than intriguing.

Cadi's gaze shifted to the driver's seat where the driver was situated. He had been dispatched with her to the garage ahead of Blake, accompanied by a team of armed Shepherds, an arrangement that both reassured and irked her. Stepping out of the elevator into the underground garage, she had been greeted by an array of Blake's guards, a preview of the escalating tensions in the world. A convoy of identical armored SUVs awaited, their formidable presence a stark reminder of the dangers lurking outside.

Soon enough, Blake joined her in the vehicle, giving the signal to mobilize. Cadi observed Blake's apparent detachment, a mixture of emotions swirling within her—puzzled by his seemingly indifferent demeanor, yet intrigued by the intrigue itself. Blake's attention was absorbed by a stream of digital information that flowed to him through the holographic lenses embedded in his glasses, a seamless blend of technology and reality.

As the vehicle surged forward, Cadi's gaze shifted from Blake to the world beyond the bulletproof glass. Outside, the streets appeared deserted for the most part, an eerie contrast to the turmoil she knew was brewing just below the surface. The government's oppositional forces concentrated their efforts on significant targets: state capitals, the nation's capital, and crucial industries. Occasionally, they passed burnt-out cars, former police vehicles abandoned when overwhelmed by civilians-turned-aggressors.

Checkpoint after haphazard checkpoint punctuated their journey, a disordered mosaic without a discernible front line. The conflict seemed to have no boundaries, no limitations. And where was the fighting occurring? The answer wasn't clear in these empty streets, in the hollow storefronts they raced past. Each block held an air of a war-torn third-world nation, a surreal scene that felt misplaced, out of sync with the nation she had known.

Amidst this tumultuous passage, Cadi's thoughts painted a picture of a world unraveled, a reality distorted beyond recognition. The juxtaposition of her surroundings with her memories and expectations created a dissonance that echoed in her mind.

Cadi's thoughts swirled in a haze of contemplation, her gaze fixed on the rapidly shifting world beyond the window. It took several gentle prompts from Blake before she snapped back to the present, realizing that he had been trying to get her attention.

"I'm sorry," she murmured, her voice carrying an apologetic edge. "My mind wandered off, and I didn't catch you calling me. I was lost in thought."

Blake's understanding expression softened her embarrassment. "Considering the circumstances, it's entirely understandable. I was merely checking in, asking how you're coping. You seem quieter today, more contemplative than your usual self. Is there something on your mind?"

Cadi's head remained slightly lowered, her fingers idly tracing patterns on her lap as she considered Blake's inquiry. Her response held layers of consideration, each word weighed against the complex tapestry of her thoughts. She understood her own youthfulness and the limits of her understanding, despite her impressive intelligence. The world was a puzzle she was piecing together, each revelation another fragment of insight.

What Cadi now grasped was the impact of the ongoing civil unrest. She foresaw the chasm it would create, a deep divide between the factions within their nation. The fringes of the far right and far left, already prone to extremities, threatened to drift even farther apart in the turbulence. Her astute perception envisioned a breaking point, where moderates from both sides could no longer wield their influence to temper the extremes.

A lamentation surfaced in her thoughts, a question that encapsulated her concerns. "Was this civil strife really necessary? I mean it's gonna cause a general collapse in the systems that we have that make our country what it is. What are we gonna be as a people if we lose that?"

Blake's eyes seemed to hold an empathetic understanding as they met hers. Cadi's expression, her words, painted a portrait of a young mind grappling with profound questions amidst the chaos.

"Do you see yourself as one of the people?" Blake inquired, his gaze locked onto Cadi's eyes.

With a nod, Cadi confirmed her perception of herself in that way.

Blake's response was measured, his tone carrying a quiet authority. "You're not one of the masses. Shepherds can never truly assimilate into the crowd. Our role transcends that. We exist on a higher plane."

A soft sigh escaped Blake's lips as he delicately removed the holographic lenses from his face. He deftly folded them, securing them within a sleek carrying case. This he stowed in an interior pocket of his meticulously tailored jacket, a tangible symbol of his polished demeanor.

He addressed the heart of the matter, his voice carrying conviction. "This upheaval, this civil disobedience, it's an uncomfortable necessity. The core values of this nation won't shatter due to these events. They might bend, but I strongly believe they will rebound even stronger than before—stronger than the initial encounter with them. Civil disobedience is a strategic tool. It's a method to remind those in power that the people hold the reins, that their voices must be acknowledged."

Cadi's counterpoint held a somber edge, her words laden with a weighty reality. "But what does that matter if there's nothing left to govern? If there's no populace left to assert their voices?"

A soft shake of Blake's head and a thoughtful cluck of his tongue signaled his disagreement. "This isn't left to chance. Every contingency has been meticulously planned for. We're not working blind. My aim is to remove Donovan Pike from the presidency, to reinstate the foundations of democratic governance that this nation was built upon. It's a step back to honor the aspirations the forefathers fought to achieve."

The dialogue painted a tableau of perspectives, each brushstroke revealing the intricate dynamics between mentor and mentee, the complexities of a world in flux, and the contrast between immediate doubts and the far-reaching ambitions that fueled their actions.

Cadi's perspective diverged markedly from Blake's. To her, the plan seemed like a tragic chess game, one where lives were pawns sacrificed in the name of righteousness. She couldn't ignore the conspicuous absence of any personal investment on Blake's part in the nation he was striving to reshape. The omission was glaring, hinting at an unsettling detachment, a detail she couldn't help but latch onto—a small, seemingly insignificant detail that reverberated with significance.

As the conversation continued, Cadi's apprehensions about Blake's true intentions grew stronger, yet she masked her concerns from him. The worry churned beneath the surface, a current of unease that she fought to conceal. "And what about the innocent civilians caught in the crossfire? What do they gain from being collateral in this clash of forces?"

Blake's response carried a note of reassurance, his words measured and resolute. "You're misconstruing my intent. Our group holds sway in most of the conflict zones. My objective isn't to sacrifice lives, but rather to steer events to safeguard Democracy."

Cadi's skepticism remained unwavering. "In theory, your intentions sound noble. But in practice, casualties are inevitable. Both sides will suffer. It just feels excessive, Blake. Like everything's spiraling into chaos."

Blake's conviction remained firm, his tone unyielding. "Rest assured, I have a tight grip on the reins. I can guide this conflict to align with my purpose—to remove Donovan Pike from power."

Cadi's gaze wandered to the muted tableau beyond the window, a contemplative silence settling over her. Her shoulders rose and fell with an audible sigh before her gaze shifted back to Blake.

"I suppose you've accounted for every possibility and have a handle on everything," she reluctantly conceded. Turning away, she resumed gazing out of the window

Blake retreated into his own thoughts, giving Cadi the space to navigate her own introspections. The remainder of the journey unfolded in silence, each absorbed in their contemplations. Cadi feeling awkward now. Eventually, they arrived at the airport they were bound for, a destination that brought a tangible sense of relief to Cadi. Stepping out of the SUV, she savored the liberation from the confines of the vehicle, the air outside like a balm after their intense discussion. A deep breath offered a cleansing pause.

With a guiding gesture, Blake led Cadi towards the waiting aircraft, an imposing cargo jet that loomed before them. The cargo hold yawned open, a utilitarian space ready to accommodate both material and personnel. Cadi had assumed that she and Blake would find their places among the crew at the back, near the loaded vehicles. However, her assumptions were shattered as Blake guided her to a different realm within the aircraft.

A sense of amazement tinged her observations as they entered a forward section transformed into what could only be described as a suite. It boasted a small open bar, two compact offices, and well-arranged sectional seating—a clever configuration designed to facilitate intimate conversations.

Blake left Cadi momentarily at the open bar, bestowing upon her the knowledge that not only could she indulge in refreshments, but she also had the liberty to order snacks or even a meal from the available menu. As he retreated to one of the two offices, he assured Cadi that the other space was at her disposal. These offices, with their adaptability, could serve as bedrooms and private havens during long flights.

As Blake withdrew and the door to his chosen office closed behind him, Cadi allowed herself a silent exhale, a subtle acknowledgment of the relief she felt. The air around her seemed to carry a different quality, one that stemmed from the release of tension in Blake's immediate presence. Inwardly, she acknowledged the sensation, acknowledging to herself the complex interplay of dynamics that was at play between them.

The flight itself transpired without event. Throughout the journey, Cadi confined herself to the provided space, neither encountering Blake nor the armed guards. Her sole source of interaction was the attendant managing the bar. Cadi procured meals and snacks, and at some point during the flight, the attendant guided her through the process of accessing movies, offering a touch of interaction.

Their descent led them to a nondescript South American airport, conspicuously devoid of other planes on the tarmac. The airport's appearance and ambiance indicated its divergence from a typical commercial hub. Nature had reclaimed the surroundings, with vegetation thriving and airport facilities in a state of disrepair. Only a few armed figures, resembling local soldiers, patrolled the distant fences—Cadi's sharp eyes discerned their presence.

The accompanying armed guards diligently unloaded six armored SUVs from the aircraft's hold, swiftly arranging them on the tarmac. Two of these vehicles promptly filled with guards and departed for an undisclosed destination. Remaining guards assumed defensive positions to safeguard the grounded plane, shielding it from potential threats.

Cadi observed an enigmatic ground crew materialize and initiate the servicing of the colossal cargo plane. This diligent crew replenished provisions for the personnel, refueled the main and reserve tanks, and ensured meticulous maintenance. As these tasks concluded, Cadi's certainty grew that the plane would be fully prepared for departure upon their return, wherever Blake's enigmatic destination might be. Interestingly, the aircraft had already been repositioned at the runway's end before the unloading procedures even commenced for the personnel and equipment onboard.

Once more, Cadi found herself in one of the SUVs, awaiting Blake's readiness to depart. It didn't take long for him to join her inside the vehicle. She had anticipated a swift reunion with him, given that he had disembarked the plane alongside her. His initial course of action was guiding her to their designated vehicle before briefly returning to confer with the individual entrusted with overseeing those stationed at the airstrip and cargo plane. The briefing seemed concise, lacking intensity or complexity, as Blake joined her in the SUV shortly after she had secured her seatbelt and settled into her seat.

The convoy pulled away from the airport, rapidly navigating toward a main road adjacent to the enclosed tarmac, which seamlessly led into the city. With this being Cadi's inaugural experience beyond her homeland, she was captivated by the world beyond the vehicle's confines. Blake couldn't help but derive mild amusement from the awe and reverence with which she absorbed the tranquil countryside slipping past their windows.

"Is this your first time leaving the country?" Blake inquired softly.

The hum of tires on asphalt provided a monotonous drone that filled the vehicle's interior. Amidst this auditory backdrop, Blake's question punctured the silence. Yet, before Cadi could respond, intermittent bursts of static erupted from the dashboard radio, followed by a voice from another vehicle in the convoy delivering a status report before signing off. Cadi allowed the clamor to subside, granting her the space to speak without contending with that distraction.

"Yeah, this is the farthest I've ventured from home in my entire life. My grandparents reside about six hours outside of the city, so up until now, that was the greatest distance I'd traveled from home," Cadi confessed.

"Where are we going?" Cadi inquired, curiosity evident in her voice. Blake didn't respond immediately, creating a pause that left room for the possibility that he might choose not to answer at all. "Don't worry about it. You'll know when we get there. As things stand now, it won't make a difference if I tell you."

Cadi found herself unsatisfied with his answer, yet there was little within her control to influence a different outcome. She glanced back out of the driver's side window, her attention captured by the passing scenery. A subtle twitch in her tail revealed her anticipation as she observed vehicles zooming past them in adjacent lanes, while they smoothly overtook slower traffic.

The roadside displayed a lush tapestry of unfamiliar vegetation, exotic and vibrant. Trees soared into the sky, while shrubs and underbrush obscured visibility beyond the immediate growth. Intermittent gaps in this verdant screen revealed glimpses of farmland and cultivated terrain, punctuated by modest-looking homes. These dwellings, neither lavish nor ostentatious, exuded a humble charm, leaving Cadi pondering about the demographics of the region they traversed. Yet, such considerations were secondary, as her fascination with the unfolding vistas held her enthralled.

"This country is truly beautiful. Though it makes me anxious for home, knowing what's unfolding there," Cadi murmured softly.

Curiosity laced Blake's response, "Really, how so? In what way does this view make you worry about home, Cadi?"

Cadi's gaze shifted from the window to Blake. A shy demeanor surfaced in response to his intense stare and the penetrating gray of his eyes. Seeking solace, she delicately held her tail between her hands, soothing its restive movements with gentle strokes.

"It's the civil war that troubles me. Our country hasn't grappled with such political and civil unrest for centuries. I'm left wondering how it will reshape things," she confessed, her voice carrying a hint of uncertainty.

Blake's eyes shuttered closed, his head drooping as he exhaled in a mixture of exasperation and resignation. "I wouldn't advise dwelling on it too intensely at this point, Cadi. Much of the combat has already ceased. My faction played a significant role in the initial upheaval, and I've been in direct contact with the leaders of those factions. Our primary objectives have faltered, prompting me to order our forces to stand down and scatter. While sporadic pockets of violence persist across the country, I'm confident these will extinguish by evening or early morning. We kindled the flames, but now we must allow them to naturally burn out, having been outmaneuvered."

Cadi found herself caught off guard on two fronts. First, the revelation that Blake's efforts had not borne fruit. Second, the swiftness with which hostilities had ceased took her by surprise.

"What were these significant goals that warranted such drastic actions? You only ever admitted getting President Pike to resign." she inquired.

"One of our primary aims, as I've mentioned before, revolved around Donovan Pike. The intention was to coerce his resignation as President, or in a more extreme scenario, to eliminate him. The second goal pertains to matters I can't divulge presently. Suffice it to say, the first goal failed, rendering our continued support for an insurrectionist campaign within the nation unviable. Different avenues are now open to me, aligning with my central objective, and this shift is part of the reason for our current situation," Blake responded, his tone devoid of emotion.

Among Blake's words, Cadi's attention snagged onto the idea of 'eliminating Donovan Pike'. The notion reverberated within her thoughts, a puzzling detail as it had never been discussed earlier. Pushing this aside, she steered her focus to another query.

"Does that also encompass rescuing my parents from President Pike's custody? Can they be freed?" Cadi's question hung hopefully in the air. She perceived a fleeting shadow of concern cross Blake's usually composed features, a momentary lapse before he swiftly regained control of his countenance.

Blake inclined his head, his gaze unfocused as he half-observed the passing landscape through the window. "Absolutely. We're diligently working toward achieving that goal. It's a process that demands time. We've encountered... complications, but we've managed to pinpoint their location, at the very least."

Cadi's smile flickered to life, a spark of reassurance kindling within her that the world might indeed regain a semblance of normalcy someday. She turned to glance out of the window once more, the scenery acting as a soothing backdrop to her thoughts. Meanwhile, Blake observed her contemplatively before redirecting his attention to the passing panorama outside his window. As the landscape slipped by, he concentrated on his mission here in South America and contemplated the forthcoming stages of his plan. He contemplated the tasks that lay ahead even after this phase was completed. The failure of the civil war to oust Pike or force his resignation didn't weigh on him as a disappointment; rather, it pushed him to rethink his strategies for the endgame.

The convoy seamlessly navigated its way through a sizable city. Cadi remained captivated by the ever-changing view beyond her window. Her eyes drank in the scenes unfolding before her, leading her to draw comparisons between what she was observing and the knowledge she had accumulated about her upbringing. This introspective exercise proved enriching, revealing cultural variations and shared human experiences.

The city swiftly slipped by, fading into the rearview mirror as the convoy diverged from the thoroughfare that had begun to resemble a highway from Cadi's homeland. Transitioning onto a surface road, the convoy surged forward with a somewhat reckless velocity in Cadi's estimation. The narrower lanes and towering concrete structures flanking the slim path created a pressing, shadow-dappled passage that felt alien to her.

The speed of their movement hindered Cadi from discerning much detail. As one element captured her attention, it rapidly yielded to another. Eventually, the convoy emerged from the constraining urban landscape, venturing into the countryside. Within minutes, Cadi managed to distinguish what appeared to be a campus, their intended destination becoming evident due to the lack of alternatives in their current trajectory. The gothic and Latin-infused architecture of a prominent building on the campus took shape before her eyes. Blake's voice supplied the final puzzle piece, identifying their location even if the purpose of their presence remained elusive.

"This is one of the largest universities in the city. The person I need to speak with is a temporary academic staff member here, teaching this semester abroad," Blake informed Cadi.

Cadi absorbed the tidbit of information, mentally filing it away while continuing to observe their surroundings. The road soon gave way to a path leading onto the university campus grounds. Cadi noticed that the two trucks preceding them from the airport were stationed at the same turn they had just taken. Unaware, she didn't realize that two vehicles had peeled off from the convoy to station themselves as overwatch, while the rest continued toward their destination. Casting a backward glance, she briefly considered them before dismissing the thought as their group came to a halt in front of one of the many buildings.

Exiting the vehicle, Blake and Cadi were joined by two escorts. As a unit, they stepped inside the nearest building, Blake guiding them toward their intended destination. Progressing down a corridor that unmistakably belonged to the building's administrative sector, they passed offices on either side. Blake navigated with the certainty of someone familiar with the layout, though this was their first time there.

At a particular door, indistinguishable from others they'd passed, Blake signaled one of the escorts to continue down the hallway. The other positioned himself by the door, suggesting he would remain outside the office. Cadi, uncertain about the roles of the two escorts, watched as Blake sought to ease her worries. His smile and reassuring demeanor helped soothe her nerves, even as her embarrassment flushed her cheeks crimson upon realizing she'd been less discreet with her tail than intended. Blake's laughter, light-hearted and warm, resonated, indicating that her small mishap was no concern.

Blake opened the door, and Cadi followed him inside. The sight of a short, balding man, unmistakably a Shepherd, drew her attention. Adjusting his glasses, he initially observed them with a measured gaze, ultimately sitting up properly as recognition settled in.

"Mr. Blake Tipis," the man greeted warmly, his smile both bright and sincere.

"Dr. Adonis Olaf," Blake responded, approaching the man to exchange a handshake.

15

In Cadi's perception, Dr. Adonis Olaf resembled a wise old gnome, his appearance carrying a certain charm. Despite his age, there was a distinguished handsomeness about him. His features, though etched with wrinkles, carried an appealing air. His height fell on the shorter side, and the thickness of his glasses suggested a possible myopia, a detail not lost on Cadi's observant eyes.

"Please, come in, Blake," Adonis beckoned, guiding them to another segment of his office.

This section exuded a homelier ambiance, a departure from the book-cluttered side where his desk sat. Positioned on the opposite end of the room were four well-worn, high-backed chairs encircling a central table. The bookshelves flanked two adjacent walls, bearing the weight of an extensive collection that verged on overflowing. Fortunately, the space surrounding the chairs remained unburdened, inviting them to settle in comfortably. Adonis extended an offer of tea, met with unanimous agreement. Taking his place in one of the chairs, he aimed to join them after serving the tea.

With a warm curiosity, he inquired, "What has prompted this journey to see me? And you've graced me with such delightful company."

Adonis's gaze shifted from Blake to Cadi, acknowledging her presence with a respectful nod.

Cadi's lips curved upward, a soft smile spreading across her face. Her cheeks, however, betrayed her attempt at composure as a flush of warmth painted them a delicate shade of pink. In a subtle attempt to shield her embarrassment, she averted her gaze, allowing her head to dip down behind her knees. Her feet, now nestled beside her buttocks after being positioned on the chair's seat, provided a modest barrier between her and the world.

Yet, despite her best efforts, her tail had a mischievous agenda of its own. It emerged from its concealment behind her, swaying with a rhythm dictated by her inner unease. The involuntary motion of her tail revealed the bashfulness that had gripped her in response to the flattering words that had been bestowed upon her.

Blake's intent to engage in the conversation was thwarted, as Adonis directed his attention predominantly towards Cadi. At first, Blake's initial wariness eased into a mild amusement, prompted by the visible reaction Cadi displayed in response to the compliment. Contenting himself with a sip of tea, he settled back, an attentive observer of the dialogue unfolding before him.

Adonis's kindly voice filled the air, addressing Cadi with an observation that carried both curiosity and warmth. "My dear, you still possess your tail. Our lineage has long since shed that trait. It's quite revealing, isn't it?" A gentle grin framed his features, his wizened eyes studying Cadi with a mix of interest and empathy.

Cadi, though silent, conveyed her response through a swift nod of her head, her acknowledgment succinct yet appreciative.

The elderly Shepherd continued, his words carrying a gentle praise that underlined Cadi's exceptional beauty. "I'm confident you'll continue to blush whenever compliments come your way. You are truly a striking young Shepherd."

Adonis's gaze deepened, as if a sudden realization had dawned upon him. "You seem oddly familiar, my dear. Pray tell, who are your parents?" The question, now directed at Cadi, signaled a juncture that prompted Blake's intervention.

Until then, Blake had intentionally omitted Cadi's name from the conversation, as if an oversight. Yet, Adonis's direct inquiry about her identity and parentage marked the point at which Blake deemed it necessary to assert himself. A calculated act, he sought to withhold a specific piece of information from the Librarian—information that could potentially unravel the truth about Cadi's origins.

The truth would inevitably emerge. Blake knew that the Librarian, with his vast knowledge, would piece together the puzzle once presented with Cadi's identity. She was a clone, after all, a living relic of the past. Blake recognized the inevitability of the truth surfacing, yet he was determined to delay that unveiling for as long as possible. As he skillfully inserted himself into the conversation, his voice bore the tone of amiable companionship.

"Adonis, my old friend, I've sought your wisdom for knowledge, not the other way around—at least, not yet," Blake interjected, accompanied by a gentle smile and a light-hearted laugh.

His words, while delivered in jest, held a subtle undercurrent of purpose, a reminder that he had come seeking answers, even amidst the unfolding rapport between Cadi and the Librarian.

Adonis delicately perched his glasses on the bridge of his nose using his fingertip, his focus unwaveringly fixed upon Blake. "What is it that you seek, Blake? You're well aware of my repository of knowledge. That's my purpose."

Blake acknowledged this fact, stating, "I'm fully cognizant. You are one of our Libraries. I'm in search of the whereabouts of our Communicator."

Adonis maintained a thoughtful silence, his gaze traversing the rim of his glasses as he first regarded Blake, then shifted his attention to Cadi. A question lingered in the air, poised delicately between curiosity and concern. "My dear, how much have you been enlightened about your Shepherd heritage and our mission on this planet?"

Before Blake could respond, Adonis's raised hand intervened, halting his words. The older Shepherd directed his focus solely toward Cadi, awaiting her response. Aware that Adonis's insistence had strategic implications, Blake acquiesced, understanding that defying the

Librarian's request might hinder his own quest for essential information.

Blake's mission to locate the Communicator hinged upon Adonis's cooperation. With crucial details held by the venerable Shepherd, refusing him was out of the question. The journey to South America and the quest for the Librarian's counsel had led Blake to this pivotal moment, and he wasn't willing to jeopardize his chances.

The stakes were too high; the Communicator's location was the key to a puzzle that demanded resolution. Without this missing piece, Blake's efforts would falter, rendering his journey to South America futile.

Cadi's gaze flickered between Adonis and Blake, her anticipation palpable as she awaited guidance. With no overt signals from either of them, she decided to take the initiative herself.

"I've only learned what my mother shared with me. It's not much," she offered, her voice carrying a hint of uncertainty.

Adonis, attuned to subtle nuances, honed in on Cadi's mention of her mother alone. This seemingly innocuous detail spoke volumes to him, filling in gaps in her narrative. Coupled with her continued possession of a tail, it didn't take long for Adonis to draw significant conclusions. Recognizing the echoes of a familiar face in her features, he grasped the truth. While younger than the individual etched in his memory, Cadi bore a striking resemblance to that person—a realization that aligned with his deductions.

Nonchalantly setting down his tea cup, Adonis leaned back, his gaze steady upon Cadi. "Our purpose here is straightforward. We are tasked with a duty—to ensure that our masters' product not only survives but is ripe for harvest when they deem it necessary."

A furrow creased Cadi's brow, her confusion evident as she probed for clarity. "What exactly is this 'product' that these so-called 'masters' seek?"

Adonis closed his eyes briefly, his fingers steepled in contemplation. "Humans. Periodically, they descend upon this realm and select humans according to their needs."

A sharp, audible click resonated as Cadi closed her mouth, grappling with the staggering revelation. After a prolonged silence, her bewilderment surfaced in words. "Their needs? But... what could these 'masters' possibly want with humans?"

Adonis's response was as direct as it was chilling. "Colonization."

Cadi's astonishment was palpable. The concept of humans being transported across space to establish colonies on distant planets seemed ripped straight from the pages of a science fiction novel.

"Wait, are you serious?" Her incredulity was evident in her voice.

Adonis maintained his solemn demeanor. "Absolutely. The beings known as the Braxit are a highly advanced interstellar species. Their civilization's demands are beyond human imagination. They seek out planets like Earth that can sustain life and provide the resources they require. If such planets already house native intelligent life forms, they use humans to displace them. This process readies the planet for exploitation following colonization."

The question tumbled from Cadi's lips, tinged with curiosity. "But why humans? Why not undertake this process themselves?"

Adonis leaned back, folding his hands across his lap. A knowing smile curved his lips. "Ah, an astute inquiry, my dear. The Braxit are an ancient race, predating the recorded history of modern humanity. They discovered this planet during its nascent phase and introduced the ancient Homo sapiens here. Humans aren't indigenous to this solar system; they hail from a distant realm among the stars. The Braxit recognized our bipedal species as remarkably adaptable, resilient, and robust—qualities unmatched by any other species they encountered. In essence, we provided a solution to their most pressing challenge: sourcing labor for their vast needs."

Cadi absorbed this revelation, awaiting Adonis's continuation. When he remained silent, her curiosity prodded her forward. "Was labor the only reason the Braxit sought to exploit humans?"

Adonis refrained from being the one to directly answer Cadi's question, and Blake's response fell slightly short of the explanation she sought.

"Have you ever noticed the persisting disparity in numbers between humans and Shepherds?" Cadi nodded, signifying her awareness.

Blake then posed a question in return. "Do you understand the reason behind this phenomenon?" Cadi shook her head, indicating her lack of knowledge. "It boils down to the fact that Shepherds have a significantly lower birth rate compared to humans. Our extended lifespans negate the urgency for prolific reproduction in order to ensure the survival of the species."

Cadi's admission followed. "I'm familiar with that aspect. My parents mentioned it a long time ago."

Blake continued, shedding more light on the topic. "You see, Shepherds are essentially genetically engineered humans. Around half of our genetic makeup is contributed by the Braxit. The remaining half originates from the humans we were intended to safeguard."

Adonis interjected, his voice carrying the weight of authority. "The fact that Shepherds reproduce less frequently than humans is intrinsically linked to the Braxit's genetic influence. The Braxit, distinguished by their notably extended lifespans even compared to Shepherds, have engineered this exchange to accompany the reduced birth rate. Humans possess a propensity for rapid multiplication, a trait the Braxit leverage to facilitate planetary colonization. This genetic contribution from the Braxit spares their own population from the risks associated with taming potentially hostile worlds."

Cadi took a moment to process the information, a thoughtful expression crossing her features. "So, in essence, we Shepherds are the bridge between the Braxit and humanity, adapting the advantages of both to fulfill a specific role in their grand design."

Adonis replenished his cup with tea, leaving it on the table. Perched at the edge of his seat, he resumed the revelation of Braxit's reality to Cadi. "The Braxit typically select tens of thousands to hundreds of thousands of humans, as well as a portion of Shepherds, transporting them to a newly discovered planet. If the existing civilization endures upon their return within a specified timeframe, the Braxit then integrate themselves into the colonization endeavor. They mold the planet's development to align with their needs and aspirations. However, if the colonization endeavor falters, the Braxit try anew elsewhere until success is achieved."

Cadi's inquiry followed suit. "What happens to the humans and Shepherds on the planets where colonization fail?"

Adonis held a deliberate pause, his gaze shifting to Blake before redirecting to Cadi as he provided his response. "They are essentially abandoned to their fate."

The weight of this revelation settled upon Cadi, and she absorbed it with a certain detachment. She recognized that, notwithstanding its inhumanity, this was perhaps the only feasible option. The Braxit's moral compass diverged from human and Shepherd values, a realization reinforced by everything she had gleaned thus far.

Seeking further clarification, she inquired, "How many planets have been subjected to this method?"

Adonis's response followed, measured and revealing. "To the best of my knowledge, the count is less than a few hundred. The Braxit's process involves meticulous exploration of new star systems, which, despite their advanced technology, consumes a significant amount of time. However, once they arrive, they establish gate systems that expedite travel within the star systems."

Cadi digested this information, the implications unfolding before her. It was a bleak and unfathomable scenario, one that underscored the vast disparities between the Braxit and the worlds they manipulated.

Cadi found herself at a loss for words. The knowledge she had just been exposed to demanded her to discard the assumptions that had formed her understanding of the world. In an instant, her universe had shrunk, while the scope of the galaxy had expanded exponentially, stretching from one horizon to the other.

Blake's timely intervention drew attention back to the central purpose of their meeting. His voice cut through the weight of the revelations, seeking clarity amidst the newfound understanding. "Adonis, I require information concerning the whereabouts of the Communicator."

Adonis adjusted his posture, his crossed legs a mirrored reflection of his composed demeanor. Lifting his tea cup, he leaned back, transitioning from the edge of his seat where he had been engrossed in his discussion with Cadi.

"Why for, old fellow? Such knowledge holds the potential to invite unnecessary predicaments. This isn't akin to times past when a pandemic could explain the loss of tens of thousands. Today, we'd need to offer an account for the presence of massive alien spacecraft in our skies and the abductions by ten-foot-tall extraterrestrial felines."

"We have our purpose, Adonis. A responsibility ingrained in our very creation. Millennia have passed without contact from the Braxit."

Adonis regarded Blake with cautious scrutiny. With a deliberate shift, he uncrossed his legs, leaning forward to rest his tea mug on the table that stood between them.

"You remain ensnared by your programming, just as I do," he observed evenly.

Cadi's gaze darted from Adonis to Blake, registering her surprise and concern. She voiced her thoughts directly, seeking clarity amidst the intrigue, "Are you suggesting you're orchestrating an alien invasion?" Blake's head shook in a gesture of denial, even as his words suggested otherwise.

"No," he stated, an unspoken truth lurking beneath his denial. "I'm seeking the Communicator to prevent Donovan from summoning the Braxit."

A single eyebrow lifted on Adonis's visage, his response laced with dry humor, "Ah, then I retract my earlier judgment. It seems you're not entirely subservient to your inherent programming."

Cadi seized the opportunity to unravel the complexities of the conversation. Her voice held a note of curiosity as she questioned Adonis, "What do you mean by that?"

Adonis's smile was tender as he addressed Cadi's inquiry. "My dear, I find myself disheartened by the gaps in your education. We're individually encoded at a genetic level with specific dispositions, talents, if you will. The intricacies of this process have eluded our understanding. Our DNA carries the blueprints for certain life roles—functions ingrained in us. For example, my memory and recall abilities are vast, a product of my genetic programming. Furthermore, any knowledge previously acquired by a Librarian is accessible to me. However, some topics remain enigmatic, veiled from our comprehension no matter how diligently we strive to grasp them. Such as the subject of genetics."

Cadi absorbed much of Adonis's explanation, though the concept of not comprehending certain aspects of the process remained puzzling. Her brow furrowed as she voiced her confusion, seeking clarity in her inquiry, "But if your memory is so comprehensive, how could you not know about genetics? What else could be hidden from you?"

Adonis leaned back in his chair, his expression both thoughtful and serene as he provided an answer to Cadi's query.

"The Braxit engineered us as a fusion of their species and humans. Every strand of our DNA was meticulously sequenced and programmed. They deliberately restricted our ability to acquire knowledge about genetics or to access detailed information about the Braxit themselves. Only Dr. Brundle stood as an exception, albeit at the cost of his sanity. Even he had to undergo immense sacrifice to tap into that knowledge. None of us have been willing to make that sacrifice. The Braxit remain an enigma within a conundrum," he concluded.

Blake interjected, redirecting the conversation to his primary objective. His tone was determined as he addressed Adonis, "Nevertheless, Adonis, I require the information about the Communicator's location. I need to locate it before Donovan can and fulfill his mission."

Adonis met Blake's resolve with a probing question that hung in the air, laden with implications. "Are you absolutely certain? Is it truly in the best interest of the people on this planet to prevent Donovan from invoking our ancient masters, summoning them once more?"

Blake's eyebrow lifted in response, conveying his intent and answering Adonis's inquiry without words. Despite outright lying, Blake sensed Adonis's doubt. However, Adonis was one to act solely on facts, not emotions. Aware of this, Blake anticipated that Adonis would provide the information he sought, confident that Adonis had no facts to refute his words.

"Well then," Adonis began, his tone carrying a mix of acceptance and resignation, "if it must be your way, Blake, I suppose it leaves no room for other alternatives."

Adonis pushed his chair back and rose, prompting Blake to follow suit. Cadi was determined not to be left behind and joined them as they moved across the office space, retracing their steps to where they had initially entered. Adonis reached for an ink pen, jotting down the crucial information about the Communicator's location. With precision, he folded the paper and handed it to Blake, who carefully stashed it in his pocket, expressing his gratitude in return. Adonis then turned to Cadi, enfolding her in a warm embrace.

"Take care, my dear. I hold hopes for our paths to cross again," Adonis conveyed gently, his voice soft and comforting. Drawing closer, he leaned in to whisper the remaining part of his farewell into Cadi's ear, hidden from Blake's view. "...Miss. Cadi," he added in a hushed tone.

Cadi's brow furrowed slightly, perplexed by the use of her name, which, to her knowledge, hadn't been mentioned during their conversation. Before she could voice her confusion, Adonis gave her a subtle wink, releasing her from the embrace. Stepping back, he allowed a smile to grace his features. Cadi quickly masked her surprise, her lips curving into a genuine smile as she expressed her gratitude for his guidance. With farewells exchanged, she and Blake left the office in unison.

Upon reaching the outdoors and finding themselves amidst the waiting vehicles, Blake turned his attention to Cadi, his words carrying a directive. "I'll have you go ahead of me. I'll catch up and rendezvous with you at the airplane."

Cadi's brows furrowed in mild confusion at the unexpected arrangement, but she chose not to press for an explanation. Blake was the leader in this venture, and she respected his authority, even if the reasons behind his decision eluded her. Without further inquiry, she climbed into the waiting SUV, settling into her seat. The vehicle's engine roared to life, and they embarked on their journey.

Observing as Blake joined a different vehicle within the convoy, Cadi's gaze followed his movements. Meanwhile, the rest of the convoy remained stationary, a clear divide forming between the two segments. As her part of the convoy began to move, Cadi's attention shifted, focusing on the familiar path they took to exit the campus and the administrative building they had just left. The convoy smoothly navigated the route, proceeding up the driveway with a sense of purpose.

The panoramic view of the surroundings spread before Cadi, her gaze taking in the scene with a mixture of shock and alarm. Ahead, at the junction they had passed on their entry, two formidable armored SUVs stood still, forming a strategic barrier. However, the situation escalated rapidly as a convoy of combat vehicles emerged from the city, closing in on the waiting SUVs. The tension in the air was palpable, and Cadi's pulse quickened as she observed the unfolding events.

Within moments, the occupants of the SUVs sprang into action, disembarking swiftly and engaging the approaching combat vehicles in a fierce exchange of gunfire. Bullets and projectiles zipped through the air, while the combat vehicles retaliated with precision, their roof-mounted machine guns blazing. The confrontation painted a chaotic tableau of conflict, with each side locked in a dangerous dance of aggression and defense.

As Cadi's own convoy drew nearer to the heart of the escalating skirmish, her vantage point afforded her a close-up view of the adversaries. The distinct features of the enemy combatants became clearer, their faces etching themselves into her memory due to the proximity. Among them, she recognized a face that struck her like a bolt of lightning—a face she knew all too well. Her father. The realization hit her like a tidal wave, mingling shock with an overwhelming urge to call out to him, to bridge the divide that had grown between them.

Yet, harsh reality interceded. The cacophony of gunfire drowned out any chance of her voice carrying across the battleground. She remained confined within the protective shell of the SUV, aware that stepping outside to call her father would expose her to the deadly crossfire. The torrent of ammunition exchanged between the two factions created a barrier even more insurmountable than the physical distance that separated them.

"What the hell is happening?" Cadi's voice pierced the tumultuous atmosphere, a mixture of fear and confusion evident in her tone.

Seated in the rear of the vehicle, flanked by the driver and a guard in the front passenger seat, she received no response. Instead, the interior was inundated with the cacophony of radio chatter, each voice contributing to the disarray.

Instinctively, Cadi's reflexes kicked in as a series of pinging sounds reverberated within the confines of the vehicle. The sound of rounds striking the fortified structure triggered an involuntary duck, her heart racing as a scream escaped her lips. Her wide-eyed gaze darted frantically, attempting to make sense of the chaos enveloping her. Amid the turmoil, a hefty impact slammed into the vehicle, jolting it and sending shockwaves through Cadi's senses. Ears ringing, her vision blurred with spots, and the acrid smell of smoke began to suffuse the air within the vehicle.

Despite the onslaught, the SUV pressed forward, determined to keep moving amidst the danger. The driver skillfully navigated the vehicle, executing a sharp turn to change direction, retracing their path to link up with the convoy that had been left behind with Blake mere moments earlier. The three vehicles that had remained with Blake's group were already en route, having taken a different trajectory.

As Cadi's vehicle converged with the others, the convoy came to a halt, the driver of her SUV promptly disembarking. Moving with urgency, he opened Cadi's door and assisted her out, his actions quick and efficient as they headed towards the truck in which Blake was located. The door swung open, granting Cadi access to the vehicle's interior. The driver's gestures communicated a clear directive, prompting Cadi to climb into the truck.

The driver didn't bother waiting to ensure her safe entry before swiftly shutting the door behind her. His figure blurred into motion as he dashed back to his own vehicle, abandoning her by the rear passenger side of Blake's SUV.

Inside the truck, Blake was engrossed in his phone conversation, his back turned to the open door. Unaware of the presence behind him, he spoke, oblivious to being overheard. "I specifically instructed you to keep me informed regarding Jack Riddle's departure from the country... I don't care about excuses; you failed to deliver his wife when I needed her... Fine, I'll make use of his daughter instead... the Librarian is inconsequential now, one of my operatives left him a parting surprise."

As the chilling words reached her ears, Cadi instinctively retreated from the open car door. Panic surged within her, propelling her into a hasty escape. Her feet carried her away from the vehicles, down the road they had traversed multiple times. The urgency of her flight reflected the weight of the sinister revelation she had just stumbled upon.

About halfway down the road, a deafening explosion ruptured the air, and Cadi's heart pounded as she turned to witness the building she and Blake had entered consumed by a fierce blast. The sheer force of the explosion threw her off balance, sending her tumbling off the road and into a nearby ditch. The impact was brutal, her head making contact with the ground, and darkness descended upon her as unconsciousness claimed her.

16

Amidst a storm of curses, Jack found himself grappling with ill fortune. The campus erupted in chaos, a deafening explosion tearing through one of the university buildings. In the disorienting aftermath, Blake and his contingent skillfully broke away from Jack's forces, slipping away from the conflict zone. Despite his burning desire to pursue Blake, Jack made a conscious choice to prioritize the well-being of those around him. He recognized an urgent duty to extend a helping hand to the survivors of the explosion, a responsibility he held above his personal vendetta against Blake.

The decision to abstain from the chase was not without its reasons. Jack's mind raced, considering the manifold ways he could provide aid in that dire moment. The devastation left in the explosion's wake was a canvas of suffering, and Jack was determined to contribute whatever aid and assistance he could muster. His heart was a blend of altruism and urgency, as he navigated through the chaos, his eyes scanning for the elusive figure of the Librarian amidst the tumultuous aftermath.

Though the prospect of first responders' imminent arrival was certain, Jack initiated his own rescue operations. With the precision of a seasoned leader, he designated one of his trusted Captains to serve as a liaison for the impending collaboration. A shrewd strategist, Jack anticipated the questions that would arise from the local authorities, well aware that the intrusion of foreign military action on their soil would demand explanations.

Upon reaching the razed building, Jack stood at the helm of a modest force, a group of sixty Shepherds under his command. Swiftly and decisively, he orchestrated a network of rescue efforts in the immediate vicinity. The dual purpose of these operations was evident: logistical and medical support. He drew a deep breath of relief, the memory of the skirmish with Blake's forces etched in his mind as a close call that mercifully spared his men from harm. A tally of casualties from their earlier confrontation revealed that four of Blake's men had met their fate at Jack's hands.

In the present moment, Jack's soldiers worked in tandem with civilian volunteers, the boundary between military and civilian blurred by the shared goal of rescuing lives. The air was thick with swirling dust, obscuring visibility and posing a challenge to breathing. Fingers ached and muscles strained as they painstakingly sifted through debris, a relentless search for both injured and unscathed survivors. The terrain underfoot was treacherous, its solidity shattered by the explosion's force, creating an unsteady foundation that tested every step.

Amid the clamor, a symphony of voices arose from the injured, their cries a haunting chorus pleading for salvation. Among the chaos, a quiet courage prevailed, as those equipped to offer aid rose to the occasion, bridging the chasm between anguish and solace. In this crucible of catastrophe, the threads of empathy and compassion wove a fabric of shared humanity, where care for the wounded was paramount.

The Shepherds, their genetic inheritance endowing them with heightened auditory acuity, were at an advantage in detecting faint calls for aid beneath the rubble. Entrusting local operations to his second-in-command, Jack assumed the role of coordinator, linked with the operational hub they had established near the city's main airport. Intelligence at his disposal painted a clear picture: Blake's forces had regrouped at an airfield located on the outskirts of the city, and with an efficient swiftness, they had evacuated the area by loading their entire cache onto a patiently idling cargo plane.

For Jack, his strategy pivoted swiftly. One of his prime objectives had become a fleeting specter, out of his immediate grasp. He shifted his focus to the actionable tasks within reach, adapting his approach to the new landscape. Navigating through the assembly of individuals, he sought out a specific Shepherd.

"Major Burke, any developments?" Jack inquired as he located his target.

"Indeed, sir," responded Major Burke, his salute crisp and sharp, an embodiment of military discipline. "Anticipate the return of our forces stationed here and a transition from active rescue to supportive collaboration with local agencies. Estimated timeline for the local responders' arrival is within the next fifteen minutes."

"Any news on our primary target? Has the Librarian been identified among the casualties?" Jack's question hung in the air as he fine-tuned his gear, his purpose twofold: assisting a passerby and absorbing Major Burke's ongoing briefing.

"Actually, sir, that's precisely what I was about to update you on. We've got positive news," Major Burke conveyed, gesturing toward an elderly man offering solace to someone swathed in a blanket. "Right there, sir. That's the Librarian."

"The young lady in the blanket?" Jack sought clarification, his gaze falling upon the pair a short distance away.

"No, sir. It's the older gentleman, aiding her in taking a sip," Major Burke clarified.

"Excellent work, Major," Jack commended, his stride setting course toward the duo.

"Though, sir, credit doesn't entirely belong to us. He sought us out, actually. It seems he was familiar with our identity," Major Burke admitted, quickly amending his words. "I mean, he recognized us as Shepherds."

Jack arched an eyebrow, a quizzical air enveloping him. "Really?" he murmured contemplatively, almost to himself. His focus returned to the Librarian, his gaze holding for an extended moment, attempting to glean more from the man's demeanor. Eventually, his attention shifted back to Major Burke. "Round up our personnel. Once the locals are on-site, let's prepare to depart swiftly. The fewer questions we're obliged to answer, the better. We must be primed to move as soon as we're able."

With a decisive nod, Jack set the plan in motion, his mind now firmly fixed on orchestrating a seamless exit from the scene.

With a salute exchanged between Major Burke and Jack, the former embarked on preparations, rallying the team for a swift transition out of the vicinity. Meanwhile, Jack directed his steps toward the elder gentleman whom Major Burke had pointed out earlier. Jack positioned himself to the side, granting the man space as he tended to the young lady in need. Patience was Jack's ally as he awaited the opportune moment to engage. Eying one of his passing soldiers, Jack swiftly delegated the responsibility of looking after the young lady, freeing the elder man from his caretaking duties and opening a window for Jack to converse with the Librarian.

Adonis, rising from his attentive posture, brushed off his pants in a gesture of collected composure. Passing the mantle of care to the assigned soldier, he meticulously cleaned his glasses with a cloth extracted from the recesses of his jacket. In a display of practiced manners, Adonis addressed Jack without turning his gaze, an aura of seasoned wisdom enveloping him.

"It seems I'm not mistaken in thinking you're here to speak with me. Am I right, Colonel?" Adonis queried, his words carrying a sense of understated authority.

Jack acknowledged the truth of Adonis's perception with a nod. Swift to realize his gesture had gone unnoticed due to Adonis's ongoing actions, Jack translated his agreement into words.

"Yes, sir," he affirmed audibly. "My journey led me here specifically to converse with you, to gather the information I require."

As Adonis slipped his glasses back onto his face and finally met Jack's gaze, the conversation took a more direct course.

"You're human, aren't you? And you're aware of our identity as Shepherds," Adonis stated matter-of-factly.

"Yes, on both accounts," Jack confirmed

"Very well, Colonel. Pose your question, and I shall endeavor to respond to the best of my ability," Adonis conveyed, his smile carrying a blend of fragility and determination.

"Thank you, Dr. Olaf. To begin, how were you aware of our identity? I've been informed that you initiated contact with my team and introduced yourself before we had a chance to locate you," Jack inquired.

With a deliberate step, Adonis approached the soldier to whom he had relinquished his caregiving role. Swift as a breeze, his hand shot out, securing a grip on the Shepherd's tail before the soldier could react, his surprise palpable in his jump. The distinctive appendage, a unique mark of the Shepherds, was still an adjustment for many.

"Your people possess an unmistakable presence," Adonis stated, indicating the tails of the Shepherds. "My assumption was that Shepherds underwent genetic alteration long ago, eliminating this specific anatomical trait. However, within the last few hours, I've encountered an astonishing mirror image of a deceased woman, and an entire unit of Shepherds, each marked with this identical trait," Adonis concluded.

The soldier, now freed from Adonis's unexpected grasp, shot him a resentful glare before returning to his task. In this tangle of tension and revelations, the Shepherds' distinctive feature became a tangible emblem of both their identity.

"We've encountered some... shifts," Jack confessed, grappling with the complexities of recounting recent events.

"It's introduced a layer of complexity we'd rather have avoided, but we're navigating these new circumstances as they unfold," he continued, reaching out and firmly clasping Adonis's hand, a bridge between their worlds. "Correct me if I'm wrong, but did you mention encountering a doppelgänger who possessed a tail?"

"Yes," Adonis affirmed, a radiant smile painting his features. "A captivating young lady by the name of—" Adonis's words were abruptly intercepted.

"Cadi," the voice of Cadi herself chimed in, her presence materializing beside her father.

Jack's gaze snapped to his right, an overt astonishment etching across his expression.

"Cadi! Where on Earth have you been? We've been so worried about you," Jack exclaimed, his voice a mix of shock and joy. He lunged towards Cadi, enveloping her in a heartfelt embrace.

Cadi, her emotions mirrored in the tightness of her embrace, sought to reciprocate the overwhelming affection radiating from her father. "Hi, Daddy," Cadi's voice wavered, muffled against Jack's chest.

Cadi never had the opportunity to inquire about what transpired that night her parents disappeared from their home. The fleeting thought of seeking this information was overshadowed by the overwhelming joy of reuniting with her father after so long apart. Resting her head on his chest, she succumbed to tears.

Blake's curses echoed with vehement frustration, marking the fourth time in the last hour he had succumbed to anger, venting his rage over the unexpected setback at the university campus entrance. Jack's forces had ambushed him when he was convinced he still had ample time to carry out his meticulously devised plans, unimpeded by the Shepherds aligned with Donovan and his cohorts.

The bulk of Blake's lament wasn't solely on the squandered opportunity, though it gnawed at him. The true sting came from losing his grip on Cadi. The realization struck him twenty minutes after their encounter, a realization that fanned the flames of his dissatisfaction. The sensation of Cadi slipping through his fingers left a sour taste in his mouth, a feeling that resonated with his broader predicament. His attack on the logistics base hadn't secured him Faye, and now, due to a subordinate's ineptitude, he had also lost control over Cadi. The growing inferno of his frustration threatened to engulf him.

Seeking recourse, Blake retrieved his cell phone and dialed the person he had conversed with upon leaving the college premises. His voice, taut with restrained anger, sliced through the air as he spoke in clipped tones, making no effort to conceal his vexation.

"I've lost my 'Key.' Arrange for the immediate delivery of the first copy," he demanded, urgency laced with fury in his words.

"I don't think we should risk that again now," Jason cautioned. "Faye is in a dangerous point. I have no idea what the original Dr. Brundle did but this pregnancy is accelerated and could kill her if we're not careful. If that happens, we could lose her as a useful Key."

"What do you suggest that I do now, doctor? I need a Key or I cannot complete my task."

"I'll think of something, Blake. Rest assured, I'll reach out to you once I've explored the available options," Jason assured him.

A brief silence filled the line as Jason's mind raced through possibilities. He wondered if Faye had transferred her Genetically Engineered Acoustic Resonance. If she had, it could simplify matters and expedite Blake's desires.

"It might be more feasible for me to acquire one of the babies after their birth. I'll keep you informed," Jason offered thoughtfully.

"Make it swift, doctor. I require a Key urgently. I'm en route to Russia to retrieve my Communicator. I'll await your call," Blake replied, the urgency in his voice evident.

The call was severed, and Blake pocketed his phone. He hoped that Jason's plan would bear fruit—not for Jason's sake alone, but also to prevent Blake's wrath from descending upon the man if things fell apart.

Jason let out a sigh of relief as he finally hung up the phone, grateful to have concluded the call with Blake. The stress inherent of his duplicitous role had been gnawing at him for years, and every interaction with Blake was a reminder of the intricate web he had woven to hide his true intentions. He never anticipated being thrust into the midst of the ongoing conflict between the two factions of Shepherds. Originally recruited to obscure traces of deceased Shepherds and humans linked to Blake's concerns, he found himself reluctantly coerced into a spying role that he never bargained for.

Leaving the workspace he had been provided, Jason traversed the corridor with a sense of unease gnawing at his core. The role he now played was ill-suited for his disposition, leaving his palms damp and his heart pounding within his chest. He couldn't shake the feeling that he was out of his depth, entangled in a situation he never intended to be part of. He took a deep breath, attempting to steady himself, yet the complexity of his predicament remained ever-present, constricting around him like a tightening noose.

Opening a nearby door, Jason entered the room beyond. His gaze landed on the occupants—Faye, Elizabeth, and Dr. Brundle.

"Hello," he greeted, his voice a blend of formality and forced warmth. Responses varied, a mixture of nods and verbal acknowledgments.

Jason's eyes swept across the room, taking in its purposeful design, tailored for the care of its patient. Monitoring devices adorned the wall, a silent vigil overseeing the bed where Faye lay. The toll of recent events was evident in Faye's demeanor, etching lines of weariness on her features. Yet, she emanated a strength that belied her exhaustion. Observing Faye, Jason couldn't help but feel a pang of guilt. Her involvement in this intricate power struggle was not of her choosing, and her well-being now hinged on the machinations of others. It was a stark reminder of the consequences that unfolded when people like Blake sought to manipulate the course of events. Jason's mind churned with the weight of his actions and the knowledge that he had become a part of this dangerous game.

Pushing aside his internal turmoil, Jason refocused his attention on the present.

"Is there anything I can assist with?" he offered, his words a genuine attempt to contribute, yet tempered by the awareness of the tumultuous circumstances they were all enmeshed in.

Elizabeth and Dr. Brundle communicated their self-sufficiency, declining Jason's offer of assistance. He moved with a measured pace toward the array of monitoring devices that provided crucial health updates. His eyes swept over the illuminated readouts, his fingers deftly tapping a rhythm of efficiency against the surfaces. A nearby cabinet yielded a syringe set, his practiced eyes assessing its usability before he secured it and shut the cabinet door. Meanwhile, on the opposite side of the bed, Elizabeth and Dr. Brundle continued their attentive administration of IVs to Faye.

Positioning himself beside Faye's bed, his presence a calm reassurance, Jason outlined the procedure he was about to undertake.

The amniotic fluid extraction was a necessary step to ensure the well-being of the developing babies.

"Today, I'll need to collect a bit of amniotic fluid for testing. It will help us monitor the babies' progress. Are you prepared for the procedure?" His gaze rested on Faye, his voice gentle.

Faye acknowledged her readiness with a subtle nod, her frailty evident in her weakened state. The weight of her pregnancy bore down on her, sapping her strength with each passing day. Jason's practiced hands moved with precision, methodically conducting the procedure. Professionalism underscored every action as he ensured Faye's comfort and safety throughout the process.

Upon completion, Jason lingered for a moment, attentively assessing Faye's condition. Satisfied that she was as stable as could be expected, he bid his temporary farewell, a responsibility calling him to the lab for further analysis of the collected fluid. His commitment to providing the best care he could, despite his dual role, was unwavering.

In the lab, a series of tests awaited the collected amniotic fluid. The gravity of the situation was not lost on Jason, his internal conflict evident in his meticulous approach. One test held particular significance—it aimed to identify the Genetically Engineered Acoustic Resonance marker, the telltale sign of a Shepherd as a Key. The results were swift in coming, but the outcome was far from desirable. Disappointment welled within him as the absence of the marker confirmed the absence of Key status in the babies.

Jason's frustration found voice in a muttered curse, his heart sinking at the realization of the challenges ahead. The delicate balance he had maintained was teetering on a precipice, and his actions were poised to determine the fate of those he cared for. With determination ignited by adversity, he knew that the journey ahead would require cunning and resourcefulness. Faye's safety was paramount, and he was prepared to navigate the treacherous path that lay before him, even if it meant betraying the very forces he had aligned himself with.

Jack held Cadi at arm's length, his eyes carefully assessing her condition. He playfully spun her around—twice—taking note of the dirt smudges and a slight bump on her forehead, but overall relieved to see her relatively unharmed. She appeared robust and hearty, a sight that warmed Jack's heart. Gently, he pulled her back into his embrace before fully releasing her, though she remained close by his side. "You seem a bit disheveled there, Kitten."

In response, Cadi playfully punched her father's shoulder.

"Missed you too, Dad. And yes, I'm definitely feeling a bit rumpled." Her attempt to brush off the dirt proved futile, prompting a wry smile from Jack. Amidst the humor, an overwhelming sense of joy enveloped him—his daughter was back in his arms. The serendipity of encountering her in a foreign land was uncanny, yet it brought him immense happiness. He couldn't help but notice Faye, Cadi's mother, in her features, a bittersweet pang tugging at his heart.

With an affectionate arm encircling Cadi, Jack's voice carried his emotions. "No doubt you've got an intriguing story to share, and I'm eager to hear it. But for now, I'm simply relieved to see you safe and sound. Your mom will be overjoyed to hear from you. She's been missing you fiercely."

Cadi's recollection of something she'd overheard Blake saying while outside the door of his SUV shifted the atmosphere. "Dad, I think there might be someone associated with Blake near where you and Mom are."

Jack's concern deepened.

"What do you mean?" he pressed, sensing that this revelation held potential complications for the safety of his family.

Facing her father squarely, Cadi's hands landed on his shoulders, the action requiring her to stand on her tiptoes.

"I mean that I overheard Blake talking to someone about Mom and the pregnancy, mentioning something about getting her," she revealed in a rush.

Jack sought confirmation, his brows knitting as the revelation sank in, thoughts racing through his mind. A hand rose to his head, his fingers threading through his hair in a gesture of concern.

"Are you absolutely sure?" Jack pressed, grappling with the implications of the news that Cadi had just unveiled, each word deepening the furrows on his forehead.

Cadi's response was unwavering.

"Yes, I'm sure," she affirmed before stepping back.

Her eyes mirrored the unease her father felt, the shared concern. Cadi had once placed trust in Blake, blinding herself to hints of his true nature. However, an intercepted phone conversation had stripped away that naiveté, revealing an uncomfortable truth.

Jack's worry escalated rapidly. Cadi's words carried certainty, cementing the situation. A spy lurked in their midst, and the safety of Faye and their unborn children was perilously compromised by this unseen traitor. The mere possibility that someone within their own facility might be aligned with the very forces they were battling was disheartening. The fact that few individuals were privy to Faye's pregnancy magnified the betrayal. If the person Cadi referred to was indeed aware of this intimate detail about his wife, the existence of a spy lurking perilously close to his beloved wife at this very moment seemed inevitable.

Suppressing the torrent of concern, Jack pushed those distressing thoughts aside. There was a pressing duty before him, a mission to fulfill—one he understood was just as vital for ensuring Faye's and

Cadi's safety. Priorities crystallized in his mind; he would execute his task first before delving into the hunt for the spy, a task that couldn't wait. "Kitten, shelve that thought for now. We'll need to discuss this more thoroughly once I've completed my current objective."

Cadi's response was swift, her shock palpable. "You're planning to kill the Librarian?" she blurted out, her voice tinged with disbelief.

Jack's reaction was equally swift, a mixture of surprise and rebuttal. "No," he exclaimed, taken aback. "Where did you get that idea?" He was genuinely puzzled by the notion that he might resort to such a drastic measure.

With a hint of uncertainty, Cadi explained, "Blake told me the President wanted the Librarian dead, claiming he had information that could ruin the President's power." Her revelation was accompanied by a growing realization that perhaps Blake's words shouldn't be taken at face value, considering her newfound awareness of his ulterior motives.

Taking a breath, Jack clarified, "It's true that the Librarian possesses vital information that we need to prevent from falling into Blake's hands. But rest assured, we don't need to resort to killing him to safeguard that information."

Cadi exhaled a breath she hadn't realized she'd been holding, relief washing over her.

"Oh, that's a relief. I actually quite like Mr. Olaf," she admitted, her gaze turning to Adonis with a warm smile.

Adonis, chiming in, added his perspective, "Indeed, your well-articulated sentiments are deeply valued, my dear."

"Wait, so you've met my daughter?" Jack inquired.

"This is your daughter?" Adonis echoed, his surprise evident.

Confirming Adonis's query, Jack nodded. Adonis's gentle laughter followed.

"Well, well, life certainly brings its surprises," Jack mused jovially. "So, earlier, you were referring to my daughter, I assume?"

"Indeed, earlier, before my building decided to meet ground level," Adonis quipped wryly, his words carrying a mix of rueful humor and resilience.

"We're fortunate that our school semester hadn't commenced yet. We were still in the midst of the break between terms. There were only a handful of people within the building, and I'm relieved to report that everyone has been accounted for and, thankfully, is alive, albeit with a few injuries," he explained, his tone transitioning from lightheartedness to somber concern.

Curiosity led Jack to probe further. "How did you manage to verify that, sir?" he inquired.

Adonis gestured towards his head, the action imbued with a sense of understanding that transcended words. "I am the Librarian. My memory captures every sight, sound, text, touch, and scent. I meticulously documented the individuals who entered and departed the building. My Shepherd senses aided in hearing their movements. When the explosion occurred, just adjacent to my office, its intent likely being to end my life as well, I employed these faculties to account for all remaining occupants. Your forces' contribution to rescue operations further aided in confirming their safety."

A sense of relief washed over Jack. "I'm truly relieved to hear that you and everyone else emerged unharmed. On a related note, how did you manage to survive the explosion?" he inquired.

Adonis responded with a bashful grin, a subtle hint of embarrassment tinging his expression. It was evident that the topic he was about to broach was a matter of privacy to many.

"We shared a cup of tea, and I've always preferred milk and honey in my tea," Adonis disclosed, a wistful note entering his voice. "However, age has brought with it a growing intolerance to milk. Consequently, I've found myself making more frequent visits to the water closet. It was during one such visit, in the restroom at the far end of the building, that the explosion tore through, demolishing both the building and my office," he revealed with a touch of resignation.

Jack's astonishment was palpable. "An incredible twist of fate," he marveled, clearly recognizing the fortuity that had spared Adonis's life.

Adonis's arms encircled his midsection, a gesture that seemed to cloak him in a protective barrier.

"If you say so," he replied, a faint gurgle emanating from his belly. Both men opted to overlook the interruption, allowing Adonis to continue with a wry smile. He eventually withdrew his arm, humor prevailing over the awkwardness of the moment. "So, Colonel, about this tail?"

A grin crept across Jack's face. "Ah, yes. The tail," he acknowledged, ready to delve into the topic at hand.

Over the next few minutes, Jack engaged in a comprehensive explanation, involving both Adonis and Cadi. He detailed the nature of the virus responsible for Shepherds regrowing their tails, shedding light on its origins and mechanics. Remarkably, Adonis and Cadi absorbed the information without significant resistance. Jack couldn't help but observe that Adonis seemed to assimilate the details with a fervor akin to a sponge soaking up water. The parallel was fitting—Jack was conversing with the Librarian, a symbol of knowledge absorption and dissemination.

As Jack delivered the wealth of information, he processed the circumstances with a sense of urgency. In the course of their discussion, Adonis disclosed that Blake had already extracted the location of the Communicator from him. This revelation stirred frustration in Jack, but he recognized the futility of dwelling on it. Time was not on his side, and he acknowledged that he had been too tardy to prevent the information from being divulged.

The realization dawned that apprehending Blake and preventing him from obtaining the Communicator was an exercise in futility. The time constraints rendered such efforts inconsequential. In the midst of this strategic recalibration, Jack made a point to connect with Donovan, providing a comprehensive briefing that encompassed every facet of the situation, including the presence of a spy within their ranks.

17

Elizabeth and Jason, entangled in the throes of a harrowing situation, boldly chose an unorthodox path. Rather than succumbing to stress in turns, they united to confront it simultaneously. Faye's pregnancy had entered its advanced stages, hovering on the brink of childbirth. With Dr. Brundle conspicuously absent, a shroud of uncertainty enveloped Elizabeth and Jason as they grappled with determining the optimal course of action.

The apprehension of Dr. Brundle at the behest of Donovan Pike wrought transformative shifts in the group's dynamics. The disclosure of a potential infiltrator lurking amidst them reached Jack, who subsequently disseminated this disquieting revelation. The spy's intimate knowledge of Faye injected an added undercurrent of tension.

In an unexpected twist, Donovan vehemently rejected the idea of a mole infiltrating their ranks, firmly believing that it was implausible for someone to have slipped in among their members. Despite this conviction, he couldn't dismiss the possibility entirely. A select few individuals raised doubt in his mind, with the clone of Dr. Brundle emerging as the most likely candidate. Despite hesitating to acknowledge it, Donovan couldn't ignore the fact that Dr. Brundle's unstable mental state raised concerns about the clone's potential for betrayal.

Suspicion appeared to coalesce around the sole individual who had successfully sown doubt in Donovan's steadfast mind—the original Dr. Brundle who had audaciously fabricated a clone of himself before his mind became distorted. Anthony. Not surprisingly, this led him to doubt the clone. Astonishingly, this very same clone was an unlikely ally and the very one they thought of as a spy.

Doubt gnawed at Donovan, a sensation he detested, yet the inherent nature of the original doctor magnified the potential threat posed by this clone. A chance on this matter was not a luxury he could afford. Donovan ensured Dr. Brundle's isolation from the rest of the group, meticulously controlling his access to specific information. Yet, Donovan's watchful gaze extended beyond the doctor alone. The luxury of blind trust had shattered, an aftermath of both his own brush with assassination and the brazen attack on their installation. Thus, a new protocol emerged—a personal escort was designated for both Elizabeth and Jason, relevant to the era of caution.

Faye's safety was paramount, a principle underscored by the assignment of a vigilant two-person security detail for her. It was Donovan's unyielding commitment to mitigate risks.

However, as the progression of Faye's pregnancy reached a juncture beyond their medical expertise, both Elizabeth and Jason found themselves in Donovan's office. With urgent determination, they laid their plea before Donovan. The core of their entreaty was the return of Dr. Brundle to the medical team, a necessity for Faye's well-being and the welfare of the impending twins. His unparalleled skill was an imperative in this critical juncture.

With synchronized determination, Elizabeth, Jason, and Dr. Brundle orchestrated the meticulous readiness of the medical facility and its staff for the impending emergency cesarean section—a pivotal procedure that held the promise of ushering Jack and Faye's babies into the world. As the pivotal moment loomed, the preparatory measures assumed an air of urgency, leaving minimal room for additional arrangements.

The foresight of Dr. Brundle proved accurate; he had anticipated the necessity of this very procedure, foreseeing the inevitable culmination of Faye's pregnancy.

The sterile, white-lit operating room hummed with controlled urgency, the air heavy with a blend of antiseptic and anticipation. Elizabeth's gloved hands moved with practiced precision as she meticulously prepped the instruments, the metallic tang of the tools contrasting with the clinical cleanliness of the surroundings. She was acting as the nurse for Dr. Brundle as he performed the procedure.

Jason stood by Faye's side, his eyes locked onto hers, his grip on her hand a steadfast anchor amidst the tumultuous sea of emotions. Faye's face bore a mixture of fear and determination, her shallow breaths punctuating the room's otherwise hushed tension.

In the sterile environment of the operating room, a longing for Jack tightened its grip on Faye's heart. As the gravity of protecting their unborn children loomed, a tidal wave of fear threatened to engulf her. In the void left by Jack's absence, the presence of Jason and Elizabeth—and by default, Brooke in the waiting room, served as her salvation, their steadying presence a reassuring counterbalance.

Yet, an ache persisted—the solace she yearned for lay in the warmth of Jack's embrace, in the tender words he would have whispered, soothing her doubts.

I wish you were here, the thought echoed within her, a silent refrain that harmonized with the distant symphony of medical instruments. She clung to Jason's hand, her fingers finding a vice-like grip as her gaze sought Elizabeth's, a silent plea shimmering in her eyes.

In the quiet chamber of her mind, a mantra arose, a lifeline of its own: *I can do this. Everything will be okay.* The rhythm of those words, like a heartbeat, throbbed in sync with the monitors that surrounded her. Each repetition was a hope she cast to herself, an aid tossed into the churning sea of emotions.

As the seconds stretched, minutes yielding to a timeless expanse, the mantra persisted. It was a lifeline of resilience, a whispered affirmation that she clung to like a sailor navigating stormy waters.

With Dr. Brundle's steady hands and the reassuring presence of her companions, Faye embarked on a passage overflowing with her courage and filled with her defenselessness. The words echoed louder in her mind, not just a mantra anymore, but a declaration of her strength.

Faye was tired. The pregnancy had sapped her strength more and more with each passing day. And as the moment approached, as new life prepared to make its entrance into the world, Faye found solace not only in her own whispered reassurances but also in the unity of the team around her. In this crucible of shared determination, Faye discovered an unforeseen wellspring of robustness, drawing from a reserve she never knew she had.

Though Jack's physical absence was notable, his spirit seemed to echo in the room, intermingled with her resolve. In that fragile yet powerful space, Faye's journey unfolded—a dosser intertwined with filaments of love, courage, and the unbreakable bond between herself, her unborn children, and the family that stood by her side.

Dr. Brundle, his demeanor a blend of concentration and professionalism, assumed his position at the head of the operating table. His hands, gloved and steady, held the responsibility of guiding this delicate dance between life and circumstance.

As the first incision was made, a mosaic of sensations enveloped the room. The soft swish of fabric, the rhythmic beep of monitors, and the occasional murmur of reassurances, meant to calm and hearten, created a symphony of controlled chaos. The tautness in the air seemed to mirror Faye's escalating heartbeats.

"How is our patient holding out," Dr. Brundle asked Jason. Jason was working as the anesthesiologist for this procedure.

Jason looked at the monitors and deduced their meanings. He glanced at Faye and gave her a reassuring smile as he answered Dr. Brundle's inquiry. "She's doing great. Blood pressure is nominal, heart rate is slightly elevated but it's understandable why. Oxygen saturation levels are good."

Elizabeth looked away from her assisting role and regarded the monitors that gave the vitals of the infants. "We can't differentiate the heart rate of the individual twins. However, the combined heart rate seems to be within tolerable levels."

Dr. Brundle nodded and continued to work. With deft movements, Elizabeth assisted Dr. Brundle as they navigated the intricate pathways within Faye's body, the procedure unfolding like a meticulously choreographed ballet. Tension ebbed and flowed in the room, intermingling with waves of hope and concern.

Time lost its grip as minutes stretched into eternity, each second laden with significance. The room seemed to hold its breath as Dr. Brundle's hands finally reached the moment of truth. With deliberate care, he gently guided the infants into the world, their cries piercing the air, announcing their arrival with raw vitality.

As the cries faded into soft whimpers, the room gradually exhaled. Faye's features shifted from pain to a blend of exhaustion and profound relief, her gaze fixed on the bundles in the nurse's arms.

Jason's grip on Faye's hand tightened as tears welled in his eyes, the moment transcending words. Elizabeth's face was a blend of emotions, a mix of professional accomplishment and empathetic connection.

Amidst the controlled chaos, life had triumphed over uncertainty. The room, once a theater of nerves, now held the resonant echoes of new beginnings.

The surgical endeavor proved to be an unqualified success, confirmation of the expertise and coordination of the medical team. The culmination of their efforts was heralded by the arrival of two healthy babies, their entrance into the world a poignant reflection of their Shepherd lineage. From their split irises to the delicate feline tails, every nuance resonated with the distinctive traits of their heritage.

Dr. Brundle's initial concern, a flicker of apprehension in the wake of the accelerated growth experienced during gestation, was eased as he observed the twins' postnatal trajectory. A sense of relief washed over him, the infants' development having seemingly settled into a more conventional pace akin to their human counterparts. His examination confirmed that the twins were now embracing the growth pattern anticipated for beings born of the union between a human and a Shepherd.

These two exquisite newborns represented a unique breed, the first of their kind, and Dr. Brundle's commitment to their well-being burned with an unparalleled intensity. Their survival, their health, and their voyage to maturity were entrusted into his capable hands for now.

With Elizabeth by his side, he cradled the twins, their small forms showing the beauty of life's delicate beginnings.

Their departure from the room left Jason behind, a keeper of care for Faye, whose recovery surpassed expectations. The speed with which her body mended itself, regenerating tissue and healing wounds, left even the experienced Dr. Brundle in mild astonishment. A mere network of delicate stitches served as a temporary mend, allowing her body's remarkable healing ability to take the reins.

Faye lay encased in a cocoon of exhaustion, the aftermath of the emergency cesarean section and the accelerated gestation etched into her weary frame. The steady beep of monitors provided a rhythmic backdrop, punctuating the placidity that enveloped her.

The room's cool air seemed to contrast with the warmth that radiated from Faye's chest—a mélange of emotions, from relief to the echoes of pain, blended in a tapestry that only childbirth could weave. Her eyelids felt heavy, as if the weight of the world rested upon them, yet she resisted the pull of sleep, determined not to miss the first moments with her newborn twins.

Through the haze of fatigue, she glimpsed Dr. Brundle and Elizabeth returning from the initial examinations, each cradling a precious bundle. The sight stirred a mixture of anticipation and yearning within her, an ache that transcended weariness. In the tender embrace of the recovery room, a fervent wish fluttered within Faye's heart—a wish that Jack could have been there, by her side, to share this pivotal moment. Yet, the resolute understanding that duty had claimed him anchored her thoughts. In the labyrinth of his responsibilities, he stood as a guardian, a watchman shielding not just her, but also the precious twins soon to be nestled in her arms.

"Are they... okay?" Faye's voice, soft and fragile, trembled with a vulnerability she seldom allowed herself to reveal.

She yearned for reassurance, to hear the words that would confirm the well-being of the two lives she had nurtured within her. Dr. Brundle's smile was a blend of professional assurance and genuine warmth.

"They're both doing remarkably well, Faye. Healthy and strong," he replied, his voice a soothing balm that eased her fears.

Elizabeth's presence beside Dr. Brundle added an air of compassion, her eyes reflecting a depth of understanding that only a fellow woman could possess.

"They're beautiful, Faye. You'll be able to hold them soon," she reassured, her words a gentle promise.

As they approached, Faye's outstretched arms were met with two tiny bundles, each swathed in soft blankets. Her trembling hands found their resting places, and a mixture of awe and tenderness washed over her. The sensation of their weight against her chest was an indescribable comfort, like a balm for her worn-out soul.

The scent of newborn skin, that delicate and intoxicating fragrance, mingled with the sterile scent of the room. Faye's fingers traced the contours of their faces, their delicate features a testament to the miracle of life. Their little tails twitched when touched. Her heart swelled with a love that seemed to stretch infinitely, a love that was both instinctual and profound.

With each breath, Faye felt herself drawing closer to these tiny beings that held her heart captive. Despite her exhaustion, the energy to marvel at their existence was renewed, a vitality that resonated through the room.

And as she held them, her eyelids drooping in a rhythmic dance between consciousness and sleep, Faye found solace in the warmth of their bodies, the cadence of their breathing. She nestled them against her, a trinity of souls bound by an unbreakable thread, a mother's love and a life that had only just begun.

Dr. Brundle couldn't contain his elation at witnessing Faye's remarkable progress. To him, her well-being was a triumph, a marvel of both medical expertise and her own accelerated healing. His professional perspective led him to speculate that it might be a mere three or four days before she could begin to reintegrate into normal activities, due to the astonishing pace of her recovery.

As Faye's eyelids fluttered closed and her weary consciousness surrendered to sleep, they allowed her the rest her body craved. With maternal grace, Elizabeth attended to the twins, cocooning them in soft swaddles and placing them in adjacent cribs, forming a watchful circle around Faye.

With a collective sigh of relief, they departed the room, leaving Faye to the embrace of restorative slumber. Their footsteps, muted echoes in the hallway, marked the transition from the flurry of activity to the hush of convalescence.

A few hours later Faye stirred, her awakening a slow unfurling from the depths of sleep. The room, a tableau of muted colors and faint sounds, gradually sharpened into focus. Moments of fragmented awareness had interspersed with rest since the twins' arrival, a dance of consciousness that painted her recovery with hazy strokes.

Dr. Brundle's expertise shone through, despite his initial focus not being obstetrics. His skillful touch had fostered Faye's journey to healing, guiding her along a trajectory that now seemed promising. The convergence of medical prowess and her innate abilities to mend her own body marked a turning point in her postnatal journey.

Her gaze shifted, settling on Jason. A weak smile that held gratitude for Jason's presence and help curved her lips. Even the haze of exhaustion couldn't dim it. And as she navigated the gentle currents of her awakening, Faye felt the stirrings of strength within her, a reminder that even in her groggy state, the journey to full recovery had commenced.

"Hey, doc," Faye's voice, a mere murmur, was the prelude to her question, a bridge between her rest and the realm of wakefulness. "How are the babies doing?"

With a gentle, focused air, Jason approached Faye's bedside, his steps a blend of familiarity and caution. As he attended to her, checking the intravenous tubing that snaked beside her, his reassurance found voice. "The babies are doing wonderfully. They're in safe hands. I'm just ensuring that you're stable enough for a transfer."

A quizzical look traced Faye's features, her lips poised for inquiry. "Relocated? Where?"

Jason gave a measured smile. His reply held an air of nonchalance, a reassurance wrapped in casual words. "You're not going far, just to a different room where your recovery can progress without interruption. A more comfortable environment, less reminiscent of a clinical setting."

Faye's brows knit. The idea of a move intrigued her. The peculiarity was noted. The notion of questioning, of probing further, flickered in her mind. Yet, she stifled the urge, her acceptance rooted in the knowledge that Jason's actions were grounded in her well-being.

Faye's intuition stirred instead, a whisper of uncertainty brushing against her thoughts. But a sense of trust, forged through days of meticulous care, kept her doubts at bay. Jason was an integral part of her medical team.

Even as Jason tended to her intravenous tubing, Faye's acquiescence remained intact. In a dance of care, Jason's deft hands inspected a port on her IV tubing. And as he administered the subtle injection of a substance into the line, Faye's eyelids grew heavy, a lullaby of drowsiness casting its spell. She surrendered to his actions.

The world around her softened, the lights dimming to a mere glimmer. The tendrils of sleep's embrace enfolded her as she felt her body sinking into the pillows. Faye succumbed to the beckoning embrace of sleep. With the gentlest of exhalations, she surrendered to the pull, her consciousness ebbing as if into a tranquil tide. In that gentle surrender, Faye allowed herself to drift, to be carried away. And as she drifted, the room around her seemed to shift, like a veil slipping between dimensions, the realm of dreams beckoning her with gentle arms.

Jason's silhouette remained, even as her consciousness waned. Jason finally checked her and found that she was asleep.

Jason called out to the two guards stationed outside the door to Faye's infirmary room. His voice carried an air of urgency, requesting one of them to step inside. With purposeful poise, one of the guards complied, crossing the threshold to meet Jason's beckoning. Engaging him in conversation, Jason wove a narrative that deftly obscured his true intentions, expertly crafting a plausible ruse.

He orchestrated a strategic positioning to draw the guard closer and use proximity as a means to lull the guard into a false sense of cooperation. In that moment, Jason seized the opportunity to execute his covert mission. He surreptitiously administered an injection to incapacitate the unsuspecting soldier. Within moments, the guard was unconsciousness.

Capitalizing on the success of his first maneuver, Jason's calculated facade remained intact as he summoned the second guard under the guise of seeking assistance for his fallen comrade. Employing the same technique, Jason replicated the outcome, rendering the second guard unconscious as well.

Jason's focus shifted to the execution of the escape plan with the guards neutralized. Swift yet deliberate, he gathered a compact bag, its contents part of his preparation. Ensuring Faye's freedom from unnecessary connections, he deftly detached extraneous cables, allowing the monitoring equipment to be stealthily shifted into silent mode.

He released the gurney's wheels from their restraint, the soft clatter of metal resounded in the room. Jason's steps were measured as he navigated the corridor's pathways. His focus was locked on his patient and their path. Through each twist and turn, he remained resolute.

Upon reaching the waiting van, the culmination of his meticulous plan came to fruition. He secured Faye to the gurney with restraints and secured the gurney into position in the van. And as the van's engine thrummed to life, Jason eyed Faye and wished he had not been forced to kidnap her.

Jason's escape was executed with eerie efficiency, a disappearance that unfolded silently, to the detriment of Faye. Within the sanctuary that should have cradled her in safety, he had managed to elude the notice of the installation's vigilant personnel. He ended up slipping away unnoticed like a shadow unfurling under the cloak of darkness. The very haven that was meant to keep her safe was the stage upon which his vanishing act played out.

The realization of Jason's absence dawned with a cruel delay, nearly two hours later. By then, the tendrils of his covert maneuver had rendered any attempt at apprehension futile. The sands of time had shifted beyond their favor, leaving the staff with an acute sense of powerlessness.

Donovan, in a state of unnerving panic, found himself in an unfamiliar predicament. Normally adept at concealing his emotions, his face now laid bare the inner turmoil he usually guarded with utmost secrecy. Those observant enough, and able to muster the courage to do so, could readily decipher the vivid display of his usually hidden expressions and sentiments.

Each vehicle in the installation motor pool harbored a tracking device, a technological aid in the determination of their location. Yet, even this measure of security had been systematically dismantled in the cargo van that had whisked Faye away. The sense of vulnerability in the facility was a lingering disquiet that reverberated within every corner.

Security measures escalated, the installation's vigilance elevated to a state of high alert. Behind the scenes, senior staff embarked on the formulation of plans, orchestrating the assembly of a search and rescue team. Faye's liberation, her extrication from the clutches of her captor, became the singular mission that galvanized their resolve.

As the installation's command moved into action, the threads of communication extended beyond its walls. Jack, a steadfast protector even in his absence, was contacted, his heart became heavy because of what had occurred. The news, a bitter pill to swallow, held a duality of emotions—fury at the audacity of the act, and a wellspring of determination to bring Faye back to safety.

Upon receiving the news that his twins were born and Faye had been kidnapped, Jack's emotions became a turbulent sea, churning with a mix of joy and anguish. He clenched his jaw, absorbing the bitter truth that the joyous occasion of new life had been violently juxtaposed with the ominous shadow of Faye's abduction.

As the gravity of the situation settled upon him, Jack's hands trembled slightly, a physical manifestation of the conflicting emotions that threatened to overwhelm him. In a secluded room, he took a deep breath, steadying himself for the conversation he needed to have with Cadi.

Entering the room where Cadi awaited updates, Jack's face betrayed the storm within, a complexity of emotions etched in every line. He shared the harrowing news with her, a heavy weight in his voice as he navigated the delicate balance of honesty and reassurance.

"Cadi," he began, his tone a mix of firmness and tenderness, "there's been a complication. You have new siblings now, twins, a gift of life and love, but your mother has been taken. It seems someone is playing a dangerous game."

Cadi, too, felt the turbulence in the air. Her eyes widened with a mix of shock and concern. The news hit her like a sudden gale, and she leaned in, absorbing the weight of her father's words.

"Taken?" Cadi's voice quivered, a reflection of the uncertainty clouding her thoughts. "Who would do such a thing?"

Her concern seemed to prioritize her mother's welfare over the arrival of a sibling. Not even a flinch marked her reaction upon learning that there were two new members of the family and not one as she had originally thought.

Jack, grappling with his own uncertainty, placed a comforting hand on Cadi's shoulder. "We don't have all the answers yet, but we're going to find her. We'll bring Faye back, and your new siblings will know their mother's embrace."

The urgency in Jack's words resonated with determination. As they faced this unexpected crisis, the bond between father and daughter tightened. The room, now charged with emotion, became a sanctuary for shared resolve—a commitment to reunite their family, to reclaim what had been taken, and to confront the shadows that had cast a pall over their world.

With every passing moment, the urgency intensified. Their collective pulse, quickened by the unfolding crisis, propelled them toward a singular goal—to reclaim Faye from the clutches of a calculated gambit that had disrupted the fragile equilibrium of their world.

18

Embarking on a journey that spanned continents, Blake dedicated two days to traverse from the lush landscapes of South America to the sprawling Russian tundra. His purpose was twofold: to seek out the enigmatic Communicator hidden within the folds of this remote terrain and then to return with her to the heart of the city.

"The Russian tundra is unlike anything I've seen," Blake muttered to himself as his breath mingled with the chilly air. "But finding the Communicator is worth every frozen step."

The Communicator was not an ordinary individual. She belonged to a very ancient lineage of Shepherds, her age eclipsing any other that Blake had personally encountered. In the presence of her time-weathered demeanor, Blake was granted the rare opportunity to stand close to the annals of history, a privilege he had never before experienced.

Blake's arrival near her modest abode did not escape notice. The house, a quaint European-style cottage, perched gracefully at the edge of a forested enclave, its front yard blanketed in a pristine layer of snow. Echoing the front yard's charm, the roof boasted matching decorations, while a welcoming plume of smoke ascended from the chimney, nestled to one side of the roof. This unassuming dwelling mirrored the unassuming ambiance of the village that lay just beyond, reachable via a narrow, single-lane road.

Standing sentinel outside her door, the Communicator awaited Blake's arrival, a delicate shawl draping over her shoulders.

"Are you truly one of the oldest Shepherds, as they say?" Blake asked, his voice tinged with a mixture of curiosity and respect.

He stood just outside the fenced in area of her yard. A weathered smile tugged at the corners of the Communicator's lips.

"Old enough to have witnessed the turning of many tides," she replied, her eyes revealing their encompassing of countless stories.

She stepped off of her porch and walked out to meet him at the end of her walkway. Blake's conduct in the presence of the venerable Shepherd was marked by an unwavering reverence. Every action he took, every consideration he extended, was steeped in a profound respect for the legacy she carried. His commitment to ensuring her comfort and well-being was not simply a duty, but a gesture of profound honor, a way of paying homage to the past that had paved the way for his own existence.

"Please, allow me to assist," Blake said, offering his arm as they navigated through the uneven terrain. "Your existence is the guiding light that shapes my purpose."

Yet, beyond the surface of duty, a deeper connection pulsed between Blake and the Shepherd. She held the threads of his purpose, her possible assistance directing him towards the aspirations that fueled his very being.

"You are more than a Communicator," Blake confessed that evening as they sat around a campfire, the crackling flames casting dancing shadows on the tundra. "You are the bridge between the present and the future I strive for."

The symbiotic relationship they shared transcended mere kinship in the broader sense as fellow Shepherds; it was a weaving of fates, a confluence of the individual roles they shared as Shepherds. Her as the Communicator and he as a Facilitator. The bond between them deepened as they felt a growing closeness through the ties of shared blood and their distinct roles within the Shepherd hierarchy.

Blake's sole intention was to linger in the village with the Communicator only for the duration necessary to persuade her to accompany him back to the states. He held a wishful expectation that this period wouldn't be protracted, yet he understood it wasn't within his authority to decide. Blake harbored no intent to coerce Emaleth; instead, he hoped she would contemplate their shared status as higher Shepherds, entwined with their genetic encoding and conditioning.

As Blake and the Shepherd ventured forth, the dynamic between them encapsulated the intricate interplay of generations. She led him on a short walk back through the village. It was as if the temperature outside was only a secondary matter to her that she ignored, despite only donning her shawl.

Emaleth, a name imbued with history and echoes of ages past, was the moniker that the Communicator bore. The name resonated amidst the tranquility of the snow-covered village. Amidst the vast expanse of the Russian Tundra, she sought a solitude that resonated with the very essence of her being. It was within this remote haven that Blake's journey led him, the threads of fate weaving their encounter amidst the tranquil setting of the snow covered village they walked through.

The trappings of modernity held little allure for Emaleth; her heart inclined towards the simplicity of life unburdened by the clamor of bustling civilization and the complexities that accompanied it. The tendrils of her existence intertwined with the natural world, finding solace in its unchanging rhythms and unspoiled landscapes.

With a lifetime that spanned just shy of three hundred and fifty years, Emaleth was a repository of memories, a living testament to the passage of time and the longest living Shepherd to date. Despite the burden of years, her countenance bore a remarkable grace, concealing the age she carried with a gentle elegance that could have easily placed her in the prime of her fifties as a human.

During their journey, Emaleth's words were measured, her utterances sparing. The rhythm of their progress was punctuated by quiet contemplation, each step harmonizing with the silent language of the forested village they traversed. Yet, the silence was not a void but a canvas upon which the unspoken complexities of their connection were painted.

The journey reached its destined culmination as Blake arrived at the threshold of Emaleth's modest abode nestled within the heart of the woods that evening. They had taken a circular path. It was here, amidst the rustling leaves and the whispered secrets of the trees, that Emaleth's voice resonated beyond the confines of her quietude.

"Your presence is the convergence of a myriad of possibilities," Emaleth's voice carried a timbre rich with introspection. "You stand at the juncture of past and future, of purpose and destiny."

Blake's response was measured, his demeanor reflecting the significance of the moment. "And you, Emaleth, are the bridge that spans those realms. Your wisdom and legacy breathe life into the path I tread."

In that brief exchange, words unfurled like tendrils of understanding, forging a connection that extended beyond the surface. It was not the quantity of words that mattered, but the depth from which they emerged.

As their journey wove itself into the fabric of the tundra, the dynamics between Blake and Emaleth evolved like the shifting seasons.

"Is it time, then, to make contact with the masters?" Emaleth's inquiry flowed softly into the air, laden with the weight of anticipation.

Blake's response held a sense of gravity, tinged with a hint of urgency. "Indeed, the moment has come—past, perhaps. Their message arrived, bespeaking the need for pioneers for a new world. We are to unseal the gate, a task entrusted to us."

The responsibility of their mission hung in the space between their words.

"It has been an age since my lineage bore a Communicator at all. Over six hundred years, and yet the mantle lay dormant. Unused. Unneeded. It is time to summon the masters, don't you think?" Emaleth's voice held a mixture of determination and reflection, as if echoing the sentiments of all who had come before her.

With a nod, Blake confirmed, "The Key has been unearthed. It rests in waiting, a sentinel of destiny, until we return from whence I journeyed."

With the path ahead illuminated, Emaleth's resolve solidified.

"Then, let us set the gears in motion," she declared, her gaze resolute as she gathered only a jacket from the sparse belongings that adorned her humble dwelling.

It was as if her actions mirrored the essence of her character—simple, focused, and uncluttered. In the face of this readiness, Blake offered time like an outstretched hand, inviting patience into their shared space. He recognized the gravity of their mission, the culmination of his pursuit for the Communicator. He was hesitant to impose urgency upon Emaleth, for their steps were guided by destiny's tapestry, and haste held no dominion.

As she prepared to depart, it became evident that Emaleth needed no prolonged period to marshal her belongings. Emaleth's readiness was evident in her simple preparations. The shawl was her sole companion on this journey, an emblem of her preparedness. Blake watched, a quiet admiration coursing through him—admiration for her purposeful simplicity and the unswerving commitment they both shared.

For Blake, this was the realization of a fervent quest, a culmination of efforts and aspirations. The Communicator was at his side, and the Key, the elusive talisman, awaited his return.

Taking advantage of Jason's help, Faye was led to the same nondescript office building where Cadi had been taken the day prior to their departure in pursuit of the Librarian. Simultaneously, Blake's convoy began its deliberate journey back to the recently touched-down airport, propelling towards the same destination. Blake's patience held firm while he waited for the convoy to complete its course, his thoughts interwoven with the precious cargo inching closer to their rendezvous point.

Meanwhile, in South America, Jack grappled with a dilemma. His intelligence unit worked tirelessly to monitor Blake's global movements, yet he acknowledged the futility of this endeavor. The fickle nature of their quarry's journey meant that by the time he arrived at any given location, Blake would have already moved on. The realization irked him, for time was a luxury they could ill afford. Cadi's presence, despite her endearing qualities, proved a handful even within the confines of their temporary South American base. The burdens she presented at home translated seamlessly to their current location. Determined to assert her individuality and take charge of her destiny, Cadi consistently challenged her father's reluctance to involve her in his planning processes. Her hope was to contribute to the search for her mother. She persistently questioned him about the twins and the details surrounding their birth, expressing concerns about the brevity of her mother's pregnancy and the potential consequences it might entail.

The mounting tension within Jack had only escalated when he had received the jarring news of Faye's abduction from their fortified installation. The volatile mix of emotions surged within him, encompassing gratitude for the safety of their unborn children, yet overshadowed by a profound sense of powerlessness.

The captor who had abducted Faye had once been an friend, a realization that deepened Jack's ire. The man he had entrusted with his wife's security, believing him to be an ally, had betrayed their cause. The gravity of the deception fueled a burning desire within Jack—a thirst for vengeance directed squarely at the turncoat Jason Conwell who had shattered his trust.

The tempest of emotions within Jack mirrored the global tumult that surrounded their pursuit. The lines between ally and adversary blurred in the chaotic dance of their mission, testing bonds and revealing hidden truths. With each passing moment, the stakes escalated, and the intricate tapestry of alliances continued to unravel in the face of an unforeseen betrayal.

Jack found solace in one thing—the knowledge that Cadi was safe by his side. Her presence brought him a renewed sense of hope. Not only had he reunited with his beloved daughter, but Cadi had also provided him with crucial intelligence about their elusive enemy.

She divulged the location of the apartment that Blake had been using as a hideout. Acting swiftly, Jack dispatched a surveillance team to stake out the area. However, his heart sank when he received their reports while he was mid-flight back to the United States. Blake had not been spotted at the watched apartment; instead, they had located the abandoned van used to abduct Faye somewhere within the city.

This unexpected twist in their pursuit added another layer of complexity to the mission. Jack immediately ordered his ground forces to assume strategic positions around the apartment building. He emphasized the need for utmost discretion, instructing them to remain concealed while he convened with the rest of the team back at the installation.

Upon landing, Jack and his group disembarked to find a convoy of vehicles and equipment awaiting their arrival. The tension in the air was palpable as they prepared to navigate the ever-evolving challenges that lay ahead.

The journey back to the installation was fraught with tension. The cityscape outside the window was a stark reminder of the chaos that had erupted in their absence. Burnt-out cars, shattered glass, and the remnants of the insurrection littered the streets, painting a grim picture of the city's recent turmoil. The acrid scent of smoke still lingered in the air, stinging their nostrils, and the distant echoes of sirens and shouting voices reached their ears intermittently.

Cadi broke the silence that had settled in the vehicle since they left the airport.

"Dad," she began hesitantly, her voice laced with concern, "I can see how much this is tearing you apart. We'll find Mom, I promise."

Jack turned to his daughter, his eyes reflecting a mix of gratitude and worry. "I know, Cadi. Having you back with me is a blessing I'll cherish forever. And your intel about Blake's apartment is invaluable. But we just received word that he's nowhere to be found there. The situation has become much more complicated."

The struggle presented by their predicament hung in the air as the vehicle continued its journey. Jack's mind raced with thoughts of Faye, his missing wife, and the unknown dangers she might be facing. He glanced out the window at the city's bleak landscape, knowing that every moment counted in their race to find her. The distant hum of generators and the flickering remnants of streetlights served as a stark backdrop to their grim task, emphasizing the urgency.

As they approached the installation, Jack knew that their battle was far from over. The missing van, Blake's sudden disappearance, and the city's volatile state had all stacked the odds against them. His resolve remained unshaken, but the anxiety in his heart grew with each passing mile. He could only hope that with meticulous planning and the dedication of his team it would lead them closer to bringing Faye back to safety.

After arriving back at the installation, Jack and Cadi made their way to the nursery where her twin siblings, born just before Faye's abduction, were being cared for by her cousin Brooke. Cadi had pined to see them dearly during her time away, and seeing them brought a sense of warmth to her heart.

The nursery exuded an air of serene tranquility, with the two infants resting in their cribs, their tiny fingers reaching out into the world as they slumbered. Cadi entered the room, her heart swelling with a tender affection as she beheld their innocence. Their eyes, reminiscent of the unmistakable Shepherd lineage, gazed into the unknown, devoid of the burdens of the world.

Approaching her baby brother and sister, she couldn't help but marvel at the familial connection that bound them. She gently extended her fingers to touch their delicate hands, her own bearing the same telltale Shepherd traits. The small tails, mirroring her own, extended gracefully from their lower backs. It was a unique characteristic that marked them as different from ordinary humans, just as she was.

Yet, as she observed these tiny lives, an overwhelming realization flooded over Cadi. Rather than a sense of isolation or doubt, her heart swelled with an unshakable acceptance. The memories of days when she questioned her own identity, grappling with the notion of ever fitting in as a 'real' girl, now felt like distant echoes of the past. Those moments of doubt and insecurity, once oppressive, had been replaced by a newfound perspective.

The recent trials, the abduction of her mother, and the relentless pursuit of her family's enemies had become catalysts for change. They had shifted her perception in profound ways. Cadi understood now, in the depths of her being, that being different didn't diminish her reality or value. She had faced danger head-on, demonstrating her strength and resilience while reuniting with her family under the most challenging circumstances. These experiences had meticulously reshaped her sense of self.

As she watched her baby siblings, their chests rising and falling in the peaceful rhythm of slumber, Cadi silently vowed to herself. She would stand as a steadfast pillar of support for them, just as she would for her mother, her father, and everyone she held dear. The twins, with their tails and all, deserved to feel unconditionally accepted and cherished. Cadi recognized that the essence of family lay in love and unity, transcending the very differences that made them unique.

With a profound sense of determination, she leaned closer to her sleeping siblings, her voice a gentle whisper in the tranquil nursery.

"You're perfect just the way you are," she assured them, her words filled with love and conviction, "and I'll always be here to protect you." The acceptance she had discovered within herself extended to them, binding their unique family together.

Cadi cradled each of her siblings, one in each hand, nestled close to her chest. The warmth of their little bodies and the rhythmic beating of their hearts against hers enveloped her. Her smile exuded warmth, a hopeful shield for the two bundles against the troubles she had recently encountered.

"We'll find Mom, I promise," she whispered gently to them before placing them back into their crib. "We'll be a whole family again soon."

As Cadi stood by the cribs, lost in her thoughts and emotions, the nursery door opened quietly, and Elizabeth, Jack's sister, entered the room. She approached her brother with a sympathetic expression, her eyes reflecting the seriousness of the situation they were all facing.

Jack turned to Elizabeth, his eyes heavy with a mixture of relief at her presence and the burden of guilt that had been weighing on him since Faye's abduction.

"I can't stop thinking about it, Izzy," he admitted in a low voice. "I should have been there to protect her, to keep her safe."

Elizabeth placed a comforting hand on Jack's shoulder and sighed. She had seen her brother go through countless challenges over the years, but this was different. It struck at the core of his identity as a husband and father.

"Jack, you're an amazing detective and soldier, and you've saved countless lives," Elizabeth said gently. "But none of us could have seen this coming. Jason was like family. None of us expected he would turn against us."

Jack nodded, his jaw clenched in frustration. "I know, but that doesn't change the fact that Faye is out there, and I couldn't be there for her when she needed me the most."

Elizabeth looked at the tiny infants in the cribs, then back at her brother. "You're torn between your duty as a soldier and your duty as a husband and father. I get that. But remember, you're not alone in this. We're all going to do everything we can to bring Faye back."

Jack met his sister's gaze, his eyes filled with gratitude for her understanding. "Izzy, I just wish I could have protected her better. That's what I was supposed to do."

Elizabeth squeezed his shoulder reassuringly. "Jack, sometimes even the strongest people need help. We'll find her, and we'll bring her back. And until then, we'll take care of those who need us here."

Jack knew his sister was right, but the guilt still gnawed at him. As he watched his sleeping children with their older sister Cadi cooing over them, he couldn't help but wonder about the challenges that lay ahead and the difficult decisions he would have to make to bring his wife back safely.

Jack left Cadi in the capable hands of his sister, entrusting her with the care of the newborns. As he exited the nursery, he encountered the person he had anticipated seeing all along. Donovan leaned casually against the wall opposite the nursery door, arms folded across his chest, lost in silent contemplation. Without a word, Jack moved to stand beside him.

After a prolonged silence, Jack finally broke it.

"I thought I'd see you soon," he admitted, his tone heavy with contemplation.

He turned to Donovan, his eyes searching Donovan's face for any sign of what he was about to say.

Jack continued, saying, "I suspected the wrong person. My prejudice against that mad scientist made me believe he was the spy among us." Jack had never truly trusted Dr. Brundle, given that he was basically the same person who had caused problems for him and Faye years ago. Donovan straightened up from the wall and started walking down the hall, Jack instinctively falling into step beside him.

"I understand," Donovan replied, his voice tinged with regret. "I felt the same way. Now I feel like a fool, and I've let you down. You expected me to protect Faye, and I couldn't even do that much."

Jack couldn't help but notice a subtle difference in Donovan's demeanor, one he couldn't quite pinpoint. Since their initial meeting in the conference room after their kidnapping by Donovan's forces, it had seemed as though Donovan was harboring something about Faye, something he wasn't revealing. Jack was growing suspicious that Donovan knew more than he let on and had a connection to Faye.

As they walked in silence, Jack contemplated whether to delve deeper into Donovan's words. Despite his suspicions, Jack refrained from pressing Donovan. He figured if the man wanted to talk about it, he would.

Donovan, aware of Jack's astute detective skills, was relieved that Jack didn't delve further into the matter. He was guarding a past that held painful memories that he didn't want to delve into.

Jack cleared his throat.

"I believe it's time we start formulating plans to rescue Faye and hunt down the bastard behind this entire debacle," Jack asserted, his jaw clenched with determination.

As Blake embarked on his journey back to the States, he found himself with few concerns weighing on his mind. His meticulously laid plans were finally nearing fruition, marked by the Communicator's acquiescence and the successful capture of Faye. Faye's presence held a crucial role in facilitating the Communicator's connection with the enigmatic Braxit, although the intricate workings of this connection remained shrouded in mystery. Blake understood one thing: the Key had to be present to enable the Communicator to transmit its message.

In the cozy confines of the cargo plane's lounge area, Blake and Emaleth occupied adjacent seats. She appeared lost in contemplation, gazing out the window, and Blake hesitated to disrupt her reverie. It felt impolite to intrude upon her thoughts without an invitation. However, Emaleth seemed to sense his desire to converse. She turned toward him, draping her shawl more snugly around her shoulders, and subtly adjusted her seat to settle into an even more comfortable position.

Blake couldn't help but be captivated by Emaleth. She stood as the eldest among the Shepherds, a fact beyond dispute. Yet, one would never guess her true age upon a casual glance. Her light brown hair flowed gracefully down her shoulders from beneath the shawl's embrace, its luster undiminished by the passage of time. Rather than diminishing her allure, the lines etched by age upon her face seemed to enhance her beauty, enchanting him with her presence.

"If I didn't know any better," Emaleth remarked casually, her tanned complexion revealing a subtle blush, "I'd think you were interested in me beyond my role as the Communicator." Her wisdom prevented her from being swayed by his apparent fascination with her, fully aware that his interest extended no further than her role as the Communicator.

Blake jolted as though he had been caught divulging a forbidden secret. He snapped out of his trance and queried, "Why is the Key necessary for communicating with the Braxit?"

Emaleth shrugged, uncertainty clouding her features. "I can't say for certain. Perhaps the Librarian might have the answers. What I do know is that to facilitate message transmission, the Key must be present."

She fell into a contemplative silence before adding, "I believe it has something to do with Genetic Harmonic Resonance. The Key and I are bioengineered to depend on each other in this aspect. It could have been a safeguard because no such setup is required for receiving messages from the Braxit, only for sending them."

Blake pondered, his hand finding its way to his chin. "I do recall learning about Genetically Engineered Acoustic Resonance. It's likely they implemented it to prevent us from contacting them when there was no real necessity."

Emaleth acknowledged his point with a nod. Her gaze shifted towards the plane's window, effectively concluding their conversation and leaving Blake to his thoughts.

The remainder of the journey passed without incident, a fact for which Blake felt grateful. He was confident that Donovan and his group of Shepherds remained unaware of his imminent arrival at the airport. His eagerness to progress with his plans burned within him. The cargo plane descended onto an undersized, abandoned airstrip some distance from the city. Despite the airport's limitations, the pilots' skills triumphed over the odds. Armored SUVs emerged from the plane's belly, ready to transport Blake and Emaleth to their destination.

The journey to the location of Blake's base with Emaleth spanned approximately an hour. During the ride, Blake couldn't help but be repeatedly captivated by the enigmatic Communicator. Memories resurfaced, and he found himself musing over the past. It struck him that the last time he felt such fascination for a fellow Shepherd, the sentiments weren't reciprocated. His desire had burned one way, while her affections had flowed toward someone else. These recollections left Blake feeling self-conscious and harboring a bitter taste of regret.

Determined to escape the memories, he turned away and fixated his gaze on the SUV's window. He remained steadfast in his resolve not to revisit that chapter of his life until their journey reached its destination.

Inside the office building, Blake had Emaleth accompany him to ensure she met with Faye, facilitating their message's transmission to the Braxit.. His sole concern revolved around delivering the message, and he brushed aside all other worries. Waiting for him in the building was Jason.

"Doctor, how is she?" Blake inquired as soon as he entered.

"If you're inquiring about Faye," Jason explained, "she's still unconscious as of my last check. I've been maintaining sedation to avoid any potential issues."

"Good," Blake responded promptly. "Lead us to her room so we can proceed."

He glanced behind him to ensure Emaleth was still following. His concern proved unnecessary; she trailed closely, her gaze shifting between the Shepherds stationed throughout the building. It had been quite some time since she had seen so many of her brethren gathered in one place. Blake trailed Jason through the building until they reached their destination. Jason opened the door, granting Blake and Emaleth entry. As Jason stepped into the room, Blake cut him off abruptly.

"I believe your role concludes here, Jason," Blake declared.

Jason's expression displayed frustration, but he held his tongue. He nodded slightly, acknowledging the dismissal, and left them to tend to Faye. Though seething with anger, he refrained from voicing his discontent. He had risked his life and damaged his reputation to bring Faye here, and the feeling of receiving nothing in return had soured his mood.

Blake couldn't help but sense Jason's growing sense of alienation, but he remained indifferent. To Blake, Jason was merely a human tool to be utilized in the pursuit of his objectives. Now that Jason had delivered Faye to him, his usefulness had run its course. Blake discreetly signaled a nearby guard, who approached him.

"Take care of him. Quietly," Blake instructed in a hushed tone once Jason had walked farther down the hallway, out of earshot.

The guard acknowledged the order and departed to carry it out. As Blake turned away, the echoing sound of a silenced gunshot reached his ears. Jason had reached the end of his journey, his presence deemed unnecessary by Blake as he moved forward with his plans to achieve his goal.

He closed the door behind him and observed as Emaleth moved toward the gurney where Faye lay. Faye appeared to be in slumber, but Blake discerned from her breathing patterns that she had likely regained consciousness not too long ago.

"Damn," he muttered softly under his breath.

Faye's eyes fluttered open as he approached, taking a position beside Emaleth. Her voice quivered with confusion.

"What's happening? Where am I?" Her memory remained hazy, with the last recollection being Jason administering something through her IV, plunging her into sleep.

Surveying her surroundings in the cramped, featureless room, Faye found little to capture her attention. A solitary desk sat off to one side, and aside from that, the room held nothing else—no chairs, no lamps, no bookcases. It was an austere chamber, housing only her, her gurney, the desk, and the two individuals looming above her.

Emaleth leaned in closer to Faye, her voice soft and contemplative. "I know you," she stated simply, her gaze lingering on Faye.

However, after a prolonged scrutiny, she corrected herself, "No... I'm mistaken. You merely bear a striking resemblance to her, but you're not her."

Preparing to initiate communication with the Braxit, Emaleth moved closer to Faye and gently took her hand in her own. Faye, her brow furrowing in concern, couldn't fathom the cryptic dialogue that the woman holding her hand had engaged in, followed by the unexpected physical contact.

"What are you doing?" Faye questioned, a rising sense of unease welling up within her. Still under the influence of the potent sedatives administered by Jason, she found herself with limited capacity to resist.

"So, how does this process work, Emaleth?" Blake inquired.

Emaleth remained silent for a moment, her attention fixed on the bewildered Faye. Several moments passed before she finally shifted her gaze toward Blake and began to explain, "I simply need her to unlock me, enabling me to send out the call."

Blake pressed further, seeking clarity. "How exactly does that work? Are there specific messages to be transmitted? We must inform them of our intent to meet and understand their requirements. It's been such a long time since we've received any communication from them, and I need to ascertain if I still have a purpose here."

Emaleth shook her head, her tone tinged with uncertainty. "No, it doesn't function that way. There's no specific message to transmit. Once I use the Key to unlock, a signal will be dispatched across the cosmos to the nearest Braxit. There won't be an immediate response, so we won't know if the message has been received. What we do know is that the portal will be opened afterward for their arrival, and that's when we'll discover if our message reached them," she admitted.

Emaleth's gaze returned to Faye, her voice taking on a gentle, almost reverent quality.

"She is beautiful," Emaleth murmured, her words filled with admiration.

Blake's eyes briefly flickered down to Faye, a trace of disdain threatening to surface, but he staunchly suppressed the impulse. He recognized her, but dwelling on it was the last thing he wanted. Faye wasn't the one he desired to recollect; rather, it was the woman whom Faye resembled that occupied his thoughts. The woman who Faye had been cloned from.

"Yes, she is," he reluctantly admitted, acutely aware of Faye's striking resemblance to someone else. "But right now, my concern is getting the message out. Go ahead, do what you need to do."

Emaleth gently grasped Faye's hands with both of her own and closed her eyes in concentration. After a moment, she reopened her eyes, directing her gaze toward Blake. "It's done."

Blake arched an incredulous eyebrow.

"That's it? It's that simple?" he asked, struggling to believe the apparent ease of the process.

Emaleth nodded with a serene smile.

"Yes, that's all there is to it," she confirmed.

Blake's inclination to voice his skepticism was cut short as the building's alarms blared insistently, immediately followed by the reverberations of an explosion.

Faye and Emaleth reacted with visceral fear, their voices merging in terrified screams. Faye, in her distress, tumbled from the gurney and instinctively sought shelter behind a nearby desk. In contrast, Emaleth scanned the room, her face etched with bewilderment as she grappled to understand the unfolding chaos.

In the midst of chaos, a guard quickly entered the room and urgently reported, 'Sir, President Pike's forces are attacking the building. They've surrounded us, but we've secured your escape."

Blake acted decisively, grabbing Emaleth's arm and leading her to safety. Another explosion jolted the building, and sporadic gunfire erupted dangerously close. Amid the ensuing chaos, Blake became unintentionally separated from Emaleth.

Blake cursed his unfortunate predicament, lamenting the missed opportunity to ensure Emaleth's safety. Dust swirled around him, obscuring his vision, while his guard remained singularly focused on safeguarding him. The guard hurriedly propelled Blake toward an express elevator, poised to transport him to a level lower than the garage. There, Blake would rendezvous with a team tasked with orchestrating his safe departure from the volatile area.

In the tense confines of the ready room, Jack stood resolute, flanked by Donovan on one side and Major Burke on the other. Dr. Brundle, Elizabeth, and Cadi were gathered as well, their presence underscoring the gravity of the situation. This meeting served as the crucible for devising a meticulously calculated plan of assault—one that held the objectives of rescuing Faye, securing the elusive Communicator believed to be within reach, and the capture or elimination of Blake and Jason.

The fate of the latter two targets hung in the balance, subject to the unfurling dynamics of resistance and the fluidity of the tactical landscape. Donovan, his stance suggestive of restraint, leaned toward capturing them, a testament to his measured approach. In stark contrast, Jack's motivations were etched in the lines of his clenched fists and the fire in his eyes. For him, Blake had transgressed the boundaries of family, kidnapping his daughter and wife, and this mission was personal. Vengeance simmered beneath the surface, a primal urge that sent adrenaline coursing through his veins.

As emotions swirled within Jack, he took deliberate breaths to regain composure, grateful for the presence of Donovan who had initiated the debriefing with Cadi.

"Cadi," Donovan began, his voice steady, "you've shared with us that there's a building housing Blake's contingent of Shepherds. Can you recall its location?"

Cadi's response was marked by a solemn shake of her head. The buildings were recognizable to her, but she had never navigated their paths before. The absence of a personal journey left her memory void of the necessary landmarks. Donovan, undeterred by this setback, gestured towards Major Burke, who stepped forth with a purposeful resolve.

"Could you provide me with a detailed description of those buildings, Cadi?" Major Burke's inquiry was both earnest and crucial.

Cadi responded with meticulous precision, her vivid recollection proving invaluable as she painted a verbal picture of their potential target. Major Burke, equipped with the information Cadi provided, inputted the descriptors into a handheld pad. With each keystroke, a series of candidate buildings emerged, each one bearing a semblance to the intricate details she had conveyed. Alongside this, Cadi's knowledge of their direction from the city center played a pivotal role in narrowing down the possibilities.

A few moments passed as Cadi sifted through the digital selection, her keen eye identifying the correct buildings from the half-dozen presented. The pieces of the puzzle were falling into place, and the elusive target was inching closer to being pinpointed.

Major Burke's fingers danced on the pad, and a holographic representation of the industrial park materialized before them. The focus zoomed in on the particular building of interest.

"Gentlemen, this is our operational target," Major Burke declared, using both the database information and Cadi's descriptors to provide a comprehensive briefing on the building's interior.

The details flowed, an intricate tapestry of information upon which they would weave their strategy. Jack, aware of the weight of their impending decision, called for a brief respite. He leaned over the hologram, his eyes scanning the representation. With each swipe of his finger, the layout of the building became clearer. It was a puzzle of precision and tactics, and Jack's mind was busy piecing it together. Beside him, Cadi joined in the contemplation. Her voice, tinged with uncertainty, broke the silence.

"Do you think Mom's in there?" Her finger pointed to a specific location on the hologram, a symbol of her hope and her fear entwined in a single gesture.

Jack's grunt conveyed agreement as he meticulously transcribed notes onto the pad before him. His brow furrowed in concentration, capturing the essence of a strategy that was unfolding within his mind. When he had encapsulated his most recent idea in writing, he shifted his focus towards Cadi, his eyes reflecting a blend of concern and determination.

"It's the most probable place he could have taken her," Jack affirmed. The room seemed to hang on his every word. "We've already secured Blake's residence using the address you provided, and he wasn't there." The unspoken weight of the situation settled among them, thick and disconcerting. Jack allowed the silence to echo his unspoken fears.

The anxiety coursing through Jack mirrored the uncertainty of their predicament. The trail had gone cold, and the dearth of intelligence regarding potential locations where Blake and his group might be operating from was a constant thorn in his side. The city's infrastructure, much like the rest of the country, remained crippled from the recent insurrection. Resources were scarce, and the perpetual alert status at their base had stretched their personnel thin, leaving few to spare for the task of scouting alternative hideouts that Blake might be utilizing.

The prospect of venturing into the unknown weighed heavily on Jack's shoulders. There was a palpable sense of unease about operating in the dark, but he knew there was no alternative. They had to act based on the limited information at their disposal. It was a calculated risk, one that underscored the relentless urgency of their mission, and Jack's unwavering resolve to bring Faye back to safety.

"Kitten, can you recall how they were positioned in there and estimate the potential forces we might encounter?" Jack inquired, his eyes locked onto Cadi's.

Cadi paused, shutting her eyes in an attempt to conjure a clearer mental image.

"I believe there were approximately twenty of them, armed and actively patrolling. In total, there were probably less than fifty Shepherds present," she recounted.

Her gaze shifted to her father, a hint of apology in her eyes. She recognized the value of precise numbers for his strategic planning, yet she admitted that her memory had faltered. At the time of her visit, her focus had been elsewhere, making it challenging to gauge their exact numbers. Of those she did recall as part of the group, around a half dozen had arrived with Blake in his convoy.

Jack hummed contemplatively while his thoughts churned.

"It'll have to suffice as a starting point for our planning," he mumbled to himself.

His mind raced, piecing together the preliminary plans. The specifics of approaching the building and executing the infiltration required collaboration with Major Burke. Determining the personnel available for the mission hinged on Burke's input. Jack couldn't rely on the same number of soldiers he had during his last mission. In South America, he had leveraged the existing Shepherd forces stationed in the country, leaving those troops behind when he and the Major returned to the United States.

"Alright, everyone," Jack called out, his voice carrying a sense of determination after a brief moment of introspection. "I'll need Major Burke, the rest of you can step out while we strategize our approach."

Donovan and the others glanced at Jack, nodding in acknowledgment as they resigned themselves to exit the room. Donovan was confident they'd receive a detailed briefing once the assault plan was solidified.

Cadi, however, approached her father and asked, "Is there anything I can do to help, Dad?" She sidled up beside him, her concern evident in her eyes.

Jack turned to Cadi, a warm smile on his face, and affectionately ruffled her hair.

"No, Kitten," he reassured her, his voice filled with paternal love. "Major Burke and I can handle this phase. We'll ensure your mother's safe return."

Despite his inner doubts, he pushed them aside, determined not to fail in his mission, no matter the cost. His jaw tightened with resolve. "For now, go and check on your siblings. It's essential that you spend quality time bonding with them."

Cadi brushed Jack's hand off her head, her feet planted firmly, and a slight pout forming on her face as she replied, "But, Dad, they're just babies. I love them, but they won't even remember this. I can bond with them when we have Mom back."

Jack understood Cadi's sentiment, but he needed her away from the planning process, shielded from the grim reality of the sacrifices that might be necessary to secure her mother's freedom.

Jack turned to Elizabeth, his eyes silently pleading for her support. His sister stepped forward and gently led a reluctant Cadi away from the meeting room, granting Jack the solitude needed to craft his plans in tandem with Major Burke. While Donovan's position could have made him a valuable asset in the planning process, his expertise lay in the political realm, rendering his assistance impractical.

Jack and Major Burke efficiently finalized their plans within the span of an hour. Jack then summoned Donovan and delivered a comprehensive briefing on their intended course of action. As expected, Donovan posed the pertinent questions, and Jack did his best to provide answers that satisfied him. Donovan ultimately approved of their arrangements and exited the room.

Unbeknownst to Jack, Cadi had quietly slipped back into the conference room during the briefing with Donovan, silently absorbing all the information exchanged. She discreetly made her exit as the meeting concluded and made her way down to the motor pool at the installation.

In the motor pool, soldiers conducted final equipment checks and geared up for the mission. They received last-minute orders and began loading into their respective vehicles, preparing to convoy to their target. Amidst the bustling activity, Cadi seized a moment to conceal herself in one of the vehicles lined up for departure, nestled among cargo boxes containing supplies needed for the impending assault and its aftermath.

Minutes later, Jack and Major Burke arrived, mounting their vehicles as the convoy readied itself for departure.

The convoy moved through the desolate streets of the city, the eerie silence broken only by the low hum of engines and the occasional rattle of equipment. The once-vibrant urban landscape had transformed into a haunting ghost town, its streets now littered and cluttered with remnants of the recent insurrection. Burned-out cars, shattered glass, and overturned debris bore witness to the chaos that had reigned here not long ago.

Colonel Jack Riddle sat in the lead vehicle, his eyes scanning the grim tableau outside. He couldn't help but recall the days when these streets were bustling with life, now reduced to this bleak and desolate state due to martial law. His jaw clenched as he contemplated the stakes of their mission.

Seated behind him, Major Burke was busy coordinating with their squads over the radio, ensuring everyone was ready for the impending assault. The crackling of voices in his earpiece filled the otherwise somber atmosphere of the vehicle. He relayed orders, reminding his teams of their roles and responsibilities.

As they approached the target building, the convoy slowed to a halt. Jack and Major Burke climbed out, their boots crunching on the debris-strewn asphalt. The imposing structure loomed before them, the building having been spared the scars of conflict.

Jack called out to the assembled soldiers, his voice carrying a tone of unwavering resolve. "Listen up, everyone! We've trained for this, and we know our mission. Major Burke will lead Team Alpha, and I'll take Team Bravo. Let's execute this operation swiftly and with precision. Remember, we're here to rescue Faye Riddle, capture Blake Tipis and Jason Conwell, and find the Communicator if the Communicator is present."

The soldiers nodded, their faces etched with determination. Squads were assigned to their respective leaders, and the teams began to move into position. The tension in the air was palpable as they prepared to breach the building and confront the unknown challenges that awaited inside.

Amid the quiet intensity, the soldiers readied their weapons, and the countdown to the assault began. Jack gave the order to execute mission a few minutes later. Explosives breached the door sealing the entrance of the base. Subsequently, a second door, identified as a potential avenue of escape, was breached to grant access to the secondary team. Their mission focused on securing the breach, aiming to prevent any attempts to exit the facility.

Jack's team surged through the sprawling building, each step a measured progression towards their designated rendezvous point on the floor that the Shepherds occupied. The air hung heavy with anticipation, their senses attuned to the smallest nuances of movement. Despite the gravity of their mission, the opposition seemed strangely subdued, their resistance barely more than a murmur.

The skirmish that ensued, though limited in scope, still bore the tension of a coiled spring. Jack's unease was palpable, the concern for his men and their objectives woven into his every move. He maintained a cautious acceptance of the exchange of small arms fire, recognizing that a prolonged confrontation with Blake's forces was not in their best interests. His priorities lay elsewhere—finding Faye and potentially locating the elusive figures of Jason and Blake.

The tumult within Jack mirrored the chaos of the firefight around him. Yet, amidst the fray, he grappled with a personal struggle that lay beneath the surface. His desire for retribution against Jason simmered, a seething rage that he wrestled to contain. The conflict between vengeance and restraint was an internal battle as fierce as any physical confrontation. He knew that impulsivity would cost more than it would gain.

As the minutes slipped away, the tide of the battle began to shift. Surprisingly, the actual exchange of gunfire had been quite brief, a mere fifteen minutes to be exact. Blake's forces crumbled, their numbers proving inadequate for the challenge.

Jack's priorities swiftly shifted once the enemy combatants were secured. His focus pivoted squarely toward finding and ensuring his wife's safety. Alongside his squad, he meticulously went from room to room, methodically clearing the remaining spaces until they stumbled upon the very room where Faye had been held.

Remarkably, Faye appeared relatively unharmed, tucked away in a corner of the room, her position chosen deliberately to be visible to anyone entering. Her training had taught her that concealing herself would only heighten the risk to her life, especially when the room's door was breached during the firefight.

When the gunfight erupted, she'd instinctively fashioned a makeshift barricade from the nearby desk, providing a meager shield against stray bullets. As the gunfire subsided, she emerged from her hideout and positioned herself in a corner where she could easily be seen. With her hands raised to her head, she waited patiently for her rescuers.

Faye's abduction had been a harrowing experience. Her fury had surged when she realized that it was Jason who had orchestrated her capture within the installation, the very place she should have been safe. Separated from her newborn babies and consumed by worry over how their father would react to her kidnapping and their daughter's disappearance, she had endured moments of profound anguish.

The overwhelming sense of relief washed over her as she recognized that the ongoing assault outside her prison door was the cavalry she had hoped for. Her heart felt lighter, but the fear of a tragic mishap loomed.

With a forceful kick, the door to her room burst open, swiftly filled by soldiers clad in uniforms she recognized as belonging to the troops under Donovan and her husband's command. Her gaze darted around the room, locking onto Jack first, resplendent in his gear, and the tears welled up in her eyes at the realization that he had come to her rescue. Her joy was short-lived, however, as she saw Jack pushed aside by a smaller soldier who rushed into the room ahead.

"Mom!" screamed Cadi as she raced toward Faye, enveloping her in a tearful embrace.

"Cadi?" Faye uttered in bewilderment, lifting her head to take in the incredible sight before her.

Her daughter, whom she had believed was lost in the world and for whom she thought she would have to fight to find again, stood before her. Tears cascaded from her eyes like a waterfall.

Jack, standing in the doorway, initially seethed with anger at the realization that his daughter had defied his orders and joined the assault team. But as he witnessed the tearful reunion between his wife and daughter, his anger dissolved into a mixture of relief and overwhelming emotion. His feet carried him slowly into the room. He opened his arms as he moved forward.

Jack's heart raced as he finally held Faye in his arms, her safety like a balm to the turbulent storm of emotions within him. Yet, his triumph was tempered by the void left by the absence of Jason and Blake. The search had only begun.

His forces rallied, each corner of the building methodically secured, each Shepherd accounted for, including the elusive Communicator. The cacophony of battle had dimmed, replaced by a sense of grim satisfaction.

The aftermath of conflict was a tapestry of victory and loss, of apprehension and relief. Jack's eyes scanned the captured Shepherds, his gaze lingering on the Communicator, a figure of significance in this intricate web of alliances and betrayals. The pulse of their mission, once throbbing with uncertainty, now beat with a rhythm of purpose. The building's walls, once witnesses to violence, now held silence.

explicitus est liber

https://writingfortheworldpress.com

Also by J. A. Springs

Chronicles of Cosmic Realms
Shadows of the Forgotten Void

elctrcsheepdrmwrks (Electric Sheep Dreamworks)
Blurred Vision
Fractured
Zero One

Essays in Systems and Being
Essays in Systems and Being

The Absurdities Anthology
How Not to Find Your Local Weed-Man

The Gifted
The Untamed Force
Next Exit

Watch for more at https://authorjasprings.com.

About the Author

I'm J. A. Springs.

Father of six wonderful children. I served twenty years on active duty, living around the world and experiencing things I never imagined I would. I spent time in societies and countries I once couldn't have envisioned as part of my future. I've done a lot—and still not enough.

These days, I live quietly, accompanied by my cats, music, and an interest in writing that consumes me. I've been writing seriously since 2021. I never set out to write in a particular genre—it made more sense to write around them instead. As for goals? There aren't many. Enjoy the first cup of coffee in the morning and see what the day brings.

Read more at https://authorjasprings.com.

About the Publisher

LLC. Lancaster, PA

www.writingfortheworldpress.com

Read more at https://www.writingfortheworldpress.com.